Totally Bound Publishing books by Nolan Vancey

The Bondgate Mysteries
Adam's Appetite

I0636138

The Bondgate Mysteries

ADAM'S APPETITE

NOLAN VANCEY

Adam's Appetite
ISBN # 978-1-80250-528-3
©Copyright Nolan Vancey 2023
Cover Art by Erin Dameron-Hill ©Copyright April 2023
Interior text design by Claire Siemaszkiewicz
Totally Bound Publishing

Published in 2023 by Totally Bound Publishing, United Kingdom.

Totally Bound Publishing is an imprint of Totally Entwined Group Limited.

ADAM'S APPETITE

Dedication

Dedicated to the real Adam B., who suggested it.

Chapter One

Adam Blythewood could have hated Roderick Utley. Like Blythewood, Utley was a man who knew what he wanted and had the initiative and resources to take it. Worse yet, wherever Adam turned during his time at Windmere Hall and its environs, he found that Roderick had been there before him, laying claim to everything that Adam would have hoped to have for himself. In another time or under other circumstances, the two might have become deadly enemies. Fortunately for both of them, by the time Adam Blythewood was in a position to meet Roderick Utley, he had gained a mite of sympathy for his rival, and his own goals, indeed his very temperament, had changed.

On the day Adam arrived at Windmere Hall, a grey, featureless morning, he knew nothing of Roderick Utley. In fact, he had never even heard the name. After the long carriage ride from London to the rocky highlands of the West Country, he would have accepted lodgings much less grand than the estate that welcomed him at the end of his journey. The ride had provided solitude for him to ponder his position. No matter how he looked at it, this was exile, a last chance for him to redeem himself in his parents' eyes before he would be cut off from his inheritance…a reprieve from the dire consequences of the path he had cut through London society before his father had engineered this abrupt departure. He had every reason to be chastened and humble, but like a keen hunter who could never quite give up the field, he took stock of every feminine creature he had encountered between the city and Windmere Hall.

Adam could not help himself. His interest in womanly companionship had long ago graduated from idle small talk in the parlour and holding hands while dancing to those pleasures that were by custom limited to marriage but in practice were frequently available by the night or by the hour, if one knew where and how to ask. The joys of Venus were the source of Adam's greatest delights, but also his downfall.

So it was that Adam Blythewood, an inveterate rake, cad and seducer, found himself delivered to dwell as a guest at the manor of Lady Adonica Windmere, the widow of one of his father's old Army friends. According to his father, Lady Windmere had only one son, close in age to Adam, a moral and upright young man whose influence, it was hoped, would rub off on him. Lady Windmere herself was, according to Colonel Blythewood, a stern, pious woman who would little tolerate Adam's foolishness. In addition, Adam's father had offered his son to Lady Windmere as a secretary, going through the Windmere family papers and organising them — Adam had little to say in the matter, of course. In this way, it was hoped that continuous work in the country would undo the bad habits that idleness in the city had bred in Adam.

Adam had sullenly acquiesced and prepared himself for a period of enforced celibacy and menial labour. He was neither old enough to take charge of his own fortune nor daring enough to break with his family entirely. Better to try to satisfy his father, for now. If this was as close to a monastery as he could manage to place him, so be it. Adam would have to make the best of it.

Adam's first impression of Windmere Hall's inhabitants did little to change his idea of the place. Gainesborough, the butler, was a man of many years and few words, lacking only a robe and tonsure to match exactly the mental picture of a monk that Adam had formed. As the old fellow led Adam through empty hallways that echoed with their footsteps, he informed Adam that the lady and her family had just finished their morning repast.

Gainesborough cleared his throat and opened the door after announcing his presence with a knock. For the first time, Adam felt hope that Windmere Hall might turn out to be a livelier place than he had been led to expect, for the parlour held five beautiful women. Once Gainesborough withdrew and closed the door behind him, Adam had them all to himself.

Sitting at the head of the room in a wing chair as if on a throne was a comely, finely attired woman. This was Lady Windmere, surely. Three maidens sat about the room, their attention on embroidery or reading until Adam walked in. Two of them, by appearances the youngest and oldest, looked up, the third staying focused on the novel she was reading. The eldest girl, tall with ravishing chestnut hair, blanched upon seeing Adam but quickly averted her gaze. The fifth woman was a maid in a neat black uniform. She was on her way out, carrying a tray and following the way Gainesborough had let Adam in.

Lady Windmere stood to take Adam's hand. "Thank you for welcoming me into your home," Adam said after they had exchanged pleasantries about his trip. "I look forward to meeting your son. I'm sure we will become the best of friends." Adam was a little confused that the young man wasn't present to welcome him, and even more so by the blank stares that returned to him from all four ladies.

"But Mr Blythewood, there must be some mistake," Lady Windmere said. "I have no son."

Adam half-smiled. Surely she was pulling his leg. "Am I not to understand that this is the home of Freddie Windmere?" he asked.

A ripple of amusement passed through the room and Lady Windmere rolled her eyes in sudden understanding. "Ah, 'Freddie' is what my late husband Sir Alfred called our eldest daughter." She gestured to the maiden who had blanched at the sight of Adam — she was now somewhat recovered — and said, "Miss Frederica Windmere, Mr Adam Blythewood."

Frederica stood and took Adam's hand, curtseying as she did so. My, but she was charming! Now that she fully occupied his attention, Adam observed her tall, fine figure, her swelling bosom and the tasteful cascade of hair that draped her shoulders and neck. Still not quite believing his good fortune, he turned again to Lady Windmere and said, in what he hoped was a tone of regret, "So…there is no Alfred, Junior?"

Lady Windmere shook her head in resignation, and in that gesture Adam read twenty-odd years of having to explain the situation. "I hope that this will not spoil your plans to stay with us?" she said.

Inside him, a smouldering desire for Frederica began to kindle. It would certainly spoil his father's plans to keep Adam away from the fairer sex, but he personally felt no disappointment at all. "I suppose I shall manage," he said.

Lady Windmere introduced her other two daughters. The three young ladies had stood and lined up during the conversation, tall, medium and short. They made a handsome set, and each was pretty in her own way, although "Freddie" was the prize. Jane, the middle daughter who had been absorbed in her book the whole time, dressed modestly and kept her mousy brown hair wrapped tightly. She returned to her book after returning Adam's greetings. Alice, the youngest and most petite in features, had long, pale blonde hair and pallid skin, like a porcelain figure. She looked Adam full in the eye, almost defiantly, while being introduced. There was something forceful about her presence, as if she were accustomed to making up for her size by will alone.

Adam had but a moment to admire the three sisters before Lady Windmere's voice interrupted his train of thought. "Very well. You've already met Gainesborough—just ask him for anything that you need. As for the rest of the help, you need not learn their names. They are far too bold as it is. After you've settled in, Gainesborough will show you to the library."

"Please, Mother," Alice spoke up. "Could Jane and I show Mr Blythewood around the grounds? We can leave him at the library afterwards."

"What a splendid idea. But I'm sure Mr Blythewood is tired from his journey." She looked to him to provide the final verdict.

"I would love to see the grounds with such charming guides," Adam said, "provided that Miss

Windmere is able to join us. I wouldn't want her to feel left out." He showed her a smile that had proved winning in the past.

Although Frederica seemed to have adjusted to Adam's presence, there was still an underlying stiffness in her manner as she replied, "That is most generous of you, Mr Blythewood. But I am afraid I have plans to occupy my time, and I am sure you will be in good hands with my sisters. Good day, sir."

Adam bowed once more before Frederica departed so quickly that even Lady Windmere had not time to utter a dismissal. Adam wondered if he had been too forward, but Jane and Alice seemed to take no notice of their sister's abrupt departure and were as eager as before to show him around. Their manner suggested that it was Frederica who had breached etiquette, not him.

"You mustn't mind Freddie," Alice said as the three of them crossed the lawn behind Windmere Hall. There was little to see from this angle but densely wooded forest and the rocky highlands that descended into cliffs along the shore. The sound of the ocean was audible, but it was too cool and misty to enjoy the sunshine very much. "You see, Father wanted a boy, and he raised Frederica as if she were one...riding, fencing, sailing, all that sort of thing."

"But not you?"

"No." Alice looked away towards the bleak cliffs. "Once he had Freddie, he didn't... One picks up a few things by observing, of course, but...well —"

"He didn't pay much attention to us either way," Jane said. She still carried her book, tucked under one arm.

Adam made a sympathetic sound and nodded as if he understood. His own father had taken "Freddie" for

Sir Alfred's son, perhaps because Sir Alfred chose to frame the situation thusly, and he had no knowledge of Jane or Alice because Sir Alfred simply never mentioned them. It was a bit sad, or would have been if Adam didn't personally yearn for a little less paternal oversight. He shrugged and said, "Fathers, hmm?"

Alice and Jane both nodded, each taking whatever meaning they chose, and the subject was dropped.

Contrary to Lady Windmere's instructions, Adam learnt the names of many of the servants that afternoon. Jane and Alice knew them all, and stopped to engage in conversation with several of them, introducing Adam and showing off the features of the grounds. Dick, the groundskeeper, oversaw the planting and tending of lawn, garden, hedges, trees and so forth, and kept a pack of docile hounds who lazily patrolled the grounds. Sir Alfred had been an avid hunter, but that was the one outdoor activity in which he could never interest Frederica, so now the dogs were practically pets. Peter maintained the stables and carriages, supervising a handful of grooms and stable boys. Anne had recently married and had left her position, but Adam might encounter Susan and Samantha, if it were the right day, and on and on. The names and duties came so thick and fast that Adam could hardly keep up with who did what.

This friendliness mainly extended to the outdoor servants — Alice and Jane were instructed to be less familiar with the household help, at least within their mother's hearing. Adam did pick up some useful information, however. Gainesborough had the reputation of a dirty old man, but he was harmless. Alice and Jane giggled at the mention of him. Adam learned that the pretty maid who served Lady Windmere was Marie — more giggling. The kitchen was staffed by—yet more giggling—until Adam was convinced that both sisters were far too silly to provide any useful information about the running of the house. The seriousness that marked Frederica's character had apparently used up the entire family's supply.

Adam knew better than to try to pick up hints about Frederica's opinions and preferences directly. The first thing her sisters would do was run to tell her that the new gentleman had been asking all sorts of questions about her. Rather he asked them about themselves, deducing Frederica's character from their answers.

Alice, at eighteen, seemed to revere her eldest sister, but from a distance, having little in common with her. Jane had a more clear-eyed view of things, even though she was apparently not very close with Frederica either. "Well, it's no wonder she's so frigid! She's almost twenty-four, poor thing, with no prospects, except, well—"

"Except?" Adam said, noting the abruptness with which Jane stopped herself. But Jane said nothing else, silenced by a look from Alice.

Jane changed the subject to the library, which they were approaching, but it was too late—Adam had caught on to their secret. So Frederica had a paramour, eh? That didn't change Adam's intentions in the least— even the bonds of marriage had not stopped him in the past, he had to admit—but it was exactly the kind of information he needed to plan his attack, his "manoeuvres" as he and his chums used to say in school. Yes, his intentions were probably all too transparent to Jane and Alice, but so far he had said nothing that could be interpreted as too forward.

Gainesborough was waiting for them in the library when Jane and Alice were done with Adam. They departed, still giggling, as the butler began showing

Adam where he was to begin, where his supplies could be found and so forth. A small writing desk had been procured and placed in the corner, along with ink, quills, fresh paper and other provisions. As Gainesborough talked, it became clear that the bulk of Adam's work would be in organising and editing the memoirs and other personal papers of Sir Alfred, gone these past four years, as Lady Windmere hoped to present her late husband's genealogical and historical work in published form, lest it be forgotten.

"It might be said, sir, that Sir Alfred was not the most organised of scholars—not by me," he hastened to add, "but by those less charitable. He was a man of deeds rather than words, if you take my meaning. And of course the last person to attempt the feat—" To Adam's raised eyes, Gainesborough cut himself off, much as Jane had done earlier.

"Tell me truthfully, Gainesborough—I am not the first person Lady Windmere has taken on to complete her husband's manuscript, am I?" The butler's stony silence was all the confirmation Adam needed. "And something happened to the prior editor?" Adam leafed idly through the pages that were stacked on the desk.

"I think you'll find everything you need, sir," Gainesborough said, then he hastily withdrew.

It must be understood that Adam Blythewood was not of a particularly scholarly bent himself. He had received a good education in English and Latin grammar and knew a smattering of French and Italian besides, and he had been told that his penmanship was excellent, but beyond that, he was not especially bookish or inclined to an interest in history, religion or art. Most of his reading had consisted of browsing illicit copies of *Fanny Hill* and the poetry of Catullus. But truth be told, this put him not that far behind many of the young men of his class and background, and as long as he satisfied his father's demands enough to stay clear of ordination in the Church or a commission in the Army, he stood to make good use of what limited talents he had. He attacked Sir Alfred's manuscript as if his life depended on it.

He began with an introductory essay Sir Alfred had composed on his illustrious forebears. True to Gainesborough's words, the author was a rather poor stylist, with a clumsy prose manner and a limited vocabulary, but once Sir Alfred had warmed to his subject, he painted a clear enough picture of a family whose fortune extended back to the time of Elizabeth and had grown with the expansion of the Empire through shipping and trade. Sir Ambrose Windmere was the man who had truly made the Windmere name, and was the first Windmere to rise to knighthood. After building his fortune in speculation, he crowned his accomplishments by opening trade with the South Pacific island of —

Just as Adam had become absorbed in the story, however, he found that a page was missing. The pages had no numbers, so finding the loose sheet meant sifting through the entire stack to see if it had been put out of order, but nothing made sense when connected to the last page. He glanced at the other pile of papers stacked up beneath the desk and on the shelves next to it — sheaves of personal letters and correspondence, diaries and assorted certificates of title, presumably the primary sources Sir Alfred had relied on in composing his history — and despaired of finding the missing leaf in all that disorder.

Adam composed himself. He had a big task in front of him, and of course it would seem intimidating taken all at once. Better to pace himself — he took a piece of blank foolscap and inserted it into the manuscript, noting the missing page so he could come back to it later. Soon he had half a dozen such bookmarks poking from the stack. He furrowed his brow. How could there be so many gaps in a manuscript that had lain untouched for years? Then he remembered Gainesborough's accidental hint. Someone else had been through the papers, perhaps a literary executor or another hireling Lady Windmere had brought in to finish the job, and for whatever reason, they had failed. *Perhaps, if this is a sign of their level of organisation, they were dismissed, and rightly so.*

Adam came to the end of the incomplete family history. After an hour or so of work, he was ready for a pause. *Thwack!* A sound from outside interrupted his reverie. Adam looked out of the window into the courtyard beneath. Miss Windmere stood with a bow and arrow, taking aim at a target. The arrow flew into it with the same *thwack!* he had heard before.

Well, well, thought Adam, leaning on the sill so he could enjoy the sight of Freddie's archery practice. He was on the second floor and had a good view — Freddie wore a plain black dress with bare arms, allowing her to move freely. Her hair was casually tied up and her mind was clearly on her bow. *Thwack!* In this candid state, Adam found her even more alluring than before, and he could not deny the pleasurable shiver he got from spying on her unseen. There was something captivating about her mannish pursuits. Adam enjoyed visualising her as an Amazon warrior, one of Diana's hunters, and he relished the thought of being in Actaeon's position, even if it meant sharing his terrible fate.

Abruptly, his idyllic daydream came a little too close to reality. Glancing across the courtyard, he saw, or thought he saw, a pale face at the window opposite him. While he watched Freddie, someone else was watching him! In a flash the face — or shadow, whatever it was — disappeared, but in his surprise, he must have made a noise, for Freddie looked up and scowled upon recognising him. With the quickness of the goddess he had imagined her, she took aim straight at him and let the arrow fly.

Thwock! The missile stuck in the frame just outside with a bang that rattled the pane. Adam fell back in such a panic that it was only afterward he remembered the window was still closed. Would the glass have protected him from such a shot? He was glad he didn't have to find out. What a woman! His heart still beating in his chest, he turned back to his desk, deciding he had taken enough of a break.

Chapter Two

Some time later, after Adam had lost himself in Sir Alfred's exhaustively detailed childhood and this time found the narrative uninterrupted, he was alerted to a visitor by a soft knock at the door. At the same time hoping and dreading that it might be Freddie, come to chastise him for spying, he felt an equally mingled sense of disappointment and delight upon seeing Lady Windmere's maid enter with a tray and cups.

"Is it tea time already, then?" he said in a bright tone. "Thank you...Marie, isn't it?"

Marie blushed that the distinguished guest should already know her name, but nodded. "Is there anything else I can provide for you, sir?" she asked after she had poured the tea.

Adam pretended to examine the tray for sugar, cream and the small cake that had been brought with the tea, but his eyes lingered on Marie's pretty ankle, just visible under the hem of her skirt, and the swell of her bosom beneath the bib of her uniform. Marie had dark hair, tucked under a lace cap, and wide doe eyes with heavy lashes and eyebrows. She tented her fingers anxiously as she awaited Adam's judgement.

"No, everything is fine," he said, to Marie's evident relief. Nagged by the earlier incident, he added, "Marie? Could you tell me something?" She nodded, eager to be of use. "The window across the courtyard, just there?" The maid went to the now-open window, trying to follow where Adam pointed. Freddie was no longer in the courtyard, having finished her archery practice long before. Adam experienced a moment of dread, imagining the pale face still in the window, watching and judging him, but there was nothing. In fact, there was nothing at all to distinguish the window in question, as they were all alike, and he had to share the sill with Marie in order to count out the window he meant.

"One, two...the third from the corner," he said, reasonably sure that was the one from which he had been spied. Marie leaned forward, and didn't shy away when he leaned closer to point it out. The smell of lavender, mingled with the aroma of hard work, came to his nose. He could hardly help but notice the curve of her bottom beneath her skirt as she leaned out.

"Yes, sir?" Marie said. When she turned back to Adam, their faces were suddenly close, surprising both of them.

"Could you tell me what room that is?"

Marie blushed again. "Sir?"

Adam repeated his question. Marie placed her hand on her bosom, fluttering her eyes at him. His worries about the mysterious face, or even Frederica Windmere's opinion of him, were fading fast in the company of this charming maiden. "Why, that's the guest bath," she said. "The bath attached to your room."

That was odd. Adam hadn't visited his new quarters yet, as the Windmere sisters had led him straight to the library to get to work. "Could you take me there?" he asked, still looking out through the window.

Marie evidently interpreted his perplexity as a deliberate tease, so she asked, leaning in, "Are you in need of a bath, sir? Before you change for dinner, perhaps?"

Adam took a chance. "Are you offering to administer it?" He placed a hand around her waist.

Marie bit her lip. "Oh, I couldn't, sir, I'm to wait on Lady Windmere. I was only supposed to bring your tea—"

In Marie's expression, Adam saw a frank desire to comply, coupled with an insider's knowledge of how things worked around Windmere Hall. He made his intent clear in the hand he had settled across her waist, and which drifted downward to feel Marie's bottom and bring her closer to him. With the other, he stroked a stray curl that had escaped her cap. "Nonsense. In the city, tea time sometimes takes upward of an hour. There's no need for Lady Windmere to miss you."

Marie wavered, but Adam could tell that she wanted to give in. "Very well, sir. She *did* say to serve you in any way you required."

As Marie ran ahead to prepare the bath, Adam turned from the earlier mystery, deciding that it could wait. It was just Gainesborough or some servant, he told himself, preparing the room, and they happened to look out of the window at the same time as him. Surely there was nothing sinister about it. He had just become excited by associating the sight with being shot at by Freddie Windmere.

Never mind that the shock of seeing the face at the window had come *before* that display of Miss

Windmere's athleticism. Even that nagging doubt went by the wayside when he opened the door and found Marie on the floor on her hands and knees, scrubbing at something. The tightness of the cloth pulled across her backside had a similar effect on the crotch of his trousers.

"Sorry, sir," Marie said, standing, "it's the queerest thing. I know this room was cleaned before you arrived, but there were some muddy footprints!"

So there had been someone here! "Queer, indeed," he said. And now Marie had erased any hope of identifying whether it had been a man or a woman. But in his present state of mind, it mattered not at all. Inflamed by lust, he shrugged it off and took Marie in his arms. "Now how about that bath?" He pressed his lips against Marie's. She responded warmly, returning his embrace.

She pulled away. "Aren't you forgetting something?" Gesturing at the empty tub, she said, "I must fetch the water!"

Thinking of how easily Marie might be pulled back into Lady Windmere's service if she were on her own, Adam said, "How often do you get a chance to relax in this place? Why not put your feet up and let *me* fetch the water?"

This suggestion seemed to shock Marie much more than the prospect of making love. "Oh, no, I couldn't let you do that, sir! Let you carry your own water? Lady Windmere would dismiss me for sure! Why, you wouldn't even know where to find the buckets!"

This was true, but Adam wouldn't be deterred and he was determined not to let Marie out of his sight…a bird in the hand and all that. "Well, can't we ask for some to be sent up? Isn't that what all these cords are for?" He reached for the ropes hanging in the corner, but Marie smacked his hands and immediately blushed again at her assertiveness.

"It won't take but a moment, I promise," she said, and the eagerness in her eyes convinced Adam that she meant it. "You just make yourself comfortable, sir, and I'll bring it right up." She kissed him again and added, "And then we can get started." Adam thought he detected a little extra sway in her hips as she departed.

Adam undressed, his loins already tingling with the expectation of a good tumble. He'd been out of sorts since leaving London, and he felt sure that this would put him right. His only fear was that Lady Windmere or another member of the family would pull Marie away for some other task. It was only when all his clothes were removed, down to his stockings, that he noticed there were no towels at all. *Well*, he thought, *time to set out the buffet*. He lay across the bed, resting on one elbow, to create an amorous tableau that he hoped would surprise and gratify Marie.

It was, as promised, only a few minutes later when he heard the sloshing of water in buckets and the tread of footsteps, but Adam grew alarmed when he realised the sound was quite a bit louder than Marie's step alone had been. Marie was speaking, at full volume, to someone with her.

Adam had no time to get dressed again. He jumped off the bed in search of a hiding place. He could just fit in the small linen closet, empty of towels, in the corner of the bath chamber. Through the woven screen that covered the door, he watched Marie enter his bedroom carrying a pair of buckets, somewhat flustered and still speaking loudly, her eyes darting from side to side. Another maid, also carrying water and a pile of towels, followed closely behind her — broad-shouldered, buxom and plain of face, she seemed indifferent to the task and insensible to Marie's behaviour.

Marie stopped short of the bath and said, "Thank you so much, Gretchen. I can fill the tub."

"Nonsense," Gretchen answered, pushing her way past Marie. She stopped, just feet away from Adam's hiding place, when she noticed the clothing that Adam had left on the floor in his hurry.

"Uh, how queer—" Marie started.

"He must be eager for that bath," Gretchen said. Then, more confidentially, but still within earshot of Adam, she said, "D'ye think he's roamin' the house, naked?" She giggled and turned bright red at the possibility.

"Ah, you never can tell," Marie said weakly. She glanced about until she looked at the linen closet, and Adam could tell she had figured out his hiding spot. She smiled and said to Gretchen, "You'd better look for him. He'll be awfully cold with nothing on."

Gretchen laughed again and turned to leave, but at the last minute changed her mind and said, "I'll just put these towels away first."

Before Marie could say a word to stop her, Gretchen had opened the door and come face to face with Adam, completely nude. She let out a little scream and swooned, but not before looking him up and down. She dropped the towels and fell towards Adam, pinning him in the linen closet as Marie rushed forward to help.

It was only a passing faint. Gretchen awoke almost immediately, pressed against Adam's naked body, and as she backed up and looked from Adam to the embarrassed Marie, she grasped immediately what was going on. A sly grin split her face and her eyes narrowed, darting between the two would-be lovers.

"Oh, Gretchen, let me explain—" Marie began.

"You were going to keep this to yourself, weren't you, Marie?" Gretchen said, not without a little admiration as she openly ogled Adam's manhood, impressive even when at rest.

"No, no, I swear!" Marie said, panicked.

Gretchen was obviously enjoying making Marie squirm. "Yes, I see it exactly. No wonder you wanted to fetch the water yourself. Who takes a bath at this hour?" She faced Adam, hands on hips, as if he were a naughty little boy caught making up fibs. "You'd better come out of there, sir. The jig is up."

Adam mustered as much dignity as he could. He stood straight and tall and marched forth from the little closet. "Well done, Marie. You've found me! That was quite an invigorating game of Hide and Seek, but now it is time for my bath." With his eyebrows he sent Marie a message to play along. "You must excuse me...Gretchen, was it? I would hate for Lady Windmere to feel that you had interrupted one of her family amusements, so it would be best if you ran along." He said it as if it were the most obvious thing in the world.

The gambit almost worked. Gretchen, out of habitual obedience, started to turn away, but she quickly changed her mind. "Now, hold on, sir, that don't track at all, does it?"

"Oh? Whatever do you mean?"

"It's plain as day you and Marie were goin' to have a bit of fun in the middle of the afternoon, innit?"

Adam shifted, his ardour flagging. Marie looked as if she wanted to die. "Be that as it may —"

"Well, there's an obvious solution that'll save us all quite a bit of embarrassment!"

Too late for that, thought Adam, but he took the bait. "Go on."

Gretchen took another look at Adam and his impressive equipment and said, "Cor, why don't I just join you? There looks to be more than enough of you to go around, sir!" She pushed her bosom towards him. It made a compelling supplement to her argument.

Adam found Gretchen's proposition entirely reasonable and spread his hands in admission of defeat, his eyes pleading with the still unconvinced Marie to accept this happy compromise, if not for him, then for the prospect of peacefully living under one roof together.

Marie's mouth gaped open. "What! But sir — "

"Now, now, I know it's a little different from what we expected, but there's no need for either of us to be selfish, Marie. Gretchen is right, there *is* plenty to go around!" This part was true. Gretchen exhibited obvious satisfaction at the prospect of being included.

"But...a bath?" Marie continued to hesitate.

"Why not? It's a big tub," Adam said.

Marie looked at the tub, then Gretchen doubtfully, but said nothing, folding her arms.

"Please, don't be jealous," Gretchen said. "Come on, let's fill the tub." She hoisted one of the buckets of warm water and dumped it in. The water roared like an echo of the surf crashing against the cliffs outside.

While Gretchen went to work, Adam embraced Marie and whispered to her, "Please don't think less of me. You see the bind she has me in. Don't worry, I still think you the sweetest of the pair, but have you ever been with another woman before? Think of it as, well, think of it as a new adventure for you as well."

Marie rolled her eyes, knowing that she was being played upon, but she appeared to appreciate the effort. "New adventure! Once a week I have to scrub down

Gretchen's bum on bath day! It's hardly a new adventure for me!"

"Is that so?" Adam said, savouring the image that brought to mind. As he watched Gretchen stirring soap into the warm bathwater, his appreciation of her voluptuous figure increased. "Well, in that case, consider that I may need help from an old hand such as yourself. Think of it this way — there won't be anything between us that you haven't already seen!"

Adam Blythewood could be very persuasive when motivated, and at last his efforts, combined with Gretchen's, wore Marie's resistance down. His scandalous nudity silently played its part in convincing her. It was a matter of pride to Adam that his slim body was as pale as a cave fish, unmarked by the sun's rays. Not for him were labours in the fields of the country — not so much as a single brick of the city's stone labyrinths bore his fingerprints. Women, in Adam's experience, found this physical evidence of his indolence and wealth very alluring. Certainly Gretchen did. Adam could hardly fail to notice her eyes wandering over his form, and he did the same, taking stock of her powerful arms stirring the soap in. Her skin glistened as the steam from the warm water enveloped her.

"Gretchen is getting a little hot," Adam murmured into Marie's ear. Taking the hint, the young maid approached her buxom colleague and gently, solicitously, began unbuttoning the back of her uniform. Gretchen registered only a moment's surprise before setting the wooden paddle aside and allowing Marie to finish undressing her. Once her black linen weeds had fallen away, revealing the white stays and stockings that encased her ample form, she turned and did the same. Marie blushed but didn't flinch away.

Both maids kept their gaze focused on the visiting gentleman, anticipating the pleasure they would each give to and receive from him in turn. Nor did Gretchen stop at Marie's foundation, surprising her by pulling her chemise down so that the young maid's breasts emerged like a pair of ripe nectarines. Marie gasped, but in response to Gretchen's cheerful grin, she could only pay her back in kind, feeling the smooth expanse of cotton pulled tightly against Gretchen's full bosom until she, too, was able to pull it down, setting her bounty free.

Finally, unable to look without touching any longer, Adam approached the pair of increasingly excited abigails. Marie took charge, snaking her arm around his waist and offering her mouth to him. He kissed her hotly, embracing her on one side and making room on the other for Gretchen, who was now stroking his chest and working her way down to his stiffening manhood. At last fully responsive to his charms, Marie urgently pulled the hem of her chemise up over her hips, revealing a thatch of hair as thick and black as her eyebrows, eager to play hostess to the distinguished visitor. Gretchen broke off her embrace to shed her own underthings, and the three of them wedged themselves into the tub together. Marie nearly sat upon Adam's lap, but he was still pressed so close to Gretchen that he could suck at one of her large nipples while caressing and squeezing Marie from behind.

"This is cosy, is it not?" Adam asked after they had settled in. The rising soap suds hid their busy hands from view. He found their soft and supple nether parts, eager and wet with more than the water of the bath, and they found his thickened root, on which they playfully traded grasps like revellers at a maypole, obviously enjoying the feeling of it getting harder and longer under their ministering touch. "Is it really true that you bathe each other?" he teased.

"Once a month, whether we need it or not!" Gretchen said.

She laughed uproariously when Marie splashed her and said, "Don't lie! There's more than one Sunday to a month, last time I checked!"

"Well, I guess we'll call this one in the bank!" Gretchen replied, and they both giggled.

"Are you trying to tell us something, sir?" Marie said.

"I think he thinks we're dirty!" Gretchen said, affecting shock. "Should we get a good scrub before we go any further?"

"That's what we're here for," Marie said, looking into Adam's eyes. She picked up a sponge and squeezed a rivulet of soapy water from it that flowed between her breasts. Then the two women began taking turns sponging each other down, in between pressing against him or "accidentally" dropping the sponges, after which they would feel around in the water, inevitably finding him or each other first.

Adam lay back, enjoying the sight, and in no hurry to press forward to a finish. As starved for company as he had been, he was yet a gentleman and would no more throw himself into rutting like an animal than he would wolf down a meal after being rescued from starvation in the desert. Before him was a veritable banquet of pleasure, one maiden sleek and slender, and the other plump and bountiful. More importantly, both were as eager as he, once he penetrated their customary reserve. He was gratified to find that the maids' bodies were almost, but not quite, as pale as his own, although their strong arms and rough hands hinted at the labour to which they were accustomed. After showing off to him, they grabbed their sponges anew and worked him over, scrubbing as if he were a ballroom floor the day before a masquerade.

At length, he could no longer put off the moment of truth, although the tub was not very convenient to pleasuring both women equally at the same time. Marie would not be put off, straddling and taking him into herself hungrily while Adam continued fingering Gretchen's split under the surface of the water. Even then the dam did not burst until he pulled out and was confronted with their bosoms pressed against him — a comparison of apples to melons, unequal in size but both delicious. It was too much — he gallantly restrained himself until their combined fingers, lips and supple breasts teased his issue forth and he spent all the credit he had built up on his journey thence. It was, he hoped, but a down payment on an afternoon of pleasure.

Adam's colloquy with Marie and Gretchen was pleasant indeed, but even the sweetest idyll must come to an end. The water in the bath grew cool and the bathers' skin grew wrinkled and prunescent.

"Ah, this is a pretty change from serving Miss Bond," Gretchen said as she luxuriated in the foam. Her full breasts floated just under the surface, round and buoyant.

"Eh?" Adam said, interrupting himself as he nibbled on Marie's ear.

"Our nearest neighbour, Pamela Bond," Marie explained. "She lives at Bondgate, an estate overlooking the cliffs... Oh, that tickles! No, don't stop, please."

"It's a right queer place, too," Gretchen went on, tangling her feet underwater with Adam's and Marie's.

"It's a big place for a single lady to hold sway over, to be sure. I'm happier here, I am."

"I'm happy you're here, too," Adam said, squeezing Gretchen to him while holding onto Marie with his other arm. Soon he was sandwiched between the two, where they nuzzled and sucked on one another as one body part or another emerged from the water.

"I didn't fit in, anyway," Gretchen said idly. "There's one thing almost all of Miss Bond's servants have that I haven't got."

"What's that?" Adam said.

"This!" Gretchen laughed, grabbing Adam's cock under the water. There was a great deal more splashing and thrashing as he found his energies renewed.

"Ladies, I must apologise, but I fear that I am done in," Adam said a little later.

Gretchen giggled. The soapy water lapped around her breasts as Adam stepped out. "No apologies are needed for me, sir! I wouldn't have thought it possible for one man to last so long. You can count on me as well pleased!" She, too, stood to dry off, streaming water from her ample figure.

Marie lay back in the tub, a smile of contentment on her face. Only her hair had been left dry. True to his promise, Adam had indeed lavished her with special attention, caressing her and whispering in her ear, encouraging her to intimate acquaintance with Gretchen before coming between them. "We mustn't leave at the same time," she said, as if remembering her obligations from a great distance away. "Gretchen, you go first."

This time the other maid gave no objection and raised no fuss. Adam enjoyed watching her towel herself off and put on her underthings, rolling stockings up to her thick knees before pulling her black uniform over her head and straightening her cap. She left, rosy-cheeked and sighing, a girl now ten years younger than when she had entered.

Adam had slowed his own drying-off to watch Gretchen leave, and when he turned back to Marie, she was looking at him with a glint in her eye. "What?"

"I think you *do* favour Gretchen," she teased. "Should you like me better if I grew big and fat?"

Adam snorted. "Don't be silly, my dear. We suffer most when we want to be what we are not. She is perfect the way she is, and you are perfect the way you are."

Marie rolled her body towards him in the tub. "But what if I want you to play with my tits like you play with hers? I know you liked them."

"Marie, what do you want me to say? Your bosoms are the most beautifully formed, most perfect ornament to your womanhood — on you. You and Gretchen are not of the same make. Should I put the dome of St Paul's on the Queen's Chapel? Let us not make ourselves miserable by comparison." He sat at the edge of the tub to cradle his lover's head.

She looked up at him. "Perhaps I should have a baby. Then I would grow as full as Gretchen. Would you like that? Is that what you are looking for...a wet-nurse?"

Her smirk suggested a jest, but Adam felt a stroke of terror and his heart quickened. Leaping up, he said, "Please, be serious! If there is one thing I have no interest in, it is fatherhood! Did you not notice how I redirected my issue when the moment came? It is for you as much as myself that I took such pains!"

"Of course I noticed. And fear not, I have no intention of ensnaring you in marriage, if such is your concern. But can I not admit to feeling a little cheated by your games? It may gratify you to spend all over Gretchen's chest, but couldn't I have something stronger than your delicate fingers to send me on my way?" She spread her legs wide in the tub, sinking to the chin and smouldering enough that Adam almost believed she could reheat the water with just a look.

The invitation was clear, and Adam's excitement grew again. Returning to the tub, he fell into Marie's arms and rejoined their coupling with a slower rhythm than before, knowing from experience that with this second wind, he would remain firm longer with less chance of a sudden eruption.

Soon Marie was gasping with the transport of climax. She lay back, satisfied, and after a moment invited Adam to straddle her so that she could take his still-firm member in her mouth. She extracted the last drops of his creative fluid, wringing him out with a groan.

At last it was time for Marie to leave as well. Adam watched her admiringly, but from the comfort of his bed, where he lay to recover from his exertions. He had made up for a few days of celibacy and then some. As soon as Marie had gone and he was dressed, he hoped to return to Sir Alfred's papers with new energy and focus. All the cobwebs had been swept from his mind and he was as sharp as a pin. All he needed was to close his eyes for a few moments, then…

* * * *

When Adam awoke, the dying sun lit the room with a golden glow. Hours had passed. He had heard a knock — or had he dreamt it? The knock came again. "Y-yes?" Adam said, sitting up and finding himself still naked.

Gainesborough's thin voice came through the panel. "Dinner is served, sir."

Chapter Three

"How kind of you to join us," the eldest Miss Windmere said when Adam arrived in the dining room after hastily dressing. Lady Windmere and her daughters were already gathered, and the soup course had been held up waiting for him. As soon as he sat in the chair indicated by the waiting servant, a young man already practised in the arts of self-effacement that Gainesborough had perfected, the other servants rushed to put out the wide, flat bowls before their contents were cold.

Adam apologised profusely for his lateness, but his words were drowned out in slurping noises as the three sisters attacked the soup. He raised his eyebrows in surprise but instead turned to Lady Windmere, who had not started, and directed his regrets to her.

"No doubt you've found something to interest you already," the lady said, to which Adam could but smile and nod agreement.

He tasted the soup, which had not gone entirely cold, and found it subtle and refreshing. "Delicious."

"It is, isn't it?" said Alice.

"It must be one of Molly's," added Jane.

"Hmm?" said Lady Windmere, who was now delicately tasting it. "Oh, the new girl? Yes, she does seem to have a knack."

"Or at least some fine recipes," said Alice.

The main course, a roast fowl, was neither disagreeable nor exceptional, and passed without comment. Evidently this was *not* the work of the "new girl." Jane and Alice peppered Adam with questions about London. Jane wondered aloud how the Windmere family library compared to others he had seen. While Adam had vague memories of seeing matched leather spines in the homes or clubs of friends, he shied from admitting that the contents of those volumes were as foreign to him as the residents of Mecca. He went on about the costliness of Sir Such-and-such's mahogany shelves or the richness of Lord Somesuch's vellum editions until he noticed Frederica, so far nearly silent, smiling wryly and deduced that he was making a boor of himself.

"Still," he concluded, changing course, "there are many impressive collections in London, yes, but I find that so many of them contain the *same* books. The libraries of the country houses — of the oldest and best families — often hold much more interest for a collector."

"And how do you enjoy the *view* from the library?" Frederica asked, addressing Adam directly for the first time since the beginning of the meal.

Adam blushed beneath her gaze. "It is, ah, very stimulating."

"Oh, indeed? The air is quite fresh in the courtyard. I frequently take my exercise there. Tomorrow I have a session with Miss Prine. She is a skilled instructor in

Greco-Roman wrestling. Perhaps you would like to watch us grapple?" Adam's heart gave a great thump at the prospect, but the vehemence with which Frederica stabbed at a portion on her plate underlined her sarcasm, and the grip she held on her knife further reinforced it.

"Ah, perhaps not," Adam said, his voice issuing as a whisper from his suddenly dry throat.

"Mother," Frederica continued, "perhaps we should ask Gainesborough to put some heavier drapes in the library windows. I would hate for Mr Blythewood to be distracted from his work."

Adam was rescued by the arrival of the last course. "Ah," exclaimed Alice, "I *know* this is some of Molly's handiwork!" The dessert was a tart, small in circumference but thick with buttery yellow custard, with a flaky bottom crust. In the centre was a single ripe, red berry. Each diner received one to themselves.

"This tart is her specialty," Jane explained.

"Please," Lady Windmere said, as if the very name of a servant spoken within her presence pained her, "let us simply enjoy them. This excessive praise is sure to go to the girl's head."

"But, Mother," Jane said, "surely it can do no harm. Molly isn't even in the room!"

"Yes, but you know how they talk to one another," Lady Windmere said, dismissing the servants who still stood by to wait upon them. "As soon as one of them hears something, they *all* know it."

Adam nearly choked on his wine.

* * * *

That night, Adam pulled the drapes against the encroaching nightfall outside his chambers. His suite of rooms, across the courtyard from the library, was on the opposite end of the house from the family's chambers. The servants' quarters were to the rear of the building, near the kitchen. Gainesborough, the butler, was accessible to him at any time by means of a pull rope in the corner of the room. It was cosy, but lacking in personal touches—no family portraits or curious heirlooms caught his attention, as the chamber had apparently never been other than a guest room.

Although the day had been long and draining, sleep refused to come, a combination of lying in an unfamiliar bed, the cat nap he had taken earlier that afternoon and, most of all, thoughts of the three Windmere daughters, Alice, Jane and Frederica. His imagination worked memories of their meeting into more speculative tableaux, all the more enticing for how many layers of clothing he chose to remove from his mental picture. But of course it was absurd—there was only one path to consummation with any of them, and it led straight down the aisle of a church. Even if any of them were inclined to stray, the watchful eye of Lady Windmere would put an end to that, and to Adam's welcome, too. Yet Frederica was exactly the kind of difficult prize that seemed most worthwhile to pursue, and her armour the most tantalising to penetrate.

Then there were the two feisty maids...their company had been pleasurable indeed, and, to be sure, he spent some of the night reliving his moments of enjoyment with them, but one still had to be cautious. He was a guest of the Windmeres, and while a man of normal appetites, he was still a gentleman, and he felt certain that Lady Windmere would be put out if she had to let any of her staff go for their indiscretion.

Tossing and turning, forcing his eyes to stay closed as if that would bring sleep more quickly, Adam was attuned to all the small sounds typical of a grand old house. Every creak and rustle sounded louder to his sensitive, unsleeping ears. But it was a sound quite different from those ordinary background noises that caused him to sit up, wide awake, every nerve quivering to determine whether it was real, or merely an impression from an approaching dream. No, he felt sure he had heard it...*the sound of the doorknob to his room being turned from the outside!*

Throwing on his dressing gown, he rushed to the door. "Marie?" he whispered through the crack. There was no response. He felt no fear—yet—for there was surely a simple explanation. Most likely Gainesborough or one of his underlings was checking on the room to make sure Adam was comfortable before turning in for the night. But when he opened the door himself and faced the darkness of the empty hallway, his nerve failed him.

Then footsteps retreated towards the central hall—not the tap of hard shoes, but a soft padding, as of bare or slipper-clad feet—and his curiosity overcame his hesitance. No servant would try a door then slip away, unless they were up to something. The possibility that it was another guest, mistaken as to which room was theirs, seemed even less likely, as he was the only one staying in this wing.

Down the hall he spied a tall, shadowed figure. As the visitor passed in front of a window, an errant moonbeam revealed a womanly form in a thin silken shift, with dark hair cascading down her back. It could be none other than Frederica Windmere! But why would she come to his room in such a state, and proceed in the dark? A night-time rendezvous? That seemed a little too good to be true—if anything, Frederica had been cool to him so far. And in any case, why would she try his door then flee? Cold feet? It made no sense. He decided to pursue her, if only to understand her actions.

She walked at such a stately pace that it wasn't hard to catch up. Adam followed Frederica to the gallery overlooking the central hall. If she heard him, she neither increased nor slackened her pace in response. The moonlight that filled the hall gave it a fairylike unreality, and Frederica an otherworldly beauty. She indeed wore nothing on her feet, and only a little bit more on the rest of her body.

"I say," he began in a whisper, lest it shatter the strange, dreamlike atmosphere in which they moved, "Miss Windmere, I—" As soon as he touched her, she turned and took him in her arms, pressing her body against his and kissing him hungrily on the mouth. For the briefest moment, his reaction was as primal as any animal's, shocked as he was by her actions, and he returned her embrace, separated from her lithe form by only the thinnest layers of silk and cotton.

"I—I didn't know you felt this way about me," he said once the necessities of breathing had separated their lips, but Frederica only embraced him all the more, leaning on his shoulder.

"Don't be silly, my love," she said. "All that matters is that you have returned."

"Returned?" Adam echoed. He could hardly think straight over the pounding of his heart and the rush of blood thundering through his veins, but something didn't feel right.

"Shh," Frederica whispered, "don't speak, Roderick."

Adam felt as if he had been shaken out of a dream. Who was Roderick? Before he could ask, Frederica turned away from him, first heading towards one corner of the hall then another, as if confused. "We're being watched, my love," she whispered urgently. She turned back towards him, and as she stepped into the full light of the moon, Adam could see that her eyes weren't focused on his but on something far away, and that she walked as if in a trance. Suddenly it all fell into place. "Tomorrow night, then," she said, and hurried away towards the Windmere family rooms.

Sleepwalking! So that's it. Adam retraced his steps towards his room. *How queer!* Yet, he thought, relishing the taste of Frederica's lips that even now was fading from his own, it wasn't entirely unsatisfying. This Roderick was certainly a lucky fellow, if he were real, and not simply born of feminine hysteria. Adam felt certain that he knew what he would dream of tonight, if he ever fell asleep.

These thoughts and more were tumbling through his mind when he passed a side table on which stood a candlestick. He hadn't remembered seeing it there before, focused as he had been on following Frederica. But the wick of the candle smouldered orange, as if it had just been blown out. It was still warm. He looked about, mystified all over again. Perhaps that had not been merely a part of Frederica's waking dream. Someone really *had* been following them!

Chapter Four

The next morning, following Lady Windmere's suggestion, Adam borrowed the coachman to drive him down to the village that stood at the base of the cliffs neighbouring Windmere Hall. The village dated back to the days of Sir Ambrose and even earlier, and was the local trading centre for those tenant farmers who owed their fealty to the Windmeres, as well as the fleets of fishermen who still plied the waters nearby. Although reduced in its importance to trade from the old days, it was still a quaint, bustling place, made up of low wooden buildings placed alongside dirt roads tramped flat by centuries of passage.

Today was one of the village's periodic festival days, so Lady Windmere had thought Adam would find it diverting to see the medieval character of the buildings heightened by fluttering banners, streamers and the peasant costumes of the villagers themselves. "Lord knows there is little enough to see on an ordinary day," she said. Unlike many such folk festivals in urban areas, this didn't seem to be a put-on for outside observers.

Adam saw no other gentlefolk like himself. It was as if he had walked into a scene from the past, and once the coachman took his leave, he was entirely on his own.

A group of a half dozen boys in archaic costume hurried towards him, chasing a girl their own age, teasing her. They wore grey coats and childish approximations of tricornered hats, and they had their faces covered, some with handkerchiefs over their mouths and noses, others blacked with shoe polish.

The girl squealed in a mixture of affected terror and genuine apprehension. She hid behind Adam momentarily until the boys caught up, at which point they circled around both Adam and the girl, chanting in raucous unison, *"Where, where is the fly without wings? Washed ashore, washed ashore! Where, where is the treasure it brings? No more, no more! No more, no more!"* Then they reversed direction and repeated the rhyme, switching the answers so that the "fly without wings" was "no more" and the treasure was "washed ashore." After this performance, the girl, hiding no longer, rewarded each boy with a kiss, and they were on their noisy way, spreading their mischief to other parts of the village.

Adam discreetly felt his pockets to make sure he had not been the target of a "tip." His billfold and pocket watch were still there, and he smiled at himself for the suspicious habits he carried with him from the city. It was not long before Adam observed that the costume of coat and tricorn was a traditional part of the festival, as there were several other boys, and a few too old to be described as such, chasing girls — and, again, some who had quite outgrown that label — in similar manner. Like most festivals, it was an opportunity for behaviour that on other days would earn a slap.

Although Adam had hoped that one or more of the Windmere sisters would join him, they had their own schedules to keep. At breakfast Frederica had hardly acknowledged him. In the light of her mysterious nocturnal visit to Adam's room and her lusty embrace of him, Adam's interest in her had bloomed into a full-fledged infatuation, making her daytime indifference to him all the more maddening. Now that he knew the ripe curves of her body, usually hidden beneath layers of silk and linen, he was determined to have her. Even as he strolled through the market, she was wrestling with her instructor Miss Prine back at the Hall, and the knowledge which had been meant to needle him served only to inflame his imagination. Damn her! How could one so beautiful be so cruel, and crueller yet, she had already given her heart to another! Roderick…whoever that was. But he was determined not to give up. The sight of the copious bounty for sale in the market inspired in Adam a new plan. A bouquet of fresh flowers might go a long way towards softening Freddie's opinion of him. There were many to choose from and he had soon gathered a handsome spray of blossoms bundled in paper.

As he passed a booth belonging to a purveyor of herbs, Adam was surprised to be accosted with a surprising familiarity. "I 'ad the plant you asked about, sir," the old woman said, shuffling her parcels to bring out a small bundle wrapped in paper, "but it's dried out. Mind you, it's been more than a month so I'll 'ave to dig up another one if you want it for plantin'. I wouldn't mind payment in advance this time. It's a lot of work to do an' then not 'ave you take it."

"I beg your pardon?" Adam said. "Have we met before?"

The old woman focused her rheumy eyes on Adam then shook her head. "Beggin' your pardon, my 'umblest apologies," she said, rewrapping the parcel and stowing it among her wares. "I took you for someone else. Not very many gentlemen come through 'ere, y'see."

Adam accepted her apology and tipped his hat to the woman, forgetting the incident almost immediately. He had other things on his mind. He inhaled the fragrance of his flowers. Despite his frustration with Miss Windmere, he was in a good mood.

As he made his way towards the other end of the town square, Adam was distracted by a roar of voices and the sight of a gathered crowd. Now, this really was more like London — perhaps a juggler or ballad singer was performing, or a cockfight was underway.

The sight that greeted him when he pushed through the crowd of villagers mystified him — in the open space a set of wooden stocks stood, and locked within it by her wrists and neck was a comely lass. At least he guessed her comely, for her face was obscured by splattered cream and crust as the villagers took turns hurling custard pies and other bits of food at her. Many had missed their mark, covering the wooden planks of the stocks and the ground around her, but more had landed on her skirt and bodice, and the girl dripped with the stuff. Members of the crowd shouted names or invectives at her that would be quite unprintable. For her part, the young woman, evidently a villager herself, took this humiliating punishment with stoic indifference.

Adam was shocked, struck by the girl's plight and the unfairness of the mob's treatment of her. He leapt in front of her without a thought. "Stop this at once!" he cried. "What is the meaning of this?"

The villagers were just as shocked to see a gentleman throw himself between them and their victim. Only as he stood, catching his breath, did Adam appreciate what he had put himself in for...the villagers, men and women, with mingled expressions cowed and defiant, held pies, rotten vegetables and other missiles in their hands. It occurred to him that they might decide that he made an even better target than the young woman they had already splattered.

"You'd better move if you don't want to join me," said the girl from behind him, but her resignation made him only more determined to put an end to this medieval display. At least in the city a woman might be paid for being made into a spectacle!

"And leave a defenceless lass to be treated this way?" Adam said with a confidence he no longer felt. He wished that he were back at Windmere Hall. The villagers looked restless. All it would take was one daring soul to throw something at him and he would be likewise turned into a mess or forced to retreat. Either possibility was humiliating. He had moved to rescue the girl, but who would rescue him?

His salvation came from an unexpected quarter — a slim, red-haired girl in peasant skirt and bonnet stepped to the front of the crowd. A basket hung on her arm. The other villagers seemed to look to her, and Adam sensed a relaxation of the tension that had enveloped the square. "Apologies, sir," the girl said, her rustic accent at odds with the Roman firmness of her mouth. "You couldn't 'ave known, but this is part of our festival. It's all in fun now, but in the old days it could get a mite bloody. One goat must bear the punishment for the sins of the flock, ye ken?"

Adam shifted uncomfortably, feeling that he had jumped in to interrupt something he didn't understand. Remembering the girl in the stocks behind him, he turned to see if she felt that this was "all in fun." Beneath the slathering of custard that coated her face, her expression was unreadable, but the woman with the basket revealed it with a swipe of her hand. The "goat" was indeed pretty, with large, soft eyes, although there was something grotesque about her imprisonment, both within the stocks and the layer of orts that covered her. "Now tell me," the girl said, saving her ire for the red-haired lass, "you promised —" She was cut off abruptly as the redhead, still smiling, pulled a small tart from her basket and stuffed it into the girl's mouth.

"Or you could take 'er place, if ye feel so strongly about it." She glowed with triumph, perhaps hoping that he would take that dare.

Now over the shock, and provided with a face-saving exit, Adam began to withdraw. "I apologise for interrupting your rite," he said. "I had no wish to offend."

"Not so fast, sir," said the woman with the basket. "Since you're 'ere, why not join in? There's no 'arm in it." She withdrew from her basket a single round tart, yellow with a pink berry in the centre. It looked familiar to Adam. "The price is only one flower," she said as she handed Adam the tart and extracted a rose from the bouquet Adam still held. She tucked it into her red hair, behind the ear.

"I know you!" Adam said. "You're Molly that works in the kitchen at Windmere Hall!"

Molly nodded in satisfaction. "And you're Mr Blythewood, the lady's new guest," she said. "Oh yes, I've 'eard all about you I 'ave, and I must say you don't disappoint." She glanced at the girl in the stocks, who had spit out the tart with which Molly had closed her mouth earlier. "Well, go on, give 'er a splat!"

Adam begged off. "Oh, I couldn't. What kind of gentleman would I be—"

"The kind of gentleman that 'as 'is way with two maids in a tub?" Molly said in a low voice, nudging him conspiratorially. Good lord! It was true—they all talked to one another! "I shan't tell. Go on, then!"

For a brief moment, Adam was tempted. The girl seemed resigned to her messy fate, and had he not indulged in worse behaviour in the city? But there was something too eager about this Molly, and her galling assurance that she had his number, such that Adam felt his innate stubbornness—the same imp of perversity that would have made him throw the tart if he had been instructed *not* to—well up, and instead he looked Molly in the eye and took a bite of the tart. It was indeed the same flavour he had tasted the night before, and while it was quite sweet, he hadn't yet made up his mind if Molly were as well.

* * * *

The incident in the village stayed with Adam after he'd returned to Windmere Hall and resumed his work on Sir Alfred's manuscript. He sought an opportunity to give the bouquet to Freddie Windmere. She was polite in accepting the flowers, but he later saw Marie carrying them to her own quarters. "A pressie from the miss." Adam had smiled wanly and said nothing, but it was another sign of Frederica's indifference to him.

Dinner that night was quiet. Adam chose not to mention the scene that had unfolded in the village square, limiting his observations to how quaint, how picturesque, how unspoiled by modernity it all seemed. If any of the Windmere sisters were familiar with the rituals of the village's festival days, they did not let on.

Afterward, Lady Windmere excused herself and Adam was drawn into an evening of games. While he was familiar with quadrille and whist, the Windmere sisters preferred a game of lottery, as many country people did. "Mother doesn't enjoy it, so we don't often get to play," Jane explained.

"I hope she feels better rested tomorrow," Adam said, thinking the lady had retired early. His sympathy brought a few knowing giggles from his hostesses.

"Oh, she's not ill. She's visiting Miss Bond."

"Your neighbour?"

"Yes, she and Mother are friends. No doubt you will get your chance to meet her soon."

Imagining a spinster or widowed dowager like Lady Windmere herself, Adam thought nothing of it, and Frederica, who had still spoken but few words to him since his attempt to make peace with her, impatiently said, "Shall we continue the play or not?" and the subject of Miss Bond was dropped.

The game became increasingly rowdy, with an abundance of inside jokes, squeals of outrage and even comical attempts to upset the game from the three sisters. Adam sat apart, a little shaken. He had been warned about the relaxed habits of the country gentry, and he didn't wonder that Lady Windmere's apparently frequent visits to Bondgate left Frederica, Jane and Alice to their own devices, and their manners somewhat lacking in refinement. It was a surprising contrast to the watchful sternness he had been led to expect, but he had no complaints. Seeing Frederica in the flush of enjoying herself and acting in high spirits made up for this defect in Adam's eyes. Once she caught him looking at her appreciatively in the middle of some jest with her sisters and she immediately straightened up, recalling her earlier standoffish attitude.

Did she remember, he wondered, her embrace of him last night, if only as a dream? Or were Freddie and Frederica two different people, one by day and the other by night? It was a fascinating conundrum. That night, after the party had broken up, he chose to stay awake, lying in bed in hopes of hearing another step outside his door, even though he was tired from the day.

At last, when his eyes had almost closed of their own accord, there it was! The knob turned, yet despite his excited anticipation, the door did not open. Frederica did not enter. As soon as he heard her footsteps receding down the hall, he opened the door as silently as possible and followed at a distance. Where would she go? What would she do? He imagined with rising ardour that she might lead him all the way to her private bedchamber and quickened his step.

The house was dark. No servants were about, and the only moving figures were the ghostly daughter of the manor and the gentleman who watched her from a distance. This time she passed the gallery and the main hall and, as if in a trance, entered the dining room. It was pitch black, and Adam caught his shins on the chairs around the table, nearly distracting him from keeping Frederica in sight. The movement of a swinging door, barely visible, guided his next steps.

Into the forekitchen he followed Frederica, his eyes adjusting to the darkness. The swing of another door, this time closer, showed him the way. In the kitchen proper, a long, narrow galley in the manner of old houses, moonlight spilled in through diamond-paned windows, giving a lustre of faerie twilight to the stacked crockery and pots on the counters. In the middle of it all, Frederica Windmere stood, her back turned as if she were absorbed in a scene viewed through the window, or in her mind's eye.

From behind, her diaphanous silk negligee hugged and revealed every curve of her lean hips and bottom. Her chestnut hair, like a cloud of ink spilled into a pool of water, descended to the middle of her back, covering the pale skin revealed by the plunging neckline of her nightdress. Adam's mouth dried up with stunned surprise, then began to water with desire. Here was an angel, a spirit, a magnificent beauty out of a dream, and she was all his…at least by night. Who was Roderick? In that moment, Adam cared not at all.

Rather than turn back to him, Frederica bent to rifle through the cabinets before her. She seemed to know exactly what she sought, even if in a daze, and she worked with the silent efficiency of one who had performed this act many times. Adam stepped closer, but his curiosity began to overcome his passion. What was she looking for?

"Oh, Roderick," she said pitiably, "where is it? Where have you left it?"

Adam took a chance. "Left what, my love?"

Frederica stood and turned back to him with unseeing eyes. She clasped her hand to her breast and said, as if to herself, "There!" She passed by Adam without so much as a glance, so near that he caught the scent of her hair in passing. How he ached for her, how tormenting was her nearness! But what did she seek?

Opening a small chest, Frederica removed from it a tray — a tray piled high with tarts! *Goodness, all this for a midnight snack!* How the Windmeres enjoyed their tarts! Yes, they were good, but Molly must have been a spell-binder to have such power over both the village and the Hall! At last understanding, Adam approached Frederica from behind. He placed an arm around her pliant waist and leaned over her shoulder, her exposed neck inviting the first kiss of what he hoped would be many. Only at the last minute did he remember Frederica's earlier words about her training with Miss Prine.

Greco-Roman wrestling, he thought helplessly as, in one smooth motion, Frederica pulled the arm he had placed around her and threw him swiftly to the floor. He was so stunned that he didn't even feel the pain of his landing until a moment later, and by then it was too late to cry out. The moment had passed, so instead, he exhaled like a punctured balloon. His heart pounded in his chest. Meanwhile, Frederica, still moving as if in a dream and unaware of what she had just done, gathered a tart in each hand. Adam scooted backward on the cold stone floor, his eyes glued to this fascinating — and dangerous — woman.

"Ah, Roderick." She sighed, holding the tarts. She now looked out through the window again. Adam was looking at her face-on, but from the floor, beneath her notice. "How I miss you," she whispered, and caressed the side of her face with one of the tarts, as if cradling it.

What on earth?

Soon Frederica was moaning as if in the embrace of a lover. She began rubbing the other tart on the opposite side of her face until both had turned to runny liquid, making a mask of custard on her beautiful features. She grabbed another, then another, pressing them into her face until only her mouth, agape and moaning in open arousal, was recognisable. Adam had never seen anything like it — well, almost never, but the girl in the stocks in the village hadn't seemed to derive any pleasure from the experience, and Frederica showed nothing but. He could not help but respond. There was something primal, naked, about it — the spoiling of both the pretty tarts and Frederica's yet prettier looks felt dangerous and naughty, and what he could see of Frederica's natural beauty was heightened by its partial coverage. Adam remembered how some of his more eccentric college mates had admired ladies wearing high-heeled boots or fur coats, sometimes to the exclusion of any other consideration. Just as a quizzing glass could focus the sun's rays into a point of blazing heat, so these fripperies could serve to intensify a lover's ardour.

Adam had thought such fancies strange then, but he understood the appeal now, and more, he wanted to participate. His manhood throbbed. Frederica's angelic beauty, her trim, athletic body, trembling with frustrated desire and sensual abandon, was all too much for him. At the moment when he was about to stand, to take Frederica in his arms, to override her, whether she thought him Roderick or someone else, the creak of the swinging door from the dining room into the forekitchen brought both of them back to reality. Afraid as one caught filching from the pantry, Adam scurried backward, knocking a set of cookbooks from a low shelf, a cascade of loose papers fluttering about him and making yet more noise than the creaking door. When he looked up, Frederica was gone, as if she had been only a dream. He stood and looked about. She was nowhere to be found.

The dining room! She must have hurried past him while he was blinded by falling papers. He raced to the swinging door to follow her but nearly cried out in shock when confronted by the glowing face of a ghost!

The scream of a woman, surprised by Adam's abrupt appearance, explained the true identity of the "ghost" immediately. "Marie!" Adam gasped, his heart pounding. The lovely lady's maid wore a night-time "mask" of skin-conditioning mud that glowed a bright greenish colour in the moonlight, and he had taken it for the visage of a prowling spirit. "Did you see anyone go through this way?" There was no sign of Frederica.

"No, sir!" she said, catching her own breath. "That is, just you. I heard a noise in the kitchen, and...my word, you scared me!"

"But you didn't see anyone else?"

"No. Why?"

She placed her hands on Adam's shoulders, and he really looked at her for the first time. Besides the face mask she wore very little, just a slip that descended to her knees and left no doubt of what it concealed. "Never mind. You must be freezing."

"I keep my room warm, but it is always chilly in the kitchen. You still haven't said what you were doing. Up for a late-night snack?" She leaned into him, pressing her bosom against his chest. He was already flustered and aroused, and Marie knew him well, to her advantage. "Perhaps I can be of service?" she offered, finding his firm manhood with one hand and caressing it through the thin fabric of his nightshirt. "Just let me remove this awful mask."

She turned to lead him back to her room, but Adam grabbed her shoulder and turned her to face him, a sudden wellspring of appetite erupting within him. "Leave it on," he growled, and kissed her hungrily. Suddenly they were all hands, groping and stroking each other through their clothes, their lips mashed together, tongues entangled.

"Oh, my!" Marie gasped, when she could get a word in edgewise. "Whatever you say, sir, but not here!" She led him by the hand to a small private chamber, close to the kitchen. In the near darkness of her room, illuminated by a square of moonlight, the mask again glowed and seemed to float in mid-air, as if it had a life of its own, teasing, pouting and yielding kisses to him, but its chief appeal for Adam in that moment was how it reminded him of the mask Frederica had made of her own face, smearing it with those mesmerising tarts. A scent reached his nose. Above and beyond the aroma of Marie's body and her excitement, he smelled the fresh bouquet that he had given Frederica but which she had handed off to Marie. The entire room, closed up during the day, had become saturated with the scent.

An incredible surge of desire overwhelmed Adam, bringing together in his mind's eye the girl he had seen punished in the village, Freddie Windmere's unladylike wallowing and Marie's frank lustiness. He pushed Marie towards the little bed in the corner. He squeezed her ripe breasts through the lacy negligee then, overcome, grabbed handfuls of fabric in his fists, tore it from her with a satisfying rip, pushing her down onto the bed and entering her with an urgency that clearly shocked Marie as much as himself.

In and out he plunged, fixated on the gap in the mask made by Marie's open mouth, the sound of her cries and the shape of her lips as they stretched open in full-throated climax. He wished he had one of Molly's tarts right now, and the mere thought of pushing one into Marie's face, of smearing it around and decorating her beauty, of custard sticking in her night-black hair while her eyes and teeth shone through, even more alive by contrast with the mess he would make of her, brought him to his peak. He pulled out and spent across her shallow belly with a strangled cry.

A few moments later, there was a knock at the door. "Marie, honey, are you quite all right?" It was Gretchen! Marie and Adam hissed each other to silence. They had made so much noise!

"Yes, dearie," Marie called. "I was—er, having a dream!" She wiped Adam's pearly essence from her stomach with the torn nightie, now a rag.

"Cor, sounds like a dream worth talking about!" Gretchen said through the door. "Shall I come in and brew a cup?"

"N-no," Marie said, shushing Adam, who was unaccountably overcome with a fit of silent laughter. "Go to sleep, and I'll tell you all about it tomorrow."

"All right. Good night, dearie."

"Oh my, sir," Marie finally said after Gretchen had departed. Adam and she lay together on her narrow bed in a daze. "I had no idea you were so zealous."

Neither did Adam, he thought to himself. Even at his most debauched, he had rarely felt such urgency, such heightened passion. What had happened? "I — I'm sorry," he said. "Did I hurt you?"

Marie giggled and squeezed him closer. "I shall recover," she whispered. "But I shan't say the same for my nightie."

"I'm sorry. I'll buy you another one. I really don't know what came over me. I was beastly, I was a brute —"

Marie hugged him closer and climbed on top of him, silencing him with a kiss. "You were a man," she said. The mask she wore had been smeared but was still visible, and her eyes shone with recent pleasure. "Don't worry, I won't tell Gretchen. She can believe I was with a stable boy."

Adam shrugged. He was in a buoyant mood. "Why should some stable boy get the credit? Invite her in. I could take on a whole bevy of housemaids." He could do no such thing at the moment. He felt raw and drained, and thought he might sleep until noon if he were allowed.

"I think I'd rather have you all to myself," Marie replied, kissing him again. She laid her head on his chest and sighed. "But I suppose I must let you go. It wouldn't do for you to wake up here in the morning, would it?"

Adam groaned. "I suppose not." With an effort, he dragged himself up and pulled on the nightshirt that had almost suffered the same fate as Marie's negligee. He bade her good night and left her sitting on the bed, naked and flushed. Where would he get something to replace the torn garment? How mad, how inflamed by lust he must have been!

After making sure the halls were again empty, Adam passed the kitchen and his mind returned to the mystery of Frederica's disappearance. She must have slipped out through the back door while he was distracted by the falling cookbooks. Remembering that shower of papers, he felt he should probably straighten them up to cover his presence.

The kitchen, darker now that the moon had passed its brightest height, was empty. Adam replaced the lid on the chest from which Frederica had taken the tarts. Splattered drops of custard and cream dotted the floor where she had stood. At least that hadn't been a dream. He turned his attention to the books and papers he had knocked off the low shelf. He stooped to replace them mechanically, his mind already on his bed and the sleep that invited him. What a day he had experienced!

Something about the loose leaves of paper caught his attention—he held one up and examined it in the faint light of the moon. The handwriting, although he could not read it clearly in the gloom, was unmistakably Sir Alfred's! And the size and weight of the paper matched the manuscript he had been editing...surely that was what had turned his attention to it in the first place! Rifling through the other loose pages, he found more. Now fully awake and amazed, Adam realised that these must be the missing pages! He grabbed them and took them back to his room.

Chapter Five

Retreating to the library the next morning, Adam avidly read the first of the wayward pages. It began in mid-sentence.

were not so understanding. Undeterred, preparations were begun for a great feast to celebrate the undertaking. According to Sir Ambrose's diary, Cliffsward "had ne'er seen such abundance." Guests marvelled at a fifty-foot buffet laden with meats, game and fruits-de-mer. Loaves of bread had been baked in the shapes of the most bizarre mythological creatures. The centrepiece was a tableau recreating the eruption of Mount Vesuvius and the destruction of Pompeii rendered in pastry. Incredibly, the records describe an outlay of four hundred gallons of dairy-fresh cream for tarts alone!

Tarts, again! What hold did such simple desserts have on the Windmeres? Adam continued reading.

Alas, the night did not go as planned. The so-called "Feast of Ambrose" became a notorious scandal, and those who attended were marked with shame thereafter, no matter how highly placed. Sir Ambrose's diary is strangely silent regarding the event itself, but he was afterward plagued with misfortune. Many of his investors deserted him, and after his prize ship sank in the bay, he became a retiring figure, moving to London soon afterwards. Cliffsward fell into decline, and it was left to Sir Ambrose's nephew Gulliver to begin the project of renewal that led to the current Windmere Hall.

An introduction of that nephew and a summary of his life, beginning at birth, followed. The narrative again broke off at the end of the page before young Gulliver even experienced his First Communion. Working backward, Adam inserted this page into one of the gaps he had found in the manuscript, but there must have been at least another page still missing, as it didn't connect to the narrative of Sir Ambrose's opening of trade in the South Pacific. There was likewise no continuation of Gulliver Windmere's biography anywhere to be found. Cliffsward, Adam knew from his previous reading, was the original estate of the Windmeres, but it had been located elsewhere and, after its decline, it had disappeared from Sir Alfred's narrative entirely. It was probably only a ruin now.

Scanning the other pages he had brought from the kitchen, he found that they did indeed fill various holes in Sir Alfred's history, but not all of them. There must have been more yet waiting to be found. *Damnation!* Adam mentally cursed the late Sir Alfred for lacking the courtesy to number the pages of his manuscript.

Who even knew how many pages might fit into the remaining gaps? He could only guess. Adam also noted that the alluded-to diary of Sir Ambrose was nowhere to be found in the library. A fruitless hour of searching had convinced him of that. He sat at the desk in frustration. His supposed victory in finding the pages had only led to more mysteries. Looking out of the window into the courtyard, he had not even the sight of Freddie Windmere to cheer him up. Not waiting for Gainesborough to commission new drapes for the library, she had moved her gymnasium to a less conspicuous part of the grounds.

Impulsively, Adam stood and made his way downstairs. Perhaps there were more pages hidden in the kitchen. He had been in a hurry the night before and had only moonlight to search by, after all. On the staircase he passed Marie going the opposite way with her tea service, complete with a gooey sticky bun, evidently intended for him. "At this hour? I'm afraid I'm very busy," he begged off, hardly breaking his stride. He barely heard her huff and stamp her foot after he continued on.

The kitchen in daylight was narrow and cramped. Beads of perspiration appeared on Adam's upper lip when he entered. Clouds of steam emerged from boiling pots on the stove and flames tickled the bottom of the rack in the oven. Compared to the cool, moist air outside, it was like stepping into a furnace. He loosened his cravat in response.

A cook busied herself managing various pots and pans boiling and fuming on the stove and didn't see him come in at first. Adam found himself unaccountably relieved to see someone other than Molly, the redhead who had made such an impression on him in the village. The cook was buxom and full-figured, no longer young but not too old, and the plain muslin dress and petticoat she wore beneath her apron did little to hide her curvaceous figure in the kitchen's sultry atmosphere. Masses of honey-blonde curls spilled from under a lace cap that could hardly contain them. Adam appreciatively watched her bustle about for a few moments until she looked up and noticed him.

"Cor!" she exclaimed in surprise, wiping her hands on a towel. "I didn't see you come in! You must be young Mr Blythewood, an' come to see me?" She approached him with a smile, as if happy for any interruption. She had a sunny, almost cherubic face, with rosy cheeks and full lips. The perspiration of hard work had given her a glow that suited her.

"Yes, indeed, and you must be—"

"Sally. Sally Jones. What's your fancy, guv'nor?" Suddenly concerned, she added, "Not 'aving indigestion, I 'ope."

"No, no, nothing like that," Adam hastened to assure her. Before setting eyes on Sally, Adam's only thought had been searching for more of Sir Alfred's papers that might have been hidden in the kitchen. At the moment, though, he couldn't think of anything less pressing. "You look as if you could use some help," he said, and it was true. In addition to the baking and boiling dishes that had so warmed the kitchen, the counter was laid out with cakes and decorating implements.

Sally dismissed the idea with a wave. "Oh, I'll manage. Mind you, if that dratted girl who's supposed to 'elp me were 'ere, it'd be a little bit easier—"

"Come now," Adam said, taking the opportunity to close the gap between him and the beguiling wench,

"I'm not afraid to put a hand in. Now, show me what to do."

Sally shook her head in wonderment. "Cor, I'll never get over it," she said, "a gentleman puttin' in time with us galley slaves. Well, God love you for it, guv'nor. 'Ere, I'd wager you can ice these cakes without 'urting yourself. That's right, just wait there for me."

Between monitoring the boiling pots and the oven, Sally deftly instructed Adam in icing the cakes — first adding a smooth layer with a flat spatula, then building on that base with a piping bag. "Like this, sir," she said, putting her arms around him to guide his hand. He didn't object, and their partnership soon became as well-lubricated as a machine. The various glazes and icing and the implements for applying them had a sensual element that Adam had never appreciated before, and the baker's job was to give the cakes a surface as appealing to the eye — glossy, glistening and almost palpably moist — as their flavours were to the palate.

"Ah, you've a natural talent," Sally approved after Adam recreated a rosette as perfectly spiralled as the example she had set for him.

To his surprise, Adam felt a small glow of pride. "I've had an excellent teacher."

"Food always tastes better when you've prepared it yourself, you'll find."

"Well, then I can't wait." Adam leaned in closer. Their two breaths mingled in the space between them. Adam could sense Sally's heart beating beneath her pillowy bosom, and felt sure that she could feel his.

"You'll 'ave to wait until tonight to get it," Sally teased.

"Tonight?"

"After dinner, of course, silly." Sally laughed. She leaned in closer and whispered huskily, "What did you think I meant?"

Adam didn't hear the swing of the door from the forekitchen until it was too late. "Too busy, eh?" said an indignant voice from behind them that he recognised as Marie's. The lady's maid had come up behind them with the unused tea tray.

Sally stepped away from Adam, the picture of innocence. "Marie! I didn't expect you—"

Marie slammed the tray down on the counter with a rattle. "I bet not, you cow! Now, you stay away from him!" Sally put her hands on her hips and began to fume. "And you—" Marie turned to Adam. "You lure me into the bath with Gretchen, and then you tear my best nightie and after all that I find you *here*, with *her?*" She jabbed a finger into Adam's chest with each word, pushing him against the counter until there was nowhere left to escape.

"But, darling," Adam said, "it's not what it looks like! I was just a bit peckish, and Sally was only showing me—"

"Peckish! Peckish!" Marie exclaimed. She hefted one of the cakes they had just made from the counter next to her and said, "If you're so 'peckish'—here!" With one deft motion, she slammed it into Adam's face. The icing he and Sally had laboured over covered him. The cake collapsed utterly and slid onto his shoulders and chest. He could say nothing, so surprised was he. Marie stalked out of the kitchen.

Adam stood, speechless, for a few moments, until Sally began to laugh, full-throated as a gong. "Oh, my word! I'm sorry, sir, but—oh, ho!—you should see yourself. 'Ere, let me 'elp you." Sally turned Adam around and dabbed at him with a towel. To herself she muttered, "Stay away, she says — who made 'er queen? I'd like to know," and assorted other opinions about the lady's maid.

Halfway through cleaning him up, Sally narrowed her eyes as if she had just remembered something. "Hold on now — did you really tear Marie's nightie?" The blood that drained from Adam's face returned with full force, and he felt his cheeks grow hot. "Tore it right off 'er, did you? Well, aren't you a naughty boy? I bet that was a change for Miss High-and-Mighty." She chuckled to herself. Now that Marie was gone, Sally's flirtatious mood was returning. "Oh, come now, sir, don't carry on. Surely that's not the first time someone's pushed a cake into your face... Really? Well, there's a first time for everything, I suppose."

Adam had thought himself incapable of flushing any more than he already had beneath the caking Marie had given him, but his heart nearly stopped in his chest as the back door slammed open and Molly, whose voice he recognised from the village, flounced in, singing happily to herself. "Sorry, I'm late, ma'am, but I've just had the most wonderful ronday-voo with me beau," she said as she entered.

Sally froze in mid-dab, and Molly did the same as she saw the scene that had unfolded without her. "Oh! I say, ha ha!" She smothered a laugh with one hand but her eyes continued to twinkle. "What brings you to the kitchen, sir?" She snorted in barely covered derision.

Sally took charge, adopting a prim expression and continuing to clean Adam's face. "Never you mind, Molly. It was just one of those mishaps, nothing to get worked up about. Maybe if I'd 'ad you to count on, it wouldn'a 'appened."

Molly raised an eyebrow. "Whatever you say, ma'am." She took an apron from a hook and put it on.

"I—er, was looking for some papers," Adam said when he had found his voice. It was the truth, so why did it sound so false? Sally hesitated not a breath before nodding along with this explanation.

"At the bottom of a cake?" Molly replied. "Guess I had you pegged wrong, guv'nor. There's some as like to dish it out, but some are 'appier on the receivin' end." Almost as an afterthought, she added, "I 'ope you didn't bother yourself tryin' to find my tart recipe. You're not the first to look for it—" She shot an indecipherable look at Sally. "It's all up 'ere."

"No, of course not," Adam said, hastening to explain that he was editing Sir Alfred's manuscript and hoped to track down some missing pages. Now that he was somewhat cleaned up and offering the truth, the words flowed easily and he began to feel back in control.

"Again?" Molly exclaimed suddenly, having opened the chest on the counter and found it nearly emptied of tarts. "How do miladies find the room?"

While Molly wondered at the appetite of the Windmere family, Sally said to Adam, "Don't mind 'er. Take whatever papers ye like, but come back tomorrow after breakfast is served an' I'm sure I'll find something else ter show ye." Her lascivious wink and the closeness with which she pressed her body against Adam's made it clear that she referred not only to the papers for which he searched.

* * * *

Having found a few more papers before leaving the cook and her assistant, Adam returned to the library and fitted them into the gaps in Sir Alfred's manuscript. Finally, he might be able to read the saga of Sir Ambrose's South Sea venture and its inglorious aftermath.

The gist of the episode was that Sir Ambrose had landed one of his trading ships on the island of _____. Sir Alfred had written it just that way, as a blank, as if it were a public figure apt to sue for libel if this narrative were published. There he had encountered a tribe of friendly natives who lived in Edenic innocence.

Here Adam knew exactly what Sir Alfred was suggesting but was too tactful to describe explicitly — the islanders must have practised that "free love" that was so attractive to the sailors who had first made landfall in that part of the world. Adam wondered again if Sir Ambrose's diary would ever turn up. The late explorer had probably been much less squeamish in his version of events!

He had been initiated into their culture as an honorary member because of his friendliness and because of the trading goods he brought, and after an idyll of some six months, he and his crew had returned to England. Sir Alfred held that Sir Ambrose had spent that time learning the natives' language and discovering the secret to their contentment and not, as Adam's sinful mind suggested, bedding guileless native maidens in a tropical paradise for the duration.

Regardless of Sir Ambrose's actual motivation, a plan had been hatched to open a regular trading route between England and the island, as there was something beyond the natives themselves that the explorer and trader had coveted. Here Sir Alfred fell into one of his typically vague circular turns of phrase, and Adam read the paragraph three times without a solid idea of what Sir Ambrose had proposed to trade. A ship had been commissioned and a crew hired while Sir Ambrose had begun planning a great feast to commemorate the successful trading mission. That was where the manuscript connected to the pages Adam had already read. He knew that the feast would end in ignominy for Sir Ambrose and exile in London. Cliffsward would fall into decline. Curiously, Adam noted that the old manor overlooked the bay. While the great house in which he was now a guest was near the water, it could hardly be described as overlooking anything. He wondered if there were still any ruins left of the old place.

By now, Adam really was starting to feel "peckish," as he had claimed earlier, but neither Marie nor anyone else appeared with the tea service. He had blown his chance, it seemed. Marie would cool down, he was sure, but in the meantime, he had no urge to face her contempt again. Nor did a visit to the kitchen seem appropriate—not yet, anyway. Recalling that the family sometimes took tea together in the parlour, Adam made his way downstairs in hopes that he would be welcome to join.

Alas, he was too late here as well, but thoughts of his stomach were pushed away by the sight of Frederica alone, sitting in the tall wing chair, so absorbed in reading a letter that she didn't notice his presence as he stood in the doorway. Adam's blood quickened with the memory of her body pressing against him the night before, the animal yearning so in contrast to the ladylike composure she exhibited today. Did the wistful smile that played across her lips indicate that it was a private missive from a lover that so occupied her? Perhaps Roderick himself?

Noticing Adam's presence, Frederica abruptly returned the letter to its envelope and the little smile disappeared, replaced by the polite, neutral expression with which she generally regarded him. As always, he saw nothing to indicate that she remembered their late-night embrace. If she had been awoken by Marie's sudden appearance in the kitchen last night, did she have any memory of Adam being there? Or was it like a half-remembered dream, nothing more?

"Excuse me, Mr Blythewood, I didn't see you there," she said.

"No, it is I who must apologise for not announcing myself," Adam replied. He had undoubtedly been staring. "I had no wish to disturb your reading."

Frederica dismissed the envelope. "Just a letter from a friend recently married," she explained. "I had not heard a word since the honeymoon... Please, make yourself comfortable."

Adam thanked her, and after an additional reassurance that he would not be disturbing her, he took a seat opposite. Frederica tucked the envelope into her workbag and resumed a half-finished embroidery.

Curiosity gnawed at him, combined with an urge that last night's adventure had stoked into flame. So, too, was there something to Frederica's waking indifference to him that made her all the more irresistible. "And how is your 'friend' enjoying marriage, if I may ask?" he said, in an effort to extend the conversation.

"Why, do you know her?"

"How can I tell if I don't know her name?"

"Then why such concern for her well-being?" Frederica continued this line of conversation without looking up, as if giving it the bare minimum of attention while she worked.

"If she is a friend of yours, then I am confident she must be worthy of my well-wishes," Adam said. If it were to be a tennis match, he was determined to return every volley.

"Do you attempt to flatter me, or yourself?" Frederica replied, gazing at him sharply.

Taken aback, Adam stammered, "I have nothing but fond hopes for *all* who enter the state of matrimony."

Frederica raised an eyebrow doubtfully. "And what, if any, aspirations do *you* have to enter that state?"

"It is a truth universally acknowledged, as they say," Adam said dismissively, "but what about you? Did you catch the bouquet at your 'friend's' wedding? A lady of your position must surely have prospects?"

Adam, pretending ease, watched Frederica closely. While outwardly relaxed, he was inwardly excited that he had stumbled on a line of conversation that engaged her. Perhaps he was getting closer to the truth. If, for example, her eyes darted towards the hidden letter when he asked about her prospects, then he would feel confident that she was hiding the truth from him. But he had evidently pushed her too far. The bloom that had risen so attractively to her cheeks drained away and she snapped at him, "I hardly see what business that is of yours, nor what right you have to impose your judgements on me. *Good day*, Mr Blythewood." She gathered her things and stormed out of the parlour, choking back a sob before Adam could say another word.

Adam stood, stunned by the force of Frederica's reaction, and turned to see the hem of her gown disappear through the door. But as surprised as he was, he got a nasty shock to see that young Alice Windmere was standing in the hall opposite the doorway, her eyes on him. How long had she been standing there? How much had she heard? Adam's voice, with which he was going to call out to Frederica to wait, died in his throat and he said nothing.

Somewhere, a door slammed. "She's going to be in there all day," Alice said flatly, then she, too, turned and left, leaving Adam with more questions than when he had begun.

Chapter Six

After a restless night in which Frederica had once again visited Adam's chamber in her sleep, and during which Adam had followed her to the chapel before she disappeared, Adam struggled to keep a cool head during breakfast. How could Miss Frederica sit across from him, uttering commonplace pleasantries — when she deigned to speak to Adam at all! — remembering nothing about the night before? Moreover, how was it that in her somnambular state she could give such vent to her passion, wailing for her beloved to return, while seeming so reserved, even frigid, while awake? Even the minor blow-up in the parlour the day before seemed forgotten, or masked behind a dreadful calm.

Adam's gaze turned to those at whose table he was a guest — Lady Windmere and her other two daughters, in addition to Frederica — each sipping coffee or chatting while a servant cleared away the dishes, and wondered how they could avoid hearing Frederica's outbursts during the night. Of course, he reminded himself, the upper classes were quite adept at leaving unheard that which they did not want to hear. This was a house of secrets, even if they were open ones. Not for the first time, Adam wondered how Frederica had managed to evade him—she had rounded a corner before him, and simply been gone when he caught up to it—and a chill went up his spine when he recalled the eerie feeling that, while he watched her, he was in turn being watched by someone else.

If Adam had been imaginative, he might have worried, but as it was, his fancy was engaged in anticipating the end of breakfast and the payment of a return visit to the kitchen to see Sally. The buxom cook had become the latest object of his fascination, and the feeling had seemed to be more than mutual, if only she could shoo Molly out of the kitchen for a while. The door that closed behind the serving maid was only one small room away from his goal. Adam had never been very patient, but this morning, the Windmeres' coffee might have been molasses, as slowly as they finished.

"You must be eager to return to work, Mr Blythewood," Lady Windmere observed, nodding to the foot Adam tapped and fingers he twiddled without realising. "You don't have to wait for us if you have somewhere duty takes you."

Sheepishly, he ended his nervous fidgeting and stood. "My apologies, milady. I should have been more forthright. I do indeed have much to do today. With your gracious permission, I shall withdraw."

Adam knew he didn't fool Alice for a second. The youngest sister watched him with a leer hidden from her mother but quite clear in its meaning to him. Whispering to Lady Windmere, Jane excused herself as well and said, "If Mr Blythewood doesn't mind, I need to retrieve something from the library. May I walk with you?"

Adam grunted in surprise but nodded and said she would be welcome. In reality, he had planned to walk around the manor then return to the dining room and, once the family was absent, thence to the kitchen. But he was caught in a trap, and was now committed to visiting the last place a true gentleman would wish to go…his place of work.

While walking, Adam stole a glance at his companion. Jane was pretty, in an unadorned way, but terribly introverted. She said nothing beyond a few commonplace pleasantries while they walked, as if whatever was going on in her mind was too compelling to break away from. For his part, Adam's thoughts were on Sally and he made little effort to keep a conversation going.

In the library, Adam's papers lay where he had last left them, and he sat down as if to proceed, but in reality, the words were forgotten as soon as he read them, chased out of his mind by images of Sally's luscious curves, her full lips and merry eyes, the strong hands with which she formed and patted her delicacies into shape. Adam's mouth watered just thinking about it.

All the while, Jane took her time, pacing up and down the room, first pulling one book from a shelf, then another, sometimes replacing the first or sometimes adding it to a small stack. While in truth Adam was only waiting for Jane to finish before he could sneak off, his gaze wandered to the ankles she revealed beneath the hem of her gown when she reached for a book on the highest shelf.

"I must apologise," Adam said. When Jane turned around — and Adam had directed his eyes elsewhere, as if in the middle of his work — he explained, "For taking up so much time and space in the library, of course." *Anything to hurry her up.*

Jane laughed and said, "Please, do not trouble yourself. Truth be told, my father's reading habits rarely aligned with my own, but I have occasion to consult his collection from time to time." The stack of books she had assembled must have struck her as distressingly small, for she sighed over it.

"Then I take it you have your own library? As much as I see you reading…" Adam said.

"Well, I have my favourites, is all," Jane said, with a half-smile of pleasant remembrance.

"Ah." Adam nodded, not really understanding. "Are you looking for something in particular? I might have run across it."

Jane thought a moment. "No, it's all right. Perhaps Alice has seen what I am looking for."

"Yes," agreed Adam, and added without thinking, "I imagine she has seen quite everything in this house."

His cheeks burned as he realised what he might have implied, but Jane only laughed again and said, "Yes, Alice is admirably…transparent."

Adam chuckled, more out of relief than humour, and agreed.

"Well, I shall leave you to your work. Good day, Mr Blythewood. No, please, do not stand on my account." It was too late. Adam had already stood as gallantly as he could, a sheaf of papers held over the bulge in his trousers that he hoped was not too obvious. A bead of sweat popped out of his forehead. When would she go?

"Pardon me, but are you quite all right, Mr Blythewood?" Jane said, smiling a little. It was but an echo of the knowing smirk Alice frequently exhibited, but enough to show that they were indeed sisters.

Adam assured her that he was simply eager to return to his labour, and that nothing fascinated him more than the distinguished history of her exalted family, and oh yes, by the way he *did* know that this was actually the second family seat, and no, he *wasn't* sure how much longer this business would take, and the answers to a dozen other questions that suddenly came to Jane as if she had taken it in mind to torment him by quiz. Finally she took her leave, and Adam wondered whether Jane suspected his thoughts, or if Alice had told her that Adam planned an assignation with the cook. If Alice were transparent, the middle sister was opacity herself.

Once he was sure Jane had gone, Adam ducked out of the library, glancing from side to side to make sure no one else was in the hall to observe him. If someone called on him at the library later, he could make some excuse for his absence, but he would rather avoid indiscreet questions or any further delay. He approached the dining room…empty, as he had been sure it would be by now. Approaching the door into the forekitchen, he hesitated for a moment. What if Sally had forgotten her invitation, or if it had been a jest in the first place? What if he had misread her signals? As desperate as he was for a good lay, coming on too strong could be disastrous.

He pushed the thought out of his mind. His experience had been enough to know when a woman was "hot-arsed" for him, and Sally was willing, he was sure. Still, he decided to take a nonchalant approach and let her lead. Far from showing himself overeager like a schoolboy on his first trip to Whitechapel, he would even be fashionably, if inadvertently, late for their liaison. Adam straightened the lapels of his jacket, wiped the shine from his forehead and imagined the tables turned, with Sally fretting over his absence. It was a satisfying picture and one that stirred his already aroused nethers. He knocked lightly on the door.

He needn't have worried. After Sally opened the door a crack and confirmed that it was he, her face lit up and she admitted him to the narrow forekitchen. "I was beginning to think you weren't coming, guv," she said. As she led him back to the main kitchen, Adam noted that she wore a fetching cotton dress that fit her snugly indeed, and that she must have pulled her stays extra tight to ensure the fit. It gave her a pleasingly sleek appearance and all the more prominence to her wide bottom and full bust. His gaze returned to her pretty face as she turned towards him and locked the door to the forekitchen with a simple catch.

She examined him as hungrily as he had taken her measure and closed with him almost immediately. Their lips met and their hands found purchase on each other's bodies. Her method was as direct and unapologetic as any man's, feeling his rump and stroking his strong chest. As he returned her attentions in kind, his already firm manhood stood at attention, eager for duty.

Sally broke off, lust smouldering in her eyes. "I sent Molly on an errand, but she could be back any time," she said.

"I'm sorry," Adam said. "I was delayed."

"Never you mind," Sally said, pressing closer again, "I think we'll still have time. I whipped up a little treat for ye, something you might na' have had before."

"Oh?"

Sally led Adam to the counter where they had decorated cakes together the day before. She had laid out an array of jugs and dishes containing custard, treacle, jam and syrup. Nearby, a pair of chairs stood by, shrouded with white sheets. "What's all this?" Adam said.

Sally pressed her body closer against Adam's. "Shall I tell you a secret, sir? I usually make an extra cake or two when I bake. Just one for meself, right? Oh, I know what you're thinking, an' you're right, an extra bite or two doesn't hurt me girlish figure, but I don't eat 'em all. What d'ye think I does with 'em?" She stood with her hands on her hips, aglow with her naughty secret. Adam shook his head. Sally leaned in close and whispered in his ear. "I sit on it." To Adam's surprised expression, she nodded. "It's quite the sensation, it is. First I hike up me skirts." She caressed her hips, miming the act. "An' then I squish it with me bum." She laughed. "It sounds mad, I know, but don't knock it until you've tried it. It's heaven, sir, when it squeezes into me fanny an' me, ahem —" She was becoming heated just talking about it, a condition Adam found quite infectious as he listened.

"Hmmm," Adam said, wrapping his arms around his new partner's waist, surprised at how arousing Sally made it sound. "That sounds…unique. Is that what you wanted to show me?"

Sally nodded eagerly and pulled the cloth from the chair, revealing a plain fresh cake already sitting on the seat. "I had to make another batch after Marie, er, gave me extra to you…"

Adam flushed at the memory of Marie pushing the cake into his face, but since arriving at Windmere Hall he had started to learn how sensual, even erotic, that could be.

Sally rubbed her hands together, pleased at his tacit approval. "It's cooled enough, I should think," she added.

The cook's descriptions had already begun working on Adam's imagination. As she turned back to the counter, revealing a good view of her ample backside beneath the pleats and padding of her old-fashioned skirt, he imagined himself in the cake's position. It hardly knew what it was in for, but the vision appealed to Adam's sense of the perverse. Perhaps she would need help pulling up her skirt before she did it, or maybe she would let him finish the job by smearing the sticky pastry around her wobbling bum cheeks. Maybe he could even lick them clean for her. His cock stiffened in anticipation.

Turning back to him, Sally twinkled merrily, perhaps sensing the hunger she had awoken in him. She held in her hand a pitcher and a piping bag like the one they had used the day before. To his quizzical expression, she laughed. "Ye have to decorate it first, don't ye?"

To Adam's relief, this decoration was hardly the painstaking operation she had guided him through before. Perhaps she was in a hurry, or perhaps it contributed to the sense of wanton abandonment, but there seemed to be no limit to Sally's liberality in adding icing, jam and whipped cream in great mounds until the cake itself could hardly be seen. With Sally's encouragement, he helped himself to the ingredients on the counter and added to the pile. It was a sticky business, and soon both their hands were coated with the liquids that had dripped or dribbled from their containers. Sally licked the excess from her fingers and Adam followed suit. This, too, seemed to excite her, and Adam thought his trousers would burst in sympathetic arousal. He surprised himself as the queerest ideas entered his head. What, he wondered, would it look like — *feel* like — if he left his sticky handprints on the full bodice of Sally's dress?

Seeming to read his mind, Sally demurely directed the prow of her breast away from him even as she manoeuvred him towards the chair, wiping his hands and her own with a towel. Only then did she allow him to embrace her.

Sally's nimble fingers found the clasp to his trousers and began working. Adam's already stiff cock strained at the fabric as it sensed its approaching escape from confinement.

"Now, don't get too excited, just yet," she warned him. Adam's trousers dropped towards his ankles. Smoothly and confidently, Sally pulled his drawers down. A breath of cool air made his prick spring upwards. With one hand, Sally massaged it appreciatively while she continued to kiss him. "After you, sir," she murmured.

"Wait —" Adam started to protest as the backs of his knees collided with the front edge of the chair. Before he could even object, Sally had gently pushed him into a seated position, on top of the cake they had "decorated." Adam's breath caught as the cool liquids spurted beneath his balls, over his thighs and between his cheeks, followed by the feeling of the spongy cushion of cake giving way and spreading out. After the initial shock, he gulped for breath and began laughing. Sally, clearly enjoying both the anticipation and the surprise, laughed along with him. She stood before him, drinking in the sight of his undignified position with her hands clasped, biting her lower lip eagerly.

"You tricked me!" Adam protested, but not too seriously. It did feel strange, but not unpleasantly so, and his prick was as firm as ever. He appreciated the glow of Sally's arousal, the flush of her cheeks and her obvious pleasure in disordering Adam's composure.

"Now, hold on, guv, don't get hot," Sally said — *Too late for that*, Adam thought — as she pulled the cover off a second chair, a stool about the same height as the seat of Adam's chair. A cake identical to the first sat upon it. She pushed the stool towards Adam so that it was directly in front of him, the cake jiggling a little as she did so. It was as plain as the first one had been, and she made a show of pulling more ingredients from the counter to pile onto it — slowly, this time, teasing Adam by pulling the hem of her skirt up to reveal a smooth calf or bending over the chair to thrust her breasts into his face while she playfully covered the cake. Treacle, custard, golden syrup, more cream and a few other things...everything she had left went on top of it, until it was at least as mounded up as the one Adam had sat on. Adam's mouth fairly watered at the sight — both sights, really.

"Oop!" she laughed as she missed her mark with a jug of custard, dribbling it onto Adam's crotch and bathing his prick in the silky liquid. Adam's breath caught, then he released a most unmanly giggle as the queer sensations surprised him. It was indeed pleasant, but strange, and the similarity to dipping his wick in a wet pussy was enhanced when Sally's strong hand began wanking him off, pulling his slippery cock back and forth.

"Ready?" she asked playfully when at last the dessert was "finished" to her satisfaction. She stood facing away from Adam, looking over her shoulder at him, and when she was sure she had his attention, she pulled up the hem of her dress, first revealing her ankles, her calves, and the backs of her thighs. With an even greater flourish she revealed her bottom, as round, full and glowing as the moon. She laughed gaily at his evident pleasure and anticipation, and with a teasing hesitance, an affected coyness that was most endearing, she lowered herself onto the makeshift trifle with a deep sigh of contentment. Her cheeks flattened against the stool as they squashed the cake and pushed all of its toppings outward until they dribbled to the floor in a puddle.

After the initial shock, Sally continued to work her bum back and forth on the slippery stool, continuing to sigh in greater and greater ardour. Was it the sight of her making a sticky mess of herself or the sound of her evident arousal in doing so that made Adam's cock throb so? Without thinking, he began rocking back and forth in the remains of his own cake as well, savouring the thought that he enjoyed nearly the same sensations as Sally. Soon, she invited Adam to caress her from behind, smearing the cake and jam all around her backside, he moving forward on his seat and she backward on hers until they were as close as a pair of spoons in a drawer, mutually enjoying each other's reactions to the sensation and abandoning all pretence of modesty until Adam was freely stroking Sally's enormous bosom from behind, she so involved in her enjoyment that she made no complaint about handprints or any other mark he left on the cloth of her dress. Their nethers were slickly lubricated by the desserts smeared between them. As Sally rubbed her fanny on his prick, grinding her food-covered arse into his equally covered groin, it was impossible to tell where the slippery cream ended and their own natural juices began.

"Oh—oh—oh, sir," she gasped, trying to find the words. "Mightn't it be time to put that sausage of yours into the oven, then?" Adam, building towards his moment of climax, couldn't agree more. Sally shifted backward onto Adam's lap, her arse already spread so that in no time at all he had slid his cock into her waiting split from behind, her full bum bobbing up and down in front of him as they heaved to and fro. It wouldn't be long now.

In the next instant, the outside door to the kitchen clapped open and the sound of a heavy weight dropping to the ground was audible. It was followed by Molly's sing-song voice calling halloo from outside. "Anybody in here?" she said.

In a rush, Sally and Adam made sure that Molly would find both of them lined up behind the baking counter, counting out tarts as if the King himself had decreed the fate of the Empire rested on their success. The true reason for their flustered appearance was one they hoped to keep to themselves.

"Cor!" Molly said in wonderment as she dragged in the full bin of flour and sat down on it to catch her breath. "You two look as if you've seen a ghost!" Well could she say that, as she was nearly covered head to toe with the white flour dust herself. She must have had a little trouble on her errand. Sally just laughed noncommittally. She and Adam stayed behind the counter, hunched over their work. Sally had pulled her dress back down over her legs, but Adam still stood trouserless, his shrunken willy exposed to the breeze, his ardour having fled as suddenly as Molly had appeared.

"Don't you want your apron?" Molly said to Sally, approaching the counter.

"No!" Sally exclaimed, then, in the face of Molly's obvious surprise, softened her answer to, "We've got it well under control 'ere, dearie... Why don't you check the butter an' make sure we're full up, eh? There's a good girl." Molly raised an eyebrow but did as she was told, making her way to the pantry to check their supply levels. Adam took the opportunity to quickly pull on his trousers with Sally's help, the remains of cake and custard squelching as he did so.

"Didn't mean to take so long," Molly said, clapping the excess flour from her hands as she came back in from the pantry, "but I just couldn't resist stopping to see you-know-who, an' well..."

"Oh, all right," Sally said, recovering some of her usual jollity, "when are we going to meet this man of yours? It mustn't be long before the banns are announced at the rate you're going." To Adam she said, *sotto voce*, "It must be serious, it's been over a month an' the same boy." She snickered.

"Fine, go ahead an' larf," Molly said serenely. "There's nothing you can say that'll trouble me today. If you're nice to me I'll arrange an introduction the next time you're in town." The way she said it made it clear that she didn't just mean the little village that Windmere Hall overlooked.

"Oh, izzat right, yer majesty? Am I to believe that you're courting a reg'lar gentleman?"

Molly preened. "Izzat so hard to believe? I happen to attract a very high-toned breed of man."

"You?" Sally snorted. "Maybe for a roll in the hay, but I don't know where you've call for such airs!"

Molly levelled her gaze at Sally and Adam as if seeing them for the first time. She seemed to have something to say, but bit it back. "Fine! Believe me or don't, it's na' concern o' mine."

Adam, conscious of the queer sensation of liquid custard dripping down the inside of his trouser legs, took the opportunity to make his departure before it ran out over his shoes, but he wasn't quite fast enough to escape Molly's vigilant eye. "Pleasure to see yer again, Mr Blythewood. Next time, borrow a smock before Sally puts you to work—you're a right mess!" Their ringing laughter followed him, red-faced, out of the kitchen.

Chapter Seven

Thankfully, Adam met no one in the hall as he returned to his chamber to change his clothes. No one, that was, until he was surprised by Alice Windmere rounding the corner, not ten yards from his destination! She was as pretty as ever — petite and blonde, with a reticence that appeared demure until one met her eyes and sensed the deep well of intense feeling that lay beneath her ladylike surface. Frankly, Adam had begun to find her unnerving, and he was in no state to conduct polite conversation, but decorum demanded he at least make an effort.

"Good morning to you, Miss Windmere—"

Alice took him by surprise, interrupting his banal greeting by hissing, "She can never love you!"

Had Alice seen the incident with Sally in the kitchen? Or did Molly have the young lady's ear? Adam's face reddened again. "Who?" he squeaked.

"My sister, Frederica, of course! I see the way you look at her — follow her about, bring her flowers—"

"Shh! Shh!" Adam attempted to quiet her outburst, before his sense overcame the fright Alice had given him. She could, of course, know nothing, because there was nothing to know. There had been nothing untoward, even if she had seen Frederica embrace him the other night. How could it reflect upon her honour when it was clearly the product of a dream or a troubled mind, and how upon his when he had only sought to aid her if need be? Recovering his poise as much as possible with drawers full of custard, he said, "I have nothing but esteem for your sister, of course, but—"

"And we have nothing but esteem for *you*, Mr Blythewood," said Lady Windmere, rounding the corner. Adam froze, and was further mortified to see that the eldest Windmere daughter, the subject of the discussion, was in the lady's company. "But come, why this dithering? Alice, did you inform Mr Blythewood of the boating excursion?"

"Not yet, Mother," Alice replied, once again the prim, soft-spoken young lady she had first appeared to be. "I only just found him."

"Well, so be it," the lady responded. Turning to Adam, she said, "We've arranged to show you around the bay and the cliffs, if you'll join us at the mooring, Mr Blythewood."

"Of course, I'd be delighted," Adam said. "If I could just take a minute to get dressed..." He pointed to the door to his chambers, where privacy and a change of drawers awaited him.

Lady Windmere looked him up and down. "Nonsense! I wouldn't have you waste a change of clothing only to expose it to the spray of the water, and I'm afraid we must hurry in any case. Pamela is expecting us, and my silly daughter took so long in finding you that I'm afraid we have no time to waste. The hour is late!" She would brook no further argument. Frederica and Alice dutifully followed, and with a yearning look at his chambers, so near yet out of reach, Adam did likewise.

It was a beautiful morning for Adam's first meeting with Miss Bond, whose yacht the party was to board. The *Cupid* was a fine forty-foot craft, white with red and black trim. Painted on the side was a keyhole-shaped insignia, the Bond family crest. Pamela Bond lived up to some of Adam's expectations. As Gretchen had said, all of the lady's servants were men, from the driver of the carriage who brought them down to the moorings to the squad of smartly uniformed tars who handled the riggings on the boat. But she was younger than Adam had gathered, a handsome woman in her mid-thirties. If she were a spinster, it appeared to be by choice, and in every word and action, she showed that she regretted and wanted for nothing. She made an ebullient hostess, and in other circumstances, Adam would have been enchanted by her at once.

Adam's discomfort had nothing to do with the new situation or company. Every time he bowed or moved, he was conscious of the squelching and sloshing of the custard that lubricated the insides of his attire, and he was mortified with the suspicion that everyone around him could hear it and was merely too polite to say anything. Luckily the thick wool trousers were dark enough that nothing showed through.

"The pleasure is all mine," Miss Bond said, taking Adam's hand and curtseying in response to his greetings. "I daresay you look a bit green—I hope seafaring has not made you ill before we've even left the dock?"

Adam assured his hostess that such was not the case, and Lady Windmere said, "Please excuse Miss Bond's forwardness. You will find that there are few subjects that are off limits to her."

Miss Bond showed no offence from this rebuke, and instead seemed to take it as a great joke, or perhaps a challenge, giving a throaty laugh and summoning her boatmen. This gang took over the rigging and sails with practised efficiency, hardly saying a word to one another or to their mistress as they cast off. For her part, Miss Bond wore her authority over them with the ease of long practice and seemed to relish the surprise Adam expressed at seeing a woman boss them around and even, when necessary, show them how she wanted something done.

"Oh, Miss Bond is quite self-sufficient," Alice said. "She needs no man to give orders to her staff." Lady Windmere raised an eyebrow to her daughter's smart remark, but let it pass, as she often seemed to do.

"Are you sure you aren't going to take a hand in steering the ship?" Miss Bond asked Frederica, who had been moping on the deck.

"I think not," she answered, then turned to continue staring out at the grey-green sea. Adam wondered what, if anything, she remembered about the night before, or if it was as forgotten as a dream. He had hardly been able to reach her in ordinary conversation, and this jaunt, which should have had a salutary effect on her mood, seemed to have the opposite.

Miss Bond couldn't help but notice Adam watching Frederica. "Miss Windmere is usually such an avid sailor," she said to Adam when she had the opportunity to converse with him one-on-one, now that she was satisfied that the yacht was well in hand. "The *Cupid* is the very boat on which she 'learned the ropes.' You should have seen her climb the riggings on her best day. She would climb all the way to the top of the mast and pretend she was a pirate, crying 'Land ho!'" She chuckled at the memory, and Adam couldn't help but smile at the image of this side of Frederica, of which he had so far only had glimpses.

"Miss Windmere is a woman of many skills, I gather," Adam said, "but perhaps she is simply tired." She had been up half the night, after all.

Miss Bond shook her head in resignation. "No, I think it is the present company rather than sailing for which she has lost her taste. I am no longer her favourite, you see."

"Oh?" Adam hesitated. What could she mean? And was it appropriate for him, a relative stranger, to hear of it? But he could not deny his curiosity.

"You see, it was I," she continued without prompting, "who arranged to introduce Frederica's archery instructor, Miss Planter, to a gentleman acquaintance of mine, a Mr Anthony." A slight smile, as of a delicious secret, played about her lips.

Adam, recalling Frederica's practising alone in the courtyard, and yesterday's letter from a friend recently married, arrived at the obvious conclusion. "And now Miss Planter is Mrs Anthony, is that it?" Miss Bond's smile broadened and she nodded with the satisfaction of an affair brought to a happy conclusion.

"Miss Bond fancies herself quite a matchmaker," Alice said, having come up to the rail next to them. "You should watch yourself around her, Mr Blythewood."

Miss Bond dismissed Alice's comment with a wave of her hand. "Pish, my dear."

"*Anne* Anthony," Jane said without looking up from the book she had been reading since their departure from the dock. The name seemed to conjure up distaste for her. She furrowed her brow and pursed her lips as she repeated the offending name.

"Pardon?" Adam said, turning to her.

"Oh, Jane, how you do carry on!" Alice said, rolling her eyes. Miss Bond seemed highly amused by Jane's disgust.

"Am I missing something?" Adam said, completely lost.

"It's just so *unmelodious*," Jane complained, finally looking up from her book. "Alliteration is one thing, and 'Anne Planter' is hardly poetry, but of all the needlessly repetitive, ungainly names she could have taken, 'Anne Anthony' must be near the top! 'Anne Anthony.' It's hideous!" She shuddered again. "I would have refused on principle."

Alice and Miss Bond laughed again, and this time Adam joined in, having heard on what trite basis Jane's objection was made.

"You wouldn't." The flatness of the objection cut through the fading merriment, chilling it. It was Frederica, who had returned from the other end of the boat and now stood before them. To Jane she said in all seriousness, "When you find the one for you, hold on to him. Don't let something as silly as a name block your chance for happiness." Then she turned to look out at the water again, like an oracle who had delivered its message then lapsed into enigmatic silence.

Suddenly, it all fit together — Adam realised the source of Frederica's heartbreak. Surely Mr Anthony was the mysterious Roderick. Frederica had set her hopes on him, but he had chosen another, and not only that, but to marry beneath him. Her own archery instructor! What a blow that must have been! And no wonder she could not stand to have the subject made light of. Were her sisters really that insensitive?

Jane blushed at the rebuke and delved deeper into her reading, barely looking up. Alice returned to sit by her mother, who had been basking in a woven chair enjoying the weather.

Adam and Miss Bond were left alone again. The atmosphere had shifted with Frederica's sombre interjection. "I should think," Adam said to her in a low voice, trying to recapture something of the earlier pleasant mood, "that being able to call oneself 'Mrs Roderick Anthony' would be sufficient to overcome any poetic objection."

Miss Bond froze, her supercilious smile suddenly a rictus covering something dead rather than an expression of genuine warmth. Overcoming a momentary catch in her throat, she said, "Thomas, actually. Thomas Anthony."

Feeling his grasp on the situation slip away from him yet again, Adam mumbled, "I beg your pardon. I must be thinking of someone else."

"So it seems," Miss Bond agreed, but doubt remained in her expression. The smile was still present, but behind it was calculation and a new sense of caution. "Now, I understand you are learning something of the history of Windmere Hall!" she said in a light, effervescent tone. Lady Windmere had come up behind them, and Miss Bond renewed playing hostess. "Bondgate is a small part of that history you may find interesting, and should be coming into view soon now that we are free of the rocks. This really is the best view of the cliff side..."

Jane Windmere ostentatiously turned a page in her novel, obviously determined not to be drawn into conversation again, but Alice, who had taken up watching the land passing by alongside Lady Windmere, thrust out her arm and pointed. "There!"

Alice directed their attention to an expanse of rocky cliffs, a sheer wall of imposing stone above which was only a lip of green turf, and at the bottom of which was a muddy brown shore exposed by the low tide. Adam had heard these cliffs mentioned and had been advised against walking in the area, but as he followed Alice's outstretched finger, he saw the same thing she did. Somebody was walking along the mud at the base of the cliffs.

It was too far to see with any detail who it was, and left to his own devices, Adam would have assumed it was a fisherman or some such, but beyond Alice's pointing them out, he was also struck by Frederica Windmere's reaction to the sight. She became bleach-white, as if she were going to faint.

"I say, Pamela, is that one of your men?" Lady Windmere asked, shielding her eyes from the sun with one hand.

Miss Bond produced a collapsible brass spyglass from her reticule and levelled it at the tiny figure. A trumpeting exhalation of breath from her nostrils reminded Adam of a bull about to charge, and she said, "I think not, Adonica! I'm afraid we shall have to cut our trip short so that I can get back!"

While Miss Bond gave the orders to her crew and they hopped to it, her guests expressed a mixture of disappointment and indifference. Adam, for his part, was mystified, having understood nothing of this exchange. Frederica still appeared out of sorts, and he had little desire to rekindle conversation with Alice. Jane, still reading her book and having not so much as looked up during the conversation, seemed to sense his question, and as he leaned to ask her, said without prompting, "The shore at low tide is quite dangerous."

"Oh?" Adam said, keeping his voice down.

"The mud is so waterlogged, and at such an incline, that it is veritable quicksand," she elaborated.

Adam sat back, accepting that explanation. "I must apologise, Mr Blythewood," Pamela Bond said to him a few minutes later. Repeating Jane Windmere's description of the dangerous sucking mud that lined the shore, she said regretfully, "Some of the locals brave the mud to dig for clams, but the shore is part of my estate, and I could hardly live with myself if someone else —" She cut herself short, her eyes darting towards the still distraught Frederica.

With visible effort adopting a more cheerful countenance, she said, "'Tis a pity, really, for I had hoped to show you Bondgate — my home — for it is visible from the bay, and most striking in the morning light. As I was saying, it is built on the former site of the Windmeres' ancestral home."

Recalling something he had read in Sir Alfred's manuscript, Adam perked up. "You refer to Cliffsward?"

Miss Bond nodded, impressed. "Yes, indeed! The Bonds and Windmeres are distant cousins. Cliffsward fell into disrepair around the time the new Hall was built — some two hundred years ago — and eventually passed to the Bond side of the family. Since you are interested in history, it would be my pleasure to show you the inside. Please, come over for tea. Adonica wouldn't mind, would she?" She addressed Lady Windmere thus.

"If you think you can pull Mr Blythewood away from his work, you are most welcome to borrow him!"

"No!" Frederica exclaimed, bringing the eyes of the entire party round to her. For the second time she had split asunder the ribbon of conversation, and even the sailors had halted their work in surprise, with only the soft sound of lapping waves filling the silence that followed. "I mean," she said lamely, reddening under the collective gaze of the party, "surely Mr Blythewood has more than enough to occupy him at Windmere Hall?"

Alice snorted under her breath. "*That* is an understatement."

A quick reprimand from Lady Windmere to her daughters brought the conversation to an end, and the rest of their trip back to the dock passed in silence. Pamela Bond slipped away quickly, perhaps more than ordinary politeness would allow, but her sharp instructions to her footman and the speed with which her carriage pulled away showed how seriously she took her duties as warden of the grounds around the cliffs.

Adam returned to the Hall with the ladies and had almost forgotten his need to return to his room until Jane, looking up from her novel, exclaimed, "I hope Sally has a custard waiting! I can't explain it, but the smell has been haunting me since we left the house earlier!"

Chapter Eight

At the stroke of midnight, Adam, who had lain awake waiting for that hour, as he had done so many nights since arriving at Windmere Hall, got up from his sleepless bed and quietly opened the door to his chamber. Looking this way and that, he crept silently down the hallway until he saw, as he did every night, Frederica Windmere drifting silently through the house like a pitiful ghost. She wore a diaphanous silk gown that clung appealingly to her, and once again Adam wondered at what he was doing. He had not touched Frederica during one of her nocturnal ramblings since she had thrown him to the floor in the kitchen, but he could not keep himself from watching at a distance. From such a vantage point, and in such circumstances, the frostiness of her daytime demeanour became as lovely as the moon...distant, yes, and undoubtedly cold, but full of a brightness that illumined and ensorcelled everything on which it shone.

What would Adam do if Frederica succeeded in entering his chamber? Would she make love to him, believing him to be "Roderick"? He had begun to feel that such a deceit was too low even for him — but if that were true, why did he still follow her? Fortunately, he had not faced the same temptation since that night in the kitchen, and he had not approached Frederica to test her awareness. He could not deny, though, that every night he spent watching her inflamed him further and made him more determined to displace Roderick in her heart, as impossible as that goal seemed to achieve by daylight.

Beyond his expectation of another midnight vigil, he had been kept awake by his inability to comprehend the conversations he had heard and been a part of aboard Pamela Bond's yacht. Clearly the marriage of Anne Planter, while perhaps an annoyance to Frederica, was not the true source of her recent dislike of Miss Bond, and Roderick had no part in the affair. Yet the distress Miss Bond had shown when he had used Roderick's name, however quickly she had covered it, spoke for itself! Along with Frederica's sudden opposition to Adam visiting Bondgate and her reaction to the villager they spotted on the beach, it was clear that something had happened to Roderick and Frederica held Miss Bond responsible.

Deep in thought, Adam almost lost Frederica as she ducked through one doorway and alcove after another. She was moving faster than usual, and if Adam weren't convinced that she still sleepwalked, he might have believed her to be fleeing from him. She looked back over her shoulder more than once, with eyes that failed to register his presence, a change from her usual reverie. Her expression held fear and agitation, but whatever she ran from was in her mind only.

Quickening his own steps to keep up with Frederica, Adam followed her as she pulled aside a tapestry and, looking sightlessly behind her lest she be followed, opened a plain door that had been concealed by the wall hanging. *How intriguing.* Keeping his distance, Adam did the same and found the door unlocked. It brought him into a narrow, winding staircase, at the bottom of which was another door. He had just missed Frederica closing the door behind her. Flying as fleetly as possible, he caught the closing door and followed her…into the kitchen!

A secret passage, Adam realised. This must have been how Frederica had disappeared before, when he had seen her rub the custard tarts on her face and been interrupted by Marie. Closing the hidden door behind him, he realised it was a plain panel that he would hardly have noticed from that side. Perhaps Miss Windmere was going to repeat her lascivious performance from before, but no. This time she slipped out of the back door and down the pathway that led towards the shore. This was different! She still wore no shoes and the grounds past the house quickly became dark. Remembering the steepness of the cliffs in one direction and what he had been told of the dangerous mud in the other, Adam's heart quickened with concern. It was no longer his pleasure to shadow Frederica and spy on her — it was now his duty to protect her or report the danger that she was in!

There was no time. By the time he awoke Gainesborough or one of the other servants, Frederica might disappear into the woods or walk unseeing over the cliff into the bay. If it came to it, he would have to wake her, no matter the risk, but at the moment it was a struggle simply to keep up with her, she who knew the grounds much better than he did and could make her way in the dark as clearly as by day. She was now running, as if she had a particular goal in mind, and Adam huffed as he rushed after her, clumsily tripping from one hole or hillock to the next, only a flash of light-coloured silk occasionally revealing his object's position in the darkness before moonrise.

At the sound of a disturbance behind him, Adam turned his head. Perhaps someone else from the family had noticed Frederica's absence and raised the alarum? He could see nothing, but the barking of suddenly awakened dogs reached his ears. Good, perhaps Dick would soon be up to join in the chase.

Turning back to face forward, Adam nearly collided with a tree, but a glimpse of Frederica's nightgown, glowing in the rising moonlight far ahead, focused his attention. The ground was getting lower. At least she wasn't running to throw herself off the cliffs like a romantic heroine, but there was still no question that in her agitation she might do something drastic. The smell of the bay came to him. They were now proceeding down rough-hewn stone stairs towards the water, their surfaces worn smooth with age.

All before him was dark. He stumbled. Cold wind whipped at his flimsy robe and his slippers came loose as he tripped down the uneven steps. Thankfully they had reached the base of the cliffs and the end of those tortuous stairs, but now Adam was plunged into the vast darkness that lay in the shadow of the cliffs. The moon had not yet risen enough to cast light on this part of the bay and he could no longer tell which way Frederica had run. Standing still, indecisive, he heard nothing but the sound of the bay lapping at the shore. Even the barking of the dogs had faded into nothingness behind him.

Paralysed by fear for Frederica's welfare, he raised his voice for the first time. "Miss Windmere! Halloo!" he called. He quickly overcame his hesitation and called again, louder. Soon he was turning his head in different directions, crying "Freddie!" again and again. Assuming she could hear him—and he couldn't imagine anyone along the shore not hearing him— would his voice penetrate the fog of her waking dream? Getting no response but the indifference of the relentless tide, he stepped forward, hoping that perhaps she was merely too far away to hear him or respond.

Adam's heart pounded, only a little because of the exertion he had made in running after Frederica. In truth he was terrified that she had already walked into the bay and drowned, or fallen from a rocky height. She could be bleeding to death at this very moment! "Freddie!" The thought made him cry out all the louder and walk faster to cover the shore.

Suddenly, Adam's foot plunged into something deep and cold that sucked at him. He had been so intent on finding Miss Windmere that he had barely noticed the ground becoming softer and wetter, and now he had stumbled blindly upon the muddy stretch he had seen from Miss Bond's yacht, seemingly ages ago. He struggled with all his might to pull his foot free, but the moment the mud released it with a great slurping sound, he became unbalanced. With his other foot, he lurched forward, dropping almost to his knee as it too sank into the miry ground. The momentum threw him face-forward to the ground, where his hands sank almost as quickly.

"Frederica!" he cried again, but now his wild imaginings fixed on a concrete possibility. If the mud had caught him off guard, how could she hope to escape it in her delirious state? *Oh God, she's already been sucked under!* The most horrific fancies took hold of him, clutched at his heart and chilled him more than the cold earth that even now drew him under. Another cry of warning died in his throat.

Oh, he was in it now! The cold, wet mud seeped quickly through his thin nightshirt and set his bones shivering. For the moment, all thought of Frederica Windmere was gone as he had to start worrying about himself. Whenever he could pull one limb free of the sucking mud, the effort caused the rest of his body to sink ever deeper. Every part of him that became coated in the thick mud grew heavier. Between the cold and the added weight, the struggle began to exhaust him. At this rate, soon he would have nothing but his head above the surface of the mud, and if that went under, he calculated numbly, he would drown!

"H—help!" Adam had been so stunned by his fall into the quicksand that he had hardly thought to cry for help. Not that anyone could help him — if no one had heard his call to Frederica, there wasn't much chance aid would find him in time. A fine effort he had made to help her, he thought, when he couldn't even save himself!

Only as the muddy water began to close on his face and he thought the cold might prove too much for him and tuck him into that slumber from which no one awoke did he feel a strong grip take hold of his arms and begin pulling him upward. First he sputtered as he could breathe again, spitting mud from his mouth and thrashing as his upper body came free. He could barely see, but a nearby lamp had cast its light on him. His saviour was little more than a cloudy silhouette, but one unmistakably feminine in shape.

"Frederica?" he said, bewildered, his voice sounding strange to him as his ears were clogged with mud. She said something to him, perhaps to soothe him. He noticed that if he stayed relaxed, it was easier for her to pull him free. Soon he was out enough that he could pull himself onto the harder earth nearby. He lay gasping like a fish taken from the water, and with a little help, he was able to crawl forward, still in a prone position, until his head rested in her lap. His rescuer, her form a black shadow in front of the small lamp, cradled his head and began wiping the excess mud from him. Once he had shaken the water from his ears enough to hear her, he caught the end of a sentence. " — all right?"

He nodded, finally clearing his mouth and nose enough to attempt a joke. "And to think I came here to save you!"

She responded with a laugh, musical and touched with relief, and added, "That was brave of you, but foolish." While Adam did feel like a fool, his rescuer's tone was but gently admonishing. The struggle had left its mark on her too, as she had braced herself against the ground and stuck her arms into the mud in order to get a good grip on him. The thin silk of her nightgown clung to her body in a way that would have revealed much if he could have seen her better. Looking up into the shadow of her face while she wiped his features of the lumpiest clods, he was struck by how unlikely it was that he should end up here, in her arms — or at least her care — but in this way!

"Oh, you're still shivering!" she said, wrapping her arms around him. Cold he might have been, but the warmth of her body, so near, just separated from him by a thin layer of fabric, went a long way towards rekindling his furnace. She must have thought so too. As she massaged him and came to feel the firm muscles of his shoulders, she grew bolder, her hands moving of their own accord across the slender lower part of his back and, from the other side, the thickness of his chest. "You've lost a button!" she observed as a pretext, her hands moving inside his ruined shirt.

In the face of such tender care, Adam hardly felt the cold at all anymore. In fact he became so warm that he had no choice but to share the feeling, rubbing his rescuer's tender flesh with his own hands, making sure that she had not injured herself while saving him nor given herself a chill. Soon the quicksand and the cold were forgotten as they both explored each other's bodies, pressed together, and what had begun as a wet, cold and frightening experience became sensual, a conversation without words, the slippery mud forming a layer that removed the friction from their relationship and through which they could touch each other freely and without shame or contempt.

Adam could no longer resist. He sat up and faced the woman who had saved his life, but whose features were still invisible to him in the half-light of the lantern behind her. The hand with which he had stroked the curve of her neckline he used to move a thick, ropy strand of mud-covered hair out of her face and leaned in to kiss her. Her lips were as warm and yielding as the rest of her, but it seemed to break the spell they were both under and she reared back as if he had tried to bite her.

"I must go," she said in hurried explanation.

"I — I'm sorry," he said, surprised, trying to hold on to the moment, but it was too late. She stood, and turning away from him, she hastened to pick up the lantern, shadowing its glare with her body.

"You take it," she said, holding it out to him but covering her face with her dishevelled hair. "You can find your way back to the house that way."

"Nonsense," Adam replied. "We'll go back together." He stood, but for each step he took, she retreated another, until at last she left the lantern sitting on the ground and took refuge in the darkness outside its radiance.

"No, I — I mustn't," she said, her voice already becoming fainter. "Goodbye!"

"Can I at least see you?" Adam asked helplessly, but there was no answer. It was only after she was gone and he stood alone in the circle of light that he thought to wonder where she had picked up a lantern.

Chapter Nine

The next time Adam met the family at the breakfast table, his heart pounded in anticipation of seeing Frederica again, and in front of her family. Would she still be cold to him, or would at last she betray by some look, some colouring of her cheeks, that they had shared something? Of course, as a gentleman he would say nothing, but what an actress she must be to maintain the marble façade under the circumstances! Perhaps it was a game to her, and she hoped for him to make a more overt advance. Frederica had given him no encouragement during the waking hours so far. Was last night a thawing of that chill between them, or had she continued sleepwalking even as she rescued him? Had she imagined it was Roderick she had freed from the bog?

To his surprise, Frederica was absent from the dining room. Lady Windmere sat at the head of the table as usual, Jane and Alice on either side. All three looked up at him when he entered. He must have had the queerest expression on his face, for before he could offer a single pleasantry or inquire after Miss Windmere, Alice said, "She isn't here," in answer to his unspoken question.

With effort, Adam sat and said mildly, "I trust Miss Windmere is not unwell?" It occurred to him that she might have caught a chill, or—even worse—she was embarrassed to see him again and might simply be avoiding him. After losing sight of Frederica the night before, Adam had returned to the house sodden, frustrated and alone. He had hoped Gretchen or Marie might be able to help him bathe again, but when he pulled one of the cords in his chamber, it had been Gainesborough who brought his water. Adam had told him to leave the buckets outside his chamber door, feigning a sore throat he had no wish to share. He hadn't really become ill, of course, but a sheltered young lady like Frederica might easily have succumbed.

"I received a message from Pamela earlier this morning," Lady Windmere said. "Frederica went to visit her late last night, and will be returning by carriage shortly. You didn't see her last night, did you?"

Adam felt the eyes of the three ladies on him—or was it simply his imagination? "N-no," he said, perhaps a touch too quickly. "I saw no one after going to bed." This was true in a narrow sense. While he had retired to his chamber, he had not actually gone to bed until after chasing Frederica down to the shore. Still, his cheeks burned at what he knew was a deception in spirit if not in letter. He glanced at Alice—Alice, who was always watching, and whose knowledge already threatened Adam's position in the house — but the young girl said nothing.

Still, that was very curious. Why would Frederica continue to Bondgate, all the way at the top of the cliffs? The whole episode was shrouded in mystery to him. What did Pamela Bond have to do with it? "Is Miss Windmere accustomed to visit Miss Bond late at night?" he wondered aloud.

Jane snorted. "Not at all. Nor during the day, for that matter."

"Jane —" Lady Windmere said in a warning voice.

"I am sorry, Mother, but it is true! There is no reason for Mr Blythewood —"

"There is no reason for us to burden Mr Blythewood with trifles that are of no concern to him," Lady Windmere said with finality.

"I apologise," Adam said. "I meant not to stir up trouble. It was not my place to ask, and I hope I have not offended."

"Nay, it is we who should apologise," Lady Windmere said. "We have only allowed our concern for Frederica — which, I am sure, you share — to make us short-tempered. How could you have known?"

How indeed? Adam nodded and was about to say something mollifying to smooth over the incident once and for all when Gainesborough appeared at the door. "Miss Bond's carriage, milady."

At once the three ladies stood to greet Frederica's return. Adam followed at a distance, torn between his wish to see her again and his fear that he should be unable to control his features. Desire and dread warred within him, but his curiosity got the better of him. When he arrived at the open front door, the eldest Windmere sister was already stepping down from the carriage—easily identified as Miss Bond's by the keyhole insignia on its door—with the footman's assistance. The servant handed her a wrapped parcel, tied together like a bundle of laundry—her night clothes, Adam realised. The dress she wore was evidently borrowed, and Adam was glad that he had held back from welcoming Frederica as the memory of the previous night flooded back to him. It was just a kiss, yet more. His skin tingled as he remembered Frederica's fingers rubbing his body, warming the layer of cool clay as it lubricated them. He was hard again just thinking about it, and the frustration of the unconsummated union nearly overpowered him. He turned to go back inside the house before he was forced to meet Frederica.

Adam needed some relief from lust's grip. His thoughts turned to the kitchen. Sally had already made her inclinations clear to him, and he had unfinished business with her. It had been after breakfast yesterday—how long ago that seemed!—so he wondered if she might appreciate another visit. But there was the matter of the other girl. If Sally hadn't sent her on an errand, there went any chance of a liaison. Still, Molly was very pretty, too, with a devilish look in her eye—or had he imagined it? Remembering the relish with which she had punished the poor girl he had seen in the stocks in the village, Adam wondered if Molly had ever been on the receiving end of such treatment. Perhaps it could be arranged. Guiltily, he found the prospect more and more appealing, so before he knew it, he was headed back to the kitchen.

Outside the dining room, he realised that it might be suspicious for him to enter directly, in sight of the other servants, but then he recalled the secret passage. What luck that he had been led through it! And wouldn't the two kitchen wenches be surprised when he appeared! He made his way upstairs and found the tapestry behind which the door was hidden. His curiosity about Frederica's night visit to Bondgate was no more, and he had a feeling that if he were to repeat his experience with her, it would not be until after dark.

He crept down from the upstairs corner room and cracked open the hidden panel where he could see but not be seen, not until the moment he chose to reveal himself. The sounds of conversation and clinking dishes greeted Adam. Luck was with him again. Both Sally and Molly were at work and so distracted that they didn't notice his arrival. They were preparing racks of tarts again. Bowls of thick cream and chocolate stood by, waiting for use. From his new vantage point, he could watch them from behind, admiring their figures quite unseen. They both wore aprons over their clothing. Sally wore a striped cotton dress and petticoat different from the one she had worn the day before and Molly a calico dress with an attractive frill on its short sleeves, covered by the apron. He wondered if its neckline had the same frill, and just how much of her décolletage it revealed? A delicious *frisson* overtook Adam when he realised that they were talking about him! Discreetly, so as not to be seen, he crept towards the bench on which the full bowls stood and watched the two cooks.

"Come on, love," Molly was saying, "I know you an' the gentleman was up to somethin' yesterday, can't ye just give me a little hint?"

"Now, Molly," Sally answered, "I wouldna' ask ye for private details of you and yer beau, would I? It's me own personal business, it is!"

Molly pouted and blew a strand of red hair out of her face as she stirred an enormous bowl of custard. "'Tis true," she admitted, "but I work here! It's not yer own private chamber, y'know!"

"When *you're* the head cook, ye can do as ye like," Sally said.

After a moment of silent thought, Molly continued stirring and said, "Well, I would tell ye if ye wanted to know... Just the other day, I was sitting on me man's lap, an' I feel this little *poke* in me bum—well, it don't take long for me to understand what that means, so I start to seeing if I can turn it into a big poke—" Standing at the counter, she writhed her hips back and forth, descending into a squatting position as if grinding down on her lover. She seemed to become aroused at the memory of it, as her ginger complexion reddened even further. Adam's cock hardened as he watched her.

Molly's eyes twinkled as she told her story.

"Oh, my," Sally said as she fanned herself. "Well, I do remember what it was like to be young an' in love..."

Molly snorted. "Love! I know you think I'm an awful slut, but don't try to tell me yer in lurve with the gentleman—" Adam blushed. "Sometime it's just a bit of fun, innit?"

Sally, smiling to herself, finally gave in. "All right, yes, sometimes I get a bit of it...but I don't owe you or anyone else the details of it, y'hear?"

Molly rolled her eyes. "Oh, fine, all right. But some of these gentlemen get up to some queer business, don't they? I once had a fella that liked to spend his load in me hair!" She held aloft a hank of her own red mane to illustrate. "Didja ever hear of such a thing?"

Both women giggled at the perversity of menfolk. Sally shook her head. "Not me, no thank you. These curls are the devil to clean!" She took her lace cap off and shook her golden ringlets as if the mention of the subject reminded her of them. Adam's heart pounded. The idea of spoiling Sally's beautiful hair, implanted by Molly's words, took possession of him. He observed her cap, white muslin trimmed with delicate lace around the edges, sitting unattended. With a jolt, the hat's similarity to a bowl struck him and he knew what he was going to do. It was a mean trick, perhaps, but hadn't he spent half the day yesterday with custard in his trousers? It was a jest, he thought, that she might appreciate.

Silently, waiting until both women were looking the other way, his heart thumping in anticipation, he tipped one of the bowls, pouring a small amount of chocolate cream into the hat. Not too much — if it was too full, Sally would cop to it too soon.

His task accomplished, Adam crept back into the shadows, appreciating the puddle of glistening brown chocolate in Sally's cap. Before he knew it, Sally returned to work, still conversing idly with Molly, ignoring the hat. *Blast it! Is she going to leave it off the rest of the day?*

But no...Sally pulled her honey-coloured hair back and, without looking, swept up the cap and put it on top of her head with one smooth, practised motion. Then she froze. All was silent, except for the pounding of Adam's heart in his chest. From his hiding place, he could see the chocolate pooled in Sally's hair, streaks of it running down the front and sides of her face and down her neck. Her mouth was agape in surprise, her eyes wide.

Molly, unaware, continued her work until she looked up and saw the mess Sally was in. Molly burst out laughing. "Love, wot've you done to yourself! Oh, ho ho ho! Ha ha!" She nearly doubled over in her amusement, at a loss for words. There, Adam thought, that was fitting payback for Sally's messing of his suit the other day. Part of him remembered the feeling of custard sloshing in his drawers, and he started to become firm again. A warm feeling of rising pleasure filled him, but it was about to get better.

"Oi, you think that's funny, eh?" Sally said, flicking a bit of the chocolate away from her face. "Don't you think we've enough work to do without your pranks?"

"What d'ye mean, love?" Molly said indignantly. "You don't think I—"

"I know you too well, is what I mean," Sally replied. "Your sense of humour is about as delicate as Mr Punch's, an' right after I told ye I didn't like to mess me hair?" She picked up a completed tart, laden with cream, and hefted it meaningfully. "Well, says I, two can play at that game."

Molly's complexion reddened further and she stood up straight. "You'd better not," she said, but her voice wavered.

"What's the matter, love? You like to dish it out, but you can't take it?" Sally stepped forward. Molly was cornered.

"But I tell you, I didn't—"

It was too late. *Splat!* Sally brought the tart down upside down on Molly's head. Cream and fruit and bits of crust flowed down her red hair and onto her shoulders, and a big dollop of filling covered half her face. "Ooohh!" she groaned as she wiped the remains of the tart away from her eyes.

Sally laughed, her bosom shaking with merriment. "Let that teach you a lesson!" she said, wagging a finger. Then she returned to work, confident that she had made her point.

Only Adam, from his hiding place, saw the look on Molly's face turn from shock to resolution. While Sally was distracted, Molly picked up another tart, already finished, and with a piping bag squirted another layer of cream on top until it was as laden as two tarts. "Oh, Sally?" Molly said sweetly. When the other wench turned to answer — *splat!* Molly pushed the tart directly into Sally's face, smearing it around while Sally stood in shock. Now it was Molly's turn to laugh.

Sally slowly wiped the cream from her eyes. When Molly's laughter died away at last, there was a brief moment of silence, in the space of which declarations of war were made. Then each turned to the table to grab what they could as ammunition, and the battle was on!

A jug of custard flowed down the front of Molly's apron, drenching it. Cream tarts plastered Sally's face and chest. Sally clutched at Molly's hair to bring her in for a tart to the face. When they had used up everything within close reach and both women were thoroughly covered in it, they grappled with each other, slipping and sliding in the puddles of spilled liquid on the floor.

Adam savoured his view of the spectacle. The thin clothing of the two wenches clung to their bodies, revealing every curve, even as the mess that covered their faces and hair made them yet more alluring to him. It required only the shortest leap of the imagination to see their wrestling as an act of intimacy, all the more delicious to him for its Sapphic implications!

"Oi!" Sally said as her gaze met Adam's, and the jostling of the two women stopped. Adam's face flushed. He had made the fatal error of poking his head out too far from his hiding place and letting himself be seen. "Wot's all this, then?" the head cook demanded, her hands on her hips. Molly likewise stepped forward. Both women were completely covered in custard and cream. Their bosoms heaved with the exertion of the recent struggle. Both Molly's red hair and Sally's beloved golden curls were plastered against their heads in sodden globs. Adam's manhood, against the better judgement of his mind, throbbed in arousal at the sight. If it were better behaved, he would not be in this situation, cornered by the two maidens he had tricked!

Sally was quicker to piece together the truth, and as both the senior kitchen staff and the first victim of the prank that started the whole chain of events, she spoke first. "I think I owe you an apology, Miss Molly," she said. "Seems we've both been played for fools." A sly expression began to overtake her face, visible to Adam even through the custard that covered it.

"Oh, izzat right?" Molly said, catching on and seeing where Sally was going with this. "Well, I guess I can accept that in the spirit with which it's offered, an' make the same apology meself." Sally accepted her high-toned apology, and the two clasped hands in a parody of genteel intercourse.

Adam cleared out his throat and stepped out from his hiding place, as it was hardly worthy of a gentleman, and he had been caught anyway. "Well, er, seeing as how you two have smoothed over your differences, and I am not needed, I shall take my leave…"

"Not so fast, sir, I don't think you're quite finished," Sally said. Molly stifled a giggle. Adam reddened as he noted that both girls were staring, wide-eyed, at the bulging crotch of his trousers, where his arousal was still quite evident. Was it only his pride, however, that suggested they were a little impressed by what they saw?

Slender Molly slunk over to Adam and draped one messy arm around him, dripping that same cream onto his suit. Against his better judgement, his prick responded, his breathing became shallower and his heart beat faster. "Now, you wouldn't want to be leaving yet, guv, when we're about to have some real fun, would ye?" She walked her fingertips down his chest, delicately undoing the buttons of his waistcoat. Upon seeing his response, she pressed herself harder into his body.

"That's right, sir, just relax and let us take care of you." Sally adopted the same smooth, mollifying tone, but the heavy cream tart she picked up suggested anything but gentle treatment.

"Now, let's not be hasty—" Adam started, but suddenly Molly's grip on him held him in place like a vice. *Splat!* Sally dumped the entire contents in his face and down his chest. Molly oohed and rubbed her hand across his soiled shirt, smearing it into his chest.

"That's not bad, sis" —Molly giggled— "but I think you missed a spot." She picked up another tart. *Wham!* Over the top of Adam's head it went, and dripped down his neck into the back of his shirt. Sally laughed approvingly. Adam, for his part, could hardly see. Molly allowed him enough freedom to wipe his eyes. She was strong for such a slim girl.

"Here, Master Blythewood, let us get that heavy thing off," Sally said, and with Molly's help, she removed his sodden coat. "A gentleman's got to be comfortable, wouldn't you say, Miss Molly?"

"Oh, quite right, luv, an' I think all these wet clothes look very uncomfortable." Molly had undone his vest and was working her hands into the waist of his trousers.

Before he could mutter so much as a protest, the two women had overcome his resistance and the sliding of his trousers down his legs was the first sign of just how far they intended to go. While Molly was busy leaning Adam against the rail so she could fully remove them, Sally had produced another tray of half-completed tarts. Molly pulled down Adam's drawers. His manhood sprang up at attention, at which the ladies reddened. Whether they were as shocked as they pretended to be, both were clearly enjoying Adam's embarrassment and arousal. Sally shrieked, "Eek, a snake! What shall we do, Molly?"

Grinning devilishly, Molly said, "Trap it, and then we'll suck its venom dry!" And at Sally's agreement, they helped themselves to the tarts on the tray and slapped them onto Adam's erect member.

"Ooh! Ow!" Adam said. They were none too gentle with him. "P-please! Mercy!" he cried.

"Oh, we didn't mean to hurt the snake," Molly said, cuddling against him again and gently stroking him through the layer of cream splattered across his loins.

"It's a good thing Dick weren't here" — Sally laughed — "or he might've chopped it off with a garden hoe!" Molly chuckled in agreement.

His ardour suddenly flagging, Adam said, "Dick?"

Molly and Sally both laughed. "Me husband, silly!" said Sally.

Adam went white with shock. "Wait, Dick the groundskeeper?"

Sally nodded with satisfaction. She removed her apron and the outer layers of clothing, pulling the custard-streaked dress over her head. Then she pulled down the neckline of her sodden shift, revealing her inviting mounds, wobbling like two great jellies in serving cups, inviting him to dig in. "But he ain't here right now, and what he doesn't know won't hurt him. What say you, Molly — can your beau spare you for a half-hour?"

Molly agreed that he wouldn't feel the loss of what he was missing and began undoing her own dress — the frill around her bust had wilted under the weight of the custard and her cleavage was covered thickly with the stuff. Adam took the hint and removed what was left of his own suit until the three stood together, he as naked as his namesake on the day of Creation, the other two in thin cloth shifts, already so soaked through with desserts that they clung enticingly to their bodies.

It was, Adam felt, better than he could have hoped for. The pairing of the two women, one plump and one slender, both eager to please and to be pleased, seemed to him to offer the full range of feminine pleasures. He soon found it was as good as it promised to be, too. It took little to encourage him to make free with his hands, stroking the rounded and curved surfaces of their bosoms, their bottoms, their thighs and legs, as they did the same, rubbing the runny custard all over his body. Their sodden underthings were a barrier that was easily removed, and soon there was nothing to hold them back.

There was more, as they turned to the remaining jugs of chocolate and custard and poured them over each other, rubbing and stroking each other until they resembled three figures of unfired clay. Always Adam's impressive root came in for special attention. The two wenches liked touching it and inspecting it as much as he enjoyed sneaking his fingers between their thighs. By the wetness of their splits, they were as teased and excited as he was, until they could finally stand it no more.

Molly was the first to take Adam in her arms and let him plunge into her, lying back on the floor and spreading her legs open. He took to it like a rutting bull, brushing her pointed nipples with his lips as if grazing in an open field while he thrust in and out. Molly shuddered and spent with a cry, but Adam wasn't finished. Like an animal awakened by the smell of blood, he next took Sally. Leaning her against the wooden table, he spanked her fat bottom with the palm of his hand, relishing the smack of its impact and getting more excited all over again with each gasp and moan that escaped from her lips. Molly sidled up next to her and, as a kindness and merciful release from her torments, slid her fingers into Sally's minge and worked her into a frenzy.

With both women side by side, their bare arses pointed at him, Adam stepped between them and with each hand grasped a buttock, squeezing and caressing as they continued to grab sweet syrups and sauces from the workbench and pour them over his head and down his chest, rubbing them in with their hands, pressing their breasts against him, and finally to pump his handle by hand as if drawing water from a well. It was almost too much.

With a gentle kiss on the lips that tasted of toffee and chocolate and a host of other flavours, Adam said, between sighs, "Sally..."

"Yes, luv?"

"I think...I am ready to ice these cakes." He squeezed her tits meaningfully.

"Oh, yes, sir?" She attempted to bat her eyelashes but was frustrated by a glob of pudding covering one eye.

"You don't think Dick will mind, do you?"

Sally shook her head. "It's been a long time since Dick had much icing in him, to be truthful." She lowered herself to her knees and briefly took Adam's cock in her mouth, caressing it with her tongue and sliding her lips up and down the shaft. It stiffened again in her warm embrace.

Molly continued to cling to him, running her hands up and down his body and nuzzling against his shoulder. She found a purchase on his backside while Sally raised her full breasts to encompass Adam's prong, which he slid back and forth, moaning in pleasure.

Just as he had reached his peak, Molly stuck her little finger into his arsehole. As if she had sprung the hidden catch inside a music box, warmth flooded his being and he spurted hot jism over Sally's waiting tits. "Oh ho, guv, now that's a shower I haven't had in years!"

For his part Adam was nearly speechless, having groaned wordlessly upon his release. Molly, pleased at herself for the part she had played in his finishing, supported him until he could catch his breath and stand without his knees trembling. As spent as he was, he enjoyed a sense of well-being and relaxation he had not felt since his arrival at Windmere Hall. If a part of him wished that it were the elegant Frederica Windmere instead of gregarious kitchen wenches with whom he sported, he was willing to keep that to himself and ignore it while he savoured the moment.

Finally, the three of them looked around the kitchen and came to the realisation of the titanic mess they had made. Their clothing was hardly fit to wear out of there, quite aside from the question of how they might clean their bodies. They laughed guiltily as one might after an episode of over-indulgence, mentally promising never to go to such lengths again, but secretly knowing that the desire for pleasure would overcome all such scruples at the next opportunity.

A small bell next to the door rang, interrupting the moment. Somewhere, on the other end of the rope to which the bell was attached, was a member of the household, or perhaps Gainesborough or another senior servant, awaiting a response.

Sally and Molly both froze. "My word," Sally said. "It's tea time!"

Chapter Ten

The carriage ride to Bondgate was brief and uneventful, allowing Adam to take in a view of the bay on one side and woods on the other. The path surmounted the foreboding cliffs that he had been warned about and which seemed to occupy so much of Frederica Windmere's fretful mind. Not for the first time, Adam had to shake his head when he recalled how changeable the woman's moods were. Despite her seeming indifference to him, at least during the day, she had become agitated upon hearing of Pamela Bond's invitation to Adam to explore her library. Yet she had nothing to say about her own late-night visit to the woman's estate. Adam had yet to puzzle out what had happened the night Frederica had pulled him from the muddy shore. He had made his way back to Windmere Hall, but somehow, she had not.

"Do be careful," Alice Windmere had said with an unusual expression of solicitude, but when pressed, she could not say of what he should be careful, at least not under the watchful, silencing eye of Lady Windmere.

After this brief reverie, the carriage passed through a pair of imposing wrought-iron gates bearing the keyhole insignia of the Bond family. Bondgate itself was a house not as large as Windmere Hall but still elegant with its tall, vertical windows and decorative gables, modern flourishes that Adam was surprised to see in such an out-of-the-way place.

Upon being led into the house by a taciturn servant in red and black livery, it was clear to Adam that Bondgate's modernity was merely a façade, for inside it were the bones of a structure yet older, perhaps even predating the site's days as Cliffsward, the original Windmere home. The tapestries and antique furniture on display showed that the Bonds had held onto the ancestral roots their cousins the Windmeres had hidden beneath a veneer of bland good taste.

"Do you like it?" Pamela Bond enquired as she entered the room and found Adam admiring a large oil painting of a storm-tossed ship.

"It is very…dramatic," Adam allowed. "I will admit to being taken by surprise." He mentioned the building's modern exterior.

"Yes," Miss Bond agreed. "I prefer not to dwell on the past…at least in public. The foundations of Bondgate actually date back to Roman times. Each generation of Bonds and Windmeres has added their own touch, hence the disparity."

Pamela Bond was, as Adam had noticed previously, a handsome woman, with jet-black hair and eyes nearly as dark. In her own lair, surrounded by medieval flourishes, he could well understand why the Windmere sisters had attributed to her a Gothic, even sinister, air. But she was still the genial hostess he had met aboard the *Cupid,* and despite Lady Windmere's tolerance of her daughters' catty remarks about her friend, he received no impression that she found Miss Bond untrustworthy. "It's a...charming combination," he said.

"Thank you," she said lightly. "I am so glad you could find time to visit me here," she went on. "I was very sad to miss you at tea yesterday."

Adam reddened at the memory of his dalliance with Sally and Molly. It had been an unlikely chain of events indeed by which he had returned to his room to clean up unseen at the same time that the two wenches had assembled a confection to send up to the family. He still felt the scrapes where he had shimmied up the drainpipe on the outside of the Hall. For the rest of his stay there, he would shiver whenever he heard the barking of the groundskeeper's dogs, who no longer seemed so docile. He cleared his throat. "Quite. And I must thank you for the invitation whilst begging your pardon for my absence then."

"'Tis a pity. Lady Windmere's cook served a delightful...well, I should have to call it a *mélange* of mixed custard, cream and *crème de caramel*. I've never had the like."

Adam shifted from one foot to the other. "I...have tasted it."

The awkwardness of the day before forgotten, Miss Bond showed him the amenities of her home, guiding him from one *objet d'art* to another, dropping a hint as to its age and provenance and mentioning some ancestor or other who had added it to the family trove. In every hall were those silent men whom Adam had seen before on the *Cupid* or driving the carriage. It was clear to him that they were practically invisible to Miss Bond, so used to their presence was she, but he found their gaze, their ever-present alertness, unnerving, and he was glad to move into chambers and corridors that were evidently more private. As Gretchen had said, if any women worked for Miss Bond, they served only in her boudoir.

Turning at last to a bearskin that dominated one wall, Miss Bond said, with some pride, "And here is my contribution."

Adam could barely hide his surprise. Had she killed the bear herself?

"Oh, no, I am hardly interested in such pastimes," she said dismissively. "It was a gift from an admirer." She looked wistful.

Adam was not surprised that such a woman would have suitors. Had none of them made a successful claim? Instead of asking such a personal question, he said of the bearskin, "An impressive token."

Miss Bond shook her head as she stepped away from the hide. "For all he roared, he was merely a cub." Whether she meant the bear or her admirer, Adam couldn't be sure, and no more mention of it was made.

At length, Miss Bond invited Adam to sit in a parlour whose redness struck him as garish. The cloth wallpaper was the colour of fresh blood, and the parts of the furniture that were not similarly upholstered were gleaming black teakwood, matching the trim and floor. Miss Bond sat across from him and leaned back insolently, appraising him. She made no disguise of looking him up and down, and he felt as naked as he had been in the kitchen the day before.

"I say," he said, attempting to play off her boldness as a jest, "am I in for a medical examination?"

Miss Bond laughed, but her frank air remained. "Mr Blythewood," she said, "I have indeed invited you here to see the Bond family library, and you shall see it. But let us first have the tea you missed yesterday." Another silent manservant brought in a tray with cups and kettle and departed after leaving it. Miss Bond poured, never taking her eyes from him as she did so, yet she spilled not a drop.

Sipping idly at her cup after she had handed one to Adam, she said, "Does it offend you to be looked at so?"

Adam had become used to the woman's forwardness, but he admitted, "I am not accustomed to being so frankly stared at."

"By a woman, you mean." Adam nodded. "It is no more than most women experience every day. Do you dislike the attention?"

Adam felt that he was being toyed with, but he mustered a smile. "Not at all. One does not mind being made an object if the gaze belongs to a connoisseur."

At this, Miss Bond raised her cup in appreciation of the *bon mot*, and something like a twinkle entered her expression. She relaxed, and Adam no longer felt like a butterfly pinned to a board. "Yes, I think we understand each other. And tell me, Mr Blythewood, do you like what falls under your gaze?"

Adam wondered at how he should answer this. Of course he had noticed Pamela Bond's attractive features, her aquiline nose and elfin chin, the romantic shadow of her eyes, her curvaceous form. She was a woman of bold gestures, even now reclining in such a way as to show off her calves beneath the hem of her gown. A trim of dark lace on her bodice contrasted with the milky white of her bosom, and when she leaned back, it exposed her neck most tantalisingly. But he knew, too, that she was an unmarried woman, and his words might be taken seriously while hers were merely banter. He had no wish to enter into a commitment.

"You flatter me," he finally deflected, "if you consider my opinion that of a connoisseur," and sipped his tea so that his eyes might show merriment without his lips being thought mocking.

Miss Bond sat up. "Come now," she said, a tad impatiently. "I am the last of the Bonds, and I quite enjoy the life I have made for myself. Please do not mistake me for some simpering debutante, desperate to land a husband. Now, tell me — how many of the Windmere household girls have you had?"

Adam choked on his tea and had to cough into a napkin to clear his throat. If he hadn't been so incommoded, he would have stood and left, or at least insisted that such an accusation, however truthful, was incompatible with his personal honour. Surely Pamela Bond didn't expect him to answer! But one look told him that she was indeed serious, and in fact she not only did not judge him, she approved! Her expression was one of eagerness, even hunger, that of the co-conspirator who relished gossip almost as much as first-hand experience.

Quickly deciding that she wasn't seeking information to pass to Lady Windmere — if the lady wanted to know what he was up to, all she had to do was ask Alice — he admitted, not without a bit of secret pride, "Five." At Miss Bond's further coaxing, he elaborated. "Two abigails, a pair of kitchen wenches and…one whose identity I am not at liberty to reveal."

Miss Bond sat back again like a cat, knowing and satisfied. "Ah, one of Adonica's daughters, eh? Which one? Not telling? Well, it isn't hard to guess. But have no fear, Lady Windmere shan't hear it from me. We keep *some* secrets from each other, you know."

Adam had no trouble believing that. Recovering his discretion, Adam said, "As to the last, we shared only a kiss." But he suspected she already knew all about it.

Pamela Bond's expression revealed nothing, but a spark of amusement crinkled the corners of her eyes. "Did you?"

Before he could follow up that enigmatic remark, a servant—whether the same one who had brought the tea or a different one, Adam couldn't tell, since they all wore the same uniform—appeared at the door carrying a lantern. If Miss Bond had summoned him, Adam knew not how, but she seemed to expect his arrival nonetheless, as they had finished their tea and, apparently, their conversation. It was time for Adam to see the library.

"Yes, I believe you will make an excellent addition to our next gathering," Miss Bond was saying as the servant led them down a set of steps. The narrow walkway was at first of cut stone with wooden stairs, but as they descended, they entered a catacomb of a much earlier age, hewn from the rock itself. "The Romans, you will recall?" Miss Bond said in reply to Adam's obvious surprise. They walked past wall sconces with unlit torches, blackened by layers of ancient soot and smoke. It became cool. They passed barred doors that Miss Bond barely seemed to notice. Some were covered with the dust and cobwebs of ages, but others appeared shiny with frequent use. Miss Bond ignored them equally, focused on their destination.

The "library" was in fact a repository of documents from the days when the site that would become Bondgate had been home to a monastery – the barred doors he had seen had been monks' cells for private meditation and self-mortification – some so old that they were scrolls rather than books.

Adam's eyes widened in amazement, and for a moment he barely heard Miss Bond's words. Even he could appreciate the wealth of knowledge accrued in this room. Idly, he wondered if Miss Bond had ever shown this collection to Jane Windmere, and what she would think of it? *What brought her to mind?*

"I don't often open it to outsiders," Miss Bond was saying. Her manservant went about the chamber lighting candles. Soon the crypt-like room was bathed in their glow. "Of course, Sir Alfred was blood. He found some of his sources on the old Windmere family here, and I imagine you will have already examined the notes he took, but many of the original documents from the Cliffsward days are too fragile to be moved. Perhaps you would be interested in a few pages of Sir Ambrose Windmere's diary?"

Suddenly, his attention snapped back…Sir Ambrose's diaries? He had searched for them in vain among Sir Alfred's notes. He should have realised they might still be here. He turned his eyes to his hostess. Noticing his eagerness, she added, her eyes flashing, "Some of them are surprisingly…stimulating."

She had already laid out the volume in question at a desk so cramped and ancient that Adam could easily imagine one of the monks of yore using it to copy illuminated manuscripts, or study the Bible, or whatever it was they spent their time on. The book was smaller than Adam had expected – small enough to be carried in the pocket of a travelling seaman – and the crabbed, close-packed words faded with age, but it was what he had been looking for. As he excitedly fit his long legs under the tiny desk, hunching over the diary, he hardly noticed as Miss Bond and her man took their leave.

Once he got the hang of reading the old gentleman's handwriting, Adam found that Sir Ambrose was indeed more forthcoming about his adventures than his prudish descendant. It was clear that Sir Alfred's judgement was sound, however. Lady Windmere would certainly never want such vivid anecdotes published, lurid as they were with the unglamorous rigours of shipboard life, including the debauchery and violence that marked sailors' shore leave. Someone else must have felt the same way, as an unknown hand had gone through the book already and scratched out most of the proper names. References to the island, whose opening was to be Ambrose's crowning glory, were similarly expunged – the blank in Sir Alfred's manuscript was not simply an example of coyness. He had truly been unable to discover the island's name or location, as the coordinates were missing as well. Either Sir Ambrose had chosen to keep them secret, or someone who had shared his disgrace after the Feast had chosen to erase incriminating memories.

The latter seemed more likely, as Adam reached the last page, describing the preparation for the ship's arrival at Cliffsward and the upcoming Feast. "A pox upon that knave, McQ_____," it read. "Nay, a pox upon me for letting _____ talk me into hiring him! Once the _____ is safely returned, I'll have S_____ dispense with him. But I have too many preparations to complete – " The next page, and those after, were torn out. Adam wondered who "McQ" and "S," the only characters still legible in the scratched-out names, had been.

Flipping to the earlier pages, Adam reflected that some of the stories contained therein were too delightful to simply shut away in mouldering pages. If he copied a few out, just for himself, surely no one would mind? Hadn't Pamela Bond teased him with their "stimulating" qualities? Adam felt his pockets — he had nothing to copy them with. Then he remembered that Sir Alfred had spent time taking notes here. Perhaps he had left behind some paper. He stood, his stiff limbs protesting as they reminded him how long he had been sitting in a cramped position, and set about exploring the library's nooks for writing supplies.

Stuck behind some older volumes, Adam found a slim book, bound in green leather. It was a fine item and different in quality from anything else he had found in the library. He flipped through the pages. It was a relatively new journal or commonplace book, and within the paragraphs of personal observations, there were names he recognised, current residents of Windmere Hall. If it were Sir Alfred's, it seemed odd that it had been left behind here.

His curiosity aroused, Adam sat back down with the new volume and brought it into the light. His blood froze, all thought of Sir Ambrose's adventures and Pamela Bond's innuendos forgotten, when he saw the name embossed on the front — *Roderick Utley*.

* * * *

I have yet to learn any more on the final resting place of the Mosca *and its treasure. However, I must now be more circumspect, as my inquiries in the village have attracted unwanted attention.*

I am being followed.

Those were the last words recorded in the slim diary Adam had smuggled out of Pamela Bond's library under his jacket. The entry was dated six weeks earlier. He leaned back in the chair in his own chamber, his thoughts awhirl. The diary was a blank-paged notebook of the kind one could buy at any stationer's, albeit of the high end, as the quality of the leather and the customised embossing showed.

He had learned much. A testimony of Roderick Utley's origins, status and his reason for being at Windmere Hall, or in Pamela Bond's library, would have been too much to hope for, but Adam now had a better idea of who his erstwhile rival had been — a man of culture and education, who had arrived at Windmere Hall with the purpose of investigating its library. He appeared to be a gentleman at liberty, and if he had spent some time with Sir Alfred's manuscript, as Gainesborough had hinted, it was apparently by choice, as a favour, while he worked for his own purposes.

The early entries in the diary were prosaic, describing the Hall and its environs, as well as individuals Adam recognised by name and description — Lady Windmere and her daughters, designated by initial, and the various servants. Adam raised an eyebrow when he noted a short aside on the charms of a certain lady's maid! An incident that Adam had completely forgotten returned to mind when he read Utley's description of the old herb-seller in the village, the one who had mistaken him for someone else – clearly Roderick Utley! Utley did not say why he had hoped to procure the plant she had offered to find for him, but there could be no doubt it was the same one she had tried to sell to Adam.

There were even frequent mentions of the kitchen and – Adam blushed – the brazenly forward wenches who staffed it. A good part of Utley's research focused on recipes and there were illustrations of various pastries and desserts, including a certain tart that Adam instantly recognised. That explained how some of Sir Alfred's papers ended up there, but had they been left as part of his work or had he felt compelled to hide them? Around the edges there seemed to be something else that Utley dared not even set down in his private notes, culminating in the reference to the *Mosca*, whatever that was, and the conviction that he was being followed, after which he had stopped writing altogether. Had he hidden the diary so his pursuers wouldn't find it? Adam hadn't told Pamela Bond about the diary after he found it, and now that he had read it, he felt justified in his caution. The Windmere daughters didn't seem to trust Miss Bond, and he wasn't sure if he should either.

How complex Adam's feelings were might be imagined when he delved further into the book and found Utley's interest in food supplanted by, or rather mingled with, his increasingly rapturous descriptions of "F," obviously Frederica Windmere. "F" seemed to press on Utley's thoughts at inopportune times, crowding out his work in favour of panegyrics to her beauty and elegance and detailed notes of every little gesture or word from her that gave him hope his attentions might be returned. All mention of other women fell away as one alone dominated his imagination. Tucked in the middle of the book was a striking freehand drawing that left no doubt. Yes, it was clearly Frederica.

No wonder she was so cold to Adam during the day! The attraction to Roderick was clearly mutual. When Adam had arrived at the Hall after the departure or disappearance of Roderick, it had surely been a painful reminder of what Frederica had lost. But by night, she could dream that Adam was Roderick. *What a muddle!*

Adam's reverie was interrupted by the familiar sound of padding footsteps outside his room. Was it so late already? The burned-down candle showed that he had been absorbed in Roderick Utley's book much longer than he had realised. As usual, the doorknob turned quietly, but in his distraction, Adam had forgotten to lock it!

The door silently and slowly swung open. Frederica Windmere stood, her blank eyes fixed on the distance, her pouting lips half-open as if on the cusp of speaking. She wore a silk dressing gown, open to the waist, revealing the thinnest chemise of diaphanous lace. Her breasts heaved in expectation. "Roderick?" she whispered. She dumbly undid the sash of her nightgown, revealing her lingerie beneath as if in a dream. This must have been Roderick's chamber, and the pair given to nightly assignations. Scandalous indeed, but hardly something Adam was in a position to judge harshly.

Frederica Windmere's beauty rendered Adam speechless. Many times when he had followed her, he had felt himself inflamed by lust, had gazed upon her as only a husband should do, had wished that he could be that Roderick she searched for. Only once, the night he had followed her down to the shore, had they shared more than a kiss, and since then they had hardly spoken a word to each other. He had wondered what she would do if he left the door to his room open, and now, through accident, he had found out.

Yet, as beautiful and available as she was, and as opportunistic as he knew himself to be in such matters, Adam could not continue this deception. It was only partly that Frederica's heart belonged to another man — a man with whom, Adam now knew, he had much in common. That had hardly stopped him in the past. It was rather the feeling that imposture was too cruel, that allowing her to believe that he was her lost Roderick was a deception too low even for him. He could take no pleasure in having Frederica under such circumstances, especially knowing that she would hate him in the daytime if she remembered the experience.

Conquering the animal urging of his body, Adam took the hands that Frederica had stretched out to him, lowered them, and as gently as possible, said, "No. I am not Roderick." He kept her at arms' length when he would have dearly liked to crush her to him.

Frederica's blank expression registered confusion, then sadness. "Where...where is he?" she whispered huskily. The first sign of welling tears appeared in her eyes.

Adam was even more torn. He had no wish to take advantage of Frederica, but causing her distress was at the moment even worse. "Shh, shh," he said. "Go to sleep. Perhaps he will return."

Frederica shook her head, first slowly, then more violently. "No... No, no!" Her voice became louder, and Adam tried to shush her again, before she woke up the house. "He is with that woman!" she hissed.

Adam gently ushered her out of the room and into the hall. "You must get some rest," he whispered. Eventually Frederica allowed him to guide her to her own room. "Good night," he said.

Frederica, still lost in her own dream, settled onto the bed, murmuring, "Roderick, my Roderick... Where are you, my love?" The tears streamed freely down her face, illuminated by the moonlight. At last she calmed enough that Adam felt he could leave her.

Walking silently through the unlit hallway, Adam found that his own chamber was dark when he returned to it. He hadn't remembered dousing the candle, and surely he hadn't taken so long with Frederica that it would have burned down completely. He entered the room cautiously so as not to bump into anything, and feeling the lateness of the hour, he decided not to bother relighting it. He removed his jacket, his shoes and trousers, and his shirt and stockings, and since it was warm, he decided to go straight to bed in his drawers. He turned down the covers and got in bed.

Only then did he find that he was not alone. Another body had already warmed the bed, a body the weight of which drew him towards the centre of the mattress. A slender finger crossed his lips and a feminine voice whispered "Shhh," before the visitor pressed close to him and covered his lips with her own.

"Alice?" Adam exclaimed, sitting up, when he realised that it was indeed the youngest Windmere sister who now shared his bed.

"Shh," she soothed him, stroking his chest with her hand, settling him back into the bedclothes. "Please be comfortable...Adam. May I call you that?" She giggled at her own forwardness and continued to explore his lean body with her hands.

His eyes adjusted and now over the initial surprise, Adam saw that the young woman had hung her gown over the back of a chair and climbed into his bed wearing a silk shift that clung to her body. She had taken her long blonde hair out of its elaborate coiffure and let it hang loosely about her shoulders and down her back. The same intensity that had unnerved Adam before still shone in Alice's eyes, but it was now coupled with a hunger he recognised.

Adam's heart pounded in his chest, no longer from shock but from reawakened ardour. Alice was young, and while shorter and more slender than her eldest sister, she was every bit as much a woman as Frederica and her purpose in visiting him was obvious.

But Adam slowed down, not least because he was curious, now that he had a moment to think. "You were watching us?"

Alice nodded, casting her eyes down momentarily. When her gaze returned to meet Adam's, she said vehemently, "It's not what you think! Yes, I have watched you all these nights. But it is for Freddie's sake. It is her that I watch over...to keep her safe."

Adam scoffed inwardly. No caretaker could allow Frederica to get into the mischief he had observed without stepping in to halt her. But he felt that she was speaking the truth. All the strange things she had said to him during the day, the times he had surprised her in the act of spying, were clearly meant to protect Frederica. But from what?

"I had to make sure of your intentions," she explained. "I suppose you have guessed some of the truth...about Roderick."

Adam nodded. "He was staying here. Working on something, like I am."

"Roderick owned an eating house in London. When he came here, he told Mother that he was searching for a long-dormant British cooking tradition, and he asked to look in the family library."

Adam thought of Sally's indifferent cooking and snorted. With that uncanny capacity for reading his mind she seemed to have, Alice said, "I know, Freddie and Jane and I thought he was touched! But he talked a good game, and Mother was hooked when he suggested that this secret tradition, once revived, would rival the French! You can't deny an appeal to patriotism!"

Indeed Adam could not. At last venturing the question he most hesitated to ask, he said, "I take it he and Miss Windmere..."

"She was mad for him. It was expected that a marriage would be announced any time. And then...he disappeared."

"Left?"

"Vanished! One day he was here, going about his business, and the next he was gone, as if he had packed up overnight. Nothing personal was left behind. Mother took him for a bounder, said good riddance and has forbidden any discussion of him whatsoever, but Freddie... Well, you see what it's like for her."

Adam had guessed as much. "How long has she been sleepwalking?"

"It started when you arrived. You look much like him, like Roderick."

"No wonder Frederica appeared shocked when she saw me! And this was Roderick's room while he stayed here, I gather."

Alice nodded. "It wasn't on purpose! There are only so many guest rooms available, and no one, least of all Mother, could have imagined —"

Adam dismissed the idea. "No matter. I know none of you would have deliberately tormented Miss Windmere. Unless…"

"Unless what? Surely you don't think —"

"I don't know what to think." A nagging doubt had surfaced in his mind, but it was too unformed to give utterance to. At least he had confirmation that Roderick, and Frederica's relationship to him, had a fixed reality outside of Frederica's dreams. "Tell me, Alice, what was Roderick's business with Miss Bond?"

Alice recoiled in disgust. "I can't imagine. She is Mother's friend. The rest of us tolerate her eccentricities on Mother's behalf. But I know Freddie is suspicious. Roderick called on Miss Bond shortly before he disappeared, and Freddie thinks she may have lured him to stay with her, or perhaps…"

Adam thought of the barred cells he had seen in the catacombs beneath Bondgate. "She thinks he may be held against his will?" He shook his head. It was too fantastical to be believed, but since arriving here, he had seen many things that would have tested his credulity in London.

"I know it sounds absurd. Miss Bond believes that Roderick was pulled into the sea beneath the cliffs, and I admit that is probably the most likely. But Freddie cannot accept that, so she wanders the halls at night, seeking him."

"But instead she found me." Adam leaned back against his pillow, deep in thought.

Alice clung to his chest. "And that is why I watched you so carefully! Only a cad would take advantage of a woman in such a state, and I had to make sure that you were not a cad."

Adam had to smile at this girlish faith in his virtue. Clearly she didn't have eyes on him all the time. "I hate to disappoint you, but there was one night, outside, that I yielded to temptation." He described the night Frederica had fled to the shore beneath the cliffs, and wondered how she had escaped Alice's surveillance.

"Oh!" Alice chuckled. "I wonder, Mr Blythewood, if affairs were quite as you imagined them that night! It was very dark, was it not?"

"What do you mean? Was it not Frederica who rescued me from the quicksand, and with whom I —? What do you know that you're not telling me?"

Alice laughed again. "Now I am afraid it is I who am not at liberty to say," she said, "but let us say that my confidence in your behaviour towards Freddie remains unshaken." She leaned in closer to him and said breathily, "However, your treatment of me still leaves something to be desired."

It was clear she had said all she cared to about the dead and sought to remind Adam that he shared his bed with someone very much alive. He responded vigorously as she grasped his cock with her delicate fingers, staring hungrily into his eyes and daring him to stop her. Alice was not a girl to be refused.

"I say," he said, controlling his ardour as best he could, "are you sure about this? You wish to protect your sister's virtue but you throw yourself at me?"

In answer, Alice pressed her mouth against his, her tongue tangling with his as she continued fondling his now-hard prick. "I care not for Freddie's virtue," she said when they paused, "but she loves Roderick, and I would have no one take advantage of her confusion. I could have shared Roderick with her, but he had no eyes for anyone but Freddie. You see? You are so much like him, but you have no such entanglements."

Adam did see, in a way, but he was still cautious. His manhood threatened to overpower him, especially while Alice exercised it so thoroughly. "I—I can make no promises—" he stammered.

Alice sat up and pulled the thin shift over her head. "For God's sake, I don't want your promises," she said, lying back. "You've thrown every maid in the house into a tizzy, and I could use a bit of tizzying myself."

Adam could resist no longer, and at Alice's invitation, he embraced her nubile body, kissing every part of her—he explored her shallow belly and ripe breasts, the graceful sweep of her neck and the long, golden hair that draped it, the curve of her thighs and bottom, tapering to legs that made up in delicacy what they lacked in length. Even her dainty feet and perfect toes he investigated with his lips and tongue. Alice received this obeisance with mingled amusement and arousal, gasping and giggling when Adam found a spot that made her ticklish or pink with longing. Like a gentleman, he made her pleasure his own, savouring the little noises she made and the reflexive coiling of her loins under his ministrations.

Finally, spreading her legs open wide and kissing the insides of her thighs, to her audible enjoyment, he made his way to that fountain of womanhood, decorated with a tuft of the same gold that crowned her being, and made a thorough exploration with his lips and tongue, like a bee collecting pollen from a flower, adding his fingers to spread her leaves like the opening of a book when necessary. To his delight and the increasing firmness of his own manhood, she responded with ecstatic cries of pleasure — thank God the guest rooms were in a different wing of the house than the family's quarters!

"Wait, please," she panted between gasps. "I can stand it no longer!" Adam sat up, still engorged, to await her pleasure. Flushed and breathing heavily, Alice turned over and folded her legs beneath her, presenting her pert bottom to him. "If you please," she said, calming a little, "I have no desire to be with child. You may do what you like at the rear entrance."

Here was a pretty challenge! It would be one thing to feed his considerable log to the blazing furnace of Alice's maidenhood, but what she suggested was more like inserting it through the chimney. A narrow channel in the best of circumstances, it would take some teasing to open the pathway for him. Two impulses warred within him — he had no wish to pain the young lady whose enjoyment he had so far savoured. Yet, he was mesmerised by the whiteness of the moon and the single eye that stared at him. His cock throbbed, eager to ram home. "Are you sure?" he asked. "I have been told that I am, er, bigger than the common run. If you haven't experienced this before…"

"Then just give me a percentage," Alice said impatiently, "but I simply must see what the fuss is all about. Let us say that if I mention 'Napoleon,' it is time to make your retreat, hm?" While Adam smiled at her boldness, she put one of his pillows beneath her stomach and made a tent of her legs, raising her backside and exposing her moistened slit at the same time. "This is the usual position, is it not?"

The lady gets what she wants, Adam thought to himself. Far be it from him to shy now. On his knees, he began with a few appreciative strokes on her cheeks with gentle fingers, soothing and relaxing Alice further. Were her murmurs of appreciation due to these efforts, or satisfaction at having her own way? Then, while smothering her rump with kisses, he massaged her pussy, continuing to pleasure her but at the same time coating his fingers with her juices, enough to coax and lubricate her waiting hole. For Alice Windmere, even the 'rear entrance' was an exclusive one, and eventually, with the aid of his slick fingers, it opened to him.

Even as Alice quivered and gasped through another minor spasm of pleasure under his handiwork, she remained cool. "Very good," she said. "Do you think me ready?"

She was ready, in Adam's opinion. He held his manhood and gave it a last pull for luck now that the way was prepared. "How came you to know so much about it?" Adam asked. "I know *this* isn't in the family library."

"I talk to the servants often... Sally is a veritable fount of knowledge, you know... Ooh!" She grunted as Adam made his entrance.

Sally! Adam blushed at the thought of what she might have told Alice. "Is it uncomfortable?" he asked.

"I—I am all right," Alice said, beginning to breathe in rhythm with him. "It is...interesting. Please continue. Ah!"

Interesting, Adam thought. A rare compliment from Alice Windmere! But her body expressed more than mere interest, and together they found a stroke that suited them both. Their silence gave way to moans and grunts of satisfaction, and there was no mention of the French tyrant or talk of retreat. After Adam was sure Alice had received her share of delight and was thoroughly spent, he released and pulled out. He had many questions yet remaining, but Alice had given him the gift of a mind for the moment blank. After a brief kiss good night, he collapsed into the bed and fell asleep so soundly that he was hardly aware of her leaving him.

Chapter Eleven

Adam had not shown Alice Windmere the diary that confirmed Roderick Utley's presence at Bondgate. Although he now trusted that Alice only had Frederica's best interests at heart, he was still unsure that they saw eye to eye on what exactly best served those interests. Did jealousy or disapproval of Roderick's love for Frederica cause Alice to send him away, or, worse yet, lure him to his watery death? If Roderick had truly perished in the bay, then who had removed his belongings from the house? His hope of gaining Frederica's favour dwindled in the next few days now that he knew the facts, and while the eldest sister still haunted his doorstep in the middle of the night, Alice had made no such return to his bed. If it hadn't been for Marie and Sally, he wasn't sure where he would find release for his natural urges. He now felt that he and Alice shared a secret between them, a secret that was a burden to him, and made him complicit in whatever actions Alice might have taken to protect her sister.

It was with mingled regret and relief later that week that Adam watched the Windmere sisters board a carriage to begin an extended holiday, one of Gainesborough's underlings handing their luggage up to the driver to secure it. It was another grey, drizzly morning. The girls carried umbrellas and wore wide hats and veils, as if heading for a funeral rather than a fashionable spa. *Ah, well,* he thought, turning away, *perhaps it's for the best. May they have better weather than Windmere Hall suffers.* In his newfound solitude, perhaps he could get some of his own work done, or at least a night's sleep.

Adam did not have to open the envelope that came to him a few days later to know who had sent it. The red paper and the gold-embossed keyhole insignia could only have come from Bondgate.

"A masquerade!" he said to himself as he read the invitation. "How quaint!" It included a calling card, on which was written the name "Zeno" in flowing calligraphy and the image of a mask. This must be the name he was to use. He racked his brains trying to think of a holiday such an event would mark, but he could think of nothing. Midsummer had passed, and Christmas was months away. Still, the idea intrigued him. He had not seen the enigmatic Miss Bond for a fortnight, even as his perusal of Roderick Utley's diary had convinced him that there was more to her than he had been told.

"Ah, Pamela does enjoy entertaining," Lady Windmere said when Adam showed her the invitation. "Yes, it is a pity that my girls could not be included, but they shall have many opportunities in Bath. Me? No, I don't expect to be included in such affairs. They are strictly for a younger set, and I suspect Pamela would like to, shall we say, show you off? Now, don't let that frighten you away. Unless, of course, you would prefer to stay and sit up with me?"

And that was how Adam found himself dusting the lint from his finest suit the afternoon before the affair. As he brushed his coat and laid out his collar, cuffs and other accessories, it occurred to him that he might be in a position to help out Frederica. When he wasn't kept up by her nocturnal prowlings, he sometimes lay awake at night imagining the darkness of the monks' cells in the dungeon beneath Bondgate—for in his imagination he had turned the stone corridors into a catacomb, then into a dungeon, without even realising it—wondering whether Roderick Utley was truly in one of them, and if so, for what purpose?

Pamela Bond seemed to command an army of unquestioning manservants. Where did they come from? While they were objects of sly innuendo to Alice, Jane and Frederica sometimes dropped hints that they were paroled criminals, toiling in exchange for pardon, or worse, travellers whose anonymity made them easy to waylay and press into service, perhaps by mesmerism. Adam had been tempted to laugh off these fancies, but in that light, Roderick Utley's disappearance had a certain logic.

Adam would look around and see if there were any clew to such dark business, or he might even find Roderick himself. If it came to nothing, perhaps he could at least confirm the official story, his tragic loss to the treacherous ocean. He imagined Frederica, at last free to mourn, needing a strong shoulder to cry on, and who should she turn to but Adam himself? Well, anything was possible.

"Now for the finishing touch," Adam said to himself as he examined his appearance in the looking glass. His wardrobe was that of a man who was ready for any social situation, and this was no exception—from a pocket in his extensive trunk, he drew a silky black band cut with eyeholes. It had seen little use since his university days, but one never knew when something would come in handy, and he was glad he had held on to it. After tying the thin strings behind his head and adjusting the velvet-lined mask so that he could see straight, he donned his silk hat and tied a matching short cape around his shoulders. A mysterious, dashing rogue looked back at him from the mirror...a nobleman come in disguise to reclaim his title, perhaps, or maybe a dapper jewel thief. Tonight, he hoped to steal only kisses, but if he played his cards right, he might learn at least one of Pamela Bond's secrets. "Smashing," he said to his reflection.

* * * *

Upon Adam's arrival at Bondgate, the carriages lined up in front and the orderly procession of guests from the driveway to the entrance along a carpeted lane told him that the festivities were already underway. He alone rode in a carriage with the familiar keyhole emblem on the door—perhaps he really was the guest of honour. It had arrived a short time before to pick him up, as Lady Windmere's best carriage was already in Bath with her daughters. Adam had thought to engage the driver in conversation, perhaps get a sense of who he was and where he came from in order to at least put to rest those suspicions about conscripts and convicts serving the mistress of Bondgate, but the man conversed as little as all of her other servants, and the drive was a short one. Although it was not quite dusk, the dark thunderheads that had roiled the coast all week continued to linger over Bondgate, threatening a storm. In spite of the lanterns outside and the warm glow emanating from the windows, it seemed as if a previously unseen shadow hung over Adam's second visit there.

Once inside, the warmth and gaiety of the welcome served to calm his misgivings. The antiquities and curios that had caught his eye and seemed eccentric before were overshadowed by the ranks of men and women in glamorous formal attire that filled the hall. After handing his hat and cape off to a servant, Adam gave the card with his *nom de fête* to the waiting master of ceremonies, who announced the arrival of "Signor Zeno." Those guests within earshot of the announcer bowed or curtseyed, or raised the glasses they already had in their hands, in greeting. It was a most convivial gathering.

Dancers filled the floor. Chairs had been lined up against the walls, many taken by partygoers waiting their turns. All wore masks, even the members of the orchestra that played for the dancers. The ladies wore the eye-covering domino masks associated with the Venetian *Carnaval*, festooned with feathers and paper streamers. The men were a diverse bunch, some with the same kinds of Venetian half-masks and some with diabolical creations of *papier-mâché* that covered the whole face. By comparison, Adam's small mask was quite simple.

It took him little time to become one with the crowd. No sooner had he entered than a flute of champagne was put in his hand, its contents as frothy and effervescent as the mood within the hall. A lady in a sumptuous black and red silk damask gown with a matching half-mask approached and offered him her hand. He took it appraisingly, and seeing the degree of familiarity with which the revellers evidently treated each other, he bent to kiss it.

"Shall I tell you my name, or would you prefer to guess?" she teased.

Adam looked about, unsure if this were a riddle or a breach of decorum. Was he Adam or Zeno? He decided to dive into the spirit of the occasion. "Should I know you, milady? Or are we to wait until midnight to unmask ourselves?"

"No, silly," she answered, waving her fan at him. "But you must recognise Dame Fortune when you see her!" She held the skirt of her gown out, so that Adam could clearly see the numbers on the black and red squares that decorated it, the colours of the roulette wheel. Understanding, he expressed his admiration for her costume. "And who might you be?" she asked.

"Only a humble player," he said. "Perhaps I shall have an opportunity to be one of your supplicants tonight."

"I think you shall," she said, hiding the lower half of her face behind her fan, which, once spread out, Adam could see resembled a hand of cards. Adam felt sure that it hid a knowing smirk, one he had seen before. She flitted away to visit one of her other guests before he could answer.

Adam watched her leave and murmured to himself, "I look forward to it...Miss Bond."

Adam sipped his champagne and walked the outside edge of the dance floor. Now that he knew what to look for, he recognised that some of the guests wore similar themed costumes, suggestive of mythological or allegorical characters. A woman in a mask coiled with *papier-mâché* serpents was Medusa. A man dressed as a harlequin wore a waistcoat of motley colours and a mask that suggested a cap and bells. Yet many more wore only simple masks like his own, so he never felt underdressed.

There were many comely girls yet seated, chatting among themselves, sipping champagne or watching the dancers. When the current number ended, he approached one who seemed unoccupied, a blonde in a silver gown, bowed and offered his hand. She readily accepted and introduced herself as "Ursula." She was a full head shorter than Adam but possessed of a fine figure and a rich, throaty laugh. As he took her in his arms, admiring the swell of her bosom and her full lips, he idly wondered if the pseudonyms under which they bantered would provide cover for an amorous connection or two later. The sparkle of her bright blue eyes behind the silver filigree of her mask and the closeness with which they danced suggested that it was a possibility.

Having come from London, Adam found himself at an advantage. While in town he was at best a passable dancer, his knowledge of the most current steps and the liveliest gossip made him here a most desirable partner, and before the evening was half-over, he had been passed from one young lady to another without a break until his feet were tired.

All of his partners quickly deduced that "Signor Zeno" was no more from Italy than they were, but it was equally obvious that he was a newcomer to the region. "I must say," his latest partner, "Sonia," a tall redhead wearing a green domino mask that matched her jade gown, said as he begged leave to sit for a moment, "when I heard our hostess had a guest from London, I thought you might be a bit, well…"

"Stiff?" Adam said, smiling. It offended him not at all. He had encountered such expectations before, and, though a gentleman of the city, he had learned not to put on airs when visiting gentry in the country, who were sometimes sensitive to their position. He was, in fact, somewhat proud of his ability to make friends wherever he went, especially of the feminine persuasion.

Sonia laughed, embarrassed, but Adam put his hand on her knee to put her at ease. "I suppose I thought so," she said, drawing closer to him, "but you're not like that at all… It's a relief, to be sure." Adam smiled modestly. The girl was quite charming, as they all had been, and he sensed that she wasn't quite ready to give up his company even as they rested. "Would you like to see more of the house?" she asked. To Adam it was clear that she asked two questions, one spoken, one unspoken. The answer to both questions was "yes." She stood and took his hand, leading him through the large archway opposite the entrance to the ballroom.

His sore feet as forgotten as his former dance partners, Adam hadn't the heart to tell such a charming guide that he had been given the tour by the owner herself before, and in any case, the place looked quite different with its fresh decorations and its halls and rooms filled with visitors. "Just looking at the outside, you wouldn't expect Bondgate to be so spacious, would you?" Sonia said, marvelling at a hall almost as large as the ballroom. Thinking of the extensive passages and cells beneath them, Adam wondered if she knew the half of it. "It's like a castle!"

There was indeed something medieval about this particular room, with its ancient axes and swords hanging on the wall and its high-backed wooden chairs in which no one sat except briefly as a joke. The bearskin Adam had seen before hung in the centre of one of the long walls. Had it been there before? He couldn't be sure. The sound of laughter was yet more gay in this room, now that the revellers found themselves out of the way and had no fear of interrupting the music of the dance.

No sooner had they entered than they were approached by another couple. "Oh, there you are!" said the woman. Like everyone else, both members of the couple wore masks, but the two women appeared to know each other. After they all introduced themselves — by their disguised names, of course — the woman calling herself "Juno" asked if they had been to see the fortune-teller. When Sonia answered in the negative, Juno put her hand on her "Jupiter's" shoulder and exclaimed, "Oh, you must see her, she's very sensitive. She predicted long years of happiness for us! Of course, afterwards, you must visit the grotto — the whole place is like a maze, very dark...secluded. It's easy to get lost." Despite her words of warning, the sigh of contentment she released made her meaning perfectly transparent, and Sonia nodded knowingly. Juno leaned into the proud chest of her gentleman, who put a steadying arm around her and nodded to Adam in a self-satisfied manner. Adam noticed a ring with a large stone on Juno's left hand. Could it be that these two were actually married…to each other? How *gauche*. But he appreciated their suggestion nonetheless.

"Oh, we should go, don't you think?" Sonia said, clutching Adam's hand with excitement. "Purely in the spirit of the festivities, of course," she added. Fortune-telling was not something Adam would ordinarily pursue on his own, but Sonia's enthusiasm, and the excitement of the evening, was contagious. And, he told himself, almost believing it, he might be able to balance his pleasure with Sonia with his self-appointed sleuthing assignment. He hadn't forgotten Roderick Utley completely.

Guided by the other couple's directions, Adam followed Sonia, keeping his attention on the green silk bow on the back of her gown, already excited to imagine himself pulling it free and unwrapping the gift contained within. Sonia looked back only once, her eyes flashing, with an enticing smile that quickened his step all the more.

They arrived at a small antechamber, almost an alcove, in which shadow predominated, like a small cave carved out of the larger house — or, Adam thought, like one of those monastic *oubliettes* somehow relocated from the basement. It had been dressed in hanging carpets woven in exotic patterns and lined with gold tassels and fringe. Behind a small table covered by a matching velvet runner sat a stooped old woman in turban, shawl and peasant bangles, picking up cards from the table's surface and returning them to a deck. The couple whose fortune she had just read stood, glowing with satisfaction in the future she had foretold, and went on their way. Soon Adam and Sonia were alone with the oracle.

"Come, my children, be seated, let Granny tell you your fates," the crone said in a creaking, theatrical voice. Sonia sat eagerly.

What could Granny reveal to them? Adam smiled indulgently. It was just a silly game, after all, an imposture only slightly more exotic than a game of pantomime. *No need to rush things.* Sonia pressed her knee against his as he sat next to her. If this helped her get in the mood, Adam could wait, the anticipation making it all the more delicious.

Adam knew little about fortune-telling, and while he had the vague idea that cards could be used, he had imagined something like the red and black standard suits that had inspired Miss Bond's costume. The old woman began dealing in a strange cross-shaped formation, some of the cards face up and others face down, and Adam saw quickly that this deck was nothing like the ones he used for whist. Instead of the ordinary faces of the royal court, the cards bore the same kind of allegorical images he had seen around him in many of the partygoers' costumes. No wonder it took the second sight to interpret them! Throughout the process, the old woman delivered her patter, but Adam's attention was drawn not to her words but to her hands, free of lines and animated by a grace that belied her supposed old age. Adam curled his lip upward knowingly, comfortable in the feeling that it was but a charade.

Sonia, for her part, watched with wide eyes, fixated on the cards themselves rather than the dealer, her grip on Adam's shoulder bringing her closer as she leaned in, expecting him to share her excitement.

In the centre of the odd arrangement of cards, the fortune-teller turned a card face up...a drawing of a man and woman, naked, captioned "The Lovers."

"A good sign," "Granny" said in her phoney crone voice, and Sonia blushed as if she had read her mind, giving Adam's hand a squeeze. Adam smiled good-naturedly. It was all right with him.

"But..." the dealer continued, pointing at another card, a tower struck by lightning, "this reverses it."

"What do you mean?" Sonia said, a ripple of alarm disturbing the surface of her pleasant mood.

"The outlook is not favourable. Your union will be ill-fated."

Sonia furrowed her brow. "Are you sure? Read them again!"

"Very well, if you insist. Perhaps we can see more detail." The seer took up the cards, shuffled them and laid them out anew. "Hmmm," she said as one card after another was revealed. "The Empress." "The Lovers," again, but in a different position. "The Wheel of Fortune." Finally, in the position "The Tower" had been in before, a man bound and hanging from a gallows. "The Hanged Man," read the caption. One didn't have to be an expert to read that. "It's not meant to be taken literally, of course..."

That wasn't good enough for Sonia, who had become more and more frustrated as each bad omen was revealed. "But what does it mean for us?" She held on to Adam more tightly as if afraid that the fortune-teller would separate them, and it occurred to Adam that she was taking this far too seriously.

The dealer shook her head as if it were out of her hands. "What the cards show, Fate has decreed. I am sorry."

Sonia sputtered as if the fortune-teller had insulted her. "W-what kind of imposture is this?"

"Calm down, it's just a game—" Adam didn't see what the fuss was about, but he frowned as he saw Sonia's accommodating mood evaporate when the peasant woman didn't tell her what she wanted to hear.

Sonia stood with a huff. "I don't like to lose at games," she said. For good measure, she took the card with the Lovers and ripped it in half, dropping the pieces in front of the fortune-teller, whose expression, buried under pancake makeup and shadow, remained opaque. "She's nothing but a fraud. Come," she told Adam. It didn't sound like a request.

Pulled by Sonia's surprisingly strong arm, Adam found himself in the "grotto" of which Juno had spoken, watching his partner gulp down several glasses of champagne in succession to calm herself. Adam had been surprised at how quickly Sonia became angry, and at how fiercely she struggled to contain herself. All around them were other pretty, amiable girls, yet there was no polite way to extricate himself from Sonia's company. How had this happened? *Damn that fortune-teller!*

Soon the champagne took its effect, and Sonia's amorous mood returned, but Adam was having second thoughts. She draped her arms about him lasciviously, and her words slurred. "We'll show that old faker," she continued. "What does she know, anyway?"

The grotto was in an older part of the building, with stone walls and stained-glass windows. Lanterns outside simulated sunlight so the designs could be seen. In another context Adam might have called it a chapel, but there was something pagan about the designs in the windows, and likewise the coloured glass that cast red, blue and purple lamplight onto the walls, as if they were at the bottom of the sea. Most of the floor space was taken up by an elaborate buffet, laden with platters of meat and sweets, decadent desserts, loaves of bread shaped like mermaids and unicorns and assorted other delicacies. Liveried servants stood by and guests hovered at tall tables, nibbling their selections of *hors d'oeuvres*. But Adam's attention was grabbed by the buffet's centrepiece, a mountain formed of cake or marzipan in a pool of liquid chocolate. The top of the mountain bubbled with the stuff, and it ran down the sides in rivulets into the basin, where it was evidently returned through some kind of hidden pump. In the garish light of the room, it made for an amazing illusion, as if one were looking at a landscape through the distance of miles and years. In the back of his mind it occurred to him that there was something familiar about this setup, but at the moment he was too distracted by his inebriated companion to think much about it. She was really getting plastered.

"Wouldn't you like something to eat?" Adam suggested, hoping a full stomach might soften the effects of the champagne. Sulkily, Sonia agreed and they approached the fantastical buffet.

"Isn't it incredible!" Sonia said, her eyes wide. Adam could only nod. The mountain overlooked a bay of chocolate wide enough that it extended to the edge of the buffet, and a few guests stood in front of it, dipping speared pieces of fruit and cake into it. "Ooh, I simply must have a try!" Sonia said, the fortune-teller momentarily forgotten. Brusquely shouldering the other diners out of the way, she stood at the edge of the chocolate pool, which was about waist-high to her, resting her fingers on the edge to keep her steady on her feet. She gazed at the pastry mountain, complete with miniature Roman villas on its slopes, with childlike wonder.

Adam discreetly apologised to the guests Sonia had pushed aside and wondered if his opportunity to slip away had arrived. Sonia had passed the point of being obligingly tipsy and he wondered if she would even miss him now that she had a new distraction. At the moment of decision, just as Sonia began dipping her bare fingers into the liquid chocolate and tasting it, Adam turned away, only to find himself bumping into Ursula, the blonde in the silver gown who had been his first dance partner earlier in the evening.

"Oh!" she said, smiling as if he were an old friend. "I've been looking for you!" Ursula appeared flushed, a nearly empty glass in her hand. It didn't take Adam long to realise that she, too, was feeling the effects of the champagne, but it at least appeared to have made her jolly rather than sullen.

"Oh?" Adam said, conscious of Sonia's raised voice behind him. She was arguing with one of the buffet attendants, a scene Adam tried to ignore.

"I'm afraid I couldn't stop thinking about you," Ursula added. She put her arm around Adam's waist and leaned in close to him, smiling lustily as she pressed her bosom against him and provided a view of her impressive cleavage. Adam was but a man, and his loins reacted as such. He was torn between the requirements of politeness — he should at least beg leave of Sonia before switching partners — and the renewed prospect of a liaison with a willing companion.

Adam had downed a few glasses himself. If he had remained sober, he might have thought through this dilemma more carefully instead of following the dictates of his lust, but the combination of drink, the *louche* atmosphere of the festivities and sheer opportunism meant that he had made his decision before he was even conscious of it, taking Ursula by the arm and muttering, "Let us go." The entrance to the dark and secluded passageways of which Juno spoke was so close he could practically taste it.

It was almost too perfect, but alas, the promise of cuddling with this well-endowed beauty was not to be fulfilled. "I beg your pardon!" Sonia's voice rang through the grotto as she noticed Adam's imminent departure. "Excuse me," she said, grabbing Ursula by the shoulder and turning her around. "He's with me!"

Adam turned as well, cringing over the *faux pas* that was occurring. Sonia stood with her hands on her hips, flushed with anger and spirits. Her once-flawless makeup was marred by a smear of chocolate dripping from the corner of her mouth that she was too drunk to notice.

"Pardon?" Ursula said casually, tightening her grip on Adam's arm. "Do I know you, madam?"

Sonia's eyes narrowed behind her mask, her words dripping with unspoken menace. "I said, he's with me. Find your own dance partner."

Reddening, Ursula would not be cowed. "I saw him first!" she said. Equally steeped in Pamela Bond's liquor, she let go of Adam's arm and halved the space between her and Sonia, looking up at her rival scornfully. "You have no claim on him, 'Sonia!'" So they did know each other!

"Ladies, please—" Adam said, sweating with the awareness that they were being watched by the circle of people who filled the room, all eager to see what would happen. For one wild moment he thought perhaps he could convince both Ursula and Sonia that there was enough of him to share, a manoeuvre he'd had success with in the past, but the situation was spiralling too quickly out of his control and the two rivals were in no mood to be conciliatory. Ursula practically dared Sonia to push her out of the way.

"I'm telling you —" Sonia took the bait and gave Ursula a small push on the shoulder.

It was the imposition Ursula had been waiting for, and she returned the push with another, much more forceful, that backed Sonia up to the lip of the chocolate reservoir, shaking the foundations of the miniature mountain and sending a tidal wave across the bay, flooding the village on the lowest slopes with brown liquid. On its return, some of the chocolate lapped over the edge and dripped onto the stone floor with a slap. Sonia turned in horror to see the green bow on the back of her skirt droop and drip down to her hem.

"My dress!" Sonia shrieked. "Look what you've done to it!" Enraged, she lunged for her rival, who waited with her feet planted apart, ready to defend herself. *Rrrrip!* After a fumbling slap fight, the bodice of Ursula's dress gave way with a tear, down to the blonde's embroidered stays.

"Right, that's it!" Ursula responded in kind, tearing at Sonia's jade gown until she found a weak spot and it too was torn down the front.

The two girls grappled with each other, tearing at each other's hair and clothes until the beautiful silver and green gowns were shredded almost completely. They pulled each other to the floor to wrestle in their underthings. At the same time, the two women covered each other with invective, words spilling from their mouths that would have shocked the guests had they heard them in their own drawing rooms. "Stay back," Ursula warned Adam after she had broken the clinch and stood up, ready for more. "This bint's had it coming a long time now."

"Shut up, bitch." Sonia pulled cruelly at a hank of Ursula's hair, nearly bending her over and thrusting a knee into her stomach. "Oof!" Ursula gasped, backing away, but she recovered quickly and took Sonia by surprise, pushing her back against the buffet table, where they continued brawling.

Sonia kicked, pushing Ursula away with her leg, and with the inspiration of a moment, she picked up a thick, as-yet-uncut pie from the buffet where her hand had fallen. She hefted it threateningly, her face split by a wicked grin.

"Don't you dare—" Ursula said. Both ladies' coiffures had been pulled out of place, their masks askew. They were flushed and out of breath, their bosoms heaving with the exertion of their scrap. Sonia was cornered, safe from Ursula's wrath as long as she held onto the gooey pie. *But what*, Adam wondered, *could you do once you had picked up a pie, but throw it?*

It was a fool's errand — Adam knew it. Why not try to stop the tide, or the fall of rain? But it was still his duty to intervene, and that was how he found himself between the two livid girls, reaching for Sonia's arm even as she drew it back to hurl the pie at her rival. As if in the languid motion of a dream, he saw it leave her hand at a wild angle and heard the splat of its landing, followed quickly by a collective gasp from the ladies and gentlemen who stood watching the scene from a distance.

Adam turned his head to follow their gazes. The pie had not struck Ursula. She looked just as gobsmacked as Adam and Sonia herself, turning to face in the same direction.

There stood one of Pamela Bond's manservants, burly in his red and black livery — no waiter, this, but one of Miss Bond's guards. The pie had struck him square in the face, and after a moment that seemed an eternity, he raised his hands and wiped the cream away. The visage revealed beneath was stern and humourless. No one was laughing. Behind him, several more of his cohort were lined up, and as one they rushed forward, taking the stunned women by the arms, two for each of them, and began carrying them away. Once Sonia and Ursula found their voices, they continued berating each other and the guards with the most unladylike invective as they struggled helplessly against the servants' iron grips.

"Just a moment—" Adam protested as another of the servants took his arm, so surprised by the turn of events that he was nearly speechless. The two girls were marched ahead of him as they continued to snipe at each other, Adam and his escort bringing up the rear. At least he was allowed to walk under his own power and was spared the humiliation of being dragged. The small crowd in the grotto that had watched the whole scene unfold stared in silence, but even before Adam was taken from the room, they began to chatter excitedly to one another, as well they might. It had been quite a shocking display.

To his further mortification, the three prisoners were guided back towards the ballroom. As they entered, the music had stopped and the collected guests watched them, a far larger group than the witnesses in the grotto. Ursula and Sonia, their masks askew and their gowns utterly ruined, ignored the crowd's stares — nothing to see here, just a pair of rowdy guests being escorted out — but Adam had never felt so embarrassed in his life. He fully expected to be taken out through the front door and thrown out of the gates, having been mixed up in such a dreadful breach of etiquette, even if only by happenstance, that he would never be welcome at Bondgate again. Given Miss Bond's influence with Lady Windmere, he might even have to leave Windmere Hall. How ironic that it would be a scene at a neighbouring house that would get him turned out, rather than the many conquests he had made under Lady Windmere's roof!

But exile was not to be his fate, at least not without another humiliation. There in the entrance stood Pamela Bond herself, in high dudgeon. Only now did Sonia and Ursula appear to quail beneath her gaze. As if at an unspoken command, the guards brought the two women in front of the mistress of the house, pushing them into a kneeling position before her, still holding them by the arms and shoulders. Adam was allowed to remain standing, but in the custody of the guard and under the collective gaze of Miss Bond and all of her guests, he thought he might rather be dead.

"Tsk, tsk," Miss Bond said, still in her Dame Fortune costume, as if she were called upon to discipline a pair of naughty children. The two ladies squirmed under her haughty judgement, still flushed, Ursula with embarrassment and Sonia with defiance. "Self-control is a virtue," Miss Bond admonished them. "If you wish to make a spectacle of yourselves, then let us find you a worthy audience." To her servants, her voice now cold, she said, "Take these pigs to their sty."

Sonia and Ursula found their voices, protesting, but Miss Bond cut them off. Approaching Sonia, she ran a finger under the tall redhead's chin and murmured, "Do you feel you are being treated unfairly?"

Sonia, cowed, said quietly, "No, Dame Fortune."

Miss Bond turned to Ursula, who shook her head, her eyes downturned.

"Good." With a quick jerk of her head, Miss Bond signalled to her men that the audience was over, and they wordlessly pressed the two now-submissive ladies out of the room—not out the front door, but down one of the many hallways.

"As for Signor Zeno," she purred, obviously savouring Adam being in her grasp, "I really did expect more from a gentleman such as yourself." Her eyes flashed behind her mask, widening in a mockery of Adam's *naïveté*.

Adam blushed, remembering with a mixture of guilt and secret excitement how the two ladies had fought over him. Was he at all responsible? He had grown accustomed to the high hand Miss Bond took with her servants, but to treat her guests the same way, to call them pigs? He now saw the dark side that the Windmere sisters had tried to warn him about. "I expect you will want me to leave at once."

Miss Bond gave a mirthless chuckle. "Would that it were so simple," she said. "I'm afraid I can't let you go now. The game is already afoot, and we play for keeps at Bondgate."

Adam resigned himself to whatever fate had in store for him. "And Sonia and Ursula?"

Miss Bond shrugged dismissively. "They, too, are in play. Perhaps if you earn them a reprieve, they will find a way to show their gratitude to you." Then she added darkly, "But I cannot make any promises as to the condition you may find them in. Good luck, Signor Zeno!"

Chapter Twelve

Separated from Sonia and Ursula, led down through empty halls and stairways by his silent "guide," Adam reflected upon the hide he had seen hanging on the wall upstairs, and at last truly appreciated the significance of the cub who had thought himself a bear. *This is it,* he thought. *Any one of these dark cells could be mine, and I'll never be heard from again.* Even the masks the guests at Bondgate wore made it easy for him to disappear. Who would even be able to identify that he had been here?

One slim hope remained — that one of the Windmere sisters, upon returning home and discovering his absence, would ask questions and secure his release. But even that faint glimmer of light dimmed when he recalled that Roderick Utley was still missing, and *he* had been all but betrothed to Frederica Windmere! Next to that, what was Adam? Frederica had no affection for him, except when in her benighted state she thought him to be Roderick. Jane ignored him, always reading. And Alice? Alice had secured that experience from him that she desired, but would she miss him when he was gone? Would her vigilance watch out for him as it did for her sister? Adam was afraid he knew the answer to that question, and he despaired.

But instead of the silence of solitary confinement, Adam began to perceive the babble of voices, the thrum of a restless crowd, at the end of the hallway. The next doorway he went through found him in a cavernous amphitheatre, lit by numberless torches and hanging chandeliers bedecked with flickering candles. It resembled an arena of the ancient world, but entirely enclosed. Opposite Adam, overlooking the chamber, was a platform upon which sat a throne, as yet unoccupied. Directly in its shadow was a wide circular hole in the floor. The rising banks of stone benches were being filled by the very revellers he and the two girls had been paraded in front of upstairs, all visibly eager for whatever was about to unfold. A cheer arose from the waiting crowd when Adam made his entrance.

As his eyes adjusted to the guttering torchlight, he saw that Sonia and Ursula had preceded him. The two women were separately bound by chains that held their wrists above their heads and their ankles apart, and they were further each chained to a structure reminiscent of a medieval rack or Roman crucifix. They were able to move but little and were forced into a standing position by the upright posts of the framework that held them. Thus were their bodies, clad only in the scraps of lingerie that they hadn't torn from each other, exposed to the crowd. Beneath the masks they still wore on their faces, it was impossible for him to see their emotions, but their ragged breaths and futile struggles testified to their mounting terror.

All this Adam observed in an instant. At the same time, compounding his shock, he was bound to a similar contraption, facing the other two. The three racks stood at the points of a triangle, facing inward, so that each prisoner was visible to the other two and every seat in the amphitheatre had a good view of at least one of them. The audience cheered again when the operation was complete. Like his fellow prisoners, Adam strained against the chains, knowing it to be a waste of energy but trying anyway, to the great delight of the masked partygoers.

A gong silenced the merrymakers. Once the crowd's chatter had subsided to a rustle of whispers, a woman clad in bright red and black squares entered and sat upon the throne, high above the ranked seating and facing Adam...Miss Pamela Bond, Dame Fortune herself. Behind her, one of her servants set down a large wheel of fortune where she could reach it easily. In a penetrating voice, she announced, "Friends, guests, as you entered my home tonight, I bade you a gracious welcome. I trust that you have enjoyed yourselves dancing, eating and drinking to Bondgate's hospitality." A roar of approval from the gathered guests confirmed that it was so.

"It is well. I have watched and approved as you cavorted and played, making and breaking assignations with the joyous freedom of children. Such games are indeed pleasurable, but it is a mistake to think of the pursuit of Love as only a frivolity. There is nothing more serious."

Her expression darkened. "Love is not without its cost — it demands total devotion, to the point of death. Up above," she continued, "you may have noticed the model of Vesuvius that was the centrepiece of the buffet in the grotto."

Adam remembered it well, and only then did he grasp its importance. *The centrepiece was a tableau recreating the eruption of Mount Vesuvius and the destruction of Pompeii rendered in pastry,* Adam had read in the pages of Sir Alfred's history of the family. The resemblance to the buffet upstairs had tickled his mind but he had been too fuddled and distracted to place the memory. But that was obviously it. Pamela Bond had read of it in Sir Ambrose's diary, or learned of that detail from Sir Alfred, and had sought to recreate it! But why?

"The citizens of Pompeii unknowingly took shelter on the slopes of the very mountain that would be their doom. They had their goddess of love, Venus, but their dedication to her was perhaps...lacking, and so they perished.

"Centuries later, the original owner of this house, Sir Ambrose Windmere, along with my direct ancestor Seneca Bond, gathered a similar group of like-minded guests for the purpose of celebrating Love and Eros.

"Just such a model of Vesuvius was constructed for the feast," Miss Bond continued. "It turned out to be an ill omen, and it was blamed by some for the ignominy into which Sir Ambrose descended, and by extension the neglect of the house that once stood here. My ancestor, Seneca Bond, was held up for ridicule, and even now the shadow of that past shame still hangs over Bondgate.

"Those of you who have heard whispers of scandal and debasement have only heard half the story. The reality is that Sir Ambrose was brought down by the jealousy of narrow-minded people who were not ready for his vision." Her voice rose in emphasis and she passionately cried, "I say that the world is ready now, and I declare this new Feast of Ambrose in honour of my ancestors! To the memories of Sir Ambrose Windmere and Seneca Bond! To Love!" This proclamation met another wave of approval. Those who held drinks raised them to join her toast, while those who had already found partners exchanged kisses or more personal greetings.

If the three prisoners on the floor of the arena had been forgotten, it was an oversight corrected in a moment. "Perhaps, like the citizens of Pompeii, my ancestors were likewise let down by a lack of devotion. Sir Ambrose should have known — on the island from which he drew his inspiration, it was the custom of the natives to sacrifice a virgin to appease the god of the volcano." Adam shook his head, again struck by Pamela Bond's sense of drama. There had been no mention of a volcano in Sir Ambrose's diary. She was embroidering the facts in the service of her point. "The lava from Vesuvius fell upon the innocent and the guilty alike, but Sir Ambrose's islanders were preserved safely. I have no desire to repeat the failings of our Pompeiian forebears, but neither are we savages. Does Love demand that the innocent suffer, or is it enough to punish the guilty? There is only one way to know for sure.

"Friends," she continued, "you know that I have sought to restore my family seat to its former glory. I have done so. Tonight's festivities will be the capstone of the *true* Feast of Ambrose!" A cheer rose up in response. At the same time, a chill of foreboding settled in the pit of Adam's stomach.

There could be only one explanation. Pamela Bond was mad, and in her isolation and obsession with her family's history, she had sought to recreate the tragedy that had brought the house low and turn it into a belated triumph. But how?

A collective gasp from the audience turned Adam's attention away from Pamela Bond, back to the gate through which he had entered. A young woman, masked and clad in a white gown, stood waiting to approach. "In all of Bondgate, I could find only one virgin," Miss Bond explained, drawing knowing chuckles from her cynical listeners. "If Fate decrees that she be sacrificed, so be it. But these other three prisoners" — she indicated Adam and the two bound women — "know what they did to deserve their fate. There can be no glory without sacrifice, no love without discipline. The longer we hold off the inevitable eruption, the more satisfying it will be."

Miss Bond turned her attention to the wheel and gave it a spin for emphasis. The pins on its rim clattered noisily as it turned. When it slowed to a stop, she continued. "Tonight, our special friends have volunteered to illustrate the caprice of chance. They may be favoured by the wheel and end up rising above this petty moment. Or they may be brought low. None can say. The only thing that is sure is that it could just as easily be any of you in their places...any one of *us*. That itself proves how fluid, how unpredictable, are the vagaries of fortune."

Bollocks, thought Adam savagely. It wasn't luck that had placed him or the two jealous rivals for his affection in this position. Perhaps it had been Miss Bond's plan all along, and he had walked right into her trap. *On the other hand*, he thought, considering the two girls, *perhaps they really were in the wrong place at the wrong time, the poor things –*

"This is all your fault, you slut!" Sonia shouted at Ursula, pulling Adam out of his reverie.

"Suck my tit, bitch!" Ursula responded, thrusting her ample chest forward in the only gesture of defiance she had available. The noise level rose again as the audience grew more excited, so the rest of the two girls' catcalls were drowned out.

"Silence!" Dame Fortune cried out, and the gong struck again. The two women became quiet. Adam glanced at the woman in white standing at the door. Of all of the "players," she alone appeared to be there without coercion. The part of her face visible beneath her mask was flushed, but otherwise composed. Was she really the innocent that Pamela Bond claimed, a saint among sinners? Adam doubted it. No one found themselves in Pamela Bond's clutches without willing it, if only in secret. By following his own desires, he had ended up here, without realising that he had been led by the nose. But her dignity stood out in this raucous crowd nonetheless.

"The game is simple. The young lady, Virtue Unstain'd herself, has before her a path of stones leading to the Pit—since there are very few volcanoes in the West Country, we have provided a substitute." Adam observed that, indeed, it was so. In his previous excitement and terror, he had overlooked the outlined pathway, so like the squares of a game board. "Each of the prisoners shall wager a number of squares on the pathway, up to the number Virtue has already travelled, against a forfeit, for one of their opponents or, at certain junctions, themselves. A spin of the wheel—which I shall perform on their behalf—

determines the outcome. If the prisoners run out of chances before Virtue runs out of squares, then their sacrifice alone is accepted. But if she plunges into the Pit..." She held out her hands as if to shrug. The audience seemed delighted with the prospect either way.

It's easy for them, Adam thought. They had only to watch the spectacle unfold. Again he peeked at "Virtue" to gauge her reaction...nothing. She was as impassive as a statue. *Probably an actress.* Her role in this little play didn't seem a surprise to her as it was to him and Sonia and Ursula.

"The first turn goes to 'Signor Zeno.'" Addressing Adam directly, she said, "Since you are the object of these two ladies' dispute, the choice is yours — which do you favour, and which do you choose to punish?"

All eyes turned to Adam, and the silence of the audience was one of intense concentration. Many visibly leaned forward, the better to hear the prisoner's response. Adam raised himself up as best he could under the constrictions of his chains, preparing an answer. Punishment? Could she possibly be serious? "I know of no crime of which these two ladies have been convicted," he said, self-conscious of how strained his voice must sound. The audience would have none of it, hissing and booing at the attempted nobility. "It is I who have transgressed against the hospitality of this house," he continued, "however inadvertently. Release them, and reserve your punishment for me."

The audience was divided between mockery and agreement, a squabbling riot of contrary opinions. The gong sounded again, silencing them. Dame Fortune held up her hand as she considered this plea, and said, "Who says the Age of Chivalry has passed?" A smattering of laughter answered her. "But it is no more for you to pardon them than it is for me. Only the wheel can bestow that. So it is decided — whatever the wheel metes out, punishment or favour, shall be shared by both ladies!"

Sonia and Ursula visibly groaned, lowering their heads as much as their chains allowed, but the crowd's answering cheers drowned out anything Adam might have been able to hear from them. An air of anticipation settled over the arena. Many of the fine ladies who sat in judgement produced opera glasses or *lorgnettes* to watch more closely. Adam got the impression that the gentlemen shared detailed opinions of the semi-clad ladies on display, comparing their charms, or perhaps wagering over some unspecified angle of the "game."

"I will spin on your behalf, sir. The wager is two forfeits against one square forward," the hostess said. The wheel of fortune was clearly marked with wedges of different colours, and Adam could tell that there was writing on the different sections, but it was too far away from him to read any of the punishments. Nor was the meaning of the various colours clear to him...which meant progress on the path for Virtue and which meant punishment for the three prisoners. Once the clattering of the wheel began, the audience turned to it with hushed reverence. It seemed as if everyone in the amphitheatre held their collective breath until at last it slowed, then stopped.

Dame Fortune leaned in to read the section on which the wheel had landed, and announced out loud, "Guilty! The sentence is 'The Siege of Jerusalem!'...And what siege would be complete without a cascade of *boiling oil?*" The audience laughed and clapped. The blood froze in Adam's veins. Could it be possible? Was this the chance that Pamela Bond's merrymakers took when they attended one of her masquerades? He had underestimated her *sang-froid*. He was trapped in a chamber of horrors!

Sonia and Ursula struggled in their bonds, helpless. Adam sickened to imagine the terror that they must feel, and try as he might, he could not close his eyes against the mental image of their lovely forms scalded and burned by instruments of medieval torture. He lunged against the chains that held him to the rack. He strained every muscle until he felt that his eyes would burst from their sockets. He yelled — he protested with as much invective as he could muster. But he was as helpless as the two girls whose place he had tried to take in vain.

All the while, two pairs of Miss Bond's silent manservants brought out barrels nearly as large as themselves. To Adam's horror, they lifted them up to shoulder height, one holding the top by a handle and the other hefting the barrel from the bottom. The arrangement was the same for each victim. He turned towards the woman in white, still standing at the beginning of her assigned pathway, and appealed to her as a last resort. "For the love of God, do something!" Adam cried, near hysteria. She remained as still as a statue, watching intently. He closed his eyes against the horror, hoping that through some miracle, he would wake up in his bed at Windmere Hall and find that it was all a nightmare, a product of his vivid imagination. If only he were able to close his ears against the sound of hysterical feminine screams!

To his surprise, Adam heard only laughter and gasps of astonishment. A smattering of applause turned into a raucous cheer. Tentatively, he opened his eyes. Across from him, Ursula was doused in thick, black sludge that coated her from head to toe and ran down her body in slow rivulets. She squirmed and spat the stuff out of her mouth where it had trickled in, but she did not appear to be in any pain. A look at Sonia showed that she was in the same situation — covered in the black liquid but unhurt. If it was oil, it was hardly boiling. The screams Adam had heard were from shock or embarrassment — perhaps even delight? — not pain. After managing to clear her eyes, Sonia saw him goggling and flashed him a smile, her white teeth shining like pearls through the oily gunk.

Adam nearly collapsed in relief. He felt like a fool for having believed that he was in the torture chamber of a Torquemada or de Sade. This wasn't the Inquisition — it was an orgy of decadence, an amusement for the bored and idle rich. Perhaps the original Feast of Ambrose had been like this, a gathering that had, in retrospect, scandalised and embarrassed its guests. It would be just like Pamela Bond to revive such an entertainment, having read her ancestor's diaries. Even if some of the audience's laughter was at the expense of his credulity rather than the girls' messy fate, he found that he didn't care. He was glad to be wrong this time.

The gong struck again. On her throne, where she still held court, Dame Fortune smiled magnanimously and spread her arms, pointing to Ursula. "Now, young lady, it is your turn. Against whom do you wager the forfeit?"

Adam settled back as much as possible in his bound position. Now that he understood the game — one of messy trials and humiliations, but laid on a foundation of sensuality — he was beginning to enjoy it. From his vantage point he could savour the sleek forms of Sonia and Ursula, slathered in the viscous liquid so seamlessly that they appeared almost nude. His nethers began to stir at the prospect of seeing more in this vein, and he had faith that Ursula would not pass up this opportunity to further degrade her rival.

"Him," Ursula said, pulling at her chains to point towards Adam. "This is all his fault, he admitted it!" Sonia nodded in agreement and the crowd ate it up. A chill went down Adam's spine and he immediately reconsidered his warm feelings towards the game.

With visible satisfaction, Dame Fortune spun the wheel again. There was a chance, Adam understood, that he would be spared if the wheel determined that the woman in white should move forward a square, but, in the brief moment the pins clicked, he mentally prepared to face the same dousing his fellow prisoners had received. He now knew that he was in no physical danger, but he wasn't sure if he could accept the loss of what little dignity he had remaining. To his surprise and relief, the verdict came, "Innocent—for the moment!" A few answering chuckles came from the audience. "Virtue, advance one square forward!" The young lady in white did so, with the solemnity of a bride marching down the aisle.

Adam had little time to breathe easily or consider the position the young woman was in before the game continued. Sonia, again uniting with Ursula, used her turn to target Adam, wagering the forfeit against two squares for Virtue. This time the result was guilt. "'The Martyrdom of Saint Sebastian!'" announced Dame Fortune. What did that mean? Adam wracked his brain, trying to remember his Sunday schooling— images of horrible Biblical tortures mingled with the woodcuts from his youthful copy of Foxe's *Book of Martyrs*. *Ah, yes*. Saint Sebastian was tied to a tree — close enough — and pierced by dozens of arrows.

Adam sighed. The suit he wore was his best formal costume, and while he had been manhandled in the course of his adventures this night, he had hoped that it might survive long enough to make the return journey to London from Windmere Hall. Now it seemed as if it wouldn't even escape Bondgate unscathed. He took a last moment to appreciate the glossy midnight black of his velvet lapels, the crenelations of his crushed-silk cuffs, and the familiar smoothness of the tortoiseshell buttons on his waistcoat. Already, a pair of Miss Bond's servants approached. Adam straightened himself up. He would be a gentleman to the last, even if they treated him as a cur.

In a trice the servants stripped him to the waist, ripping his beloved waistcoat and silk shirt from his body and casting them to the ground in a heap. It was not at all like the valet service at the Plaza Hotel — it was more like the treatment a court-martialled soldier might receive before getting his forty lashes. Adam shuddered as the cold air struck his torso, but did he not also quiver a bit in anticipation? Hadn't he wanted this? Something in the back of his mind had told him that Bondgate was, beneath its genteel surface, a place where his ungentlemanly desires might be satisfied. The hardening of his nipples and the growing warmth in his loins were his body's answer to the approaching culmination of those unspoken lusts.

While the servants were busy with their task, a group of revellers, both ladies and gentlemen, descended from their seats and lined up a few yards away from him. So it seemed that there were opportunities for participation for the crowd! Did he see among them "Juno" and "Jupiter," the friendly couple to whom he had been introduced earlier? With everyone masked, it was difficult to say, and it made little difference anyway. Several of the guests jeered Adam or appraised his exposed chest lasciviously — both women and men. All were at least united in their relief that it was he and not they in his position.

This moment of mutual appraisal was short-lived. To the growing excitement of the small band that faced him, another servant pushed a trolley laden with desserts in between them and Adam — their target. Soon the trolley was empty, all of the cream-covered tarts and pies in the hands of the partygoers.

"Ready," announced Dame Fortune. "Aim... Fire!" *Splat! Splat! Splat! Splat!* Not all of his assailants were gifted with exacting aim, and others were foiled by the awkward weight and shape of the pies, but enough hit their mark that Adam was soon covered in cold, runny cream and custard. The pies stung mildly when they hit, and the combination of the impact and the cold liquid tightened every nerve in his body. A young lady's pie flew exactly into his face, blinding him, and her laughter, singing above that of the small band of throwers and the larger audience, affected him queerly.

To his surprise, his manhood hardened in his pants. As the custard dripped down his chest and into his trousers, he was reminded of the humiliating but exhilarating experience of the boat ride — his first encounter with Miss Bond, he realised — and the simultaneous mortification and voluptuousness of being made into a sloppy mess in public. The first time, no one had known, and the experience had been coloured by his fear of discovery, but this, the sheer abandon of it, the utter shamelessness and even the loss of his beloved waistcoat in the service of hedonism, was intoxicating. There would be no turning back.

"Well, well, well!" Dame Fortune said breathlessly as Adam shook his head to clear his eyes and nose. "As always, some players enjoy the game more than others!" She cooled herself with the playing-card fan. Members of the watching crowd chuckled, relaxing. Adam had thought that the audience had taken delight in the "players'" messy punishments, but how many of them, he wondered, secretly wished to trade places with him now? How many of the ladies, so prim and proper, undoubtedly set to return to a daily routine of sewing and playing the pianoforte, were moist with secret ardour? How stiff were the cocks of their male partners? Adam felt sure that the "game" was for most of them only a prelude to warm them up for their more discreet couplings later. As long as he found an opportunity to take part, he could accept being part of the show.

Yet his heart jumped, his breath caught, when he noticed Virtue watching him. She turned away when he made eye contact. Was she amused or embarrassed on his behalf? Why should it matter?

The game continued. Dame Fortune made it clear that the ups and downs of the wheel still held sway — that one player was hot for action or got the crowd excited made no difference, at least officially. From one turn to the next, sometimes Virtue advanced along the path or one of the imprisoned trio took their forfeits. As one punishment after another was meted out, with allusive names like "The Great Cask of Cologne" and "Hannibal Crossing the Alps," and all of which involved covering the participants in messy desserts or pouring sticky liquids on them or into what remained of their clothing, Adam continued to get excited when it was his turn. He savoured the view when it passed to Sonia, who withstood the punishments with stoic indifference, and Ursula, who became an audience favourite with her tendency to squirm and squeal in disgust.

He wagered recklessly, betting on himself and happy to lose. With his dignity forfeited, so were his inhibitions. He couldn't help but wonder what would happen when the game ended, however. Miss Bond had made it clear that the redemption of Bondgate somehow rode on the results of the contest, but in what way he knew not. That the "guilty" should be punished in place of innocent Virtue seemed important, but what would actually happen if the girl in white were thrown into the pit? What did Miss Bond mean by the volcano's eruption? All Adam knew was what he suspected — that, like Sonia, Pamela Bond did not like to lose.

Soon Virtue was standing nearly in front of Adam, a little less than halfway towards the rim of the circular pit. The more squares she advanced, the more squares could be wagered, so the game that had begun slowly seemed sure to proceed to a rapid endgame. Ursula fell victim to another forfeit that involved the audience coming down to the floor again as one of the servants wheeled out another trolley of desserts. "The Martyrdom of Saint Peter," so like the earlier "Martyrdom of Saint Sebastian." Adam watched as the buxom girl, already covered head to toe with sticky slop, was again pelted with pies until she was barely recognisable, shaking and shuddering. *With disgust*, Adam wondered, *or pleasure?*

He was certainly enjoying it — and so was one of the audience, a young man who apparently wanted more than what was strictly on offer. Adam watched him heft his pie, aiming towards Ursula, then, changing his mind, look appraisingly at Virtue, the young lady not far from him. Adam saw, as if the wheels in the man's mind turned before him, how tempting was Virtue's still-spotless gown, so like a bridal gown, a fairy-tale gown. Before he could call out a warning, the guest made as if to throw the pie in her direction.

The cad didn't get the chance, as the vigilant guards had caught his arms before Virtue even registered alarm at his actions. The pie splattered on the ground as they lifted him bodily, carrying him towards the lip of the circular hole in the floor. "That's quite a naughty thing to do," Pamela Bond chided him as she noticed the scene unfold. "I only ask that everyone wait their turn and let the game unfold in its own time. I'm afraid guests who can't follow the rules must be punished." How well Adam knew that!

Against the young rake's protests that he had only pretended to throw the pie in jest, the guards carried him to the rim of the pit and unceremoniously threw him in. Adam could see nothing but shadow from where he was chained. How deep the pit was he could not tell, and he could hear nothing over the uproar of the crowd. A moment later, a pair of slime-covered hands gripped the edge of the stonework and the young troublemaker pulled himself up with the assistance of the same guards who had thrown him in. He was covered head to toe with unidentifiable muck. It looked like the mingled runoff of everything that Adam and the two women had been doused with, and perhaps it was. The young man raised his arms in mock triumph—what else could he do, as he had been caught in a most ungentlemanly act?—and followed the guard who ushered him out one of the floor-level doors, to the amused jeering of the fellows who had presumably egged him on in the first place.

Adam shuddered at the pitilessness of Pamela Bond's justice. So this was what was in store for the young lady portraying Virtue—Unstain'd, but not for long! He glanced at her and saw that she had blanched. Perhaps even she had not realised until that moment that the symbolic sacrifice would involve such a cost to her dignity! Far from the trap door in the stage to which she was surely accustomed, the Pit beneath Bondgate was a sump into which all that house's debauchery and decadence had drained, the mire of sinfulness more literal than any preacher would have suspected!

Suddenly, the girl, at first frozen to the spot, made to bolt away like a frightened doe. "Stop her!" Miss Bond cried, standing as if she would leap down into the arena herself. The guards were as ready for her as they had been for the young rake and took hold of her just as easily. Pamela Bond, uneasily resuming her seat, appeared as stricken white as Virtue herself, although whether angry at her game being upset or something else Adam knew not. The guards kept the young woman in place, though she periodically squirmed in their grasp, searching for weak spots in their hold on her.

"The game, once begun, must be seen through," Miss Bond said once she had regained her composure. "We are all of us, in the arena and in the audience, part of it. Look above you," she said to the seated gentlefolk, "and notice the gutters suspended below the ceiling." Adam too looked up. In the gloom of the high-vaulted ceiling, above the hanging chandeliers, he could barely make out a grid of connected pipes he hadn't noticed before. "Those are connected to the model of Vesuvius above us. If Virtue loses, a valve will open and we will all suffer the deluge of chocolate from the model upstairs."

The audience looked uncomfortable at that news. The calculations of the game looked a little different to them now that they were to be involved. "Yes, that's right," she continued, pleased with this final surprise. "As Virtue descends into the Pit, so do we all. I would hate to end the party on such a note, but be aware that no carriages will be available at this time of night, so you will all be forced to walk home." Adam was stunned along with the audience. Was he to walk back to Windmere Hall in his current state? Would Pamela Bond really do such a thing to her guests, stranding them? Apparently, she would. To the grumbling and protests that arose, she shrugged. "Into every life, a little rain must fall, is that not so? Yet it is Virtue's nature to slip through the bonds of punishment, leaving others less innocent to their fates, so let us hope for her continued triumph." She sat back and signalled for the game to continue as if she hadn't just unleashed a skunk in the parlour. "Carry on. I believe it was Signor Zeno's turn?" For their part, the audience members suddenly took a more intense interest in Virtue's success.

Adam felt himself torn. He had no personal investment in Miss Bond's game, and was indeed tempted to spite the hostess for the position in which she had put him in any way he could. What was another layer of mess to him now? It would even be funny to watch Miss Bond's carefree guests — among whom he had counted himself until recently — forced to find their way home drenched in chocolate. If that meant the young lady in the white dress lost as well, so be it — she was technically his competition, and unless he misunderstood, his own freedom would come at the price of her humiliation.

On the other hand, he sympathised with Virtue and her apprehension. Although he knew her not, he imagined that she, like he, had come to Bondgate without any idea what to expect. While he had been caught in Miss Bond's web and put on display, there was still hope for her to get away clean, so to speak. At first it had seemed obvious that the audience, like the young cad, had desired to see Virtue soiled and degraded, but now that their fates were intertwined, they pinned their hopes on her. Perhaps this was the change of heart that Miss Bond hoped to dramatise.

Finally, Adam had to reckon with his own surprising enjoyment of being made into a messy spectacle. He could not deny it — his body would not let him — he was aroused. How could he be sure that the young lady in white was really any different from Ursula or Sonia, her virginal persona all for show? He didn't know her, or even who she was. How could he be sure that Virtue Unstain'd didn't also secretly wish to be stain'd, to be stripped bare, to experience the public debasement that had already been Adam's? Adam hadn't known how much pleasure he would take from being the centre of attention. Pamela Bond had a knack for bringing such covert desires to the surface, so perhaps Virtue was no victim, but another of her subjects. Maybe this was her fantasy, with Miss Bond in a supporting role, rather than the other way around. If so, who was he to withhold it?

All of these thoughts went through Adam's mind in a flash. Finally, he decided that he could only do what Pamela Bond asked of him. He would take his chances and let Fate decide. "Dame Fortune," he began, his voice developing in strength and passion as he went on, "I believe Lady Virtue is at the halfway point. I wager all the remaining squares."

The audience showed their tentative approval with less enthusiasm than before. Adam knew that many of the men and women were considering their own fine attire and looking at the state Adam, Ursula and Sonia were now in. Would they end up the same? To them — and to Virtue — Adam's play no doubt seemed reckless. Dame Fortune didn't appear eager to take up the wager, either. Perhaps she had hoped to draw out the suspense a little longer. She spoke carefully. "And what sacrifice is it to you if you lose? We can all see how much you're enjoying yourself."

"That's my business," Adam answered. "I'm playing by the rules you set forth."

Dame Fortune appeared to gauge the audience's reaction before deciding. "No," she said. "It's not an even bet. Not even the three of you together. What else do you have to offer?" She leaned forward hungrily. Adam wondered if Roderick Utley had seen the same greedy expression on Pamela Bond's face before he disappeared, but he knew at that moment what he had to do.

"Take me instead," he said after a deep breath. "If Virtue loses, let me pay her penalty."

Tentatively, the audience grasped what Adam was suggesting and began to applaud, their eyes nervously on their hostess. "I see," she said at last. "Heads I win, tails you lose. How can I refuse such a bet?" Seeing the audience's enthusiasm for the prospect, she relented. "Very well. I will spin on your behalf."

An almost electric tension filled the air. Something urgent hung in the balance of this. From beneath the layers of gooey, sticky confections that covered him, Adam watched the Mistress of Bondgate, still unsure what was ultimately meant by this ceremony. Was Adam, in fact, still in some kind of danger? Or had he been merely taken in by her theatrical flair? No matter what he tried to tell himself, his body buzzed with suspended excitement and apprehension as he watched the final spin.

The wheel seemed to turn more slowly than ever, the click-click-click of the pins echoing through the otherwise silent arena before finally coming to a stop on a green wedge. Adam held his breath while he waited to learn what it meant. Miss Bond turned from the wheel to her audience and her captive "players," beaming. As they, too, realised the significance of the result, many in the audience cheered, while others oohed and tittered with delight. They knew something Adam didn't know. Virtue appeared to have fainted, still in the grip of two Bondgate servants and now supported by them. Dame Fortune seemed as surprised and pleased as the crowd, and she stood to announce the results.

"Success! The gods have looked favourably upon our sacrifice, and the lava is held at bay! The curse of Ambrose is lifted!" Adam could only imagine the emotions surging within Miss Bond, but her cool façade briefly slipped, revealing a mingled sense of triumph and relief. She sounded almost choked up, and Adam thought he saw the glint of tears in her eyes. Did she really believe this? What an enigma that woman was!

Yet did he not himself feel lighter, more expectant, knowing that whatever the result was, it was taken as a good omen?

Even as Miss Bond unfurled this theatrical palaver, her burly manservants stepped forward to release the three prisoners from their chains. After wiping his eyes to see better, his first action was to look about for the young lady in white. Both she and her escort were gone, the door through which she had come closed after her. He took a moment to examine his stiff wrists now that he could lower his arms. He was a mess — layers of custard and chocolate covered his body and filled what was left of his drawers, his trousers having been sacrificed to one of the many punishments. His hair was stuck together with treacle. He felt like a spoon left in a dirty stew pot overnight.

Sonia and Ursula had fared little better. Aside from the difference in their heights and figures, they were unrecognisable, covered head to toe in the same slop as him. Sonia dabbed at the stuff, as if she could recover her dignity by rearranging the matter slightly and holding her head up high. Ursula made a show of flicking some of it off, wiping her limbs of it and shaking like a wet dog. Both women stepped away from their posts and headed in his direction.

Did Adam imagine it, or did Sonia even smile a bit at him? "Thanks for getting us off," she teased as she passed.

"Speak for yourself," Ursula said saucily. "The night is young." She pressed herself against Adam's slippery body, the two of them like salmon finding each other mid-stream. Her stays and chemise had been torn from her body, exposing her luscious breasts. Her pronounced figure needed no elaborate foundation to keep its shape. Adam, already excited, said nothing, but his hands acted of their own accord, returning the young lady's embrace.

"Come on, now," Sonia chided her erstwhile rival. "He's not for us, anymore," she added with a meaningful glance up at the platform on which Dame Fortune still presided.

Ursula, pouting, reluctantly let go. "I never get to have any fun."

"Don't be too sure," Sonia replied, directing her attention to a band of young swells who had gathered around the exit gate to pay their compliments to the ladies and, Adam imagined, perhaps win their favour. But from that he was distracted by the guards guiding him towards the platform. Skirting the circular Pit in the floor, Adam wondered if he was to be thrown in after all.

"It would hardly make a difference now," Miss Bond said, following his apprehensive gaze. "No, I think we shall find other occupation for you. Congratulations on your victory – you have paid the price so that my other guests may be spared. The green wedge, as you may have guessed, is more than redemption for the name of Ambrose Windmere. It is a reward for stalwart players. Follow the rose-strewn path behind you, and collect your reward, 'The Pleasure Dome of Kublai Khan.'" The audience members who hadn't already gathered around Sonia and Ursula or left to find their own gardens of delight applauded politely.

Adam was surprised by a silk robe draped about his still-slimy shoulders by one of the mute henchmen. It clung to his body most strangely but did convey a sort of eccentric dignity. He turned and found that, just as

Dame Fortune had described, there was a line of scattered rose petals leading him through one of the archways. He hesitated only long enough for the servant to bow and gesture to the pathway. It was as clear as anything else had been this night.

Once past the chilly corridors hewn from the stone itself, Adam entered a more finished hallway with wood panelling on the walls and velvet drapes hung thickly about, and a floor of inlaid marble and *pietra dure*. The smoky torches were replaced by more elegant candlesticks in hanging lanterns. There was still only one way to go—forward—for any branching passageways were either locked or hidden behind the drapery. A veritable kaleidoscope of feeling entered Adam's mind as he explored the tunnel. Hesitation turned into anticipation and back again as he wondered exactly what kind of "reward" could be in store for him. It could be a trick, another euphemism for a humiliating drenching with slime or custard. But his hostess could hardly ruin his costume any more than she already had, and he doubted he could face a greater degradation than he had just experienced.

He tingled at the memory of it, and flushed a little—if only to himself—to admit that it hadn't been so bad, and in fact, he wouldn't have complained if it had continued longer, or if he had been joined by the two teasing ladies whose fighting over him had got him into the mess in the first place. What did Sonia mean, "he's not ours"? Was he to meet someone else? Was *he*, perhaps, the prize for that person's skilful play? Adam gathered that there were many levels to the games played at Bondgate, and tournaments within tournaments. The image of the Wheel of Fortune, so like the roulette wheel at a more typical casino, spun before him. He remembered the supercilious pleasure Dame Fortune—Miss Pamela Bond herself, his hostess—had taken throughout the game, dispensing messy and humiliating forfeits to those guests who had willingly placed themselves in her hands, and he wondered, *Am I now to be a plaything of the lady of the house herself, up close and personal?* The idea filled him with a mixture of eager anticipation and anxiety. It would be a pleasurable duty indeed to satisfy her, but would he be able to live up to her high standards? And though he barely dared to ask the question, even to himself, he wondered if Roderick Utley had won a similar "prize," and would Adam follow him to the same end, whatever that had been?

At last he came to a single wooden door at the end of the long hallway, standing ajar. The message was clear. At the last moment, he knocked on it, even as he pushed it forward to face his reward.

Adam had steeled himself against all manner of surprise, whether it be a bounty or another nasty prank, but when the lady on the other side of the door turned to face him, he still found himself caught off guard, and was at a complete loss for words. Finally, he sputtered, "You?"

Chapter Thirteen

Adam found his manners almost immediately. "I am sorry, milady, I did not mean to be rude. What I meant to say is —"

" — That you were expecting Miss Bond, perhaps? I am sorry to disappoint you, then."

It was the young lady in white from the arena, "Virtue Unstain'd" herself. Her voice was familiar to Adam, but he was unable to place it in this strange setting, and the mask she still wore covered her face enough that he could not identify her, if indeed they had met before.

"No, it isn't that at all," he stammered, self-conscious of his undoubtedly ridiculous appearance. Clad only in drawers and a robe that stuck to his body, he was still covered head to toe in rapidly cooling slime.

His interlocutor was a true lady, however, and gave no notice at all to his state, treating him as if they had just met for tea in the sitting room of Lady Windmere.

"I take no offence," she said lightly. "You must realise that 'Virtue' is but the role I played in the evening's drama. I prefer to be called Zerlina." That "Zerlina" was yet another alias remained unspoken.

Adam bowed with as much dignity as the situation allowed. *So, the game is to continue.* He was, after all, still wearing his mask, too, however little it covered. "Signor Zeno, at your service."

"Is that so?" Zerlina purred, her smile of anticipation reminding Adam very much of Pamela Bond. "Then I bid you welcome to 'The Pleasure Dome of Kublai Khan.' Have no fear, our hostess has many playful names for her rewards and forfeits, but as to the outcome of the game, she is true to her word." Behind her on a stand was a large cake of several tiers, with elaborate frosted minarets and pillars spaced evenly with thick rosettes of pink and green icing. As Adam's eyes adjusted to the soft, gauzy light of numerous candles, he saw against the far wall a sidebar laden with more desserts, almost as varied and abundant as the one he had seen upstairs in the grotto. The room was of tile. In addition to the buffet, it was furnished with evocative drapery and screens and a number of low couches and ottomans, like a fantasy of the *Arabian Nights*.

"And are you part of my reward," he asked, "or am I to be part of yours?"

Zerlina blushed, an attractive flushing of the visible parts of her cheeks that was accompanied by a sudden deep breath that swelled her bosom against the tight restraint of her bodice. "Both, perhaps?" she said with a smile. "Dame Fortune would be the first to admit that the movements of the human heart are beyond even her machinations. But we do make a handsome couple."

"Handsome, perhaps, but not yet a couple," Adam said. "Before me stands a princess, yet I remain a frog. I have been debased by Dame Fortune. Perhaps I should clean up first?" He looked about him, wondering if there were a wash basin nearby.

"There is a chamber in which you may bathe connected to this one, but..." Zerlina smirked again, her eyes sparkling behind her mask. "Is that the proper solution? You must wash before you can approach me, is that it?"

"Of course."

"Perhaps... But perhaps not." She trailed her fingers across the icing of the enormous cake thoughtfully. "If we must be equally matched before such contact would be...appropriate...then allow me to put you at your ease." She extended a finger and dragged it across the surface of the cake, taking a spill of icing along with it. "If I were to be...a frog, too, so to speak...well, perhaps we could wash together...afterwards."

"You'll spoil your costume," Adam observed, not quite believing what he heard. As excited as he was by the idea of remaining in his current state, of putting his filthy hands on Zerlina's clean dress, or pressing his custard-coated body against the white of her skirts, of exploring and besmirching the frilly underthings that lay under her currently spotless gown, surely she was jesting.

Zerlina strolled around the cake, examining it from different angles, before licking the glob of icing from her finger. "Hmm, yes, I suppose. You went to some lengths to safeguard my, ahem, purity in the arena. For all the good it did."

"Oh?"

"When the guards grabbed that unruly guest, he dropped the custard tart he held, and it splattered me." She held up the hem of her skirt. In the dim light, Adam could barely make out a dot, slightly more yellow than the surrounding fabric, the stain left by a single drop. "So you see," Zerlina continued, "the damage has already been done."

"A mere speck," Adam said.

Zerlina shook her head. "You are very gallant to pretend to overlook it, but it is too late. It is beyond cleaning, I am afraid." She grabbed a handful of the elaborate cake and drew it across the offending spot on her skirt, burying it below a more obvious streak of coloured icing. "Simply ruined." She turned her gaze to Adam expectantly.

Adam's heart quickened, but he remained calm. "I suppose it couldn't be helped."

She stepped towards the laden sideboard. "Indeed, accidents *do* happen." With that, she nudged a thick trifle from the edge of the buffet so that it fell to the floor. Although the majority of the dessert lay wasted at her feet, a splash of cream had arced across the front of her skirt as it descended. It stood out tantalisingly, glistening and sweet, against the embroidered lace and baize. She held her hands to her face, her eyes wide and her mouth a perfect O of surprise.

"I think I understand," Adam said, closing the distance between them. He looked around. The tables and sideboards were laden with pies and desserts of all descriptions. "I can see that in a chamber such as this — so closely packed with delicacies — there are many opportunities for…misadventure."

Zerlina nodded. "Yes, quite."

"All it would take is one act of clumsiness on my part—" He lifted a thick cream tart in one hand and held it in front of her face. The gelid cream quivered as it hovered over her cleavage.

"Just one," Zerlina agreed, biting her lip in expectation.

At the same time that he leaned in to kiss her lovely neck, he tipped his hand minutely, upsetting the balance of the thick tart. The foamy top layer swelled then crested as the sea of custard beneath it burst forth in a wave. The bright yellow custard spilled over the edge of the pan and doused Zerlina's chest. The top layer followed once the initial surge of custard had spent itself. In an instant, she wore it like the shieldmaiden of some epicurean legion. She touched it with mingled curiosity and astonishment. "Oh!"

"Is it cold?"

Zerlina trembled. "Yes, a bit, but I think it shall warm up shortly." She took Adam's free hand and guided it to her breast, where it lay against her custard-coated skin. Her heart thumped, deep within.

After Adam set down the empty pan with more care than the poor trifle had received at Zerlina's hand, she chose something else to give him—a fluted goblet of heavy cream. Looking away from him but keeping his other hand around her waist where it had settled, she presented the elaborate configuration of her hair to him. Following her lead, Adam poured the glossy white cream over and through her coiffure until the liquid turned it into an almost sculptural mass, like the stone braids of Helen as rendered by Michelangelo. She quivered in hedonistic pleasure and pressed backwards into Adam's waiting arms. He tightened his clasp about her waist and burrowed into her shoulder, savouring the mingled flavours on her skin.

"Again," she whispered. Adam was less selective this time. The first dish he grabbed, a gooey chocolate torte, landed upside down on Zerlina's breast, and Adam rubbed it in until the boundary between smearing chocolate and caressing Zerlina was thoroughly blurred. He had now pressed his body against Zerlina's gown, leaving the mark of his earlier "punishment" at the hands of Dame Fortune, but it mattered little. There was no turning back, no limit, no refusal of anything. She became his blank canvas, the muse who drew his inspiration to ever greater heights.

She turned to face him, kissing him for the first time, their tongues jockeying for position as they attempted to find an angle to accommodate their masks. When they broke off and Adam attempted to remove his own smaller mask, perhaps encouraging Zerlina to do the same, she stopped him. "It's better this way," she murmured, and Adam was reminded that Bondgate was not the outside world, and the cover provided by the masks made things possible that would not have been permitted elsewhere.

He nodded and looked over his fair partner. Custard and other creamy and sticky liquids had splattered her bodice and skirt, and his fondling of her bosom had made of her exposed cleavage a tempting prow that shone with oil and perspiration. But she was not yet his equal in coverage, so with her encouragement he hefted a sizeable parfait of meringue and assorted coloured puddings and spread it across the back of her skirt while she bent over the table.

"I cannot feel it… Are you still there?" she said, looking back at him with a wicked gleam.

"Fret not," Adam returned. "I can attest that the effect is most becoming." He dug handfuls of *crème fraîche* from another dish and added them to his partner's backside.

"Perhaps if I had not so many layers in the way, I could enjoy it as much as you," she suggested.

"Indeed," Adam said, taking the hint. "I should not want to take my pleasure at your expense." He pulled her heavy skirt out of the way, shifting the layers aside until only a white silk petticoat, trimmed with lace, hugged her legs and backside. Just one thin piece of fabric stood between them. The white expanse, like a sail, was a view most alluring to him, representing a journey from which he would never return the same. The pirate fingerprints he left on it as he caressed her round buttocks felt like a profanation of something holy. She sighed in obvious enjoyment, encouraging him to continue, to go farther. There was no question the white was a flag of surrender, of his surrender, and he had only to take it up to make his enslavement by desire complete. He raised the white silk curtain to reveal her bottom and stocking-clad legs.

He had been a gentleman once, but now he was filthier than the lowliest mudlark, and that was what made him desirable. She, too, wanted to be made dirty, and he wanted nothing more than to satisfy that desire, fouling her lacy underthings and splattering the pure expanse of her pale skin until it was the same as his, mingling and blending together in a common medium, like the most primitive pre-animal beings in the primordial ooze.

"Do you like what you see, my love?" Zerlina asked, bringing Adam out of his reverie.

My love! he thought. *Oh, we are moving quickly!*

Priapic, rampant and as horny as the rhinoceros in the Botanical Gardens, Adam grunted his assent. "Oh, yes, but it needs just the right touch!" From the table by him, he grabbed another pie, and *splat!* He slammed it into her bottom, eclipsing it. A halo of blueberry and cream and crust splattered across her silk petticoats and dark purple streaks dripped down her quivering legs.

"Oh! Ohh!" she cried, as if she had spent already, bracing herself against the table. Adam hoped that her enjoyment was genuine and not merely an act for his benefit, but then he remembered how straited were the lives of the young ladies in his class. Just as young men found outlets for their urges in the back streets and clubs of London, perhaps this was a similar taste of sensual freedom for her. In any case, she urged him only to continue.

"I can wait no longer," she gasped, dropping her skirts back over her splattered petticoats. She presented the back of her dress to him, inviting him to undo the laces that held it in place. He did so quickly, with an expertise that might have made any virgin bride suspicious on her wedding night, but Zerlina had no more time for false naïveté than Adam, and she quickly stepped out of the heavy gown. She stood before him, still masked, in a silky chemise, supported by embroidered stays, and stockings and slippers — mostly white, like her gown had once been, but they would not stay so for long.

Although Zerlina's hair was thickly plastered with cream, and though her cleavage was full of custard that had run through the front of her garment and down her legs, and though her backside and legs were blue with the syrupy remains of a pie, she was as yet still cleaner than Adam. Together they set about remedying that.

Adam placed a torte, thick with chocolate icing, on a stool, and invited his lady to sit. She lifted the hem of her chemise and did so, pressing the cake outward with her bare buttocks, and giggling as it tickled her nethers where it pushed out between her thighs. Then Adam proceeded to add to her decoration, making up for the layers of clothing she had shed with bastings of custard and lashings of cream. When her cleavage could hold no more, she invited Adam to loosen her stays and set her bosom free. Custard, cream and syrups ran down her body to the floor until the chemise clung to her body like the victor's robe that still clung to Adam' own. Soon she was dabbed in every colour of the rainbow and she shook with suppressed laughter.

"Well, Pygmalion, are you satisfied with your creation?" she asked, posing as a modern-day Venus.

"I can take no credit. You are more radiant than any Galatea," he said, taking a bow.

"Indeed, truly so, and more varied in material," she said, appraising the hues of yellow, white, brown and more that covered her. "I look like one of those painted statues they dug up in Greece."

"But this clay is still wet," Adam said, getting down on one knee and easing the chemise from her shoulders. A handprint remained in the smeared liquid where he caressed her. "It will take a furnace hotter yet to fire it."

"I believe I can provide that" — she giggled — "but at least I am already well-glazed!" They both laughed, and after kissing her again, Adam helped to remove her sodden chemise.

"Are you at last satisfied that we make a suitable match?" Adam said, not without a little desperation. There was hardly another inch of her form that could yet be decorated, and his own ardour was hardly a whit less.

Zerlina stood and appraised herself, Venus emerging from a foam not of the sea but of the kitchen, and she pronounced it good. "I feel like a new woman," she said, taking Adam by the hand again.

"Not too new, I hope," Adam said, "for I feel that the woman I have come to know already has far too much of my affection to replace."

"Oh, you do have a tongue of silver. Come, let me taste of it once more."

"Better yet, lie back and allow me to lick you clean."

"It is too much! Can one man have so much appetite?"

"If the meat be sweet… And I believe I know where to start." After Zerlina was made comfortable upon a long chaise, Adam freed himself from the robe that ridiculously clung to his body. He knelt before her, gently spreading her thighs wide and resting her legs on his shoulders, opening the way to that ultimate garden of pleasures towards which their banter had tended all night. As Adam promised, his tongue was gifted indeed, and he did more than just clean her maidenhead… he coaxed and caressed it and nibbled at it like the most delicious sorbet served to a sultan in his harem. As he did so, he stroked Zerlina's thighs and rear. If he were a shipwrecked sailor sucking the juice from a melon on the shore of a deserted island, he could not have found this banquet more satisfying. Zerlina's murmurs and coos, then her gasps and moans of passion, gave wings to Adam's inspiration. He truly enjoyed giving service for its own sake, and derived almost as much pleasure from Zerlina's passionate response as if he were experiencing it himself.

Finally, Zerlina clutched at the arms of the chaise, holding on lest she be bucked off by the throes of erotic transport. "Oh! Oh! Please, no more! I must — I —" She struggled to make sense of her words. They caught in her throat, fighting against the urge to cry out wordlessly — they tumbled out disordered, disconnected like pearls cascading from a broken string. All she could do was grasp Adam's shoulders and lift him to her, bending forward to meet his mouth and pull him on top of her. She pulled at his drawers as if she were afraid they might be on fire.

Then he was united with her, riding the swell and ebb of the great tidal sea inside them both, finding her rhythm and matching it — the depths they had plumbed before were only the shallows, and now a great riptide pulled them both under. At last they reached nameless communion with each other, beyond words, beyond manners, beyond expression. It didn't take long. As keyed up as they both were by the extensive games of the evening, by the parrying and banter leading to this moment, it was a glimpse of paradise as brief as it was intense. Against Adam's will, he erupted like a bolt of lightning at the fiery centre of a raging storm.

"Oh! Oh — oh…oh, Adam," Zerlina murmured, catching her breath. At first Adam thought nothing of it, but as the storm cleared, replaced by that rainbow glow of satisfaction that followed such moments, and his wits returned to him, he remembered the mask that he still wore.

"Yes," he said gently, returning to a seated position next to her. "I am Adam. So you know me, miss. How can that be, when I am a visitor to these parts?"

His lover had already realised her mistake and rolled away from Adam, laughing it off. "Ah, of course you are Adam, and I am your Eve, for is this not Eden, and have we not remade the world anew?" But her voice was unsteady, and Adam knew that this was merely a cover.

"I apologise," he said. "Of course you are right. I meant no harm." But the moment was already over, and Zerlina had already stood and found something to cover herself with, a robe similar to the one Adam had been given.

"I—I must go," she said, her nerve having been apparently lost. "The dawn—"

"Yes, the dawn," Adam agreed absentmindedly. He hated to admit it, but the moment was over for him, too, all too quickly, and with her words, "Zerlina" had left him yet another mystery whose meaning was unclear to him.

Chapter Fourteen

The bronze tub with which Adam had been provided in the adjacent bathing chamber was more than big enough for two, and as he washed himself, he was acutely aware that, after running the gantlet of Pamela Bond's trials, he had apparently stumbled just before the finish line. Beside the tub lay two towels and two robes, but in Zerlina's absence, only one of each would be needed. Had he erred, or said the wrong thing, or had his partner simply had enough, flinging him off as soon as she was done with him, as Alice had done? Finding the door to the "Pleasure Dome" now locked, he passed through a different door into a waiting bedchamber. Beyond questioning anything now, he settled — alone — into the large bed and soon fell into a deep, dreamless slumber.

The next morning a tray with a moderate breakfast — nothing like the baroque creations he and Zerlina had spoiled the night before — waited for him, and he found a new suit of clothes in the closet. After dressing, he was unsurprised by the appearance of one of Miss Bond's servants. It was time to go.

Unsure whether he was expected to keep wearing his mask when he left, he kept it in his pocket and made for the carriages. He soon found that the masquerade was indeed over. No disguises were in evidence, and all he found were handsome young men and women, taking their leave and politely avoiding any discussion of the night before. The carriages were already lined up in front of Bondgate's main entrance, the operation carried out by Miss Bond's faithful troops. One of them directed Adam to wait as a pair of ladies passed him on the way to their ride. His would be next.

Lost in his own thoughts, Adam experienced a jolt when he saw the faces of the two ladies through the window of their coach. Although they wore no masks, he felt confident that he was face to face with the women he knew as Sonia and Ursula, and, furthermore, he could tell by the recognition in their eyes that they knew him as well! They offered him a nod that was polite, if sardonic, for they clearly enjoyed the look of surprise he must have worn at that moment. Here they were, the two rivals for his affection, both bound to be disappointed, travelling together and with all the outward civility and decorum of any two ladies he might encounter in London! Were they sisters? The carriage rolled away, taking that particular enigma with it.

Suddenly awake to the possibility, Adam looked all around him, scanning the faces of the remaining guests. Would he know Zerlina if he saw her without her mask? Maybe, but there was no one about who was the right height, the right build...no one as magical, as intoxicating... Adam shook his head. *Be rational*, he told himself. *If she is here, she will not let on.* The best he could hope for would be a secret sign of recognition, like what had passed between him and Sonia and Ursula.

But what if that wasn't at all what he had thought? What if he had made a fool of himself last night? Adam's mind still whirled and turned over the events of the last half-day, as if it were all a curious dream brought on by over-indulgence of spirits. He tried to recall if anything he had eaten or drunk might have been adulterated with hashish or absinthe, but he felt no physical after-effects, except general fatigue…and a tired groin that suggested at least that part had been real. He got into his carriage, still pondering it.

The carriage was empty except for a paper package wrapped up with string, like one got from the laundry. His own name was on the tag — his Christian name, not "Signor Zeno." It had obviously been arranged beforehand with the knowledge of which carriage would return him to Windmere Hall. Out of curiosity he unwrapped it and found, to his surprise, his velvet-lapelled evening suit, the one that he had thought hopelessly ruined! He inspected it carefully, at first suspecting that he really had dreamt of his experience in the arena, of his clothing being roughly torn from his body and trampled in pools of sticky ooze. But, no! Close examination showed where new thread had been used to repair the torn seams. The laundering was impressive and quite thorough, but even more incredible was the speed and fineness of the repair work!

Adam replaced the suit in the paper wrapping, pleased to find that it had not been lost forever, but realising that it brought up a new question. When Frederica Windmere had returned from her impromptu "visit" to Bondgate a few weeks before, she had carried with her just such a paper-wrapped parcel as he now held. He had assumed it contained her dressing gown, dirtied by the mud at the shore of the cliffs, but was there more to it? Had Frederica participated in something like the "games" Adam had played last night? Could she—but no, it was too wild to speculate. Frederica was, he felt, at least a few inches taller than "Zerlina." He would have known her, he felt sure. Yet the girl had known him, and there was something naggingly familiar. If not Frederica, then who?

* * * *

Windmere Hall remained quiet in the sisters' absence, and with Lady Windmere's frequent calls elsewhere, Adam nearly had the run of the place to himself. It suited him, in this case. He needed the time to come to terms with his recent adventure and rest up from his exertions. As he continued reading and writing in the library, his mind returned to the masquerade's hostess, the mistress of Bondgate herself, Pamela Bond. Such a fantastical creature she was! A lady of *outré* tastes and macabre desires, apparently driven by a sense of fatal duty to her family line...a character out of a Gothic novel, albeit one that could only be purchased "below the counter" of any reputable bookseller. He had learned much during his visit, yet still found himself no closer to determining whether Roderick Utley was in Miss Bond's clutches. Bondgate was even more of a maze than he had suspected on his first visit. He could search the place for months without being sure of finding anything, even if Miss Bond were open to such an invasion. Adam sighed. Of course, there remained the possibility that Utley really had drowned or fallen afoul of the bay's sucking, muddy shores. But even if that were true, why would he have been there alone? No, the man's disappearance didn't add up, and Adam felt no closer to solving that particular mystery.

Invariably, even as he tried to keep his attention on his work, Adam's tired mind returned to the enchanting stranger with whom he had concluded his night at Bondgate, the young woman who called herself "Zerlina" and who seemed to know him and to anticipate his every desire. Unable to help himself, he relived the words they had exchanged, the thrilling, sensual game they had played together and their deeply pleasurable coupling. By comparison, the more dramatic scene in the arena and the tantalising pleasure Adam had experienced at the hands of Miss Bond and her minions faded to an errant daydream, a queer occurrence whose only significance lay in the fact that it had brought him together with Zerlina. Zerlina, who had been his "prize" for victory — or perhaps she had been the winner of a different game, with Adam as her reward. Who could say? Adam gathered that Miss Bond's masquerade balls — and he was sure that there had been others, and would be again — were frequent scenes of such one-time liaisons. Ordinarily he would simply add it to his fund of memories and move on to the next, but this time? This time, something that went beyond the shock of breaking a taboo or the novelty of an unfamiliar place lingered in his memory and teased his imagination. What could he do? Simply wait for an invitation to the next ball, in the hopes of seeing Zerlina again? He wouldn't be at Windmere Hall forever.

A light tap on the library door brought Adam back to the present. Was it tea time already? "Enter," he said offhandedly.

Gretchen bustled in with the usual tray of tea things, as cheerful as ever. "Good afternoon, sir," she said. They exchanged pleasantries. The plump maid was even more chatty than usual, commenting on the grey weather and the emptiness of the house.

Adam agreed absently, but while she set out a cup and poured hot water over the waiting leaves, Adam was struck by a sudden thought. "I say, Gretchen, could I ask you something?"

"O' course, sir," she said, eager to be of service.

"You mentioned, er, earlier, that you were originally in Pamela Bond's service?"

Gretchen blushed. Adam knew that she remembered as well as he did the context in which she had told him that. They had both seen and touched each other's naked bodies intimately, a shared experience that wasn't easily forgotten and which even now changed their relationship to each other, no matter how layered with formal clothing and manners they were at the moment. She nodded.

"Can you tell me," Adam continued, gathering his thoughts as they went, "what it was like serving Miss Bond?"

Gretchen demurred, casting her eyes downward. "She was a fair an' fine employer. I'm happy serving Lady Windmere, I am," she added hastily, "but I've got no complaints about Miss Bond, sure."

"But you left her service," Adam pressed on. "You weren't sacked, were you?"

Gretchen's already ample chest swelled with indignation as she rose to her full height. "O' course not! I left of me own free will! Miss Bond was happy to give me a reference and recommended me to Lady Windmere!"

"Then why did you leave?"

Gretchen cringed at being put on the spot. "You should know better than to ask me that! A girl's got to keep her mistress' secrets, don't she?"

"Of course, of course," Adam said. "But I've been to Bondgate, and I saw just what you meant about her servants all being men." This appeared to relax Gretchen slightly, and Adam invited her to sit, adopting a conspiratorial tone. "Still, Miss Bond must have a lady's maid or two?"

"Yes, o' course," she said. "There were a few girls who waited on Miss Bond privately. We had quarters, separate from the men, on the top floor near the Miss'. They had their own rooms — more like a barracks — down below. But there weren't any funny stuff between us, no matter what you might think!"

"Perish the thought," Adam agreed. He couldn't see Miss Bond countenancing any "funny stuff" between her servants. His excitement rising as he realised that he might be getting closer to the heart of the mystery, Adam asked, "And these other girls? Did you learn their names?" His mouth was suddenly dry. "Did — did any of the girls call themselves Zerlina?"

Gretchen shook her head, her brow furrowed in concentration. "I don't think so, sir."

Perhaps this was a dead end. Regretfully, he brought his mind back to Roderick Utley. "These men," he went on, "where did Miss Bond hire them? From the village?"

Gretchen looked surprised. "Oh, no, sir. I came from the country meself, but not from 'round here—she don't hire anybody from the village."

"So they come from different places, from the country, like you?"

Gretchen shrugged. "I dunno, sir. They don't say much, as you likely found out."

Adam nodded. "Even amongst themselves?"

"Not while they're working, anyway. I wouldn't know what they're like alone."

Adam chuckled. "The mistresses of this house seem to think Miss Bond's manservants are all escaped criminals."

Gretchen shook her head. "I wouldn't know about that, sir, but—" She stopped herself.

"What is it?" Adam had become so accustomed to the secrecy around him that he was sensitive to any possibility of ferreting out information. "It's all right, you can tell me." He put an arm around her. They were speaking in very low voices and it was just the two of them.

Gretchen seemed torn by her duty and a desire to confess something. Her mouth worked silently as if she were searching for the words. *This could be it*, Adam thought. Maybe she had even seen Roderick Utley at Bondgate!

She finally blurted out, "There was one time—it was the reason I left, in fact—it made me feel so queer I didn't think I could stay—"

"What happened, Gretchen? Go on."

Now that she had begun, the words spilled out of her in a torrent, free from the weight of keeping her former mistress' secrets. "I hadn't been there very long yet, and truth to tell, most of the time I wasn't serving

Miss Bond directly, I spent polishing her…things." To Adam's raised eyebrows, she continued, "She had a lot of boots, and…oh, other things, saddles an' riding tack an' the like, made out of black leather, an' Lord, did she like to see 'em shine. Well, one night a visitor came to Bondgate real late, an' one o' the girls who had served Miss Bond longer told me to get up, that the mistress would have need of all of us girls. There were six girls who had been serving her a long time, an' they needed a seventh. She told me, 'Tonight you're Alcyone, remember that,' an' gave me clothes to put on." She shook her head in astonishment at the memory. "It weren't my usual uniform, no, sir!"

Intrigued, Adam murmured, "Well, what was it?"

Gretchen blushed again. "To tell the truth, there weren't much to it at all, just a corset and drawers, but all black and shiny like the stuff the mistress liked to keep around. Me legs were completely bare! They gave me a pair of shoes with heels like that" — she held her fingers about six inches apart — "well, I could hardly walk! And a sort of mask that covered me face. It was all so strange, an' I don't mind telling you it didn't leave much to the imagination!"

"It sounds very flattering," Adam said, giving Gretchen a playful squeeze, at which she blushed all over again.

"Oh, I suppose you would think so, but I never in my life would've chosen it, an' then after I'm dressed, I join the other girls, all seven of us looking the same, wearing masks, an' the one who'd been there the longest waits for a sign from the mistress. Then we go in to one of the red rooms, an' all the furniture's been taken out except for this black chair, almost a throne, an' there's the mistress, sitting on it like a queen, dressed in the same shiny black stuff, except she weren't wearing a mask, an' instead of those tall heels, she's got these long boots on, and a red silk cape draped behind her, an' she's all made up like a china doll, with one o' those black dots an' everything." She pointed at her cheek, indicating a beauty mark. "She made quite a sight, but I guess we all did. 'Well, ladies,' she says, 'it's nearly showtime. Just follow my lead.' An' she smiles like we're about to have a lark. The head girl nods and starts passing out these long black whips, like a coachman's. Well, sir, I never held a whip in me life, but the mistress just has us line up 'round her holdin' 'em, and that's that, I guess.

"Then the door opens an' a couple of Miss Bond's men bring in this man, the one who came to the gates I gather. He looks like a real gentleman, handsome an' wearing fancy clothes—like yours—but in a terrible state."

"Had you seen him before?" Adam asked.

Gretchen shook her head. "I never seen 'im before in me life. As I was saying, he looked awful, like he hadn't been sleeping or eating, with bags under his eyes, but when he sees the mistress on her throne, he lights up, an' says 'Pamela!' an' tries to come forward like to embrace 'er, but her men hold the fellow back. He called her by her first name, so I knew he was on familiar terms with her, but she acts like she doesn't know him. She puts on this face like the whole thing just bores her. She finally says to the head girl, 'Maia? Who is it that disturbs my solitude?'" The maid did a credible imitation of Pamela Bond's haughty voice.

"'Pamela! It's me, Clemenzo!' the fellow says.

"The mistress looks surprised an' says, 'Oh, my dear Count, I hardly recognised you. What brings you to

Bondgate so late?' Like we all just happened to be sitting around in our skivvies.

"Well, the fellow says he can't get Miss Bond out of his head, an' he's been going mad without her, can't live without her, he says. The mistress just listens — no effect on her at all, like he's a stranger.

"An' then you'll never guess what she says! 'Would you mind repeating that,' she says, *on your knees?*'

"So then he gets down on his knees an' starts to go through the whole thing again, an' the first time he calls 'er 'Pamela' she gets real frosty an' says, 'Miss Bond' will do, an' he corrects himself, but he looks like he's going to cry — then he says he'll do anything to be with her.

"An' that's what she's been waiting for, an' she gets real smooth again an' says, 'Anything?' An' the Count says 'Anything! Just let me be near you!'

"Then Miss Bond smiles real wide an' says, 'Would you be willing to forsake your old life and live here if I allowed it?' an' the Count nods his head an' says, 'Oh, yes, it's my dearest wish!' An' Miss Bond says, 'Even if you couldn't see me every day? I'm a very busy woman, you know.' The Count says yes, an' she says, 'Would you live among my servants and do whatever I ask of you?' An' the Count agrees. By this time he'll agree to anything, an' she says, 'Will you go to bed and get up when I command you and eat the food I give you and wear the clothes I give you?' An' the Count seems to think about it, but I guess he's come too far to turn back, so he says yes. 'Will you allow my sons to undress you?' An' at first the Count isn't sure, he thinks maybe he's being sent to change, but she raises an eyebrow an' says she means right there, an' the Count can't say no, so the two guards strip the fellow down to his drawers an' take his clothes away, an' then Miss Bond says, 'Will you allow my daughters to discipline you?'"

"Good Lord, you didn't—"

Gretchen reddened, eyes cast downward, then nodded. "He didn't even hesitate. She's a sorceress, she is. Me an' the other girls surrounded him an' took turns whipping him—like I said, I never even used one before, but Miss Bond, she says, 'Harder! Harder!' until one of us drew blood. But he never cried out, not once. Finally Miss Bond has us stop an' we line up again. The Count, he looks terrible, I mean even worse than he did before, and just when he looks like he's going to collapse, Miss Bond looks real warm and opens her arms and tells him to come forward. So he crawls forward an' she says, 'Are you satisfied with your position?' He says, 'Yes, thank you, Miss Bond,' an' she says, 'From now on, call me Mistress unless I tell you otherwise, do you understand?' an' he says, 'Yes, Mistress.' Finally she says, 'You may kiss my foot,' like she's doing him a big favour, an' after he's slobbered over her boot for a minute, all the time telling her 'Thank you, thank you, Mistress,' she signals to her guards an' they take him away. An' once he's out of the room, she just laughs and laughs an' the other girls all start laughing too, an' after when we're changing, the head girl tells me that's how Miss Bond finds all her male servants. They're all lovestruck slaves."

"Incredible," said Adam.

"An' it wasn't long after that I asked to be excused from Miss Bond's service," concluded Gretchen. "She weren't angry about it at all an' wished me luck, an' like I said she was happy to recommend me to Lady Windmere, an' I've been here ever since."

"Have you told anyone else of that night?"

Gretchen looked aghast at the suggestion. "No, o' course not, sir. I mean, it's shocking, innit? On the outside she seems like such a gentlewoman, but..." She trailed off. "I never would've imagined, would you?"

"And you didn't...enjoy...whipping the Count? Not even a little?"

Gretchen looked not shocked, but bewildered. "I'll tell you, I don't understand it, sir. *He* certainly seemed to enjoy it, and Miss Bond was having a good time, but I don't think men and women were meant to whip each other like that."

"You were offended on moral grounds?"

Gretchen shifted. "Well, I didn't say that, sir." They had been sitting quite close. Adam was aware of her nearness, her scent, and despite her protestations, she had become quite animated while relaying her story. The blush that inflamed her cheeks brought her to life, and while Gretchen was no beauty, she had a pleasantly wide mouth and full lips. Adam had enjoyed watching her speak on such an alluring subject and he found himself picturing her in the uniform Miss Bond had made her wear. It was intriguing, to say the least. Perhaps burying his face in her enormous breasts, then savouring the embrace of her thick thighs around his waist would free his mind of distracting memories.

She chose her words carefully. "I couldn't respect a man like the Count, who would crawl on his belly an' be a woman's slave. It's topsy-turvy. Isn't a woman supposed to be soft, and yielding and obedient?" She pushed her bosom forward, smiling warmly, as if to emphasise those positive qualities she saw in herself. "I like a man who sees what he wants, and takes it, but can remain a gentleman." The hand she laid upon Adam's knee made clear who she had in mind.

Feeling the sap rising within him, Adam took Gretchen's hand, kissed it, and said, "I know just what you mean. But my, it has become frightfully warm in here. Perhaps we could find some place that is less stifling."

A crooked smile split Gretchen's features. Drawing the hem of her skirt a little higher to reveal a bare, stockingless calf, she said, "I thought you'd never ask, sir."

Gretchen proved herself to be slightly less innocent than she claimed, even if Pamela Bond's methods had been too aggressive for her tastes. Guiding Adam through the empty hallways, she led him to a room he recognised, although he chose not to let on.

"How'd you fancy a tumble in Miss Windmere's bed?" Gretchen said with a naughty grin. "She'll never know."

Adam was tempted. The closest he had come to Frederica's bed was when he had guided her in her sleep back here during one of her episodes. But he, too, had a naughty streak, and thought of something even better. "Take me to Alice's room," he said, and Gretchen had no objection.

Alice's bedchamber was smaller than Frederica's, but the canopied four-poster was big enough for the two of them. After the delay of conversation and walking around, neither needed much encouragement to begin undressing. Gretchen invited Adam to untie the laces of her dress and giggled at his surprise when he discovered only bare skin beneath, with neither stays nor shift.

"You planned this," he said as he allowed her to pull down his drawers, his semi-erect cock beginning to swell with anticipation already.

Gretchen declined to give a direct answer, only saying, "I can't let Marie have all the fun, can I?"

Soon Adam was completely naked, and after he climbed into Alice's bed, he savoured Gretchen's melon-sized breasts, claiming her abundance by the hand- and mouthful. They fondled each other freely now, he kissing and caressing her pliant nipples and she his now-hard prick. At Gretchen's suggestion, he turned and buried his face in the thatch of hair between her legs, and she in turn took him in her own mouth, as much as she could fit, caressing his shaft up and down with her lips and tongue.

It was pleasant indeed, and over all too soon. They dressed quietly, Adam knowing that he had been led to this by a wench craftier than she let on, but, finding it agreeable to be led so, he had no complaints. "Sir," she said before they parted, "you know that story about Miss Bond was a fib, don't you? I, er, just hoped to excite you a little. I hope you don't think less of me."

Adam nodded as if it were silly to even broach the topic. "Of course, worry not. You succeeded... A marvellous piece of invention." Gretchen smiled in relief before she left, Alice's bedclothes tucked under her arm.

The story she had told him was receding in his mind, anyway. At the forefront of his thoughts, he turned over and over again the curious fact that while he had enjoyed Gretchen's company, it was not the buxom maid who occupied his thoughts during their coupling, but a girl he knew only through a mask, and whose real name he still knew not at all.

Chapter Fifteen

"I say, Mr Blythewood," Lady Windmere said a few days later at tea, "you look a bit tired. Are you so drained by your work in the library?"

"Or in the kitchen?" Alice Windmere added with a smirk.

The three Windmere sisters had returned from their holiday. Jane was all aflutter from taking the waters and looked refreshed, but Frederica was as moody as ever and Alice had lost none of her knowing sarcasm. She had mentioned before that she was on good terms with the kitchen staff, so perhaps she really did know of the furtive liaisons Adam had continued to have with Molly and Sally, or maybe she was just guessing and using her half-knowledge to needle him. He had learned enough to trust that she would not directly betray his confidence, at any rate.

Adam ignored Alice's innuendo and addressed the lady of the house. "I apologise, milady. There is simply so much to do and observe at Windmere Hall that I have not enough hours in the day to absorb it all. And the records I have uncovered in your library are most fascinating."

"Oh? Do tell," Lady Windmere said in a tone that suggested she hoped he wouldn't continue.

"Well, yes," Adam said, oblivious to her lack of interest. "It seems that the Hall had quite a reputation for hospitality in the last century. The dinners were apparently something special. There is even a guest book signed by Johnson, with a flattering reference to a banquet he attended here, although I recall no mention of such in Boswell..." Although he knew better than to mention it, Adam had Roderick Utley's diary to thank for pointing him towards this titbit of information. Warming to his subject, he said, "Just think of it! It could very well be possible that Johnson himself sat at this very table!"

"I don't think so, sir," Marie said, taking the tea things away. "Mr Johnson doesn't ever leave the village and I'm quite certain he's never taken tea here. I'd remember!"

"*Samuel* Johnson, Marie," Jane said, lifting her eyes from her book for the first time.

"I hate to correct a lady, milady, but it's Eli — he lives down in the village, sure."

Jane rolled her eyes and continued reading.

"Please leave us," Lady Windmere said abruptly. Marie nodded and bustled out of the parlour without another word. "I apologise, Mr Blythewood. It seems the help these days simply has no sense of boundaries. She will be dealt with."

"Please, that isn't necessary on my account—" Adam started to protest, but Lady Windmere cut him off.

"Every year they take more liberties," the lady fretted, speaking more to herself than to Adam, "and these last few weeks, it's as if something's got into them!"

"Or some*one*," Alice added. This time Adam shot her a dirty look. She was playing with fire, and he knew that it would be he who got burnt if Lady Windmere discovered their intimacy.

"Now, look at Bondgate," the lady continued, ignoring Alice and turning her thoughts onto a track they had frequently trod in Adam's presence. "Miss Bond's servants — so efficient! So capable! So *quiet*!" Lady Windmere didn't always agree with her near neighbour, but she had never expressed less than admiration for Pamela Bond's troupe of serving men.

Adam wondered if she would still feel that way if she had seen the side of them that he had, being taken roughly in their custody and given over to the treatment he had experienced at the masquerade, and, for that matter, if Lady Windmere had the will to employ Miss Bond's methods of keeping them in line. Although he had not pressed the matter, Adam was sure that the story Gretchen had told him was true, notwithstanding her recanting it later. Allowing for the possibility that Gretchen had misinterpreted what she had seen, too many of the details — the masks, the fanciful pseudonyms, Pamela Bond's tendency to manipulate and stage-manage, even the ubiquitous red and black colour scheme she favoured — fit perfectly with what Adam had seen of her former mistress. Had Roderick Utley become obsessed with Miss Bond and willingly joined her service, like the Count Gretchen had observed?

Lost in his own thoughts, Adam had begun to ignore Lady Windmere's effusion. "I wonder how she manages them?" she said, not for the first time.

Frederica Windmere, who as usual had remained silent during tea, looked flushed and agitated, as she almost always did when the subject of Bondgate was raised in her presence. Lady Windmere, seemingly oblivious to the connection between the subject of conversation and her daughter's mood, continued to prattle on.

"I say, Miss Windmere," Adam said when it seemed that there was a break in the stream of praise for the Bondgate servants' work ethic and respect for class boundaries, "did you have a lovely time at Bath?"

The eldest sister recovered some of her poise at this change of subject and replied, "It was fair, I should say, but I occasionally missed" — here she glanced about, then continued as if she had changed her mind about what she wanted to say — "Mother, and my home, of course. It is pleasant to be back." She did not speak as if it were pleasant.

Adam thought he saw Alice blanch during that split-second pause, but when he looked at her, she had returned to an expression of studied indifference. Jane continued to read, and Lady Windmere was looking towards the window, as if turning her thoughts to her neighbour's estate had made her want to gaze upon it. It was a strange moment of silence, a sagging of the conversation in which the participants almost, but not quite, expressed what they were actually thinking.

Frederica stood. "Mother, may I be excused?" Lady Windmere released her with a gesture but without even turning her gaze from the window.

At that signal, almost an afterthought, and with the tea service cleared, it was time for all of them to stand and disperse. Frederica was already gone, Jane clapped her book closed and tucked it under her arm, preparing to leave, and Alice gathered her work bag to take with her. Lady Windmere, still lost in thought, noticed the exodus and turned her eyes absently to Adam as he stood. "Johnson, do you really think so? My, my."

Adam caught up with Alice in the hall. She turned to him blandly, complacently, as if hearing him out were a chore on the same level as Lady Windmere's rebuke of Marie the serving girl. "Yes, Mr Blythewood?"

How she infuriated him! "Now, see here, Alice —"

"Miss Windmere, if you please."

Adam's retort caught in his throat. He choked it back and brought himself under control. "I gather that you take issue with some of my actions," he said.

Alice shook her head. "Of course not, Mr Blythewood. What you do on your own time is your business."

"But it seems that you are trying to provoke me when we are in the company of your mother and sisters. If it is as you say, then what have I done to earn your spite?" When no answer was forthcoming, he went out on a limb. "You're not jealous, are you?"

Alice scoffed. "Jealous! Of a kitchen wench and a scullery maid? That is a conclusion to which only a man could jump!"

Adam caught her arm before she could leave. "Then something else has happened, I am sure of it. Do you regret the evening we —"

"Keep your voice down, please!" she hissed, pulling free of his grip but stepping closer so that she could speak face to face. "I resent this line of questioning! As if everything in this house revolves around you!"

"Then, please help me to understand. It is not only you but your sisters who seem to treat me differently since your holiday." A suspicion that had nagged at him since then demanded to be given voice. "Did you really go to Bath?"

Indignation was the dominant feeling to which Alice's face gave expression, but Adam could have sworn that there was something else mixed in, an awareness that she had been caught. "I don't know where you'd get an idea like that," she said with a huff. "I think perhaps the time you have spent alone in this house has activated your imagination."

Or perhaps the time he had spent in a neighbouring house, Adam thought but did not say. He quickly apologised. It was an accusation for which he had no foundation, only a faint notion, and in any case, he had nowhere to lead with such a line of questioning.

"This is what I'm talking about," Alice said, somewhat mollified. "I should like to be able to take my pleasures like a man does, enjoying myself and moving on, but it seems impossible to have a pleasant evening with a gentleman without introducing complexities that serve to drain all the fun out of it." She folded her arms, and suddenly Adam was reminded by her petulance that she was, for all her worldliness, still in some ways a youth, needling him out of a mixture of malice and boredom. "I thought you would be different, since I happen to know that you are *no gentleman*."

Adam reddened, unaware that his character had been judged so harshly. "The fact remains that we both have secrets. If you choose not to confide in me, please at least respect my privacy."

Alice snorted. "Have no fear from me," she said. "Mother is so distracted that you could sport with the kitchen staff in front of her and she would not notice, and the rest of us have our own concerns. So by all means continue to stuff Molly to your heart's content, with my compliments." She gave a mocking curtsey.

"I'll have you know," Adam said, in a final weak attempt to regain the upper hand, "that I have put an end to, ahem, *stuffing* Molly and Sally." That was true — he had found his interest in the pair waning since returning from Bondgate, whether he took them on alone or together. During his last time with Molly, he had found that he could climax only when the red-headed cook invited him to pour a jug of clotted cream over her face and chest. That would never be a permanent solution, and he had taken it as a sign that it was time to move on.

"Good for you and them," Alice sneered. "I hope for your sake that the lack of an outlet for your high spirits does not cause you too much discomfort. I daresay that you shall find a way to relieve the pressure."

Adam chose not to dignify that barb by responding directly. "I see. Well, thank you for your candour. I shan't keep you any longer." He strode away with as much dignity as he could. However, it was not Alice who lingered in his mind but Zerlina, the mysterious woman he had met at Bondgate, and the real reason, even if he chose not to acknowledge it, that the women of Windmere Hall had begun to pale by comparison. Alice was much too petite to be Zerlina, and he knew that she would never have allowed him the freedom to enter her front door as Zerlina had, preferring he use the servant's entrance, as it were, but there was still a resemblance, a gentler version of the sardonic humour that Alice wielded as a rapier. Perhaps Alice was right—it was not she or her sisters who had changed, but Adam, and since that night of intrigue, he had become fixated on the identity of the mystery woman. He felt silly. How could they help in such a hopeless quest when they had not even been there? And were not the guests at Bondgate sworn to secrecy and anonymity, in any case? How would he begin to describe Zerlina, or even recognise her if he met her under more common circumstances?

These questions consumed Adam's mind as he rambled through the corridors of Windmere Hall so aimlessly that he was surprised to stumble upon Frederica Windmere sitting in the window overlooking the green. She had been weeping, and no amount of sudden straightening up could hide the streaks of tears on her cheeks or the redness of her eyes.

"My apologies, Miss Windmere. I did not mean to disturb you."

Frederica sniffed and put away the handkerchief into which she had been crying. "Not at all," she said, attempting a sad smile. "Please, won't you sit down? I daresay I wouldn't mind the company."

They sat in silence for a few moments. Adam's mind was in such a whirl—about Alice, about Pamela Bond, above all about the mysterious Zerlina—that it seemed a long time before Adam could marshal his thoughts about Frederica. They were strangers, after all, despite how much Adam knew about her. The time he had spent with her she would not remember. Only a month ago he would have done anything for the audience he now had with her, but her importance to him had faded, and for seeming minutes, he had nothing to say.

"You mustn't mind Alice," Frederica finally said. "She is really a sweet, devoted girl, but she has such a temper!"

Adam dismissed the very idea, as if Alice's words had not stung, unsure how much of their row Frederica might have overheard. It was not the first time he had found himself on a woman's bad side, but he wasn't usually trapped in the same household with her. "She is quite protective of you. It must be gratifying to have such a fierce advocate for your interests."

"Oh, it is," Frederica allowed, "most of the time. Sometimes it can be rather exhausting!" Adam nodded, and to his surprise found himself sharing a quiet laugh with Frederica. It was the first time since her return that he had seen her smile, and the effect it had on her appearance was like the sun shining on a garden in bloom.

"I wish—" Frederica said, then halted.

"What were you going to say?" Adam asked, hoping to sound solicitous rather than inquisitive.

Frederica shook the thought away. "Oh, it's nothing. I was just thinking. I know—knew—someone you would probably get along with very well."

Roderick, Adam knew. He was surprised to hear this much from Frederica. The emotion in her voice was still raw. He must have been close indeed to the surface of her thoughts. He wondered if she could countenance hearing his name out loud, or if she would instead close herself in her room again if he mentioned the missing man.

Instead, he nodded, and said, "It is difficult to be separated from the ones we love." Did he refer to Roderick, or to Zerlina?

Frederica smiled sadly. "Am I so transparent? Or have my sisters bent your ear to my woeful tale?"

With a gravity and sincerity that surprised him, Adam assured her, "Your sisters want only what is best for you. If they revealed something in confidence to me that they should not have, it was only because they sought to help you, I am convinced of it."

"They pity me," she said. "Very well, then, for I am pitiful."

"Not so! Believe me, I stand impressed by your forbearance. Many women would not bear up so gracefully under the strain."

Frederica sighed. "Do you really mean that?"

Adam nodded. To his surprise, he found that he did.

"And here I was prepared to believe the worst of you. You should hear what they say about you in the village." Adam blushed, and Frederica followed suit when she saw his reaction. "But I don't believe a word of it! I admit that I was rude to you upon first meeting. You didn't deserve that from me."

"No, it is I who should apologise. Will you think less of me if I acknowledge that much of what you have heard of me is true? Adam Blythewood — rake, cad, wastrel. It is only public knowledge."

"Well, you have been nothing other than a gentleman to me."

Adam smiled wanly. If only she knew! But he felt something, a small tingle of pride in knowing that he had tried his best to treat her as she deserved, that he had not taken advantage of her when she, thinking him to be Roderick, threw herself at him. Even that strange night beneath the cliffs, when he had thought to be with her? According to Alice, the situation was "not as it seemed." Did that mean that someone else had taken Frederica's place? Mysteries within mysteries! Still, the tiny spark of satisfaction at living up to someone's good impression of him, for once, lingered.

Frederica stood and straightened her gown. "I should allow you to get on with your work now. You have been a great comfort to me. Thank you, Mr Blythewood." The tears were gone, and she did look brighter and more refreshed than even a trip to Bath had rendered her. She appeared almost happy, though Adam knew it would take more than one polite conversation to truly revive her spirits. Uncovering the truth about Roderick Utley was the only sure way for her to heal. Even if it were unpleasant, it was preferable to the uncertainty under which Frederica currently laboured. Adam had a piece of the puzzle, but it wasn't enough. There was only one way to solve the mystery — he would have to return to Bondgate.

* * * *

Circumstances did not allow Adam to return to Pamela Bond's estate right away. His messages to her were answered with the information that Miss Bond was currently abroad. An excursion to Bondgate to see for himself stopped at the gates, locked and unoccupied. Not a soul was there to acknowledge his presence.

Adam also saw little of the Windmere sisters. At first, he thought perhaps Frederica had returned to her frosty distaste for his company, but later found that she had standing appointments to practise her fencing with a Miss Priestley. Like the wrestling instructor Miss Prine, Miss Priestley was a woman of good family and low fortune who had found employment as an itinerant teacher of physical culture, travelling about the West Country providing services to those young ladies of society who wished to take their gymnasium in the home. Adam had never seen either of them. He at first wondered that they were never invited to join the family at tea or dinner, but he gathered that they were of the upper class of servants, like a governess or other hired help, and that explained the matter. Jane seemed relieved that Freddie had at last regained interest in something following her prolonged funk, and Alice encouraged her and even took to following her to these sessions to provide moral support. Needless to say, they were off limits to Adam or any other gentleman observer.

In the meantime, Adam ensconced himself in the library, following the trail of clews laid down for him by Roderick Utley. The *Mosca,* for which Utley had been searching, putting himself in danger, or so Utley had believed, remained elusive. Adam determined the name was Italian for "fly," but beyond that, its relevance to the Windmere family or the history of the area was a mystery. Perhaps it was the scientific term for an insect native to the region, but of what value it could be he had not the slightest idea. His mind felt fuzzy, as if he had been running in circles. Once again he scoured Sir Alfred's pages, but after scanning a page for the third time without registering its contents, he realised that the name he sought — Zerlina — would not be found on it, and he closed the book in self-reproach.

Adam's thoughts were interrupted by Marie. "I thought you might like a cuppa, sir," she said.

"Thank you, Marie," Adam answered, "but it isn't tea time yet, is it?"

"Not quite, sir, but a gentleman does get hungry, doesn't he?" As she bent over to set the tray on an end table, she eyed him suggestively, making sure he got a good look down the open neck of her uniform. She wore no stays or shift, and the neckline of her bodice revealed her pink nipples, like a pair of cherries topping two scoops of sorbet. The strings of the little tie that kept the collar closed hung free, like a pair of open arms. She smiled invitingly, the tea already forgotten.

Adam returned her smile, but he felt himself straining to make the appearance. "Oh, I, uh, just leave it there, please." He bent towards his papers, making a show of scribbling on the parchment with a quill.

Not to be deterred, Marie approached him and bent over his shoulders, gently caressing him as if her intentions hadn't been perfectly clear. "What's the matter, sir? Am I not comely enough for you?"

Embarrassed, Adam said, "Yes, Marie. You're a lovely lass."

"And didn't we have fun the other day in the laundry room? And in your bedchamber, and in the carriage house?"

Smiling fondly, Adam agreed that yes, those had been pleasant liaisons, but habit alone had driven his actions—he had swallowed his misgivings and gone through the motions ultimately because, if he were not a prolific lover, the victor of numerous amatory conquests, then what was he? "No" had never yet been in Adam Blythewood's vocabulary, least of all refusal to himself.

But he could no longer keep up the pretence. It took reserves of energy he no longer felt within him. "I—I'm just very busy and fatigued right now, Marie. I—I'm sorry." He shrugged her off and turned to his papers.

Miffed, Marie stamped her foot and retied the bow on the front of her uniform, hiding her charms away again. "I see how it is, sir. Don't worry, I won't bother you again." She stalked out of the library, leaving the tea tray behind and closing the door a little too loudly.

"What's come over me?" Adam wondered. He hadn't turned down an opportunity for lovemaking since…well, since ever. "I must have caught a chill that has dampened my ardour," he concluded, shrugging it off and assuming that he would look Marie up later and be as good as new.

Yet when his thoughts returned to Bondgate and Zerlina, he became as excited and passionate as ever. He tapped his foot, pumping his leg up and down while seated as an outlet for this excess of energy. He found it difficult to work, his thoughts distracted by memories of Zerlina…her appearance, her conversation, her body. He wondered idly when, or if, he would be able to meet her again. Roderick Utley was forgotten, and mention or thought of Bondgate sent his heart racing because of its association with Zerlina. Had he not, even as he sported with other women in hopes of displacing Zerlina from his thoughts, relished those memories in order to maintain his arousal? It had been foolish to even try to forget her.

"Oh my Lord," he said out loud, sitting bolt upright as the realisation struck him. "I must be in love!" How ridiculous! How unlikely! He chuckled to himself, thinking how amusing this would be to his old college chums. Adam Blythewood, the least likely ever to settle down, in the snares of affection! And the funniest part was that he had no idea who the girl even was! He whooped with laughter, glad that no one was around to hear him. How mad! How absurd! But it could not be denied — he was infatuated.

Finally, his laughter ran down and he settled into a general state of amusement. Completely unable to work, he remembered the tea Marie had brought. There would be no further assignations with her, he realised. He had no interest in her, or anyone but Zerlina, now. He supposed he owed her an apology for dismissing her like that, but he knew now that his heart belonged to only one woman. Still, he was thankful for the distraction the tea provided — preparing it would keep his hands busy. He picked up the teapot and opened the lid, and started laughing all over again.

The teapot was empty.

Chapter Sixteen

Adam stared at the card in his hand, his mind still fogged from being roused in the middle of the night by a loud knock on the door of his bedchamber. Before he had quite awoken, he had half-believed it to be his lost Zerlina, stepped full-bodied from his dreams into waking life. Then he had thought perhaps it was Frederica again, but she had stopped her nocturnal wanderings after her return from Bath. It had been weeks since he had followed her on a sleepwalking jaunt. Nor was there so much as a servant waiting when he groggily stumbled to the door...only the red card with the embossed keyhole insignia that had been left on the floor for him.

"*Come alone – hurry,*" it read in a feminine hand. There was no signature, but who else could it be from? Perhaps Pamela Bond had returned from her travels and learned of Adam's desire to see her, but why contact him in the middle of the night? Why the mystery? Perhaps, he dared not hope, it was not Miss

Bond at all who summoned him, but the woman he knew as Zerlina. Only one conclusion was possible — whatever motivated the message, it was urgent. The demand for secrecy spoke for itself. Adam drew on his clothing and, card in hand, hurried downstairs.

A single lantern was visible outside the front entrance of the otherwise dark house, illuminating a horse, freshly saddled and tied by its reins to a hitching post next to the wide, curving front drive. No steward or stable boy stood by to assist Adam, but the meaning was clear. Evidently, whoever had brought the message from Bondgate had also left instructions for a horse to be readied.

Adam knew the road that led to Bondgate, having traversed it himself as a passenger, and the horse seemed to know his destination, but the experience of riding alone, awkwardly holding a lantern in one hand as his only source of light, while the thick forests of the upland country took on an ominous shadow in the gloom, was quite different from the daytime. A chill passed through him, but whether from the wind or his own mental state, he could not say.

The road wound through the forest, around tight turns that obscured Adam's visibility. When he had been a passenger, the coachman had always taken such turns slowly, in case he should run up against another carriage coming the opposite way. In the dead of night, accompanied only by the rhythm of his mount's galloping hooves, Adam let such caution fly to the wind.

It was in just this state of mind that Adam proved the wisdom of the coachman's careful approach. As his horse flew around another bend, now overlooking the rocky cliffs that overhung the bay, a dark blur appeared in the rear corner of his vision, bursting forth from a side trail in the woods and quickly overtaking him — another rider! Adam's own horse shied, rearing at the intrusion by the larger black stallion and nearly throwing him off. Adam was as capable a rider as any in his class, but his hurry and fixation on his goal had allowed him to be taken by surprise. He reined in his mount with his free hand and, holding the lantern high, got a good look at the aggressor who threatened to push him off the road — it was immediately obvious that this was no accidental collision!

The rider wore a heavy woollen coat of an old style, like a sailor's peacoat, mouldy with age, along with a similarly antique tricorner hat. His face was masked with a scarf or handkerchief. In the crazily swinging shadows cast by Adam's lantern, the combination of the attacker's ancient apparel and his black steed gave him the appearance of a ghost or revenant, a *Commandatore* burst forth to drag Don Juan down to Hell. Adam Blythewood was hardly superstitious, but his worldly heart skipped a beat when confronted by such a terror. Even had he been able to make out the figure in greater detail through the shock of its sudden appearance, the mutton leg of a pistol the attacker drew from the inside of his coat and levelled at Adam drew all of his attention like iron filings to a magnet.

No sound did the highwayman make — no threat, no demand for plunder, nor even a curse of vengeance — before pulling the trigger and blasting at Adam. The shot went wide, missing Adam, but the already startled horse reared again, this time successfully throwing him. For a brief instant Adam was weightless, suspended between the black sky and the blacker ground, until the rocks beside the path came up beneath him and knocked the wind from him. But he could hardly catch his breath before he was falling again. The horse had thrown him over the edge of the cliff, and it was all he could do to clutch at the wet stones of the cliff face in the darkness to stop his descent—the lantern had gone out, flown from his hand as easily as he had flown from his saddle. Stilling his ragged breath as best he could—someone had just tried to kill him, and nearly succeeded—Adam looked up to see a shadow blocking the stars, as if his assailant were looking over the cliff to make sure of Adam's death. If only Adam could silence the pounding heartbeat that he was sure was as loud as a thundering drum! Satisfied, the shadow drew back, and soon Adam heard the beat of hooves, his attacker's mount and his own—one flew to Bondgate and one to Windmere Hall, but which was which?

* * * *

"Good heavens!" exclaimed Lady Windmere the next morning upon hearing about Adam's perilous night-time excursion. "Brigands, in our own woods! 'Tis monstrous!"

In the bright sunlight that illuminated the breakfast table, the scene of the previous night seemed like a vivid nightmare to Adam, but the cuts and bruises that covered his arms and back proved its reality. Thankfully, Adam's handsome face had suffered not a scratch, as he had verified in the looking glass first thing after making the long walk in the dark back to Windmere Hall. As the house had still been quiet, he had chosen not to raise an alarum, but now it was in an uproar with the knowledge that an attacker rode freely through the woods between the Hall and Bondgate. The Windmere sisters had been planning another short trip by carriage, a plan now put in doubt by Adam's report.

"Surely it has been at least a century since any highwayman operated hereabouts," Jane said, her eyes wide.

"The fellow looked to be at least that long out of place," Adam replied, describing the old-fashioned garb the attacker had worn. Now, in the day, he could downplay the seriousness of the event, but inwardly he shuddered at the memory. Keeping the incident a secret didn't seem a wise option—what if one of the three sisters, or Lady Windmere herself, had been attacked?—even though it opened him up to questions he was ill-prepared to answer.

Lady Windmere doubted that Miss Bond was behind the card that Adam had been given, but a messenger was dispatched to Bondgate, just in case. Adam suspected this would come to naught, and indeed, when the messenger returned, he reported that Miss Bond was not yet back from her latest journey. No one there knew of any message to Mr Blythewood or anyone else, but the captain of Miss Bond's guards promised to sweep the woods in hopes of flushing out the would-be assassin. The card itself Adam could no longer find. It had apparently fluttered over the cliff when Adam was thrown.

By turns, every servant in the house was called forth. Only one had anything constructive to add, but that merely served to deepen the mystery. The horse Adam had ridden had wandered back to Windmere Hall, and Peter, the keeper of the stables, confirmed that it was one of theirs. Neither he nor any of the boys he supervised had saddled it or knew of its being let out, however. "I wouldn'a chosen 'im for a midnight ride at any rate," he said. "'E's so skittish, 'e'd shy at 'is own shadow! 'Tis a wonder you did na' break your neck, sir!"

The process of interrogation and investigation took most of the day and turned up nothing more than that bit of information. Just before dusk, a messenger arrived from Bondgate with the intelligence that no strangers had been found or detected in the woods, but that patrols would be sent to keep the road safe. All of this served only to confirm Adam's suspicions. There was no highwayman out to rob unsuspecting passers-by, because Adam himself had been the only target. Between the anonymous card and the deliberate choice of a skittish horse, a trap had been laid for Adam, and he had stepped right into it. He kept that opinion to himself, but remembering the last words of Roderick Utley's diary—"*I am being followed*"—he suspected that the same forces that had led to Utley's disappearance were closing in on him. But why?

Chapter Seventeen

"Where, where is the fly without wings? Washed ashore, washed ashore!"

The enigmatic rhyme had run through Adam's mind all morning the next day, distracting him from his work on Sir Alfred's manuscript. He had awoken with the words echoing in his fogbound mind, as if they had been pursuing him in a dream. Where had he heard them, and why did they suddenly seem so urgent? If he could place their original context, perhaps he could understand why they had been brought to mind, or at least lay them to rest. Already on edge from his recent brush with danger, this minor annoyance was enough to drive him completely mad.

At least he had the solitude of the library to ponder the question. Deciding that there was probably no danger in travelling by daylight, the Windmere sisters had gone forward with their plan to visit some family friends in a neighbouring town for the day.

Adam's musings lasted until tea time, when they were interrupted by a knock on the library door. When he opened it to answer, the tray had been left on a side table in the hall. Marie no longer even wanted to see him, apparently. Adam sighed. He could hardly blame her. He brought the tray to his desk and poured himself a cup.

"Where, where is the treasure it brings? No more, no more! No more, no more!"

The treasure...well, that was clear enough, Adam thought, blowing on the hot cup to cool it. Roderick Utley had been looking for some kind of treasure, and thought that the search had put him in danger—the same danger that Adam seemingly now faced. With a shudder he again recalled the dark-coated figure who had attacked him. *"Where, where is the fly without wings?"* he heard in his mind...in the voices of children. That was it! Adam sat up and set the teacup down as he remembered the boys in the village, childishly costumed in the very same manner as his midnight attacker. The odd rhyme, their ring dance and them chasing the girl...all of this scene he had completely forgotten after meeting Molly and the crowd around the stocks.

It was flimsy, but perhaps there was a connection—his sole visit to the village had made it clear that the old ways had lived on far longer there than at Windmere Hall, or perhaps even Bondgate. While Adam had been naturally suspicious of Pamela Bond's involvement with his attack, it was possible that the attacker's costume held a significance that might be explained in the village. He gulped down the cooling tea and went to find the coachman.

As it happened, the Windmere sisters had taken the family carriage for their trip, so Adam was forced to ask for a horse from the stables. The thought of riding again so soon after the attack made him uncomfortable, but Peter assured him that the chestnut mare he supplied him with was a steady, dependable animal, not like the skittish mount Adam had unwittingly taken before, and that there was nothing to do after a fall but return to the saddle as soon as possible. "'Tis the best thing for ye, sure," Peter said.

Nevertheless, Adam's stomach was sour, as if tied in a knot, as he carefully took the path downhill towards the village. Was it because it brought to mind still-fresh memories of the attack, or was he nervous about what he might discover there? In the back of his mind, the thought of running into Molly again and witnessing the spectacle of a "goat" receiving punishment in the stocks filled him with a disquieting mixture of dread and enticement, but Peter had assured him it was not a festival day. In fact, he told Adam, Dick the groundskeeper had earlier taken Sally and Gainesborough down to the village in his wagon to run some errands, and he had found the village quiet as the tomb—a choice of words Adam found scarcely encouraging.

It wasn't quite that dead. A few vendors peddled their wares in the market square when he arrived, but the stocks stood empty and there was no crowd, only a handful of idlers and customers at the stalls. Molly was nowhere to be seen. Knowing that Sally was here reassured Adam, in a way—the younger cook was surely holding down the kitchen in her superior's absence.

There were, however, quite a few more women in the market than there had been before he had started browsing, emerging from their little houses and storefronts and appearing from behind corners. Could Adam have been correct in thinking that they were watching him? *Don't be ridiculous, old man.* He was probably just on edge, noticing the maidens all the more because they were not the one he sought. The universe was taunting him.

But sometimes the universe delivered. Standing at the edge of the square, tied to one of the posts in front of the public house, was an enormous black stallion. Could it be the same horse his attacker of a few nights before had been riding? It had been dark and Adam had been taken by surprise, but there couldn't be too many horses of this stature in the area, not without it being common knowledge. He approached the beast carefully, lest it shared its rider's spirit of malice, but other than a standoffish snort of its nostrils, the horse gave no notice of Adam, allowing him to look him over. Yes, this could very well be the same animal. Would the man who had attacked Adam be so brazen as to reappear in public with the same mount, confident that Adam wouldn't come to the village? There was only one way to find out — Adam tied his own horse to a post and cautiously entered the pub.

The interior was close and smelled of stale pipe smoke. There was nothing fancy or pretentious about it, and while smaller than the taphouses he frequented in London, it also lacked the fussy artifice of those cosmopolitan institutions. Adam noticed that the only woman in the place was a middle-aged server, undoubtedly the wife of the proprietor. The lack of any other feminine company for once calmed his mind.

Finding an open space at the bar, he ordered a pint and glanced around, wondering if he could discover by sight the black horse's owner, or who he should ask first about it.

As his sight adjusted to the gloom, he became aware of a pair of rheumy eyes upon him. At the other end of the bar sat Gainesborough, the Windmere Hall butler. Of course! Peter had mentioned the butler coming to the village with Sally while she did her shopping, and Gainesborough had clearly taken the opportunity to duck in and treat himself. Adam acknowledged him and raised his glass, as if to say, "Have no worries, mate, your secret is safe with me." Gainesborough smiled half-heartedly and raised his glass in return.

"My, my, isn't this a haffectionate gathering?" said a burly man who bellied up to the bar between Adam and Gainesborough. "An' here's me, just harriving with the toasts already underway! Me usual, darlin'."

Gainesborough murmured a greeting to the newcomer, giving a name Adam didn't catch over the rising din of the barroom, then returned to drinking in silence. The newcomer quaffed the pint that came to him and turned his attention to Adam. "Well, hallo to you too, then. Glad to see yer back and about!"

Adam returned the local's inquisitive gaze. He was a big fellow with thick arms and a thicker chest, a farmer or blacksmith perhaps. Coarse brown hair sprang from his jowls and scalp in equally patchy fashion, and his already ruddy complexion became outright crimson on his nose. Recalling the old peddler woman who had previously mistaken him for Roderick, Adam said, "I'm sorry... Have we met?"

The man looked more closely at Adam and, as his eyes focused in the dim light that filtered through the dingy front window, proclaimed an oath. "Beggin' your pardon, sir, I had you for someone else. But by the deuce, you look just like him! Eli Johnson at your service, sir!" The man's familiarities melted away, replaced by the workingman's obsequious manner towards aristocracy.

The name tugged at something in Adam's memory. "*The* Eli Johnson?" Marie had mentioned the man as a fixture in the village for some thirty years.

Adam introduced himself and when Johnson added everything up, he became just as jovial and friendly as he had been before. "Aye, I hope ye find our little village a welcoming place," he went on, sucking down a second pint as quickly as it could be served. But something still seemed to nag at him. "Now, hold on, if ye be the Adam Blythewood staying at the Hall — then ye must be the rake who fooked Sally, an' in the kitchen, no less!" He roared with approving laughter, slapping Adam on the back. "Well done, mate! She's an 'ot one, she is!"

Adam reddened, his stomach tightening, shocked that his escapades should be so well known even in the village. "I — er, how did you happen to hear —" Adam stammered. Sally might have been unusually forward, but Adam knew she was married, and doubted that she herself would have spread it about. But Molly, perhaps…?

"Cor, don't be so modest! If it were me, I'd be telling everyone!" He slapped Gainesborough on the back, causing the butler to choke on his beverage. Adam narrowed his eyes as it became clear who Johnson's source was, but Gainesborough averted his gaze towards a suddenly fascinating game of darts occurring on the other side of the room.

"Well," Adam said primly, "I daresay there is a little bit more to it than you may have heard," but he did not deny the allegation, hoping instead to change the subject. "Come, let me buy you another." A third glass had been emptied in front of the local, and Adam was sure that his offer would be taken up.

Soon Adam had Johnson's confidence and peppered him with questions about the area, about Windmere Hall and Bondgate. "Aye, there's a queer lot about there," Johnson said, but would offer nothing else.

The man eagerly lapped up details of Adam's past exploits in London and elsewhere. The relish Johnson took in such tales almost overcame Adam's own wish to forget those adventures, and he was careful to avoid any mention of the Windmere sisters or Zerlina. Those stories were not for common ears.

"I couldn't help admiring the stallion tied up outside," Adam mentioned almost casually. Despite the ease with which Johnson had entered into conversation with him, Adam was finding it difficult to concentrate thanks to a pain in his belly, a slow-burning fire that no amount of ale seemed able to put out. With effort, Adam nodded in the direction of the window, turning his head to make sure the object of his interest was still there.

Johnson smiled broadly and knowingly, answering, "Ah, ye like Thorn, do ye? Aye, he's a fine one, he is."

"Do you know who owns him?"

"Why d'ye ask? ...If you're looking to buy, I'm afraid he's not for sale. He belongs to me niece, ye see, an' she's ever so attached to him."

Adam hid his excitement. "Oh? Perhaps it is to your niece that I should address my inquiry."

"I hope to introduce ye to her, when she arrives. She were recently thrown over by her beau."

"Oh? Hm, very unfortunate," Adam said warily, wondering if he was to be the object of a matchmaker's designs.

"Aye, he left for the city, an' its temptations were evidently too great for him to resist."

"It's happened to many a young man," Adam sympathised.

"You should know!" Johnson roared and he slapped Adam on the back, his high spirits returning. A moment later, a thought seemed to occur to him. "Hmm, a gentleman looking to buy... You wouldn't have taken old Thorn for a test ride the other night, would ye?"

"A test ride! I assure you, I have never" —he nearly said 'set eyes upon,' but corrected himself—"sat upon this animal. Do you mean to tell me someone has ridden him without your—er, your niece's permission?"

"Aye, that's exactly what I mean! The night before last, he was taken from his stables. At least, that's what me niece thinks, as he was returned before morning, but the signs he had been tired out were there, and there were burrs on his coat that me niece would never leave without brushing out!"

"Shocking!" Adam agreed, again hiding the fact that he knew, or strongly suspected, Thorn's whereabouts of the night in question.

"There are some as say," Johnson said as if sharing a great secret, "that Seneca's ghost has been known to walk the village at times, borrowing whatever he needs an' putting it back the next day. Some say it, anyway." He winked to show what he thought of such notions.

"Seneca? The Roman?" Adam started to wonder if the ale was stronger than he had thought, and perhaps he had misheard what seemed like a preposterous statement.

"Seneca Bond, sir. Do ye not know the story?"

Adam was all ears, and following Mr Johnson's hint, he had the barmaid set up another round for the two of them, to keep the local raconteur's tongue sufficiently loosened.

His thirst quenched, Eli Johnson began, "Ye may have heard tell that these shores are an hattractive lure for locals."

Thinking of the man Pamela Bond turned her yacht around in order to shoo away, Adam said, "Yes, I gather it's rather unsafe to dig for clams there, isn't it? Because of the tide?"

Johnson snorted derisively. "That's what Her Majesty says, at any rate. No self-respecting fisherman of Windmere would consider that bay more dangerous than any other — to swim in, that is... No, Miz Bond just doesn't want anyone poaching off her land."

As a landowner himself — or one who would be someday — Adam's hackles rose at the suggestion that Pamela Bond didn't have a perfect right to prevent poaching on her estate, and he said so. Johnson took no offence at the disagreement, in fact seemed to expect it, and went on. "Ah, but have you seen any of Miz Bond's men bringing in clams themselves? Or anything else, for that matter?"

Adam had to admit that he had not. But it was the principle —

Johnson waved away such airy notions. "Like I was saying, none of the locals fear to swim in the bay, and the idear that the beach turns to quicksand — well" — he sneered — "that's another of the Bond family's little legends."

"Well, I don't know —" Adam said, his mind returning unbidden to the night he had nearly fallen victim to the sucking mud himself.

"The truth is, there wouldn't be anything beneath those cliffs worth diving for if it hadn't been for Sir Alfred's great-great-great-grandfather."

"Sir Ambrose."

Johnson nodded knowingly. "Aye, so that part you know. He built this place, he did, and more importantly it was one of his ships that crashed against the rocks and sank in the bay. And what he had on board — well, some say it's still at the bottom of the bay, and that's what Miz Bond wants to keep people away from."

Adam suddenly made a connection between this legend and the dancing children whose rhyme had seemed so insensible to him. *"Where, where is the fly without wings?"* "This ship wouldn't have been called the *Mosca*, would it?"

Johnson nodded again. "Well, I say, sir, you don't disappoint! Aye, it was indeed Captain McQuirt's folly that broke up on the rocks, an' Sir Ambrose's treasure that went down with it. That's why people still dive for it, and why Miz Bond tries to keep 'em away. It's become a bit of a game."

Pamela Bond does enjoy her games, Adam thought. *But what about Johnson?* "Why are you telling me this?"

Johnson gave him a crooked grin. As much as he relished gossip, he clearly found enjoyment in keeping things to himself. "Let's just say I've a vested int'rest in your well-bein', sir."

Adam remained mystified, but he had become used to swimming in a solution of secrets. "And all this is somehow related to Seneca Bond's ghost, which you want me to believe still roams the land at night?" Adam still thought it ridiculous, but inwardly he shivered when he recalled how antiquated was the dress and appearance of the highwayman who had attacked him. A vengeful spirit? It had seemed real enough at the time.

"Aye, who do ye think it was that owned the *Mosca*? Seneca Bond was Sir Ambrose's cousin, and a partner in the South Seas venture, an' when the ship sank, an' Sir Ambrose fell into disrepute, well—" He spread his hands. "How'd that affect old Seneca?"

Adam remembered Pamela Bond's monologue about her disgraced ancestors and her desire to revive the Feast of Ambrose. Perhaps it was never Sir Ambrose, but her ancestor Seneca, whom she hoped to lay to rest? "So Seneca Bond still walks the earth as a spirit, is that it? The local bogeyman borrowed your niece's mount?"

Eli Johnson shrugged with the unconcern of one who knew what he believed. "I can't prove it didn't happen... But have ye guessed what Sir Ambrose's treasure truly was? And why no one will ever find it by diving to the bottom o' the bay?"

Through the fog of drink, Adam's mind began to stitch together the facts he knew and the hints that Johnson had let drop. *Think, man!* Adam knew that it shouldn't have been this difficult—clearly Johnson was a more practised tippler, and his relative size left ample room for his drink to settle. By comparison, Adam was as a gallon to a hogshead. He remembered the old peddler woman and her wares—

"The plant," Adam murmured.

Johnson slapped him heartily on the back again. "Well done, sir! How long have you been at the Hall, and figured out sommat that has eluded Miz Bond for how many years?" He laughed, a deep throaty chuckle, and signalled the barmaid to return to them.

"How are we holding up, sir?" the barmaid asked Adam when she returned. To his glazed eyes, she had gained some charms that he had missed while sober. She was curvy and plump, with a wide sensuous mouth that promised pleasures beyond the merely aesthetic, and a mischievous gleam in her eye. Adam's stomach gave another lurch. "Go easy on him, love," she said to Johnson. "These gentlemen you dig up ain't got the stamina, you know."

What did she mean by that? And why was he being stared at so? The bar had filled with silent women, from young innocent maidens to experienced matrons like the barmaid, while he and Johnson spoke. They filled the chairs, perched atop stools and stood against the walls. More loitered outside the door, waiting for their turns to enter, and all had their gazes fixed upon one thing...Adam himself!

A creeping dread had begun to mount, climbing Adam's spine with a tingle, and threatened to turn to alarm. "What's going on?" he asked his drinking companion. "Earlier, you mistook me for someone else."

"Aye, I did," Johnson said. "But you ain't him. Now, as I was saying," he continued as if he didn't appreciate having his colloquy interrupted, "the good captain's ship sank, an' with it the herb Sir Ambrose had harvested in the South Pacific. Word has it that the herb was what made the natives so pliant-like, so willing to give service, if you catch me drift — so *horny*." He leered at Adam and nudged him in the side to make his meaning clear, bruising Adam's kidney. "Drove the sailors mad with lust when they tried it. You can imagine how desirable such a thing would be for import—lots of people would pay good money for an herb that made men stiffer, their ladies hotter. Sir Ambrose had the daft idear to show it off to his fancy friends—"

"The Feast of Ambrose."

Johnson nodded. "You've about put it together, sir. Turned out the West Country wasn't ready for Sir Ambrose's elixir, an' it all came crashing down on him."

"And now Pamela Bond sits in the Windmeres' ancestral seat."

"An' all the time that missing treasure drives her mad."

I wonder. Eli Johnson knew a great deal, but he had probably never been inside Bondgate or attended one of Miss Bond's "game nights." Had she recovered Sir Ambrose's herb after all? Did that explain the orgiastic revels Adam had witnessed and taken part in?

There was something else, a connection that Adam's befogged mind was close to making, but his train of thought was interrupted by the opening of the door and a familiar voice ringing through the barroom. "Go on then, let me through! Oh, there you are!" Gainesborough shrank guiltily at the sound of Sally's voice and quickly sucked down the remains of his pint.

The crowded room tilted and blurred as Adam turned to see the cook, carrying in one hand a basket laden with produce and in the other a cloth bundle from the market. Seeing him, she couldn't resist laughing and approached him, her bosom wobbling beguilingly.

"Cor, sir! Who'd of expected you to sink to this depth so quickly, eh? No offence, Eli love. Just shows what can happen when you fall into bad company!"

"Shally, I—"

"No, save it, sir! Marie told me how you've thrown her over, and I must say I don't approve. Now, she's a grown woman an' can take care of herself, but couldn't you have let her down any more gently than that? An' without so much as a present to send her on her way?" She shook her head, tsking like a disappointed parent. Gainesborough had meekly taken his place by her side. He would be no help.

"Now, shee here—" Adam stood, a mite too quickly, as his knees gave way and he was forced to lean on his new friend Eli for support. Sally burst out laughing, her merriment echoed by the assembled women who filled the room. Gainesborough must have made his escape. Adam and Eli Johnson were the only men still in the room. How much had he drunk, and how strong was the ale that it should render him so drunk so quickly?

"Oh, don't mind, sir!" Sally proclaimed. "I'd say you're in good hands right where you are. Shall I tell Lady Windmere that you'll be late for dinner? Such a shame," she said, turning to leave with her parcels. "I've picked out the freshest lamb!"

Lamb, thought Adam blearily as he was hemmed in on all sides by eager women. *Perhaps it is a festival day after all? And if so, who is to be the goat?*

Adam recognised the panicked feeling that threatened to overcome him, of being trapped. He had experienced it before, when Pamela Bond's henchmen had grabbed him prior to hauling him into the arena.

Under other circumstances, he might not have found it unpleasant to be manhandled by this feminine mob, but he was in the grip of his own obsession...Zerlina, whom he was sure was not among them. And would being at their mercy mean the stocks? It was too humiliating to contemplate—the masked games of Bondgate were one thing, but what if Frederica or one of her sisters should come upon him in such a state in broad daylight? His drunkenness and embarrassment at Sally's hands were bad enough. He had made a fool of himself quite enough for one day!

Suddenly a thought occurred to him. He stared dumbly at the dregs of the strong ale in the bottom of his last pint. Why had Eli Johnson told him all about the aphrodisiac herb unless it were to be used? "Poison," he muttered.

"Pizen?" Johnson exclaimed. "What the deuce are you on about, mate?"

Adam looked at the faces of the girls who pressed forward, each lit by open, wanton lust. Had they, too, been dosed with the Ambrosian herb? "Master Johnson—Eli—which of these maidens is your niece?"

Johnson looked surprised. "Why, none of them. I don't know why she ain't here yet." Looking over the heads of the crowd, a glance out of the window showed that Thorn, the magnificent black stallion, was gone. "She must've decided not to come in." Johnson looked disappointed.

"I don't know what your game is," Adam said, determined to take back what little control of the situation he could, "but I must take my leave. Good day!" But despite his words, the crowd was now far too close for him to simply walk away.

Johnson chuckled. "Are ye sure? I think yer about to be the luckiest gent in the village! ...That is, if ye be the Adam Blythewood I heard so much about!"

"That was the old Adam" — he sniffed — "and I no longer want anything to do with him!"

"Oh, well, yer going to have to explain that to these disappointed girls, I fear," Eli said. Those self-same girls, at least those at the forefront of the crowd who most closely surrounded him, were now freely touching him, laying their hands on his arms and shoulders and cooing into his ear, promising the pleasure they hoped to give him, stroking his thigh. His vision was filled with lustful glances, pearly teeth emerging from supple, full lips, and breasts shuddering with the anticipation of lascivious delights. What would have been a paradise not so long ago was now as detestable to him as Bedlam.

"Please, I must leave —" he began to appeal to the eager girls, but his hesitance made them all the bolder, grabbing and clutching at him, stealing kisses, tousling his hair and pinching his backside. "Oh! I say!" Before their attention threatened to overwhelm him entirely, and knowing that Johnson would be no help, he ducked to the floor and crawled out between the waiting girls' legs before they could catch him.

Outside, the daylight that had seemed so gloomy before nearly blinded him. The girls inside, sensing a game, had chased and grabbed at him as he crawled between their legs as if he were a pig escaping the sty. "Don't let him go!" they called to their sisters who still waited outside, and forewarned, they grabbed at him, picked him up and tore at his jacket and shirt, laughing at how feisty, how "hard to get," he was being.

"Come on, now, love, am I so ugly?" one teased him, taking the liberty of stealing a kiss.

"So skittish!" another said, pulling up her skirt to tempt him with her charms. Still under the influence of strong drink, the scene whirled around him, the image of the girls doubling and tripling before narrowing back down to one.

Desperately swinging his elbows with a force that he would have considered inappropriate to take with a lady under other circumstances, Adam broke free and took off at a run from the gathering crowd of furies, leaving his mount behind. He closed his ears to their taunts and cries of disappointment, thinking only of making his way back to Windmere Hall.

Finally free of the crowd, Adam allowed himself to slow down and catch his breath. Painfully conscious of the pooled ale that sloshed in his belly, he fought off a wave of nausea. He looked up, finally ready to get his bearings. Alas! He was in the open square of the village, face to face with the stocks, still empty. But for how long? He looked around — he was still free, for the moment. But that meant he had gone around the village in a circle. A lusty mob of wenches stood between him and escape.

"You must have a twin," said a mocking feminine voice.

His heart still pounding, Adam located the source of the taunt. "Sally!" It was the Windmere Hall cook, standing beneath the awning of a shop. Gainesborough stood by her side.

"Bit off more than you could chew?" she said. "Have no fear, sir, let Sally direct you." She laid her hand protectively on his shoulder and pointed with her other hand, directing his eye. "Through there, love, between those two buildings. You won't be seen in the shadows, and beyond it lies the path up the hill."

So it was to be an escape on foot. Hearing the approaching voices of the feminine mob, he took off, panting and sweating, grateful for any assistance. Only when he passed under the eaves of the close-built houses where Sally had directed him did he remember that Sally's husband had driven them in the wagon. No matter…as the light once again broke in on him from above, he saw the path she had described, clear and open. His troubles lay behind him. All that stood between him and the safety of Windmere Hall was a long climb up the rocky hillside.

Chapter Eighteen

Adam was only partway up the hill when he heard the maidens of the village behind him, still on his trail. Would they ever give up? Doggedly, he picked up his pace again, but the ascent was more arduous than he had judged, and between his weariness and the effects of drink—the worst nausea and dizziness had passed, only to be replaced by a headache that was almost worse—he knew that he would collapse long before he reached the gates of Windmere Hall. The pursuing voices grew louder behind him.

To Adam's left, the noise of the surf in the bay continued its interminable rhythm. Impulsively, he broke from the ascending path and climbed over rocks and bushes until he found himself on a downward course towards the beach. Perhaps there he would find solitude and quiet. He wanted nothing more than to lie down until his headache passed, and he rued the day he had ever set forward on his campaign of sexual conquest. Was this a divine punishment for his recklessness? All the repayment for his sins had returned to him, with interest, it seemed!

When he set foot on the quiet beach, Adam's leather shoes sank into the sticky brown mud that covered it. He was too tired and dishevelled to pay much mind. His jacket had been nearly torn from his back, and his shirt's collar had been loosened, his cravat untied. Sweat stuck the remaining fabric of his clothing to his flesh.

"Stay back!" he cried to the wenches who followed him down the hill. By contrast to him, they were flushed with excitement and eagerness, Adam's flight all the more delicious to them for the challenge he presented. What would it take, he wondered, to satisfy them, short of tearing him to pieces like so many Maenads? "I know that you have been drugged," he said, nearly in tears, pulling himself through the thick mud. "Lie down a while, let it wear off, I beg you!" A few of the boldest girls were picking their way through the marshy soil, holding their skirts away from the mud with a daintiness that their lusty pursuit of him thoroughly contradicted.

"Drugged?" said the nearest girl with a laugh. She was only yards away, sunk up to her ankles in the mud into which Adam had so desperately thrown himself. "No one's drugged me, love. What are you on about?" Her pretty grin faltered in confusion.

"Oi, guv, we just wanted to see that giant todger o' yours," said another girl who was a few feet behind her. "We didn't expect yer to be so modest!" The first girl nodded in confirmation, obviously under the impression that Adam was only pretending shyness. More girls, still laughing and flushed with desire, followed the vanguard, crowding onto the muddy beach, jostling for a peek until almost half of them had fallen over, wrestling each other playfully. It was a scene Adam might have dreamt of in the past, but now he wished only to be in his own bed, resting.

Suddenly, before Adam could summon the energy to renew his protests, the girls in the lead gasped and shrank away, their faces drained of colour and their gazes directed to something behind and above Adam. They began to withdraw, the front line first, then the crowds behind them as they saw what the firsts saw. "Party's over, ladies," said one of the leaders dully.

"I bet it weren't so big, anyway," said another, picking herself up from the churned brown morass and turning away.

Turning his head with effort to look behind him, Adam saw what the girls had spotted — one of Pamela Bond's henchmen, in a full tunic bearing her keyhole insignia and a broad hat like a musketeer's that covered his face. The man stood on one of the rocks that jutted from the cliff face. Where had he come from, and how had he climbed up there so quickly before being seen?

"Wait!" Adam cried as the guard began to turn away. Now that the village girls had left off their pursuit of him, curiosity took hold. As quickly as his tired legs would carry him through the now knee-deep mud, Adam hurried towards the rocks upon which his rescuer stood. He would have had to climb the rocks soon in any case, rather than follow the path back to the village, as the tide was beginning to come in. The breakers in the bay had grown taller, and each time the water rolled in, it came a little closer to where Adam stood. He remembered the supposed fate of Roderick Utley and increased his pace.

"I should thank you," Adam said breathlessly as he got closer to the guard, who stood patiently awaiting him. The broad brim of the hat still covered his face in shadow. Adam could read no expression, neither one of sympathy nor of haughty disdain. "How did you come to arrive so quickly?" Adam grasped the outcropping of rock and began to pull himself up. The silent sentinel was now only yards away from him.

The guard wheeled and seemed to walk directly into the cliff face! In astonishment, Adam almost cried out, but his breath was too short from the labour of climbing. Instead he redoubled his efforts and clambered up the rocks to the spot where he had seen the guard disappear. When he reached it, there was a narrow break in the rocks, a vertical crack in the cliff face left by some antediluvian motion of the earth, a natural passageway! It was invisible from any other angle, and was probably easy to mistake for a shadow when seen from the bay.

In the darkness of the recess Adam could just make out the tunic of the guard, like a crimson butterfly seen at dusk. A single gloved hand gestured for Adam to follow. What else could he do? The events of the day had become more and more like a dream, and he could do naught but see it to the end, obeying the guard's summons as if he were in a trance, or...

...Or sleepwalking! Adam realised that he must be retracing the steps Frederica Windmere had taken the night he had followed her! They had come down to the beach, they had made love — or at least he had made love with someone, if not Freddie — then she had disappeared! This must have been the passage through which she came, and unless he missed his guess, it was by this entrance that she became the overnight guest of Pamela Bond!

And what of Adam? Was the guard leading him to Miss Bond? He could imagine the sardonic smile she would shine upon him if he came before her in his present state, all the more humiliating because it was separate from her masked Bacchanale and its amorous implications. But he had no choice. He was exhausted, and ready to go wherever this guard took him, even if it was to collapse in a monk's cell or worse.

The fissure in the cliff gave way to hewn stone similar to the upper passages he had explored before, but even older, with multiple turns and branches through which the guard led him. He was now beneath the dungeons of Bondgate, he was sure of it. The passage along which they travelled ended in a small chamber with a low couch and a single torch. With a gesture, the guard invited Adam to lie down. He did so gratefully, while still confused as to his purpose here. His gaze was drawn to the flicker of the torch. Momentarily, his view was blocked by the shadow of his saviour, leaning over him, offering a ladle of water. He sipped eagerly.

"Rest now," the guard said, speaking for the first time...in a woman's voice! Next he felt the brush of tender lips against his own, and a pair of ungloved hands gently bidding him to stay in his reclined position. Adam's heart leapt in recognition—his Zerlina!—but the release of tension and the weight of his exhaustion finally overcame him, and the last thing he saw as he descended into unconsciousness was a purple gown, with yellow ribbon trim, laid out on a chair where his beloved had left it when changing into the livery of one of Pamela Bond's servants.

* * * *

A period of delirium followed. Afterwards, Adam could hardly have said whether he saw Zerlina as she nursed him back to full strength, or whether he had dreamt it and attributed her identity to his unknown saviour. His questions, when he had the strength to ask them, she demurred to answer, putting him off until he had recovered. Of Pamela Bond or her male servants he saw nothing, at least that he could remember.

How long did he languish in the catacomb? With no rise of sun or moon, in his feverish state, he had no way of knowing. Sleep alternated with moments of wakefulness, and whenever he awoke, she was there.

After a particularly refreshing doze, Adam was awoken by a rhythmic bumping and clip-clopping, like the ticking of a clock. For the first time in what felt like days, he became alert, awakening fully. He was in a moving carriage! Still in a darkness like that of the Bondgate dungeon, he realised the window curtains were closed. Opening the one nearest him, he found the light of another grey morning nearly blinding in comparison. He was on the short road between Bondgate and Windmere Hall!

Recovering his memory of the past few days in a rush, Adam felt his person. He was wearing a suit much like his own, but not his own. Looking about the cab, he found a package on the bench next to him, wrapped in paper, like the one he had received before — and like the one Frederica had carried home after spending the night at Bondgate. A common souvenir, apparently! Folding back the wrapping, Adam found the remains of his poor suit, including the jacket that had come through so much peril, but had finally given up the ghost, clean but nearly shredded.

A note in a feminine hand accompanied the package.

I regret that I could not do more to save these, as I am not as gifted as Miss Bond's seamstresses. It is enough that I could help the dear man who wore them − Z

Z − for Zerlina! So he hadn't imagined her presence! A warmth and sense of well-being flooded Adam, a sense of acceptance − and yes, love − that he had scarcely known before. What did it matter if he could never wear those clothes again? It hardly mattered to him now. They were as inconsequential as the desiccated leaves of last autumn in the face of newly budded spring blossoms.

Adam barely had time to wonder how he would explain his absence before his arrival at Windmere Hall. The response surprised and gratified him more than he could have expected. Before he had even set a foot on the ground upon the carriage's halt, Frederica and Alice had rushed from the front door to greet him, followed at a stately distance by Jane and Lady Windmere. Frederica stopped short of embracing Adam, but her cheeks were flushed and her eyes gleamed wetly as if she were overcome. Had she been worried about him? Alice followed her sister nearly as urgently, with eyes dry but full of questions. If Adam had to guess, her expression was one dominated by relief above all other affects.

After a halting, awkward start in which neither Frederica nor Adam knew what to say first, the elder sister composed herself and said, "Welcome back, Mr Blythewood."

Taken aback by the vehemence of Frederica's welcome, if not her words, Adam bowed as if they were met for the first time and said, "I trust that I have not caused undue worry with my absence."

Before Frederica could react, Alice exclaimed, "Well, you can't blame us! You've been gone for three days!"

"Three days!" Could it really be possible? Adam looked from one sister to another — Jane had finally caught up, making it a trio, with Lady Windmere looking on haughtily from behind. Adam broke into a smile, thinking this a jest, then was gratified by the realisation that he had actually been missed. He controlled his features when he saw how worried the Windmere ladies had been. He had clearly caused them no little anxiety. At once he became grave and said, "My humblest apologies. I fell ill, and were it not for…a fortuitous meeting…I cannot say what my fate might have been."

"Yes, clearly we owe Miss Bond our thanks," said Frederica stiffly as she observed the carriage with the keyhole insignia roll away.

Adam's rebuttal caught in his throat. He *had* been the guest of Miss Bond again, hadn't he? The fact that he hadn't seen her, at least that he remembered, didn't change that fact. Before he could formulate an answer, the conversation was redirected by Lady Windmere, who simply said, "Thank goodness," in a perfunctory way. "I should hate to engage yet another secretary to manage my late husband's papers."

Taking the hint, Adam headed towards the library rather than his guest lodgings, but once Lady Windmere had left, he found that the sisters were not quite through with him. Free of her mother's oversight, Frederica gave vent to the anger she had been nursing—not towards Adam but towards Pamela Bond. "That woman!" she swore, stalking back and forth with her fists balled at her sides. "After she insisted that she hadn't seen you! I don't believe her cheek!"

"You...went to Bondgate to look for me?" Adam was rather touched by her concern.

"Well, yes," Alice said, surprised that Adam didn't know. "When you disappeared, we assumed you had paid Miss Bond another visit, and when you failed to return, well..." She glanced at her sister, who, while in high colour, had controlled her temper with great effort. "It's happened before."

"But she insisted that you hadn't been there," Frederica repeated, "and that she had no idea where you might have gone. *She* had the nerve to feel insulted by me! Ooooh!" She raged in exasperation at the memory.

"But did you not check the village? Sally saw me—"

The girls looked back at Adam blankly. "Mother had to let Sally go," Alice explained.

"Sally, fired? Whatever for?" Adam said once the situation sank in. Of course, he knew a few reasons why she might have been sacked, and they knew it, too, but Lady Windmere's attitude to him did not suggest that was the reason.

The sisters appeared embarrassed to even have to bring it up. *So it was money*, Adam thought. *Was she asking for too much?*

Finally, Jane said, "It's worse than you think. Sally was embezzling from the kitchen funds."

"No!"

"Yes!" Alice supported Jane's story. "She had two different ledgers and everything! Well, as soon as it came to Mother's attention, she was out of there, and her husband, too! And lucky she was for Mother not to bring in the constable!"

Adam thought of the village's medieval punishments and wondered that Sally hadn't got off lightly! Still, he had just seen her, doing the shopping, with the butler —

"What about Gainesborough?" Adam suddenly asked.

"Oh, I don't think he had anything to do with it," Frederica said. "He's as loyal as they come, and he lives like a monk. What would he do with money?"

"I don't mean that! He was with Sally in the village the last time I saw her, and I know he saw me. Didn't he say anything?"

The sisters looked at each other. No, obviously none of them had thought to question the head servant. "Let us ask him," Jane said, pulling one of the omnipresent cords. A chime sang distantly elsewhere in the house.

Soon the elderly butler stood before them. "How pleasant to see you again, Mr Blythewood. Can I be of assistance?"

"Yes," Adam said, controlling the urge to raise his voice. "Can you tell me why you did not inform Lady Windmere and her daughters that you had seen me in the village once it became clear I was missing?" It sounded so strange to Adam's own ears to speak of himself in such a manner, seeing as how he could hardly remember the episode in question. The time he had spent "missing" was nearly as mysterious to him as to his hosts.

Gainesborough looked from Adam to the young misses and back again. An almost imperceptible widening of his eyes was the only suggestion that the question took him by surprise. "No one asked me, sir." Filling the silence that greeted this bland declaration, he continued, "Will there be anything else?"

Chapter Nineteen

My dearest Zeno,

How I thrilled to receive your missive! No, I have not forgotten you or the night we spent together. You must forgive my sudden departure then. It grieved me to leave you so abruptly, but there are things I must keep to myself as yet. Alas, my relationship to Miss Bond is one of those things I cannot reveal, but rest assured my heart belongs to you. I do not know when we will next see each other. For now, it would be better if you did not search for me at Bondgate, but letters addressed there will find me.

Carry my love with you until we meet again,

– Z

Adam's half-remembered experience and the note included with his suit had proven two facts to him. One, far from being a guest of one night at Bondgate, Zerlina was apparently a resident there, perhaps even a prisoner. She might be there right now, sheltered behind the mocking smile of Pamela Bond and her army of servants, waiting for a return visit that Adam was currently incapable of paying! Two, he knew that Zerlina returned his feelings, that it had not simply been another night that they had spent together. The note, which Adam kept on his person and frequently unfolded to scan again, confirmed that. It had taken little time for Adam to write a return message, trusting that he could send it to Bondgate and she would receive it.

The reply had arrived the next day, and in the days since, he had pored over it more times than he could count, committing not just the words but the individual pen strokes to memory. Once that contact was established, it was as if the floodgates had opened. Adam poured out not only his feelings of affection and gratitude for his mysterious saviour, but his worries and concerns as well. Letters he sent in the morning were answered by the afternoon, or the following day at the latest. Despite her continued secrecy, Zerlina revealed a generous, thoughtful disposition, counselling patience in the face of his fervid search for answers. She had little detail to add to the illness she had nursed him through, only confirming Adam's garbled memory of the days he spent in her care. As for Roderick Utley, whom Adam naturally asked about?

Yes, I recall Mr Utley, although I never saw him with Miss Bond outside of a few social gatherings, certainly not the intimate meetings you suggest. Of course, if that had been the case, I would not have been present, my position in regard to Miss Bond being what it is.

... my position in regard to Miss Bond being what it is. With Zerlina unable or unwilling to divulge her

relationship to the mistress of Bondgate, Adam's fancy took wing along its own extravagant paths, and he imagined her as everything from one of the "girls" Gretchen had described to an imposture by Miss Bond herself, writing in the name of one of her servants for her own cruel purposes. In his darkest moments he wondered if he would find himself before Miss Bond on his hands and knees like Count Clemenzo, so lovesick and obsessed that he would give up his very freedom. No, he thought, while "Zerlina" might be a pseudonym, the woman herself was flesh and blood. He got the impression that her letters were written without Miss Bond's knowledge. From the chatter of the Windmere sisters, he had gathered that Miss Bond had come and gone again, off on her extensive travels, during the time that Zerlina had exchanged letters with him. She could not be Miss Bond's puppet. He had to believe that, or go mad.

While Adam had thoughts only for Zerlina, the women of the household hadn't forgotten him. Sally was gone, an absence that noticeably improved the quality of meals as Molly took over, but with her new authority, Molly had gained a new boldness and she often appeared at Adam's door, ostensibly to gauge his satisfaction with the menu but in reality teasing him with reminders of the fun they'd had together with Sally. "You know where to find me, guv — I can always use some more cream filling," she said as she ended one visit. Clearly, the rumour that the young gentleman had no more time for liaisons meant nothing to her. Marie, put out by Adam's rejection of her, no longer came to serve tea, but the gregarious Gretchen, taking her place, had no qualms about talking his ear off during her visits, and as guileless as she was, he regretted chasing her off.

It was in fact Gretchen who brought him the next piece of the puzzle. She had found the curious, crumbling document sewn into the lining of an antique dressing gown that she had been mending for him to use in his recuperation from illness. Adam had begged off, not feeling that such soft treatment was necessary, but the yellowing paper was indeed fascinating. He never would have known what he was looking at without the hints Roderick Utley and Eli Johnson had given him. It was a shipping manifest from the *Mosca* that Utley had been looking for, the very ship Ambrose Windmere had commissioned to bring back his treasure from the South Seas. In addition to the cargo — "200 lbs. cocoanuts, 350 lbs. bananas, 5 doz. bales herbe," and so forth — there was a roster of the crew. Heading it up was a familiar name.

Seneca Bond, agent of Sir Ambrose Windmere
Nahum McQuirt, captain
O. Brockmire, first mate

...and so on.

In another document, the brief history of the *Mosca* itself became clearer. It was a Spanish three-masted brigantine, seventy feet long, that had been "liberated" by privateers — possibly Sir Ambrose himself, Adam thought, reading between the lines — and refitted for commercial service.

Seneca Bond. Pamela Bond's ancestor, whose ghost supposedly haunted the woods surrounding Windmere Hall. Did all mysteries finally return to centre on that woman? Adam consulted the family tree

Sir Alfred had put together. He had looked at it many times already, but for the first time, he paid attention to the branching point at which the Bonds split off from the main Windmere line. They had once been close enough to conduct business together. But what if Sir Ambrose had harboured a viper in his own nest? According to Utley, the *Mosca* had sunk and dashed Sir Ambrose's ambitions at the worst possible moment, but because of it Cliffsward had fallen into the hands of the Bonds and become Bondgate. Could there have been deliberate sabotage?

* * * *

Adam remained a guest among the Windmere sisters. Freddie no longer walked the corridors at night, but her sadness seemed to have grown deeper, covering her during the day like a snowdrift. When she wasn't throwing herself into her training with Misses Prine and Priestley with renewed vigour, she moped about, frequently joining Jane in the sitting room, staring at the same page in the novel she held for hours as she vainly tried to copy her sister's prime occupation.

Despite the anxious mood that prevailed, Adam was at least able to sleep undisturbed through the night — once he could fall asleep. The same daydreams about Zerlina that distracted him during the day turned to tantalising fantasies at night that kept him tossing and turning in bed for hours until sleep overtook him.

He would dream, half-awake, that Zerlina had slipped into Windmere Hall through some secret passage and stealthily entered his bedchamber to lie with him. In these lascivious fantasies, he relived tasting her tender lips, exploring every curve of her body and listening to her melodious voice as they exchanged pledges of love with each other. How he yearned to be with her again!

On one such night, Adam experienced his dream even more vividly than usual. It was as if he felt the weight of Zerlina's slender body and the warmth of her breath, savoured the fragrance of her sex. She stroked his chest, unbuttoning his nightshirt, and in turn he ran his hands over her body, feeling it through the chemise she wore. His cock stiffened and he arched his back, electrified with longing that coursed through his whole body. His phantom lover responded in kind, pressing her breasts against him, their firm nipples grazing his skin through the thin fabric.

She leaned over him, kissing him gently, then more passionately, their lips pressing together. Her tongue caressed his and her long hair brushed his neck. "I'm ready, Adam," she panted, rolling back and spreading her legs wide, inviting him to take her.

Still half-awake but enjoying his dream more than usual, even as part of him knew that he would awake alone, he whispered, "It's Zeno, remember?"

Perhaps it was the jolt of his partner reacting to his comment that woke him completely, or perhaps the sound of his own voice pulled him out of his trance. "Zeno? Oh, ha ha! I say, really?" The mocking laughter was not that of his beloved. Even in the darkness, he awoke with a shock and recognised his bedmate for who she really was.

"Alice?" Adam exclaimed.

"Well, I thought so when I left my chamber to find you," Alice said, teasing, "but if this be *your* dream, who knows? Who would you like me to be?" She pressed close again, her hot breath raising the little hairs on Adam's neck and her fingers stroking his still-bare chest.

Adam would have none of it, and before his body betrayed him, he moved to light a candle and put some space between himself and Alice Windmere. The halo of light revealed the youngest sister, ravishing and nubile in her current state of dishabille — her silky hair, unbound, lay tantalising over her shoulders and chest. Her slim body was clad only in a silk shift trimmed with rose-petal lace that provided more than a hint of the inviting curves beneath. Adam first met her smouldering eyes but returned his gaze to this slight garment. It looked familiar.

"Where did you get that?" Adam said, indicating the lingerie.

Alice stretched one arm over her head and extended her leg, affecting a glamorous pose and hiking the hem up another inch. "This old thing?" she drawled. "Do you like it?"

"I asked where you obtained it," Adam said coolly.

"It's the strangest thing," Alice said, affecting puzzlement with a finger to her lip and her eyes cast upward, as if searching the heavens for the correct answer. "I was out front with Freddie the other day while you were gone, and a courier approached the house with a package from a dressmaker in London — a very posh establishment, from the sound of it. Well, it seemed silly to summon Gainesborough for such a trivial matter, so I offered to accept it. I went straight to my room and opened it right away, and found this inside! It fits marvellously, don't you think?" She posed again.

In other circumstances, she would have had Adam at her command if she would only surrender her charms to him, but Adam knew her too well by now, and he only wrinkled his nose in disgust and indignation. "Was there no name on the package?" he demanded. "I happen to know that it was addressed to Marie."

"Oh, I saw that," Alice said, "but I assumed it was a mistake. How could a chambermaid afford such a thing? A gift? What kind of cad would order something this fine for a dirty slut like Marie?" Once again, her knowledge of Adam's affairs was turned against him.

"Take it off," Adam said, his temper threatening to boil over.

"No," Alice said stubbornly.

"Take it off."

"Maybe you'd like to tear it off me," Alice said, eyes wide with feigned fear. "Go on, I dare you—give it a good rip, right down the middle. Ravish me like one of your serving wenches! I won't scream...unless you want me to." Adam folded his arms, aware that she would win either way by getting him to react. It was clear that if he refused to make love to her, she would take her pleasure where she could, in mocking and humiliating him.

As angry as he was becoming, Adam was almost grateful for the soft knock on the door that interrupted them—almost, as he now realised how it would appear to anyone who entered his bedchamber at that moment. Fists clenched in frustration, torn between the door and the all-too-solid woman in his bed, Adam mouthed for her to hide herself, his expression pleading. Just this once, was it too much to ask? Alice rolled her eyes and got under the counterpane, pulling it up over her head. Only then did Adam go to the door.

Adam opened the door only a crack, expecting to see a servant, but his already racing heart stumbled when he saw Frederica Windmere waiting in the hall. Many times he had seen her thus when she had come to him thinking him Roderick, but this was different. The spark of awareness lit her eyes. She looked from side to side alertly, not as one who walked in a dream but as one wide awake and not wishing to be seen.

"Miss Windmere!" Adam said in a breathy whisper, unable to think of anything more meaningful at just that moment. "Wh-what a surprise!"

"Call me Freddie, please...Adam." In the shaft of light released by the opened door, he saw her blush. "I apologise for visiting so late, but I couldn't sleep, and...and I saw the light in your room..." Adam well knew that his chamber was on the opposite end of the house from the family's rooms. She would have had to have been on her way already when he lit the candle. Had she heard Alice, he wondered, or perhaps even followed her here?

"I was...reading," Adam said lamely. He opened the door no further.

"May I come in? ...Just for a moment," she added quickly, seeing Adam briefly freeze with panic and undoubtedly attributing it to his sense of propriety.

Adam reluctantly opened the door wider and nearly gasped. Beneath her robe, Frederica wore a mantle of white chiffon thin enough to reveal more than a hint of her swelling bosom, her dainty waist, her perfectly formed limbs. On her feet were heeled shoes that made her nearly as tall as him. To Adam's imagination, it looked almost like a bridal ensemble, and perhaps it had been for an earlier generation of Windmeres. On previous nights when she had sleepwalked, Frederica had revealed as much or more, but the hint of purposeful adornment, as if she had considered the effect she would have, made her that much more alluring. His voice caught in his throat as he invited her in.

"I hope you don't think that I am angry with you," Frederica began, "for being at Bondgate, I mean."

It hadn't occurred to Adam, and he said so.

"Miss Bond just...sometimes, she brings out the worst in me. I have a tendency to overreact."

"It's understandable."

The smile with which Frederica favoured Adam seemed to warm the room. "You do understand, don't you? All this time, and I judged you so harshly—"

Adam blushed. He was about to say some self-deprecating demurral when Frederica lunged forth, taking him in her arms with a strength that caught him utterly off guard. Her lips pressed against his, not only cutting off but driving from his mind whatever he had been about to say. She closed the door with her foot and guided him towards the bed, still caressing and kissing him like one starved for affection too long.

"Miss Windmere, please!" Adam said when he could draw breath. Had her mania taken on a new intensity? "You must come to your senses. I am not Roderick Utley!"

"I know!" she gasped, still holding him close to her. "I am wide awake, and I finally know what I want— you!" Her red lips came at him again, an assault Adam narrowly avoided. How he had hoped for this moment just weeks ago! Yet the timing could not have been worse. Still trapped in her embrace, he turned her away from the bed like a dancer leading his partner around the floor.

"I realised that you had gone to Bondgate for my sake," she continued. "I couldn't ask anyone to make that sacrifice for me. It showed me how wrong I had been about you." More kisses followed.

Where to begin? Adam could hardly put his thoughts together to explain the real reason he had been at Bondgate. Would such an explanation even make sense to Frederica? "But—but Roderick—" he said weakly, fighting the rising tide of arousal within himself. Whatever his feelings for someone else, his body was responding to Frederica's presence.

"Yes, I did love Roderick," she said in an excess of emotion, turning Adam back towards the bed and its incriminating Alice-sized hump beneath the covers, "but I accept now that he is gone—gone, I know not where, but surely forever! Did not your visit to Bondgate prove that he is not there?"

"Er—"

"Then do not resist me, I beg you!" she cried. "Please, Mr Blythewood—Adam. You may think me as cold as a marble statue, but hot blood courses through my veins the same as any other woman. I too have desires that must be satisfied! I know what I want, and I know you want it too. You've lain with Sally and Molly and Marie. Surely I am not less attractive than any of them? Please don't tell me you've found your scruples only now."

"Mmm—Frederica—please,   you—mmm—mustn't," Adam gasped between the kisses that smothered his face. He did hate to disappoint anyone, especially a lady. But the choice was taken out of his hands when Frederica finally wrestled him to the bed.

He landed with a thump, Frederica on top of him, with a force that brought a surprised "Oof!" from beneath the counterpane.

Frederica felt the presence of another body at once and stopped, cocking her head like a dog that has heard a fox in the underbrush. To Adam's horror, moving as slowly as a dream but too quickly for him to stop, Frederica drew back the covers and found her younger sister gazing back. Alice's expression was almost grave, unremorseful but without the malicious smirk she usually showed Adam. The two sisters stared at each other, Adam a bystander for the moment.

Finally, her face white and her voice controlled, Frederica said, "I...I see how things stand. Pray, forgive this intrusion." She stood as if to leave.

"Please, Freddie," Alice said, "don't go. I was just...returning something of Mr Blythewood's." She sat up and began to remove herself from the thick bed covers.

"Oh, indeed?" Frederica said, her surprise curdling into anger. "Just as Mr Blythewood was only 'reading'? Do not insult me, Alice."

"I tell you the truth," Alice said, standing. "I came to return this, which rightly belongs to Mr Blythewood." She drew the chemise over her head and handed it to Adam without breaking eye contact with Frederica. She stood between the two of them, now completely naked, as if it were the most natural thing in the world. Adam dumbly took the garment, standing apart from the two sisters with the feeling that a galvanic charge now arced between them, a static electricity that, when discharged, would burst like a bombshell.

Alice broke the silence first. "Forgive me, sister, for saving you from a decision you will surely regret," she said.

Far from taking this in a conciliatory spirit, Frederica blossomed into anger. "You speak to me of regrets, yet it is you I find in Adam's bed? You have finally gone too far, Alice!"

"You're only angry because you found me here first! Or am I to believe it is your custom to rouge your cheeks and dress as a vestal virgin before bed every night? That's not what I recall — "

"You forget your place, Alice! You've no right to follow me or question what I choose to do — " The two began squabbling, their raised voices overlapping.

For his part, Adam blushed, knowing now what Alice thought of him — or had he been right the first time, and her anger was a by-product of jealousy?

In the face of Alice's impassivity, Frederica's cheeks flushed. Her bosom heaved and she said through clenched teeth, "Of all that I have suffered, how is it that I should be cursed with such a sister — "

For a brief, flickering moment, Alice looked hurt by this statement, but it was nothing compared to the anguish Frederica expressed. Alice was not one to back down or to be sentimental, however, so she pressed her advantage, leaning closer to her sister, and said, "How can you say that, Freddie, after all I have done for you?"

Frederica's eyes widened, and Adam realised something that should have been much clearer to him before — Freddie was afraid of Alice. "What — " she said haltingly, her eyes beginning to glisten with tears, "what have you done for me, sister?" There never was a bleaker hopelessness than in the way she spoke the word 'sister.'

"Only what you were too weak to do yourself!" Alice spat. "You're pathetic. Look at yourself! Throwing yourself at a cad like this? It was bad enough when you thought him Roderick, but to be wide awake and beg for his cock like a common whore—"

This time Frederica did not hesitate. She drew her hand back and slapped Alice's face as quickly and smoothly as she had thrown Adam in the kitchen weeks before. "How dare you," she said in a voice dripping contempt. "I beg for nothing—I am a Windmere, and I command!"

Alice straightened up. The side of her face Frederica had struck was red, but she showed no emotion. "That's right," she said. "Don't be afraid to draw blood."

Shaking, Frederica found herself unable to say anything more. She drew her thin robe around herself like a cape and stormed out.

Adam, stunned by what he had just seen, stood rooted to the floor. Alice touched her reddened cheek. She appeared satisfied, even triumphant.

"I don't know what you're so pleased about," Adam said when he found his voice. "I ought to take you over my knee myself for that stunt."

Something glowed in Alice's eyes that almost made Adam step back. "You won't," she said. Then she, too, left, as proud in her unclothed state as if she wore the raiment of a queen.

Chapter Twenty

It was as much to escape the continuing chill between Frederica and Alice as to help Lady Windmere that Adam found himself patrolling the grounds a few days later. As Lady Windmere had sacked the groundskeeper, Dick, along with his wife Sally, she found to her chagrin that the hounds Dick had once kept tame relished their new freedom from oversight. They heeled to no one, not Dick's underlings—who were unable to keep up with the trimming thanks to the hounds running wild—not Peter's stable boys, nor even the Windmere sisters, and as the "man of the house" it fell to Adam to bring them into line, armed only with a short whip to snap and his own authoritative voice. Lady Windmere was certain that this would be enough, but Adam was not so sure.

"Yes, give them a good talking-to," Alice said, her eyebrow raised. Adam knew that Alice thought him too spineless to handle such a job, which made him more determined.

It was, to Adam's surprise, Jane who offered to go with him, and after the pack rounded on them, he found her to be as good a climber of trees as he himself. The two of them sat in the boughs of a large ash tree, observing the dogs that circled below. "They are really quite playful," Jane insisted, against any evidence that Adam could see, but in the face of her sympathy for the animals, he kept to himself the wish that he had brought a pistol along with him.

Adam had torn his trousers while climbing the tree to escape the dogs. Examining them at leisure in its branches, he gave vent to a few choice words. "Blast it all!" He abruptly reddened when he realised how close Jane was to him. It was not like him to swear in front of a lady.

Jane smiled. "I think you can be forgiven for expressing your true feelings in such a situation." Looking at the rent in his trousers herself, she suggested that Gretchen would be able to mend them. "I would offer, but I am no seamstress myself, unfortunately."

Eventually, the dogs grew bored and moved on, perhaps to chase a rabbit or lie in the sun and lick their own nethers. Adam cared not, as his back and legs were stiff from maintaining their crouched position in the branches. He descended first and helped Jane after she handed him the shoes she had removed to hasten their earlier escape.

Instead of putting her shoes back on, she held them and walked through the now-lush grass in her stocking-clad feet. "I rather enjoy the sensation — don't you?" she said.

"Isn't it a bit wet?" Adam said. The ground from which the grass sprang felt spongy beneath his own shoes.

Jane grinned. "That is the very sensation of which I speak."

Adam had no response to that. "Well, you'd better put them on before we return to the house — I should hate it to be thought that I allowed you to run wild or tried to take advantage of our isolation."

Jane laughed. "I could credibly claim that I fought back like a wildcat," she said, pointing to the tear in Adam's trousers. "I think you overestimate the responsibility which has devolved upon you. We are, after all, already alone on the grounds without a chaperone." She walked nearer to him. "And perhaps you have underestimated me if you think walking barefoot constitutes 'running wild.'"

Adam was suddenly aware of Jane's nearness, and he was not deaf to the hint she dropped, but Adam had sworn to put such conquests behind him. It was unfortunate, but the shy middle sister was far too late in seeking his attention, and he now had thoughts only for the fair Zerlina. He coughed to cover the awkwardness of the situation and cast his eye about for any object of interest. "I say," he said, picking up his pace, "what a delightful-looking garden. Shall we have a look?"

Behind him, Jane made a sound that might have been a sigh or grunt, and the next thing he knew she was next to him on the way to the colourful spot, her skirts held daintily above the long grass.

The plot was a neat square, perhaps five feet on a side, bordered on the outside by rich violet flowers in full bloom. "How charming," Adam said, internally wincing at the false cheer he gave his voice. He took care to keep himself on a different side of the garden from Jane, and as she sought to close the gap, they ended up circling around the border of the garden, looking at it from all sides while neither acknowledged the dance of avoidance. "Did you plant these?"

Jane shook her head. "Nay. I don't recall being in this corner of the grounds for a long time. I would say that Dick must have planted it for his own reasons, but see? The edges are still trimmed neatly and the weeds have not overtaken it like they are beginning to everywhere else." Once it was pointed out to Adam, it was obvious. He knew that Gainesborough was still in the process of hiring a new groundskeeper to bring the existing crew back into line. But this little plot was neat as a pin.

"Hmm. Perhaps some villager has made this spot their own?" But for what reason, neither of them could guess.

In the centre of the square, blocked from view by the purple flowers unless one were standing very close, was a patch of a leafy green plant—apparently not weeds, since they were all the same, and they looked as carefully cultivated as the flowers. Both Adam and Jane noticed them, but while Jane readily identified the flowers as gladioli, she professed not to recognise the little green stems.

"There is something unpleasant about them," Adam observed. As they stood there and the wind picked up, he smelt the fragrant aroma of the gladioli, but noticed an acrid odour beneath it, something that made his stomach clench, as one did when tasting a food that had previously disagreed with one.

"It's the herb," Jane said, stepping closer and filling her own nose with the mingled scents.

At the word "herb," Adam recalled the little dried plant that the old woman in the village had tried to give him, and the herb that had supposedly been brought from the South Seas aboard the *Mosca* before its wreck just short of the cliffs. He said nothing, but tried to recall the herb-seller's bundle. Yes, it might have resembled this, the living plant, at one time. "Do you know what it is?" he asked.

Jane shook her head. "I'm more familiar with flowers," she said, but she waded through the front rank of the lily-like gladiolus blossoms and plucked one of the green herbs. It could have been something as ordinary as parsley or mint but for the rank smell it exuded, and Adam felt sure that it wouldn't make a pleasant addition to any recipe. "I've got a book back at the house we could consult... And perhaps Gainesborough will know who has been tending this garden."

* * * *

Jane's bedchamber was near Frederica's, but Adam had never seen it. It was as filled with books as he expected, several of them borrowed from Sir Alfred's library but many more that he had never seen that must have been Jane's own. They filled a small set of shelves and overflowed onto an otherwise tidy desk and most every other flat surface in the room. Jane chuckled and shrugged when she saw Adam taking it all in.

She murmured to herself, trying to locate the book she had in mind, pulling one or another from the shelf by its corner and replacing it, then sifting through the piles she had left in other places.

"It's a green cloth cover with gilt edging," she said, giving Adam permission to enter and look through the piles himself. He did so, gingerly at first, as handling her books in this setting seemed to him as personal as rifling through her laundry, but it was quick work to determine that none were the title they sought, and most were not even the right colour. Almost all were, as Jane had said when they first met, novels of romance or intrigue, give or take a few nonfiction books on diverse subjects.

Finally, they gave up. "I'm sure it will turn up," Jane said. "I may have returned it to my father's library by accident." In the meantime she offered to hold on to the herb so that she could identify it when the book was found. Despite his curiosity that it might be the herb Sir Ambrose had brought with him from his travels, its unpleasant scent — which seemed not to bother Jane — made him happy to leave it with her.

"I'll check when I return to the library," Adam said, feeling that perhaps it was time to return to his real job, especially as he had so bungled the mission to tame the hounds.

After a change of clothes, leaving the torn trousers for Gretchen to mend, Adam returned to the library. After the first few days of working there, he had concentrated his attention on the papers Sir Alfred had left him and the few books that pertained to his work, so in this survey, it was like taking in many of the books' titles for the first time. Sir Alfred had collected many works of history, geography and travel, and the typical scientific works an educated man might be expected to have, but the botany book in its green and gilt cloth was no more here than it had been in Jane's room. Adam was surprised, however, to find a few books on subjects considerably afield from what he had considered Sir Alfred's primary interests, books on theatre and costuming, and a book whose cover he stared at for quite a few minutes — *Cartomancy: On Divination and Prophecy Through Cards*. Flipping through its pages, Adam instantly recognised the layouts and card illustrations he had seen in the tarot-dealer's deck at Bondgate.

Chapter Twenty-One

Well, thought Adam the next morning, *there really is no time like the present to get an unpleasant duty over and done with.* He tied the paper bundle with a neat bow of string. He shook his head when he recalled the scene with Alice and Frederica a few nights before. How strange it was that Alice should strip herself in front of him, yet *he* was the one who felt embarrassment about it! Neither woman had had much to say to him since then, for reasons of their own, and Adam sensed that there was still an unspoken chill between the two sisters. Jane's company had made it a little easier to bear, but he could not help feeling that his time at Windmere Hall was growing short, whether or not he finished editing Sir Alfred's manuscript. He was running out of friends in this place.

How strange, too, that the incidents with both Marie and Alice had centred on a negligee. He left his chamber like a man leaving the comfort of his prison cell to march to the gallows. The halls were empty, as it was early yet. He hoped to find Marie before she began her daily duties, and he had slept poorly, so there was little to be gained by waiting.

Knocking on Marie's door, he felt a flutter of arousal, bringing back as it did memories of the furtive passions he had shared with the eager maid. But it was a mere echo of the excitement he had once felt for her, and he was reminded all over again that this would be an awkward encounter. What if Marie interpreted the gift he brought as an attempt to renew their liaisons? Would she be angry if she felt that he was toying with her affections? For a split second he thought perhaps he should simply leave the parcel at the door, but it was too late — he had already knocked.

"Coming, miss —" said a voice from behind the door. When it opened, Marie stood before him, dressed in a quilted house coat rather than her uniform, and the rest of her words caught in her throat. Her eyes widened. "Oh! ...I didn't know it was you."

"No," Adam said, his usual fluency escaping him. "I'm sure you weren't expecting me." He looked down the empty hallway in both directions. "May I come in for a moment?"

Marie allowed him in, but immediately turned to her dresser, pulling out stockings and other unmentionables from which Adam politely turned his eyes. If she suspected that Adam was here to pitch woo, she was going to make him work for her attention. "Well?" she prompted him. "I'm afraid I haven't much time. I, uh, woke up late." She did not look as if she had risen in a hurry. Her hair and face were already made up.

Adam's answer was forgotten when he noticed a vase of familiar purple flowers on the side table. "What an attractive bouquet," he said, stepping nearer to it. "Gladiolus, unless I am mistaken?"

"Hmm? Oh, I'm not sure," Marie replied, turning to watch Adam examine the blossoms. "Miss Windmere gave them to me. I thought perhaps they were from you?" A small smile curled her lips. Adam, too, remembered the last time Frederica had passed such a token to Marie, and he remembered that had led to the reason he was here now. There was no question—the flowers in the vase were the same he and Jane had found growing the day before.

"No," Adam said, "they weren't from…" His words trailed off as he spied the corner of a book just visible on the floor, beneath the table. It was bound in green cloth, with gilt highlights. He bent to pick up the volume and ignored Marie's prompt to finish his sentence. She still gazed at herself in the mirror, unaware of what had distracted Adam.

It was indeed a gardener's guide to flowering plants. There could be no doubt it was the book Jane had looked for in vain. He thumbed through its pages. "Yes," he said over his shoulder, as much to confirm Jane's identification as to continue the conversation. "They're gladioli." The picture looked just like the flowers before him. "'In the language of flowers, gladioli represent faithfulness, dedication…and infatuation. Sometimes to the point of obsession.'" He furrowed his brow.

"Do you often carry that?" Marie asked, looking over his shoulder at the book. "Just in case you are called upon to identify flowers?" Her smile had become merrier, perhaps suspecting that he really had sent her the flowers and was putting on this act for her benefit.

Adam shook his head. "Of course not. I found this beneath the table. You didn't put it there?"

Marie looked at the cover. "I've never seen it," she said. "You say it was here?"

Adam explained that the book had gone missing from the library. "It's nothing to be concerned about," he said when it seemed that Marie was about to become defensive. "If you borrowed it, I'm sure the Windmeres wouldn't mind."

"But I tell you I didn't!" Marie said. "By all means, return it to the library — I'm sure I don't know who left it here!"

"Fine," Adam said, taking the volume back, unhappy that the conversation had taken such a fraught turn before he had even come to his main purpose for being there. As he moved to put the book under his arm, its pages came open and a folded piece of paper slipped from between them. Marie bent to pick it up and Adam thought nothing of it. When he shifted the package and accepted the paper from her, however, it felt familiar.

"What is it?" Marie said, noticing the queer expression on Adam's face. Adam set down the book and the package he had brought, unfolding the paper. It was a sheet of parchment with a familiar handwriting in ink on one face. He had handled enough of Sir Alfred's manuscript to recognise the weight of the paper he used just by feel, but what was it doing in this book, hidden in the maid's room? Adam grew more agitated as he read.

Among Gulliver Windmere's improvements of the land upon which the updated Hall would be built was the clearance of a pestilent weed. The plant, which once covered the hills, was known to be poisonous to horses or sheep who grazed upon it, and certain locals used it as a purgative, brewing it into tea to induce vomiting or to sicken their enemies. Gulliver saw the removal of this scourge as both necessary to make the landscape fitting for his new manor and a boon to his tenants, removing a source of mischief from their midst...

Adam ignored Marie's questions. His mind was reeling. *Brewing it into tea to sicken their enemies.* Adam looked up in shock, mulling over the implications of what he had just read. He turned to Marie as if seeing her for the first time. The day he had descended into the village, only to be mobbed by lusty maidens, he had thought that the ale had been tainted, and that Eli Johnson had unwittingly — or perhaps purposefully — lured him into drinking enough that sickness had followed. His recollection of that afternoon was scrambled enough that he couldn't have been sure.

But reading about the tea had brought back a memory. The day he had fallen ill, he had taken his tea in the library, like he always did... It had been left in the hallway for him. Had he noticed an unusual flavour? Adam, recalling the sequence of events leading up to his extended stay at Bondgate, felt a wave of nausea all over again. He had thought he might never drink ale again, but where in his confusion he had blamed the drink that he had taken in the pub, in hindsight he remembered he had started to feel unwell before he began drinking. "I was poisoned," he muttered.

"Poisoned!" exclaimed Marie. "What makes you think you were poisoned?"

"Where did this come from?" Adam demanded.

"It fell out of the book," Marie said, as if Adam were being daft.

" — which was in your room," Adam continued.

"I told you, I didn't — "

"You prepare the leaves for tea time, yes?" Adam said, pacing, in his mind examining every angle, trying to come up with a reason he shouldn't make the accusation that was screaming to be put forward.

"Y-yes, but — "

"Gretchen serves me, but *you* still make the tea. And this weed that the manuscript describes, Gulliver Windmere *didn't* completely wipe it out. I know for a fact that it still grows down by the bay, and there is a cultivated patch of it on the grounds — side by side with these gladiolus flowers, in fact!"

Seemingly mystified by Adam's implication, Marie spread her hands and said, "If you say so, sir."

It must be the noxious weed that Adam had encountered and taken for the "herbe" brought back from the South Seas by the *Mosca*. But far from having aphrodisiac qualities, it had sickened him! "Why did you do it, Marie? Did you think it would increase my passion, that we could renew our affair?"

"What!" Marie reared back in indignation, but Adam continued relentlessly, working out the logic of the scenario.

"Or was it revenge? Did you know that the herb was poisonous, and you were trying to punish me for breaking off with you?"

"How dare you — "

"If I were to search this room, would I find a store of the herb, or do you keep it on your person?" Marie cowered against her dressing table as if he might search her by force, but he relented. She probably had it hidden somewhere he would never find unless she admitted it. "I repeat the question. What did you put in my tea?" Adam held out the paper as if it were a key piece of evidence in a trial, and thrusting it into the defendant's face would make her crack.

"I've never seen that paper before in my life!" Marie exclaimed. "I couldn't have prepared the tea that made you sick—I wasn't even here!"

That was news to Adam. "Where were you?"

"I can't tell you that." Marie froze, but became animated once she came up with a good retort. "Not that it's any of your business, but you can ask Miss Windmere if you don't believe me... And why would you accuse me? I had Gretchen switch places with me so I wouldn't have to see you! Did you not even notice I was gone?"

Adam was confounded. Marie hadn't been there? The reasons for his suspicions were obvious to him — he had thrown her over rather brusquely, and she might have struck back in jealousy—but face to face with her, he realised how petty that sounded. While she had sometimes given vent to her pique at having to share him, he had no reason to think she would try something so malicious.

Adam mumbled something. Marie's eyes narrowed. "If that is all, sir—"

Reminded of his original purpose, Adam presented the wrapped package he had brought with him. "No, that is not all. Here," he said curtly, all pretence of charm gone.

"What is it?" Marie said suspiciously, folding the paper back. Adam had rewrapped it since Alice had discarded the original packaging.

"It's to replace the one I…the one you had before," Adam said. "I'm sorry." Whether the apology was for tearing her nightgown or for accusing her of poisoning him was not immediately clear.

When she saw the silk negligee, Marie's cheeks reddened and her nostrils flared. "You've got some nerve, even for a gentleman! I don't see you for weeks, you accuse me of theft and poisoning, and this is supposed to make me open my legs to you?" She tossed the lingerie to her bed without looking at it. "Who do you think you are?"

The answer caught in Adam's throat, interrupted by the approaching sound of footsteps in the hall. He folded the page of Sir Alfred's manuscript back into the book and held on to it. The footsteps stopped at Marie's door. There was a knock.

"One moment," Marie said to the waiting caller, making sure her housecoat was buttoned to the neck. By the time she opened the door, the flush of anger that had rouged her cheeks was gone. Adam was chastened to see Frederica dressed in travelling clothes. "Mr Blythewood was just leaving. The draft must have blown the door closed," Marie said lamely.

"I'm sure," Frederica said, raising an eyebrow. She turned away as if she could not bear to watch Adam debase himself further. "Mr Blythewood, no doubt you'll understand, Marie's services are required…elsewhere at the moment, so I shall have to ask you to continue this some other time. Good day, then."

Chapter Twenty-Two

How long Adam stewed in the library, his hands folded pensively while he stared into space and considered the mess he had made of things, he knew not. He had watched the Windmere sisters board their carriage earlier, and the house was quiet. Where they went was a mystery to him. There was a knock at the library door. "'Allo?" It was Gretchen with the tea service. Since Marie had begged off serving Adam, the other maid had been happy to fill in, even if Adam didn't provide the attention to her that he once had. Gretchen was, above all, even-tempered. No wonder she had found Bondgate and its environs altogether too dramatic for her.

She also brought with her Adam's mended trousers. He complimented her on the nearly invisible stitching she had made, and had a thought. "Did you learn to do this at Bondgate?"

Accepting his praise humbly, she bowed her head and replied, "No, sir, I was always good with a needle an' thread, even in me village... But Miss Bond put me skills to good use on a reg'lar basis, she did. All of her girls had to know how to sew, an' we spent a lot of time mending and tailoring her menservants' uniforms."

After a pause, she asked, "Something wrong, sir?" Adam was sniffing the brewed tea with a wrinkled nose. Since realising he had been poisoned before, he had resolved to be alert when eating or drinking anything else at Windmere Hall. It smelled like ordinary black tea.

"Er, no, not really," Adam said, setting the cup down. "Gretchen, did you prepare this yourself?"

Gretchen stood with her hands folded. "O' course I did, sir. Molly don't have time to bother with such things now that she's got the kitchen to herself, does she?"

"What about Marie? You're sure she didn't prepare it?" Despite his uncertainty, he wasn't quite ready to trust the senior maid.

"Oh, no, sir, she's left already with the misses."

Adam had seen only one carriage as he watched from the second-floor window, the one the three sisters had boarded. "Are you sure about that? She isn't following the misses later?"

"Oh, no, sir," said Gretchen, quite unable to understand why Adam should want to know. "She's a proper lady's maid, the misses bring her with them an' they ride in the carriage together. Truth be told, I wouldn't mind it meself at all to serve in such a way, riding in style an' wearing me mistress' clothes —"

Adam sat up with a jolt. "What do you mean? Please, out with it!"

Gretchen blushed. It was clearly not something for common knowledge. "Between you an' me, sir, Miss

Frederica often takes Marie with her, an' Marie borrows a dress from Miss Jane when she needs to look presentable." She spread her hands, as if washing her hands of responsibility for this unorthodox arrangement.

"But I observed the coach depart myself," he protested. "There were clearly only three ladies aboard!"

"Begging your pardon, sir, an' I shouldn'a said anything, but since the cat's out of the bag so to speak, 'twas Marie who accompanied Miss Frederica and Miss Alice on their errand. Miss Jane didn'a go with them."

Adam was thunderstruck. Jane had stayed behind! How could he have been so blind? Mentally he compared her size, her general shape — yes, only the invisible barrier of class prevented Marie and Jane from trading clothes. And if they did this frequently — yes, they certainly could have made this switch when they went to Bath. But why the deception?

Adam stood at once. "Thank you, Gretchen. You have been very helpful, but I just remembered an urgent matter."

"You're welcome, sir," Gretchen said. As Adam rushed from the library, she added, "I hope I haven't caused a problem for the misses!"

"Quite the contrary," Adam said over his shoulder. He was already in the hallway, and before he knew it, he was running at a steady gait, his heels sped by the elation of hope. Oh, how he wished it were true! But it was so fanciful!

Adam reached the wing containing the family's rooms before he was even conscious of his goal. He had bypassed the parlour with barely a glance into the empty room. If his suspicions were correct, the one he sought would not be out in the open. He stopped at the door to Jane's room, which he had only entered for the first time the day before. It was closed, as he had suspected it would be.

Pushing down the instinct to hammer on the door as loudly as his own heart beat in his chest, Adam paused to calm himself. He could be wrong — no need to make a scene — but if Jane were in her room, surely it was him that she hid from. Why else maintain the fiction that the three sisters had left together?

Putting himself in the position of the elderly Gainesborough, Adam cleared his throat and knocked as discreetly as he had heard the butler do many times. If Jane was present, she must have taken tea. It was only natural for one of the servants to retrieve the service after its use.

He heard footsteps in the bedchamber. The door opened, a simple movement that thrilled him far more than he could have expected, but that excitement was nothing compared to what he felt upon having his theory confirmed and seeing Jane Windmere on the other side of it. Whomever she expected, it was not Adam, for her eyes widened and her voice caught when she took sight of him. She was speechless.

"Miss Windmere," Adam panted, his heart rising in his chest as he looked at her, her face, her figure, with new eyes. It was more than the run from the other end of the hall that took his breath away. She waited, wide-eyed, for him to recover enough to speak. "Jane, you must forgive this imposition," he said.

"Wh-what is this all about?" she said, her voice trembling. But she did not expel him from her room, as she had every right to do. She waited to hear his explanation, and Adam recognised in her face the same mixture of apprehension and longing that he felt.

"That is a fine gown," he said, casting about for the words that would unlock his throat and settling on a commonplace far simpler than the feelings he truly hoped to express. Jane blinked. *What an anti-climax,* Adam thought desperately to himself. *She must think me the greatest ass in Creation.*

"Thank you," she said.

She did look fine in it, more than fine, but Adam for once found himself dumb, inarticulate, unable to put his thoughts into words. It was the first thing Adam had thought of, but the more he looked at the dress — purple, with a trim of yellow ribbon — the more certain he became that he had seen it somewhere before. "If I may be so bold, it looks better on you than the last time I saw it." It was, he realised, the very same dress he had seen cast aside in the dungeon under Bondgate when Zerlina had traded it for the livery of one of Pamela Bond's servants.

"I am not sure I understand your meaning," Jane said. The colour rising in her cheeks indicated otherwise, but she maintained her composure.

"No. Perhaps you did not realise that I was conscious enough to see and recognise it while you were nursing me back to health. Nevertheless, it was wise to wear it only on a day you did not expect to see me."

Jane turned away from him with a chuckle, and spoke with a lightness that Adam did not find credible. "Ah, Mr Blythewood, I — I think perhaps your illness made you feverish. Surely there are many purple gowns. How could you have seen me while you were at Bondgate?"

"How indeed?" Adam stepped towards her. It was possible that he was wrong, that he was making a fool of himself, but Jane's temper betrayed her, contradicting the light words she chose. Usually as mild as a spring meadow, she seemed agitated, flustered, as if that meadow were overshadowed by a gathering storm of passion. While turned away from him she picked up the book she had been reading, holding it before her like a shield, or perhaps to keep her hands steady.

Adam gently lifted the book from her grasp. It was the same volume he had seen Jane reading frequently — it was one of her favourites, she had told him — but the way her eyes darted between it and him suggested that it was far more important to her than he had suspected. Keeping an eye on her, as if she were a skittish wild creature that might bolt at the first provocation, he opened the cover and examined the title page.

The Romance of Zeno and Zerlina
By E. B., a Lady of Devonshire

It was a thick book, its pages foxed by frequent use. This was a well-loved volume. As he riffled the pages in wonder, it fell open to the page Jane had marked. Adam held up the makeshift bookmark, half a pasteboard card from a tarot deck that still bore the caption, "The Lovers."

Stunned to see this souvenir of his night at Bondgate, Adam needed no more confirmation. He dropped the book on Jane's bed and turned to face her. The young lady stared back, her eyes wide and watery, uncertain of Adam's intention, her neck stiff with the effort of holding her head up and meeting his gaze,

whatever came. "Adam," she choked, "I can explain—
" She faltered. Her eyes filled with tears.

"My Zerlina!" Adam gasped, taking Jane in his arms
and pressing his lips to hers. She melted into his clasp,
overcome by the same unspoken emotion that united
them. Adam felt her heart thud against her ribcage,
beating in time with his own. How well he knew that
tattoo, and how little he had expected to find its source
again! And, he now realised, it had been Jane—
"Zerlina"—who had rescued him from the muddy
beach on the night that Frederica walked in her sleep
all the way to Bondgate! It was true—he knew it and
felt it as his warm lover returned his kisses. Tears
flowed freely on both sides, tears of relief and joy that
what was secret was now revealed to the sunlight.

"Can you forgive my deception?" Jane murmured,
still enfolded in the arms of her mate.

"Forgive!" Adam said incredulously, holding her at
arm's length so he could see her expression. "There is
nothing to forgive! I have found you, that is all that
matters!" And he renewed his embrace.

"I never meant for any of this to happen," Jane
sobbed. "Freddie convinced me to go to one of Miss
Bond's balls to look for Roderick while she and Alice
were away. She thought Miss Bond had held him
against his will, you know—but I could find no sign of
him. Miss Bond discovered me and enlisted me in her
games... But then you were there—oh, it was a
temptation I could not fight off under the
circumstances!" Her face burned crimson at the
memory.

Adam hastened to reassure her. "You did nothing
wrong. And I have come to know my heart. I love you,
Jane."

"Are you sure it is not Zerlina that you love, or 'Virtue'? Beware, Adam, I know as well as anyone how easy it is to lose oneself in fantasy."

Adam shook his head. "I have been a fool to be so easily thrown off by a mask and a fancy gown—and I have been a fool for other reasons as well—but you wrong yourself when you disown your own charms so. 'Zerlina' is but a name. Tell me truthfully, as Zeno did I please you?"

"Oh, very much."

"I am the same man whether I wear a mask or not. And in my entire life I have never met anyone like you. Say you love me, too, before I die of prolonged tension."

Jane renewed her embrace. "Oh, I do, I do!" More tears of happiness flowed. Finally that generous heart of hers turned outward again. "I feel terrible that I had to keep it from you. It was as great a torture for me to withhold the truth as it was for you not to know. But you must understand, I could hardly make an affair public while Freddie's Roderick was still missing. How could I bear to be happy while she was so miserable?"

The two sat down together on the edge of the bed, their ecstasy tempered by the observation. Roderick Utley's disappearance still cast a shadow over their union. "I feel that my presence has made things more difficult for her," Adam mused. "It is obvious that my attentions were unwelcome."

"You look much like him," Jane observed.

"So I have heard. How absurd it is," Adam said, "that we both should go to Bondgate in search of Roderick Utley, only to find each other!" He proceeded to describe his parley with Pamela Bond and his discovery of Utley's notebook, with its fragment of Sir

Ambrose's narrative and how the trail had gone cold after Miss Bond's masked ball. "Miss Bond is an enigmatic creature, as you know," he concluded, "but when she says she knows not of Mr Utley's whereabouts, I believe her. In fact, I wonder if the solution to the mystery is not quite a bit closer to home." He related his discovery of the missing botany book in Marie's room and the folded manuscript page describing the strange herb they had found together.

Jane pondered this new information, her passion for the moment subdued as the thoughtful, level-headed girl Adam knew came to the fore. "It is clear we have both discovered pieces of the puzzle independently," she said. "Perhaps together we can find a solution and at least put Freddie's worries to rest."

"I should like nothing better," Adam agreed.

Jane nodded. "One thing you must know," she said, and the truth began to spill out. There was no longer any room for secrets between them. "When you thought we had gone to Bath—well, you know now that I stayed behind. Marie went with Freddie and Alice in my place, to assist them."

"I just learned that. It was the clew I needed, in fact."

"But they did not go to Bath, as we all claimed. Freddie and Alice looked for Mr Utley among his old haunts—his club, his apartments, his office. No one could say where he was. His city friends had not seen him since he left for Windmere. The journey was a dismal failure."

"For them, perhaps," Adam said, unable to forget that it was their deception that had made his encounter with Jane at Bondgate possible. "And they are attempting another foray today?"

Jane nodded. "Not as far as London, however. Freddie received word that a man resembling Roderick was seen in a village north of here...but to be honest I don't expect them to have much luck. Freddie has grown desperate. They should return this evening."

Adam nodded glumly, but he could not contain the ever-renewing delight he felt at having found his love. "Should we not make good use of the time until they return?" He gave her a playful squeeze.

"Quite right," Jane said. "We should pool our findings so that if they return empty-handed, we shall be ready to make another guess as to Roderick's whereabouts." Seeing the crestfallen look on his face, Jane realised what Adam had meant, and laughed. "Oh, you thought—" She returned his embrace and gave him a kiss. "Have no fear, I have no intention of neglecting *that* bit of unfinished business!"

Adam hardly thought he could contain himself, and told her so. "We have the house to ourselves—"

Jane smiled warmly. "I am afraid you must restrain yourself a little while longer, as we have much to discuss... We have waited this long, and my eagerness has but grown. Self-control is the spice that makes indulgence all the more delicious, is it not?"

"You sound like Miss Bond," Adam said, arching an eyebrow.

A sly look crossed her features, the half-smirk that was the true birthright of the Windmere sisters. "Perhaps she has rubbed off on me... Tonight," she said, and her eyebrow rose to a nearly devilish degree. What that expression promised, Adam could only guess at, but the warmth of it was enough to keep his furnace stoked for the rest of the day.

Chapter Twenty-Three

The evening meal with the Windmeres proved to be even more stimulating than the fancies that took over his idle imagination during the afternoon. Adam was busy in the library when their carriage returned in the late afternoon. The page he had recovered from Marie's room found its place in Sir Alfred's manuscript, which was somewhat gratifying even if he still had no idea who had used the herb to poison him. Upon hearing the sound of the horses on the drive, he rushed to the window overlooking the front entrance to watch the three women emerge from the coach. From his vantage point he could not tell whether their day had been a success or a failure. It was another hour before Gainesborough rang for dinner and Adam was face to face with Jane again.

The fact that Adam knew Marie had gone with Frederica and Alice in Jane's stead was a secret between Adam and Jane. Jane maintained the fiction that she had experienced the same long, gruelling day as

Frederica and Alice. On the other hand, since Frederica and Alice had both spoken with Adam about Roderick's disappearance, the only barrier to stating the truth about their trip was Lady Windmere's still-standing ban on speaking the missing man's name. Of course, Adam realised, the lady didn't know about Marie and Jane changing places either, since she would likely not have approved of the sisters' attempts to find Roderick. The servants were aware of Marie's substitution—Gretchen had known all about it, after all—but it did not seem hard to keep Lady Windmere in the dark.

Frederica's and Alice's expressions were unreadable. Whether they had overcome their differences or merely papered over them in the name of their secret doings, Adam had no idea. Currently, the story the sisters had told their mother was that they had visited the village and had been out surveying the grounds in preparation for a garden party. Alice was saying, "In any case, we shall be quite unable to host an outdoor *soirée* until Gainesborough finds a suitable groundskeeper…and until *someone* masters the former keeper's hounds."

How fluently Alice lied to her mother! It was all Adam could do to keep the layers of misdirection straight. Fortunately, he was not called upon to speak or to know anything about the sisters' plans, and whenever he did enter the conversation, it was to offer some bit of information or to remind Alice that no one had had any success with the hounds, and his failure was hardly unique. Jane, sitting across from him, would remind him with a look not to say too much, her eyes widening slightly, her mouth set. An occasional nudge of her foot against his under the table would send a shock through his nervous system, and the more strongly Jane desired his silence, the more forceful would be the motion. Adam cared not, and in fact found himself tempted to draw her discipline just to feel her presence more closely.

During the initial course, a cooling soup, something curious occurred. Jane dipped her spoon into the broth and, with her eyes holding Adam's gaze, held it before her lips and blew on it. The pucker of her lips as she blew resembled a kiss. Then, when she was sure that the others were attending to the conversation, she tipped the spoon into the collar of her bodice, shivering a bit with the sensation, then put the empty spoon in her mouth.

Shock electrified Adam. He could scarcely credit what he had seen, and thought he might have even imagined it, until the second time it happened. The cool soup again funnelled down the collar of her dress. This time, pretending to eat it, she cleaned the spoon with her tongue, making sure Adam got a good look. Jane's eyes twinkled as she took stock of Adam's surprise and arousal, and cemented it with another surreptitious stroke of her now-unshod foot on his ankle.

"Is something amusing, Mr Blythewood?" Alice's voice cut through Adam's reverie. She had been relating a trying moment when the hounds had cornered the three sisters in a muddy patch of the grounds, he was sure, but her words were easy to ignore once Jane began the display that was, in all likelihood, the reason a smile had emerged on his face in the first place.

"So sorry," Adam said, focusing his attention on Alice — with difficulty, as at just that moment Jane had renewed stroking his calf with her stocking-clad toes —

and rejoining the conversation. The last thing he wanted was to call attention to Jane's amorous gestures – she might stop, for one thing – but neither did he want it thought that he found Alice's tribulations humorous. "No, I was, er, just recalling a lively verse of Alexander Pope I came across this afternoon." He hoped he wouldn't be invited to quote it at length. Jane adapted the same supercilious expression the other two habitually used upon him, a form of camouflage that kept Alice from asking her any awkward questions.

Alice was no more interested in hearing his thoughts on Pope than she was in anything else he had to say that did not bear on her or her family, so after a withering glance, she continued where she had left off. "So, as I was saying, there we were on the moor, the hounds baying on one side and nothing but a rocky ledge on the other, when Jane said the funniest thing." She stared directly at the middle sister. "What was it you said, Jane?"

Jane looked like a doe surprised at a turn in the lane, too shocked to move. Her wayward foot was no longer anywhere near Adam's. Of course Jane had not been there that afternoon. The entire story was fiction. It was unlike Alice to shake the foundations of an illusion she herself had spun, but perhaps it was worth it to her to put a scare into her sister. Adam never knew quite what the youngest Windmere was thinking. For her part, Lady Windmere looked expectantly from one to the other, curious only to hear the *bon mot* her daughter had come up with.

"Wait," Jane said, finally catching up with the conversation. "Why must everything happen to me?"

Lady Windmere looked from one to the other, straining to see the wit in these remarks. At last, Alice let her off the hook, sneering at about one-tenth the capacity Adam knew she was capable of, and saying, "Ah, well. Perhaps you had to be there."

The meal and the conversation continued. In no time at all, Jane found opportunities to tease Adam whilst escaping the notice of her family. Pats of butter, spoonfuls of gravy and numerous fresh garden peas found their way into the bodice of Jane's dress, even as her gestures became more lascivious. Adam found his manhood hardening, the crotch of his trousers bulging at the seams. If only it were his cock instead of a silver spoon that Jane stroked with her tongue! All along, the knowledge that Jane tantalised him beneath the watchful eye of her family and the risk of being caught made the game all the more arousing.

Adam's imagination began to work, picturing the winding, sloping path that each spoonful of dinner travelled, tracing the contours of Jane's ripe breasts, interrupted momentarily by the bulge of a pert nipple, constrained by lace and linen that only became tighter as it dampened, running down the graceful curve of her belly, perhaps stopping to collect in the hollow of her navel before at last pooling in her lap, the mound of her womanhood teased and tingling in anticipation. How much could her clothing hold, he wondered, before food began to drip out and make her pastime obvious when she stood up? That was part of the game, of course, but the expression of pleasure Jane wore, deepening with each addition to her dress's ballast, told Adam that it was worth the risk.

Before long it struck Adam that this form of pleasure was entirely one-sided. As much as he enjoyed seeing his lover indulge herself so, should he not attempt to reciprocate? He was hardly as skilled at dissembling as the Windmeres, but had he not had his share of escapades and conquests beneath the noses of chaperones far more vigilant than Lady Windmere? Surely he could find a way to gratify Jane's ardour as she was gratifying his! The sight of Jane abandoning herself to sensuality inevitably returned his mind to the night they had shared together in the hidden chambers beneath Bondgate. With it came the memory of his clothes being torn from his body, of his skin being slathered with pastries and gelatines, his hair thick with whipped cream, the feeling of his drawers being filled with custard. His skin prickled, felt electrified, and his hard cock strained against his trousers. Were he to stand up, there was no doubt that his arousal would be visible to all. Jane's smile became all the more maddening in the promises it held. How she was enjoying making him squirm!

Gingerly, Adam scooped a few peas into his own spoon with the intention of following Jane's example. He had just determined that he could drop them discreetly into the neck of his own shirt when he heard his name. He jumped in surprise, dropping both the peas and his spoon to the floor, where it settled beneath the table with a clatter.

Reddening as the girls laughed at his clumsiness — Jane most of all — Adam excused himself, waving off the servant who bent to assist him. Adam lowered himself to the floor, peering beneath the table and feeling for the dropped spoon. As his eyes adjusted, he observed the skirts of the sisters and their mother. *Best not to take too long,* he thought, but he privately savoured the view. Jane's stocking-clad toes, in particular, drew his attention, a feeling that must have been mutual, as she lifted one of them to his face, caressing him on the nose. The surprise made him jump again, this time bumping his head on the underside of the table.

More laughter greeted him when he emerged from beneath the table. "Did you find what you were looking for?" said Alice, unusual merriment in her voice.

"Ahem. Yes." Adam grunted, handing the dirty spoon to the servant who exchanged it with a clean one. "Ah, where were we?" he said, eager to move beyond the embarrassing episode.

The polite titters that greeted his emergence from beneath the table—even from the prim Lady Windmere, who did her best to keep a straight face—told Adam that something had changed. He never did find out why his name had been called, as the ladies had all become distracted. He smiled hesitantly, unsure of the source. "Aren't we a merry crew!" he said, only adding when the ladies continued grinning, "…did I miss something?"

"Only a spot with your napkin," Jane said, reaching across the table to wipe something from his nose—brown gravy, he saw when she was through. The dam burst on their hilarity and he joined in on their laughter.

"But in all seriousness," Lady Windmere continued when the group's spirits had settled, "perhaps Miss Bond will be able to send some of her men over to help with the grounds. I shall ask her when I see her."

At this, Frederica showed a livelier interest than Adam would have expected. "So it's true, then? She is returning to Bondgate?"

"Has returned," Lady Windmere confirmed. "Oh, I haven't spoken to her yet, but I received word that her retinue came back earlier today. I'm surprised you didn't see them pass through the village."

"Hmm, they must have arrived after we left," Frederica said, blushing. "We were only there a short time."

"Well, of course she simply *must* come to our little picnic, so we can welcome her back," Alice said, adding, "when she has time to see us, of course."

Lady Windmere nodded, distractedly, a little more like her old self, Adam thought. "Yes, she has so many interests to occupy her." *If only you knew,* thought Adam. "If I know Pamela, she will first want to take a turn around the bay on her yacht."

"How perfect." Frederica sat back. "The sailing should be quite clear tomorrow."

Lady Windmere smiled indulgently. Adam did not, at the time, think it odd that the Windmere sisters were suddenly so gracious towards Miss Bond. He had eyes only for Jane at the moment, and ate little of what was in front of him. Whenever the other ladies' attentions seemed directed elsewhere, he made eyes at her, hoping to convey without words the yearning that he felt for her company. In return he felt another stroke of her foot against his shin. It was the only part of him she could reach due to their relative positions, but it was enough to drive him mad with anticipation. The secret smile she wore only for him told him that was just the way she liked it.

Chapter Twenty-Four

Jane cleaned her plate, but uncharacteristically begged off dessert, and only Adam knew how little of her food had made it to her stomach. Where, they had wondered together, would be the best place to *rendezvous*, somewhere they wouldn't be caught or even suspected together? Either of their chambers was out of the question—too obvious. So too was the library. The sitting room was likely to be occupied, and anyone could just walk in on them. So where? Places of assignation were discussed and discarded. The carriage house. An inn in the village. Inside a butter-churn. None were satisfactory.

If they had been at Bondgate, Adam had observed, dozens of out-of-the-way nooks could have served, even the famous grotto "Juno" and "Jupiter" had found so pleasing. Windmere Hall was more modern, a barn of large rooms with few hiding places.

"Why?" Jane had laughed. "Were you hoping for a dungeon? Would you have me inside an iron maiden? A magician's cabinet with a secret panel?"

"A secret panel!" Adam had snapped his finger as he remembered the passage between the chapel and the kitchen. Recalling it, there was a level area, a landing where the staircase had turned. Jane knew it, of course, but remembered it as little more than a dark and dusty shaft.

"The chaplain's stair? Won't it be cramped?" she protested.

"Think of it as cosy."

"Do the stairs still creak? We shall be heard!"

"What large house doesn't make a few noises? Let them take us for mice."

"Mice, at Windmere Hall! Slander!"

"Then I shall be even quieter than one as I nibble you." She had pushed his face away, laughing, but in the end, she had come up with no better suggestion.

So Adam found himself later that evening in the empty chapel, a blanket over his arm, awaiting the young lady who infatuated him as no other ever had. Hopefully she had found—

"Candles!" she announced, entering the chapel as she held up a pair of sticks in brass holders, one of them lit already. "I went the long way around the house," she said, explaining her long absence.

Adam nodded, remembering how Alice's eyes had followed him about the grounds for weeks. It seemed, however, that she was less concerned with her middle sister's whereabouts, as Jane reported that Alice was nowhere to be seen.

"Well, better for us," Adam said, recalling—perhaps a little guiltily—how he had bought Alice's silence. He was less afraid of her revealing their secrets than of her sneering judgement. There was, however, still the unknown poisoner among them, and he watched his steps much more carefully than before. How incredible the recklessness with which he had previously conducted his affairs in the house now seemed to him! That was before he had known how high the stakes were.

Together he and Jane entered the passageway behind the tapestry and descended the stairs. In the glow of the candlelight, Jane's face looked angelic, and Adam detected a rosy eagerness that matched his own. They could have been entering a scented bower instead of an unfurnished back stairway. If it was paradise, it was because they made it so for each other. When they reached the small landing, Adam spread the blanket on the bare wood and Jane lit the second candle with the first, setting them on the stairs above. The two lovers sat on the first step above the landing in the middle of a golden circle of light outside of which nothing else existed.

Now that they were ensconced together, and the naughty excitement of hiding away had passed, a rising tide of eager anticipation took its place. After they gazed into each other's eyes until they both giggled at the solemnity of it all, their lips met, and they embraced each other. It was for this that they had hidden from prying eyes in the first place.

There was, too, a surprising timidity between them, an innocent shyness, even though they had thoroughly explored each other as masked lovers before. Hesitantly, as if there were still a danger of rejection, Adam put his hands around her waist, and she likewise put her arms around his neck and felt the expanse of his back through his jacket. As they became sure that no servant or spying relative would intrude upon the hidden landing, they became freer with their hands, stroking and petting each other as their kisses became less chaste.

Pausing, Jane looked up at Adam, her eyes twinkling in the candlelight, and pulled away from him, stretching herself.

"Don't tell me you have become cramped already," Adam said, reluctant to end the meeting so soon.

"Not by the space here, which is as cosy as you promised," Jane answered. "But something in my dress is poking me."

Adam raised an eyebrow. "Oh, is that so?"

Jane nodded. "It is."

"Well, we can't have that."

"If you helped me rid myself of it, I'd be ever so grateful." She didn't specify if she meant the intruding object or the dress itself, but Adam felt sure they understood each other.

"Why didn't you say so?" Adam said, working his fingers through the laces that held the back of her dress together. Far be it from him to allow a lady to feel discomfort when he could offer assistance.

Soon the offending garment and the layers of petticoats beneath it were removed, and Adam saw revealed the results of the arousing game Jane had played with him at dinner—the soup, gravy, and other bits of her meal that she had spooned into her bodice had left streaks of colour through the inside of her chemise and even run through a striking pair of cream-coloured drawers and down her legs. The cleavage revealed by her top shone in the candlelight with the oil from the gravy. Helping her remove her shoes, he noticed that the liquid had even pooled in the toes of her stockings, and he no longer wondered how he had ended up with a smudged nose when he had bent beneath the table at dinner.

"Better?" he inquired, taking deep delight in looking her over, almost as much as if he had filled her underthings with food himself. What a picture she made!

"A little," she said, lifting her arms to examine herself and running her hands up and down her torso, taking measure of the mess she had made. "But I think perhaps there is still a pea or a grain of rice in one of the folds inside. Do you think—"

Adam did not have to be asked twice. A fierce animal desire, like that he had experienced in the "Pleasure Dome" at Bondgate, seized him, sparked by the contrast between Jane's outward elegance and the creative way she found to tease him. He took her, already damp and slick from that dinnertime foreplay, in his arms, more passionately than before, leaning to her neck and shoulders to kiss the expanses of bare skin she had exposed. A robust kitchen aroma filled his nose. What she had hinted was true—he would enjoy this dinner much more the second time around.

Soon the stays and chemise were likewise gone and he licked greedily at the flavours marinating on her skin, caressing her supple breasts and burying his face between them, toying with her hardened nipples, inhaling the intriguing blend of scents she wore. He had never cared for peas, but every one he found he popped into his mouth and savoured as if it were a grape offered by Aphrodite herself. No more would so much as a grain disturb his princess' comfort.

All the while, Jane lay back against the stair, petting Adam's hair. A smile played across her lips as she took her own pleasure from his enjoyment. When he raised his head, his lips now smeared with some of the same sauces he had wiped so daintily from the corners of his mouth earlier, he made to take off his jacket, to join Jane in her near nakedness, but she bade him stay a moment. She lay down on the blanket on the floor and invited him to kneel between her spread legs. "A gentleman should leave his coat on," she suggested, "until after dessert." Keeping her gaze steady upon him, her cheeks flushed and her eyes smouldering as if she would burn through him, she eased down the waist of her once cream-coloured silk drawers, revealing something soft and pink, just peeking over the top. It was one of the tarts that was Windmere Hall's specialty, tucked away for who knew how long. Had she been sitting on this, letting it melt into her pussy, all through dinner, or had she added it later, before coming to join him? Its advanced state of liquefaction suggested the former.

Seeing Adam's eyes bulge in wonder and perhaps reading the question, Jane sighed and said, "I've been warming it up for you. Now eat your fill, my love."

Delicately, so as not to further destroy the still-visible roundness of the tart, pressed flat against the triangle between her thighs, Adam pulled her drawers the rest of the way down. They were thick and wet with custard and Jane's own essence. As an appetiser, he ran his tongue through the custard that coated the silk...heavenly. Jane, now only clad in streaked stockings, could hardly wait, now that her surprise had been revealed. She stroked her thighs with obvious longing, trying to preserve what was left of the tart for her love but clearly eager to at last be taken.

Adam was only too happy to oblige, wrapping his strong hands around Jane's hips and bottom and bending down to enjoy this "dessert" in full. Enough of the tart was intact that he could press his whole face into it, smearing it around both his mouth and the insides of Jane's thighs, spreading the excess onto her legs, and at last finding the little doorway to her pleasure, buried in custard and cream, with his tongue. Jane stiffened a little, arching her back and gasping quietly, confirming that he had found the spot, and he went to work.

The near silence made their lovemaking more intense, more passionate and more desperate than it had been at Bondgate, where they were free to make as much noise and as much of a mess as they cared to. Now, too, Adam was fully conscious of his partner, knew her identity and life apart from their coupling, and felt to the full the depth of his love for her, not just lust, or the dazzle and excitement that had taken hold of him at Bondgate. Jane was the only woman in the world now, and he the only man. The fact that neither he nor Jane could give enthusiastic cry to that did not make it any less true, and while he finished pleasuring her, he was overcome by a sense of joy that was, among the intrigue and uncertainty that daily stalked the house, surprising but certainly welcome.

After Adam had worked Jane to a frenzy, she invited him to lie on top of her, undoing his trousers with an urgency that replaced the cool playfulness with which she had teased him earlier. "Now" was the only word, half-whispered, half-moaned, that he could understand from her, but he agreed. Already firm while he had lapped her womanhood with his tongue, he now felt as if he had grown a third leg that threatened to rip his trousers at the seam. Freeing it, feeling the cool air upon it and the touch of Jane's greedy hands stroking it, nearly caused him to erupt. Then they were united, rocking together and surging back and forth, until finally the heat that centred on their loins and expanded outward to make his skin feel as if it were crackling in a fire became unbearable. Jane, with an unerring sense of timing, relaxed and gently pulled him out before his volcano began its flow of lava, and now it was her turn to taste him, stroking and nuzzling his manhood with her tongue and fingers, until he could contain himself no longer. She was doubly drenched.

They lay together, exhausted but happy, their churning breaths calming and their pounding heartbeats receding into the background, no longer ringing in their ears together. At last, Jane suggested they leave separately. "I'll see you in the morning," she said, kissing Adam on his nose. A serious note entered her voice. "We must tell Frederica. It may be painful for her, but it would be much more so if our affair were to be discovered."

Adam nodded, to both observations. He watched silently as Jane towelled off the excesses of their love with the blanket he had brought, then dressed. One could hardly tell anything in her attire was amiss, especially if one saw her in the shadows. "Why don't you go through the kitchen?" she suggested. "If anyone sees you, tell them you had an urge for a late snack." They smiled at the secret truth in that excuse.

After Jane left through the upper door into the chapel, Adam waited a few minutes then crept down to the panel in the kitchen. The noises beyond it told him that it was not as empty as they thought. He cracked open the panel. The first sight that came to him was of a board laden with different cakes and desserts. Someone was busy. On the other side of the kitchen, working feverishly by herself, was Molly.

In weeks prior, this would have struck Adam as an opportunity for mischief, and he was brought back to the day he stood here watching Sally and Molly until he had been "invited" to join them. But now, spent as he was, and with ardour only for Jane, he was merely curious. He would have to exit through the chapel after all. Closing the panel behind him, certain that he had not been seen, he wondered if this were part of the preparation for the *soirée* Alice was planning, for why else would Molly be so busy?

Chapter Twenty-Five

For the first time in weeks, Adam awoke with a clear head and a sense of purpose. In Jane he had found his Zerlina, and with that mystery cleared up, the others that had hagged him fell away. Not that they were unimportant, but they now seemed much smaller obstacles than they had before, and strengthened by his love, he was confident that they would soon be resolved.

In a similar light, recalling the affairs he had pursued at Windmere Hall before that discovery, he could only laugh at the foolish lad he had been, so easily distracted, hunting for satisfaction in all the wrong places. There was only one for him now, and as soon as he found her again, he would tell her so. Did he need to tell her? He had made his feelings abundantly clear the day before, but it was a new day and he had the urge to tell Jane all over again how he felt. No doubt about it, he was in a carefree mood.

Descending to the breakfast table, only belatedly did he notice how high the sun was, and observed that the dining room was empty. Not so much as a pot of coffee greeted him, and his growling stomach confirmed that it was indeed later than he was accustomed to taking his breakfast.

He was mildly piqued that he hadn't been called for the morning repast, but as yet it wasn't enough to put a wrinkle in his brow. Perhaps Jane had instructed the staff not to disturb him, allowing him a rare morning to sleep in. No matter...he had the freedom of the kitchen, and there were usually some fresh rolls or fruit available.

The emptiness of the kitchen gave him the first sense that something might be wrong, like the faint vibration at the outer edge of a spiderweb, but was he the spider in this case, sensing a disturbance that put him on alert, or was he the fly, already having stepped in the wrong place without knowing it?

The assortment of cakes and pies he had seen Molly preparing was gone. There was at least a bowl of oranges on the otherwise empty counter. Adam idly peeled one as he walked towards the family wing, hoping to find Jane. So far he had seen not a soul. Had the family gone to visit Miss Bond, perhaps, leaving him to shuffle Sir Alfred's papers? Adam would rather be alone with Jane than go to Bondgate, of course, as he no longer found Miss Bond as fascinating as he had before, but he would have been lying to himself if he didn't admit feeling left out. Still, it was rather unlike the Windmeres to not at least let him know the day's plan, and that feeling of wrongness nibbled at him, dulling his appetite.

He ate mechanically, pondering these matters, when, while rounding a corner, he collided with a body in the midst of the same distracted search. Adoration mingled with relief when he realised that it was Jane, and she, too, seemed agitated and relieved to see him. After they both finished laughing at the surprise that they had given each other, Adam asked what was going on.

"I *did* instruct Gainesborough to let you alone this morning," Jane explained, "since you've been working so hard. I thought to arrange a time at which we could together announce our intentions, and figure out how to break the news to Freddie... But when I came down for breakfast myself, I was the only one at the table! Then I went to your chamber to find you, but...well—"

"We must have passed each other," Adam concluded. "So you know nothing that might have taken the family out of the house?"

"Not that I was told of," Jane said. They headed to the parlour to either wait or decide on a course of action. It seemed too good to be true, that the house would empty out, leaving him alone with Jane again so soon, but even he could not deny that something out of the routine was happening, and that the air seemed heavy with impending, unspoken disaster.

"Perhaps Miss Bond—" Adam began, but both agreed that there was no reason for the two of them to be excluded from a yachting excursion. Adam had been invited before, after all, and he didn't think the incident at the ball would preclude Miss Bond from socialising with him again. That wasn't her style.

For that matter, it didn't seem likely that Frederica would jump at the opportunity to see Miss Bond, feeling as she did.

"She still believes her to be responsible?" For Roderick's disappearance, he meant.

Jane nodded sadly. "I haven't had much time to see her lately, but I think so. I described what I had seen at Bondgate — with a few omissions, of course — but it wasn't enough to convince her, combined with her own failure to find the track in London."

Adam gazed idly out of the window. "No wonder Frederica was in such a temper when she returned." A temper that had only lifted at intervals, and with great difficulty. Still, she had seemed recently animated by purpose.

Jane sighed. "I think she gave Roderick up for lost, after that. She put a good face on things, but beneath it yawned a chasm."

Adam nodded glumly, recalling how Frederica had thrown herself into her athletic pursuits. Was it possible that she now trained with some goal in mind? And there was the sudden interest in Pamela Bond's return home. The solution to the mystery began to stitch itself together in Adam's mind. "I wonder," he said. "Tell me, you know your sister best. Is her mind turned towards vengeance? Do you think it possible that she would attempt some manner of violence against Miss Bond?"

Jane shook her head. "I don't know. I don't want to believe it. But who knows? Roderick's disappearance has left her desperately wounded."

Adam recalled the day he had arrived at Windmere Hall, and saw frozen in his mind's eye the instant Frederica had whirled like Diana and fired an arrow at the library window from which he had watched her. That Frederica, the one he had first met, had seemed capable of murder. After that, she had moved her practice range.

Adam described the situation as he saw it. "And Miss Bond will be out on her yacht today — out in the open!"

Jane clasped her hands over her mouth. "My God, I hope you're wrong —" But the fear in her eyes told him that she thought it was possible.

"We had better hurry," Adam said, and the two of them rushed from the room.

* * * *

Please let me be wrong, Adam repeated to himself as they flew from the house towards the grounds. *Please let me be wrong.* He would rather be thought a slanderer than let Frederica, maddened by her emotions, commit murder.

The archery range now stood by the edge of the forest since Freddie had moved it from the courtyard. He and Jane had passed by it while walking the grounds just a few days ago. How different everything seemed now!

The range was empty. The targets stood forlornly, the lanes open. No one was present, but the case of bows stood open, and the quiver of arrows was missing. "We've no time to waste!" Jane cried. "She must have gone up to the cliffs!" The day was as perfect as Frederica had predicted, and the view of the bay would be quite clear.

They had crossed the archery range when a woman emerged from the trees to block their path. "Turn back, if you know what's good for you," she said. She wore a coarse shirt and breeches like a schoolboy would wear for football, and her face was familiar to Adam.

"Let us pass, Miss Prine, before you make a terrible mistake," Jane said.

"Wait," Adam said, "*this* is Miss Prine?" Frederica's wrestling instructor, short, blonde and pugnacious, was the woman introduced to him as "Ursula" at Bondgate.

"At your service, sir," Miss Prine said, giving the words a sardonic twist. "I'd stay out of this if I were you, but I won't hesitate to throw you down myself." She adopted a crouching stance. After seeing how she had handled her rival that night at Bondgate, Adam knew what she was capable of, but he was guided by an instinct higher than self-preservation. It was the obligation to save Frederica from a misjudgement that would destroy her life if she were allowed to carry it through.

"You go on," Jane said. "I can handle her."

"What!" Adam exclaimed. It was hard for him to see how his bookish lover could handle herself against a trained fighter, and he had no wish to see her put herself in harm's way. "But—"

Jane leaned in and kissed him. "I may have learned a thing or two watching Freddie practise," she said. "Don't worry about me, just head for Freddie when I've got Miss Prine distracted."

Dubiously, Adam approached the wrestling instructor as if to parley. Miss Prine stood her ground, preparing to lunge at him. "Don't take a step farther, sir."

Jane launched herself like a cannonball from behind Adam, tackling Miss Prine and bringing her to the ground like a footballer while the wrestler's attention was drawn to Adam. In an instant they were a tangled heap of grappling limbs on the grassy lawn. "Adam, run!" Jane exclaimed between grunts and cries of pain.

Against all his instincts to stay and help his outmatched paramour, Adam flew up the path to the cliff peak, trusting that Jane knew what she was doing and that any injury she sustained would be temporary. *What a woman!* he thought, and through the tangle of fear for her safety and anxiety that Frederica might already be a murderer, he felt a curious elation that such a brave young lady should choose him. What had he done to deserve such a blessing?

"That's quite far enough," an imperious voice commanded, dousing his reverie with cold water. Up the path stood a tall, redheaded woman in a jacket with a *croissard* over breeches, holding a sabre extended in the *en garde* position.

"Sonia," Adam said, recognising her as the other woman who had fought over him at the masquerade ball. "Or should I say Miss Priestley?"

"Call me Susan," she said, lowering into a defensive crouch and blocking the path. The blade she held out was no practice foil — it was a real blade with a sharp edge that gleamed in the sunlight. "It's nothing personal, you understand. The Windmeres have been very good to me. When an injustice has been done to one of them, I'll do anything in my power to set things right."

"You've got it all wrong," Adam said, desperately looking about for some way around the swordswoman. "Miss Bond didn't abduct Roderick Utley."

"Miss Frederica thinks she did," Miss Priestley answered, "and that's good enough for me. Now turn back." Her sinuously waving blade drew Adam's gaze towards it like a snake charmer's flute.

Adam backed up until he was nearly in the woods bordering the path. His choice was to head back down the path, admitting defeat, or enter the thicket of trees that bordered it, an environment in which he couldn't hope to move quickly enough to skirt around the fencing instructor. He had made a few passes with the blade as an undergraduate, but he knew he was outmatched, and without a weapon of his own besides.

As he backed into a tree his hand fell upon a loose branch that had fallen into the underbrush. It was thick and still green with sap, and might serve as a club if he could get into position. Hopelessly outmatched he might be, but could he do less than his darling Jane, who had thrown herself into combat for the sake of her sister's soul? He had no choice. Buoyed by her love, he hefted the fallen limb and lunged towards Miss Priestley with a cry that came out more desperate than intimidating.

No matter...Miss Priestley stepped back, parrying his crude lunge with her sword. It nearly struck the stick from his hand, but he maintained his grip and kept swinging. At his first parry of a stroke from his opponent, the branch was cut in half. Now he was on the defensive again. His attack had been brief indeed, and as he leapt back and back again in the face of the whirling blade, he tripped on his own feet or against a tree root and fell backward. Susan Priestley stood over him, a blur except for the brilliant clarity of the sword point only inches away from his face. He panted, his heart pounding. Would she kill him? Her loyalty to the Windmeres suggested she might.

Thud! Suddenly, Miss Priestley's iron grip on the sword loosened and the weapon tumbled from her hand. She went slack and collapsed forward. Behind her stood Jane, breathing hard and with wild eyes, another thick branch in her hands.

Adam pushed the unconscious Miss Priestley off of him and stood. Jane's clothes were torn and her face and chest covered with mud. Her hair had been pulled from its ties and stood wildly in all directions, but she was all in one piece. "Told you," she panted. "Now, hurry."

Chapter Twenty-Six

At the peak of the cliffs stood a cloaked figure, perched on the edge of the rock overlooking the bay. "Wait!" called Adam. The bow and arrow were visible in her hands — she was only awaiting her target to come into sight to let loose a volley. Perhaps Adam was disoriented by the ordeal of fighting against both Miss Prine and Miss Priestley, but he realised he was closer to the hooded figure than he thought, as she was a good deal shorter than Freddie Windmere. The impression was confirmed when she turned and showed her flashing eyes, framed in her pale face by light blonde hair.

"Alice!" Jane exclaimed, hurrying up the incline behind Adam.

It was indeed the youngest daughter of Lady Windmere. "Don't try to stop me, sister," she said defiantly, turning back towards her view of the bay. "Miss Bond has much to answer for. If Frederica is too weak to take her revenge, it falls upon me to do it for her."

"Miss Bond is innocent!" Adam protested, gasping for breath. He wondered if he had the strength to overpower the armed girl. The nocked arrow and the fury in her expression made a convincing deterrent.

"Innocent?" Alice scoffed. "I think you of all people should know better than that. It's fitting, isn't it? Aboard the *Cupid*, Pamela Bond shall be pierced through the heart."

"But both Adam and I have thoroughly investigated Bondgate," Jane protested. "Mr Utley is nowhere to be found! Miss Bond may have her secrets, but this is not one of them!"

Alice curled her lip and looked at Adam and Jane, awareness of their relationship dawning. She accepted the realisation coolly. "You always were the trusting kind, Jane. But I didn't expect a man of the world like Mr Blythewood to be so easily taken in."

"It's true," Adam said, catching his breath. "Roderick went to Bondgate to complete his research. Where he went afterwards, I don't know, but Miss Bond had nothing to do with it!"

"Nothing? Even as she has claimed that Mr Utley must have perished in the surf? A convenient ruse!" Alice watched the yacht through a spyglass with the bow tucked under her arm. "See, even now she is enjoying a liaison aboard the *Cupid*, probably laughing at poor Freddie's misfortune while she sports with Roderick!"

"No!" Jane said. "Think what you like about Miss Bond, but Mr Utley was a gentleman! He would never do something like that to Freddie!"

"See for yourself." Alice held out the spyglass.

"I see Miss Bond coming on deck," Jane said. "But aside from her crew, she is alone... No, wait. Someone is coming out of the forecastle. No—it cannot be!"

"Did I not tell you so? Roderick Utley is under her power. He will do whatever she commands. Such is the power she holds over men."

Jane appeared shaken. She lowered the spyglass, nearly letting it drop from her fingers. "Nay, Alice. Her companion is *not* Mr Utley."

Alice grabbed the spyglass impatiently. "What nonsense is this—who else could it be?" As she gazed through it, her pale face reddened. "Mother?"

Unable to make out the scene on the yacht in any detail without magnification, Adam waited until Alice set aside the spyglass. Taking it up himself, he could clearly see the two women leaning on the aft rail of the yacht's deck, taking in the view, unaware that they themselves were being watched. He failed to see what was so striking about the sight. He knew that Miss Bond and Lady Windmere were friends, and he wondered that Alice and Jane should be so shocked by it. As he watched, the two ladies appeared to be deep in conversation. Their hands met on the railing they shared, and clasped. They embraced one another...their lips met, not the polite greeting kiss of two friends, but continuously, rapturously, like lovers. Adam was stunned—so this was the secret of their relationship!

"So you see," he said, conscious of the bow and arrows Alice still held, "there is no reason to suspect Miss Bond of perfidy in Mr Utley's disappearance."

Alice shook with rage. "Be that as it may, it is disgusting! How could she? With our mother—"

"Calm yourself, Alice," Jane said, putting her arms around her mortified sister. "Father has been passed these four years. If Mother is lonely, and Miss Bond makes her happy, who are we to take offence?"

"It could be nothing more than a dalliance between two curious people, after all," suggested Adam.

Alice shook her head, wrestling with a truth she had evidently long put out of her mind. "No, we should have realised this was the case," she said. "The three of us chose to be wilfully blind, but it is clear that Mother and Miss Bond have been more than friends for some time. But for her to keep this from us — her own children!" She burst into sobs, leaning against her sister's shoulder.

Adam had nothing to add. This was between Jane and Alice. Privately, he thought it a bit rich for Alice to take umbrage at this news after making it clear how little she thought of conventional morality, but it was of course a different matter when it applied to a close family member, let alone one's parent. She would get over the shock, and come to accept that love could blossom in the most unlikely places, between partners who to the outside world seemed mismatched or against the grain of nature.

Jane eased the bow away from Alice, whose thoughts of vengeance seemed to have evaporated. At last, her spleen vented and her tears drained, Alice dried her eyes and said, "But what are we to do? If Miss Bond had naught to do with Mr Utley's disappearance, then we are back to knowing nothing. It is hopeless!"

"Perhaps not," said Jane. "Where is Freddie now? We expected to find her up here, but instead it was you."

"This seemed like the opportune moment," Alice confessed. "I knew that Miss Bond had a rendezvous planned with her lover, and I knew that Freddie would never take action against her, no matter how convinced she was of Miss Bond's guilt. All that training," she sighed, "but Freddie never had a heart for violence."

A defect obviously not shared by Alice, thought Adam.

"Perhaps not to strike an enemy," Jane said. "She has swallowed far too much grief and kept it all within herself. I fear for what she might do if it is never let out."

"I too," said Alice. "I had hoped to secure her happiness at the price of my own, but I see that I was wrong in my assumptions."

"But the question remains. Where is Frederica, if not here?"

"I sent Freddie to the village to shop with Molly to take her mind off her troubles and keep her busy," Alice explained. "The picnic we told Mother about was more than just a cover story. I hoped that it would distract Freddie while I prepared vengeance on her behalf."

"Hmm, well, I suppose she can do no harm to herself there," Jane allowed. "Perhaps we should go down to join them. We shall have to tell her what we have learned about Mother sooner or later...if only to convince her of Miss Bond's having nothing to do with Roderick."

"I suppose you are right," Alice said. "In the meantime, I trust Molly to keep her occupied. She is a simple girl, but fond of Freddie."

Adam snorted involuntarily, then excused himself. "I do not mean to speak out of turn, but are you sure we are referring to the same Molly? In my opinion, she is not simple at all...but perhaps I have seen a side of her she does not share with the family."

"I have no doubt you have seen many sides of the help," Alice said, her smirk returning, but she composed herself. "Begging your pardon, Jane." The middle sister was blushing almost as much as Adam.

"No," Adam said haltingly, "it is true, and I can only hope for the chance to outgrow the reputation I have earned for myself. I owe you the truth, Jane, and if you want to hear it, I shall relay it to you — all of it — and let you decide my fate."

Jane squeezed his hand in reply, indicating that it could wait. Frederica still seemed uppermost in her mind. "What did you mean, though? Do you not trust Molly?"

Adam thought about it. He had only known her as the lusty and sarcastic wench he had found so desirable at first, but it was obvious that the family did not know that Molly. Of course, they wouldn't. Like all the other servants, she was meek and deferential in their presence, perhaps more so than the long-time help that Lady Windmere thought so ungovernable. He had not thought her particularly malicious, however.

But perhaps he was wrong. He recalled the first time he had seen her, lording it over the villagers on the day of the festival, humiliating the poor "goat" locked into the stocks. He had a sudden thought, recalling the sight of Molly in the kitchen late the night before, preparing a wagonload of cakes and pies, and Sally's words to her echoed in his memory. "*I know you too well... Your sense of humour is about as delicate as Mr Punch's.*"

Then there were the strange things that had been happening to him since he had finally broken off his liaisons with her — the note that had lured him out onto the road the night he was attacked, the poison in his tea, the incriminating botany book placed in Marie's room. A person in the Windmere household could have easily had access to all of those things.

Adam began to wonder if it had even been Sally who was skimming off the kitchen budget. What if Molly had schemed to push her out of her position to take her place? "When Sally's embezzlement was discovered," he asked, "how did it come to light?"

Both women thought. "I remember Molly asked to speak to Mother privately," Alice said. "She was carrying the ledger, and seemed to be confused about the totals not adding up." The foreboding Adam felt began to show itself in Alice's face as well.

"And was Sally allowed to speak in her own defence before she was sacked?"

"Certainly not!" Alice said. "Mother was thrilled to have the chance to be as decisive as Miss Bond! It was the very same day that Molly was our new head cook."

Adam nodded. "I suspect Molly knew exactly what she was doing to arrange that change of staff."

Jane was not quite convinced. "That Molly is ambitious, I can believe, and perhaps even a bit underhanded, but would she really seek to cause mischief with Freddie? What on earth for?"

"I'm not sure," Adam said, but a chill crept down his spine. "I have my suspicions about the rider who attacked me on the road and the sickness that overtook me in the village. I believe that herb we found the other day, Jane, was introduced to my tea deliberately. Those misfortunes befell me only after I ceased my, ahem, friendship with Molly. Furthermore, when I first met her, she claimed to have a gentleman lover whom no one had seen. What if, either by herself or with assistance, Molly had been able to make it look as if Roderick had left the Hall, abandoning Freddie, while actually keeping him to herself?"

Alice scoffed. "I think you've been reading one of Jane's novels! Roderick, held prisoner by the kitchen wench? Why, that's as ridiculous as — as — "

"As ridiculous as a plot to assassinate your sister's rival with a bow and arrow?" Adam said. There seemed to be nothing outside the realm of possibility now. "You yourself suspected that he was a captive of Pamela Bond. Perhaps it was not his fate, but the agent of it, in which you were mistaken."

"But Miss Bond is a woman of means!" Jane protested. "How would it be possible for Molly to achieve such a thing?"

"I don't know. But the womenfolk of the village are stronger than we give them credit for. I was nearly made their plaything once myself, and Molly has a way of getting what she wants. Maybe she had help. But if she drugged him the same way I was drugged, she very well could have got him out of the house through stealth and cunning."

Jane, still sounding doubtful, asked, "Do you really think she's capable of it?"

Adam confirmed that he did. "As absurd as it sounds, I think we must admit the possibility that Molly sees Frederica as a rival whom she would love nothing more than to humiliate."

"A rival?" said Alice. "In what possible way could they be rivals? She's a kitchen wench, and Freddie is a lady!"

"Molly — at least in private — has a high opinion of herself. It is clear from Roderick Utley's diary that he knew her. Used to her importance in the village, she could have found it unbearable to lose Roderick's attention — however fleeting it had been — to her better. I don't think it's enough for her to win Roderick and keep him for herself. She won't be fully satisfied until Freddie knows she's been beaten, and Molly can gloat over her victory." The more he laid out his reasoning, the more convinced he became.

"And Freddie is with her now!" Alice exclaimed. "What have I done?"

"We must find out one way or the other," Jane said. "There's another set of stairs down to the village just up here," she pointed out.

"Wait!" Alice said. "We might need help."

* * * *

"You tied them up?" Adam said, impressed all over again at Jane's resourcefulness in the face of danger.

"And a right strong job she did, indeed," Susan Priestley said, rubbing her chafed wrists now that Alice had untied her and Miss Prine and apprised them of the situation.

"I am sorry," Jane said loftily as the five of them descended the steps cut into the cliff face, "but I'm afraid you left me little choice in the matter."

"No hard feelings," said Samantha Prine. "You were doing what you thought was right."

"We all were," Jane said, cementing a reconciliation with her wayward sister. All were on the same team now, Miss Bond forgotten, and for the moment they took Adam's concern for Frederica's safety seriously. But he had been the first to admit that it was all speculation — he had so far accused Marie and Frederica of crimes they had not committed, so his deductive skills were not to be relied upon without external support — and no more rash talk of murder or vengeance would be bruited, not until some proof was found.

The beach was occupied when they reached sea level. Few of the villagers could resist the opportunity to take advantage of the clear weather, if only in the form of fishermen repairing their nets and washerwomen laundering clothes in the runoff from the streams that drained into the bay. A few curious onlookers took note of the dishevelled gentlefolk coming down from the manor without so much as a carriage or valet, but there was no change in the daily routine.

Likewise, the pathways of the village were strewn with booths for the market day, with peddlers hawking their wares of fish, flowers and fresh fruit to anyone who came within earshot. But it took no time at all to see that Frederica and Molly were nowhere to be found. That did not surprise Adam. It was the stocks that occupied the other end of the town square he had in mind, and he directed his party thence. If Molly had kidnapped Roderick, then what further humiliation could she inflict on Frederica than to trap her in those stocks, to expose her to the catcalls and abuse of the crowd, abuse that Molly herself seemed to be an expert at stirring up? Adam could imagine the cruel delight Molly would take in such a coup.

To his mingled relief and frustration, the stocks stood empty. There were no puddles of custard or fragmented crusts to indicate that it had seen any use that day. "What now?" Adam asked himself. Then he spied a familiar face — Eli Johnson, the garrulous labourer he had met during his last visit to the village, sat on a barrel idly smoking a pipe. The older man hailed Adam as soon as they recognised one another.

"G'day, sir!" Johnson said. "Ye look a mite worse for wear, if ye don't mind me sayin' so, sir." The lines around his eyes crinkled with merriment.

"Yes." Adam chuckled, aware of how he and his feminine companions must look at the moment. "I say, do you think you could give me a bit of guidance? I'm trying to find red-haired Molly."

"Molly McQuirt?" Eli said in surprise. "Is she needed at the manor? 'Tis an awfully big party sent just to fetch her, innit?"

"No, 'tis more of a personal matter," Adam evaded. McQuirt, the old fisherman had called her. Adam didn't think he had heard Molly's family name before, but there was something familiar about it.

"We were hoping to surprise her," Jane offered.

"Surprise 'er! Well, Miss, I wager you'll succeed at that," Eli said, looking the group over again.

While Eli Johnson scratched his chin thoughtfully, another voice spoke up. "I know where she is." It was a young, handsome woman who had stepped up behind them; Adam thought she seemed familiar, but couldn't quite place her. "Are you going to kill her?" She pointed at the sword Miss Priestley still carried.

Eli coughed. "Ahem, Mr Blythewood, Hazel Hathaway...my niece."

Suddenly Adam recognised the maiden's dark eyes. She was the girl Adam had seen in the stocks on the festival day! She looked different, of course, clean and standing up straight. Adam bowed. The other ladies of his party nodded. "No, of course we're not going to hurt her," he hastened to explain.

"Hmm. Too bad," Hazel said. "I *might* have taken you to 'er, but I don't know…"

"Now, Hazel," Eli said, "I'm sure if Mr Blythewood wants to see her, he's got a reason, an' besides we've got a duty to help the manor people…"

"Quite right," said Jane, stepping forth. Beneath the layer of filth that coated her, she cut a ladylike figure. "It's not for Mr Blythewood that we seek Molly. It's for our sister, Miss Frederica. Please, Miss Hathaway. Can you help us?"

Hazel Hathaway seemed to be affected by being addressed as a lady, and Adam knew she could have no love for Molly. "Well, seeing as how you came to my defence before," she said, a reference that produced quizzical looks from Jane and Alice, "I suppose I can be of help. Right this way, all of you… Are you sure you're not going to kill her?"

Chapter Twenty-Seven

"Are you sure Miss McQuirt lives here?" Adam said after Hazel had led them out of the village and back up the hill into the woods. Again, the name McQuirt nagged at Adam's memory. Where had he seen it before? He had a suspicion that they were being led on a wild-goose chase.

"I coulda showed ye where Molly *lives*," their guide said, "but I thought ye wanted me to take ye where Molly *is*. This is her secret place — not many people know where it is, except the boys she takes here, like she took my Archie."

"Archie?"

Hazel's cheeks coloured and she assumed a girlish demeanour as she recalled, "Aye, the apprentice carpenter in the village. He was me love, or so I thought. We was set to be married. Then Miss Molly McQuirt gets her hooks into him, puffs him up an' convinces him his talents are wasted here, an' off he heads to the City. One letter I got from him, sayin' he'd found a new love, an' then nothing more. Maybe he did find someone else…but I still think Molly knows where he is."

"And Molly repaid your suspicions by making you the goat?" Adam said. The scene he had witnessed in the town square was starting to make sense.

"A great laugh she thought it was, but she still wouldn't tell me anything. I hate her, I do," Hazel expressed with great vehemence.

The group stepped up their pace through the tangled roots of the forest floor as they each individually faced their fears for poor Frederica.

"And to think, I put Freddie into Molly's hands!" Alice said ruefully.

"It's not your fault," Jane reassured her. "We all trusted her. Lord! When I think of how many of her tarts I ate, it makes me sick! I quite stuffed myself on them!"

"We all did," Alice agreed. Adam said nothing, ashamed that he, too, had gorged himself to satiation with Molly in a very different way.

Hazel hushed their chatter. She had stopped at the top of a ridge overlooking a small, run-down cottage, apparently an old wood-cutter's homestead. The overgrown weeds and overhanging tree branches hid the dilapidated structure, and it was obvious to Adam that the place could remain unknown indefinitely, off any of the beaten paths. It was an unwelcoming love-nest, but a private one. Only a puff of smoke from the stone chimney gave an indication of life.

"We must be close to Windmere Hall now," Jane said, observing how far they had come back up the slope.

"The back side of your grounds are not that far," Hazel said. "Just over the other side of this rise. I saw Molly with Miss Frederica earlier, in the village... I'd bet anything she's brought her here now."

"All this time and I never knew this was near us," Alice whispered, a surprising admission from one who always seemed to know everyone's business. She wrung her hands. "By God, if she's done anything to hurt Freddie—" Miss Priestley put her hand on Alice's shoulder, gripping the hilt of her sword with the other. She and Miss Prine would stand together with the Windmeres.

"What do you think?" Adam said quietly. "A knock on the door, or—?" He was out of his depths, and tactics were not his strong suit. He liked to say that he was a lover, not a fighter...now he would be both.

Jane took charge. "Miss Priestley, watch the front door, over there. Alice, see if there is a back door. Miss Prine, you come with the rest of us. We'll assume the best but prepare for the worst." They nodded and took up their separate positions.

Adam insisted on leading the party, minus Alice and Miss Priestley, to the front of the cabin, if only to be the first in harm's way, if it came to that. Once all was in readiness, he knocked as if they happened to be in the neighbourhood and this were just an ordinary visit. From within they heard voices in quiet conversation.

After a moment of suspended breath in which all of them entertained their own private apprehensions, the door opened. Molly appeared surprised to see them, but not unpleasantly so. "Mr Blythewood! How gracious of you to pay us a visit! I suppose I have Miss Hathaway to thank for showin' you out to me summer house!" She smiled at her own witticism, but the look she shot at Hazel gave the only hint that this was an unforeseen complication.

"I'm looking for Miss Windmere," Adam said, brushing aside any hint of coyness. "Is she here?"

Molly opened the door wider and invited Adam to see for himself. The interior of the little cabin was plain, but every horizontal surface was laden with Molly's famous tarts, as well as a variety of pies, cakes and other sweets. Adam was put in mind of the famous witch's hut visited by Hansel and Gretel. The little woodstove whose chimney had been visible from the outside flamed away, a tea kettle sitting on top. Seated at a deal table was Frederica Windmere herself, who appeared almost as surprised as Molly to see Adam and the rest of them.

She set down the teacup she had been drinking from and stood, saying, "Mr Blythewood! I assure you I am not in need of watching over!" Then she saw the rest of the party and became perplexed. "Jane—Miss Prine? What have you been doing? Is something wrong?" More than their arrival at this out-of-the-way place, she seemed struck by the condition of her sister's clothing, uncharacteristic as its implication of arduous physical activity was to her. Of Hazel Hathaway she asked, "Who is this?"

Jane approached and embraced her sister. "Thank God! Are you all right? Did Molly force you to come with her?"

Freddie laughed uncertainly. "No, of course not! What on Earth are you talking about? Molly invited me to sample some of her new creations to add to the menu at the manor, and to see this most picturesque cabin her great-great-grandfather built—did I get that right, Molly?"

"Great-great-*great*-grandfather, in fact," Molly said with good humour. "This is where I think up all me recipes. It's nice and private." Again, she seemed to lean on the final word while glaring at Miss Hathaway, who narrowed her eyes in barely suppressed fury.

Adam looked around. It was hardly a full kitchen, just the little woodstove, not a place one could cook more than a tray of scones, but the array of desserts Molly had brought here—surely the same ones he had seen her preparing the night before—did speak of Molly's personal touch. There was a rear door, and next to it a small window with square glass panes. Looking through it, towards the rise Hazel Hathaway had pointed out, Adam suspected it was within an arrow's reach of the cultivated square of flowers and herbs he and Jane had found earlier.

Suddenly he whirled and stared at the tea sitting on the table, next to a half-eaten tart of the kind he knew so well. Unable to fight his suspicions, he blurted out, "Miss Windmere, don't drink any more of that tea!" It, or the tart, could be poisoned.

Now it was Molly's turn to laugh. "Whatever do you think of me, Mr Blythewood? I thought we were— ahem—friends. What have I done to so earn your distrust?" She approached him and began to put her arm around him as she had done so often before. It was a gesture of familiarity he had once welcomed, but now he recoiled as if from a snake. He had his Jane, his Zerlina, and no more did he find Molly or any of the others tempting.

"I don't know what to think," Adam said, brushing her aside. Remembering the reason for his suspicion in the first place, he demanded, "Where is Roderick Utley?"

Frederica gasped and coloured at the mention of her missing paramour's name. Molly grew pale and silent as if to balance out their reactions, but she quickly recovered her poise and laughed off the question. "How should I know?"

Miss Prine, who had been chomping at the bit to get involved, exploded, "Come now, this is no way to get information! Let me have a moment with her — " Molly recoiled from the intimidating wrestler until Adam held up his hand to wait a moment.

Frederica approached Molly, a hurt expression on her face. "Molly, what do they mean?"

Molly laughed again, edging backward towards the little door. "It's her, Miss Freddie!" she said, pointing to Hazel. "Her beau took off on her, an' she blames me! It's her that's been filling Mr Blythewood's ears with lies about me!"

Hazel looked ready to scratch Molly's eyes out, held back only by Jane and Miss Prine. "I know you did something to drive me Archie away! He disappeared, just like Mr Utley, an' you know more about it than you're saying!"

Molly glared at Hazel, shooting invisible daggers at her. "Well, if you can't hold on to your man, that's got nothing to do with me," she said acidly. "An' as for Mr Blythewood, he can't accept that I don't want to see him anymore, an' his jealousy's driven him mad! Otherwise he wouldn't be so receiving-like to your slander!"

Once that accusation would have ruffled Adam, but he now realised that it reflected the mentality of his accuser far more than it did his own, and that indeed it was Molly who had made the attempt on his life a few days earlier, not Marie. It was as if the scales had fallen from his eyes and he saw Molly for who she was. He held no anger for her, only pity that she had made such a small thing of the life and the talents she had. It was as good as a confession coming from her.

Again, Frederica approached her, beseeching her as she would a close friend — a friend, who, by the look on Frederica's face, had suddenly become untrustworthy. "Molly, if you know something about Roderick, you have to tell me!" She was near tears, clutching at Molly's skirt as if by refusing to let her go she could force her to tell the truth.

Molly's once-pretty face was disfigured by a vicious sneer. All at once her hatred of Frederica became visible and she spat out, "How could I know anything about Mr Utley? Isn't he the beloved of the great Freddie Windmere? How could anyone else stand up compared to her? Why, Roddy would barely look at a poor kitchen wench when he could have you, isn't that right? Well, let me tell you, missy, I got something you'll never have, and Roddy wanted it, but when I wouldn't tell him the secret of me family tart recipe, he thought he could just drop ol' Molly! Well, I made sure to hold his interest, that's all! Why shouldn't he pick me? I may not live in a bloody mansion, but my family's as old as yours 'round here!" She stuck her hands on her hips defiantly. Frederica crumpled in desperation.

"That's right!" Adam interjected, seizing on the clew that had helped him put the puzzle together. "Nahum McQuirt was your ancestor, wasn't he? The captain of the *Mosca*?"

"Oh, you've figured it out, have you?" Molly said. "I guess Sally was wrong about you. There is more to you than that enormous tallywacker!" She leered at Jane, who clutched Adam more tightly. "'As he given you a taste of it yet, luv? It's a sensation, I'll tell you!"

"Enough!" Adam said, his face crimson. "We were talking about Captain McQuirt. It was he that brought back Sir Ambrose Windmere's haul from the South Pacific, wasn't it? And when Sir Ambrose disgraced himself with the 'Feast of Ambrose,' it was Captain McQuirt who assisted him, not Seneca Bond."

"Aye, that's right! And old Cap took the blame while Sir Ambrose whisked off to London an' rebuilt his fortune! The McQuirt name wasn't worth a spit after that, an' Nahum was just a broken-down degenerate!"

"And that's why Captain McQuirt made one last run to the South Pacific, to prove that he wasn't mad! And he almost made it back with the treasure intact—"

"Only he ran aground just off the cliffs," Molly agreed. "He had redemption in his grasp, only for it to be taken from him, just like that." It had happened centuries ago, before any of them were alive, but Adam sensed that Molly identified with the old captain, had probably heard his story many times growing up, passed as it was down the line, the resentment behind it growing and festering with each generation. How else could one so young hold on to such an old hatred?

"Redemption is not outside your grasp, Molly," Frederica said. She had dried her tears and grasped Molly's hand with sincerity. "Tell us what happened to Roderick. I promise to be forgiving."

It almost worked. Molly appeared to calm down. She looked from one stunned face to another. Was she looking for compassion, or understanding, or perhaps vindication, proof that she had been right all along? Pulling her hand away from Freddie's, she said, "Oh, you'll be forgiving! Well, I ain't pleaded guilty to nothing, an' I ain't about to! You can take your forgiveness an' shove it up yer arse!"

In a single quick motion Molly found one of the thick tarts resting on the tea table and thrust it into Frederica Windmere's face. The dessert exploded in a spray of cream and custard, running down Freddie's swanlike neck and settling like a snowdrift on her bodice. Surprised and blinded, Freddie staggered backward, where Miss Prine barely caught her before she fell to the floor. In the confusion, Molly made to escape, but Hazel Hathaway was too quick and blocked her way. She stood before the door, refusing to budge. "Get out of the way, Hazel," Molly said.

"I've waited a long time for this," Hazel said, picking up her own pie. *Splat!* She hurled it at Molly, striking her in the face and splattering her chest, the orange custard a shell bursting across the blue sky of Molly's cotton dress. Molly pushed Hazel away, her bosom heaving with the shock and the frantic panic of a cornered animal. She wiped the custard from her eyes quickly, only to be surprised again—Frederica, who had cleared her own eyes, turned the kitchen wench to face her and thrust another pie into her face. A spill of bright yellow lemon joined the orange. Molly had outdone herself coming up with bright colours for her desserts, and now she would wear them, one after another.

There was nowhere for her to run, and far too many women in the room who had their own grudge to settle with her, or who simply couldn't resist the opportunity to pile on. One after another, they pelted Molly with the abundant pies and tarts that had filled the room. She tried to fight back, splattering her attackers in a like manner, but they outnumbered her, ganging up against her, pushing tarts into her face, her chest, her bottom, weighing down her skirts with thick custard, dumping bowls of trifle over her head, clotting her luxurious red hair until it was a lank, colourless mop, plastering her until she resembled a statue moulded in aspic. She could do little to stem their onslaught and was soon unrecognisable beneath a multi-coloured coating of runny cream and other bits of dessert. The other women weren't in much better condition. Hazel Hathaway, who had the most to repay her for, had taken special delight in rubbing Molly's face in whatever messy food she could find, hardly flinching as she was caught in the crossfire herself.

Once started, the band of furies could hardly stop themselves. Whether it was Hazel or Frederica who made the first rip in Molly's clothes, Adam, watching from the rear, could not be sure, but the sound of tearing fabric seemed to drive all of them into a frenzy, and it was followed by more. First the bodice of her dress then the skirts were ripped away, revealing those pink charms which became pinker yet when smeared all over again with the tarts that remained. Molly howled with indignation but could no sooner push one of her tormentors away than another would grab hold of her and she was punished with more of the fast-melting, runny desserts.

"Stop! Stop!" Adam cried. While such a spectacle was hardly uninteresting to him, he felt that the key point had gone missing. "We still don't know where Roderick Utley is!"

Molly, coated head to foot and now gripped in the strong hands of Miss Prine and Miss Priestley, laughed. "An' now you'll never know, will you, luv? So much for your vaunted forgiveness, Miss Frederica!"

There was a brief pause during which the only sound audible was the heavy breathing of the ladies after their exertion...and, somewhere in the room, a slow *drip, drip, drip...*

"D'ye hear that?" Hazel said, the first to acknowledge the sound.

"It's coming from over here," Jane said, pointing to a corner of the room.

It was clear, now that the floor was ankle-deep in melted custard, that the old cabin wasn't built on entirely level ground. The spilled liquid was draining into that corner Jane pointed out and disappearing through a crack or hole.

"There's a trapdoor!" Adam exclaimed, realising that there was a partial outline made visible by the drainage. Pulling back the corner of a rug that covered it, Adam revealed the complete outline and a ring set into the planks. Molly squirmed in the tight grip of her captors, but said nothing.

Adam pulled on the ring and found that the trapdoor opened easily. More slop drained quickly into the hole. Through the black square he saw a crude wooden ladder and the walls of a root cellar, and he smelled something yeasty and moist. "A light!" he cried, for he could also hear muffled sounds of movement. Jane handed him a candle lit from the stove, and Adam climbed the ladder down as briskly as the slippery rungs would allow.

The light revealed to Adam a chamber of horrors. It had once been a root cellar, with earthen walls shored up by beams, but it was now the prison cell of a forlorn-looking man, stripped down to rags and tied to a chair. He was nearly as covered with old food as Molly herself. She had apparently taken him prisoner to satisfy her lusts in a manner with which Adam was all too familiar. A cloth gag filled the prisoner's mouth.

Now that he stood before him, Adam could hear his muffled cries for help.

Setting the candle down, Adam rushed to the man's assistance, removing the gag and setting to work on the ropes that bound him. "Miss Windmere, come down if you please," Adam said with considerable self-satisfaction.

She did so, cautiously, and with mounting horror once the situation was clear to her. "Miss Windmere, may I present to you Mr Roderick Utley!"

The freed prisoner and Frederica both at the same time reacted with surprise. "Pardon?" said the man in a raspy voice. Frederica shook her head in frustration. "That's not my Roderick!" She nearly swooned but Adam let go of the prisoner to support her. At the same time, Hazel Hathaway rushed down the ladder, crying, "Archie? Is it really you?"

It was. Hazel and her beau embraced, reunited, their ecstasy at being rejoined only serving to heighten Frederica's misery and Adam's consternation. How could it be so? He had solved the mystery — or so he thought! Now he was no closer to helping Miss Windmere than he had been before!

"Oh, uh, the other one's in there," Archie said sheepishly when he could free himself from Hazel's passionate embrace, pointing to a dark wooden bin in the corner, hidden in the shadows. Adam's candle illuminated the area once it was brought nearer. It was a box of painted wooden planks, something like a grain bin, but spacious enough to hold a large dog, or a very small horse, or —

"Roderick!" Frederica gasped, nearly clawing at the box with her bare hands now that hope had been rekindled.

"Oh, it were dreadful, it were," Adam heard Archie saying to Hazel as he searched for the clasp that would open the wooden cell, "almost every night she made me wallow in slop like a pig before makin' me, well..."

Finally the small gate was open. A gush of something like pudding flowed out, covering Adam's shoes. Already filthy, he stepped in farther to see if he could make out the prisoner. Indeed there was a man, about his size, covered head to toe in brown muck, such that at first only his eyes were visible. He too was gagged, and tied by the wrists to the top beam of the bin. He must have been standing waist-deep in the stuff at all times. Was there no limit to Molly's perversion?

"Roderick!" Frederica cried with mingled relief and horror. "What has she done to you?" She rushed past Adam to embrace her long-lost lover, ignoring the gunge that covered him.

"Help me get him down," Adam said, doing his best to untie the slippery ropes. The knots were much firmer than those that had held Archie in place. Finally, frustrated, he cried, "Send down a knife!" The next thing he knew he held Miss Priestley's sword in hand. He shrugged. It would have to do. Eventually, Roderick Utley—for indeed it was he—was freed, and after determining that no one else was being held prisoner in the cellar, Adam sent the two freed men and their lovers up the ladder, following them with one last look behind him, and a shudder that such a fate had been intended for him as well.

"Aye," Molly said when challenged, "that was my idear, but then I got a better one. I was going to trap Miss Frederica an' keep her down there, too. I would've been doing you a favour, Miss, reuniting you with your Mr Roderick an' all."

"She's mad," said Miss Priestley, who had come in while Adam was in the cellar and been quickly brought up to speed. Cleaning the blade of her sword, she furrowed her brow as if she no longer wanted to be in the same room with Molly.

"She's not mad," Hazel said. "Just very, very selfish. An' I think I've an idea what to do with her, begging your permission, miss."

"I don't care what you do with her. I never want to see her again," Frederica said. Her eyes were only on Roderick, to whom she was whispering tender words of love while she cleaned him up.

The two men had been completely stripped. Searching the cabin, Jane and Adam found the clothes they had been wearing when they were abducted, hidden along with Mr Utley's luggage that Molly had spirited out of the house. Jane also found a heavy grey coat that she gave to Miss Priestley to help Molly cover herself, as her clothes had been shredded until she wore little more than tatters.

Distracted by helping Roderick, Adam recognised the archaic peacoat a second too late. "Wait!" he cried, but Molly had thrust her hand into the deep pocket and pulled out an antique pistol. Adam knew it at once as the weapon that had been fired at him by his attacker — Molly herself.

"Get back!" she exclaimed, her eyes wild, having taken her captors utterly by surprise. Everyone froze. It was a fraught moment. The old pistol probably had only one shot — if it were even loaded — but Molly was desperate and it was no time to take chances. "That's right," she said, a sly smile forming on her face. She edged backward, finding the knob of the little back door by feel, not breaking eye contact for a second.

Adam feared that she might shoot Frederica or Hazel as a parting blow, but she kept her head. "Ta ta, Mr Blythewood!" she laughed when only her head and the barrel of the pistol were still in the room, the rest of her body having preceded them through the door. "It's been a lark, but here's where Seneca's ghost gets another chance to ride again!" She slammed the door behind her.

It had all happened so fast that it was only after Molly had escaped that Adam remembered their original plan.

"Alice—" Jane suddenly said, having reached the same conclusion. It was as if a spell had broken, and Adam, Jane, Miss Prine, and Miss Priestley rushed to the door to look, leaving the pairs of reunited lovers to bring up the rear. After much squabbling, they finally went through the door in single file. Molly was gone, but there was no sign of Alice, either.

They turned their heads from side to side, climbing up the hill, for surely that was the direction they had gone. Just as Adam reached the top he heard barking in the distance, rapidly approaching, followed closely by a woman screaming. He could just see the shadows of the Hall's undisciplined hounds, chasing a figure in a heavy grey peacoat. She fired once, wildly, the report echoing through the wood, but doing little to slow down the pursuing dogs.

"Wait! Wait!" Molly cried, in desperation climbing a tree to escape their jaws. "Why must everything happen to me?" The dogs circled, continuing to bark at their quarry, scratching at the tree trunk in eagerness to bring her down.

Over the hill sauntered Alice, pleased with herself, the mistress of the hounds. To Adam's and Jane's disbelieving expressions, she said lightly, "Well, perhaps I could have reigned them in myself sooner... You must permit me my little jests, sister."

Once they were confident that Molly was disarmed and she was again taken into custody, with Hazel, Archie, Miss Prine and Miss Priestley escorting her back to the village to face justice, Adam, Roderick and the Windmere sisters turned to make the short walk back to Windmere Hall. They looked over each other and all laughed at how messy and bedraggled they appeared — all except Alice. "Have no fear, sister," Jane said archly. "Your day is coming...sooner or later."

Frederica took one look back at the house of horrors and tore herself from Roderick Utley long enough to face Adam. "Thank you, Mr Blythewood," she said, and she kissed him, in a sisterly way, on the cheek.

For once Adam had nothing to say, but only bowed. The satisfaction of seeing Frederica happily reunited with her true love was the only thanks he needed. He was pleased as well when Jane Windmere took his arm and offered him a much less chaste kiss on the lips. It was a relief to be finally on good terms with Frederica, as it seemed obvious that he would see much more of her from now on, as her brother-in-law.

Epilogue

Months later, Adam Blythewood sat with Roderick Utley in the library of Windmere Hall in a rare moment of relaxation. So much had changed for both of them. The double wedding by which they became joined to the Windmere family, his beloved having decided that the name "Jane Blythewood" was sufficiently euphonious, had gone off brilliantly. Pamela Bond had given away the brides in the late Sir Alfred's stead, perhaps secretly proud of her role in bringing both couples together. Adam had not been entirely surprised to find that Mr and Mrs Thomas Anthony, guests of the wedding, were the "Jupiter" and "Juno" he had met at the Bondgate masquerade ball. Once they understood the situation, even Adam's parents had approved the match, and so far, Jane had lived up to every hope of marriage Adam had dared express, while he did his best to do the same.

While he and Roderick were frequently separated by the demands of their work — Adam had indeed completed the revision and publication of Sir Alfred's history of the Windmeres, and Roderick was near the completion of his monograph on the West Country's culinary traditions—he had found Utley to be everything he could have hoped for in a brother, as well as the upstanding gentleman friend and guide his father had hoped he would find at Windmere Hall.

They had filled a pleasant afternoon with conversation on a variety of subjects, sport, life in London and the fresh delights of marriage. After they had traded inquiries on the well-being of Frederica and Jane, the conversation inevitably turned to that strange experience that had brought them together in the first place.

Sally was back in her position as head cook, of course, and while the meal they had polished off earlier didn't compare to the dishes Molly had once prepared—in addition to being sacked from the kitchen of the Hall, the punishment she had taken in the stocks from her fellow villagers had, Adam hoped, served her a lesson in humility—with Roderick's guidance, Sally's food had become quite palatable. Understandably, the famous tarts were no longer served at Windmere Hall, but Roderick in particular had no appetite for them anymore, having been stuffed to the gills with them while Molly had made him her plaything.

Adam let the ash drop from the tip of his cigar into a tray, then took a pensive sip of brandy. How strange to be together in this situation in the very room from which he had first spied on Freddie and flirted with Marie! And now to be an established gentleman with no eyes for anyone but his own beloved bride! The man he had been when he had first arrived seemed like a stranger to him, those events as distant as the dawn of time. Yet there were still some mysteries that nagged at him, and he would have his curiosity satisfied.

"I say, Rod," Adam said, "did you ever find that herb you were searching for? The secret aphrodisiac the McQuirts were said to put in their tarts?"

Roderick smiled ruefully and tapped his own cigar before answering. "No, I never did."

Want to see more like this?
Here's a taster for you to enjoy!

Suiting Saffina: Taming Saffina
Flora Dain

Excerpt

*"Come back here. Bring me grog, damn your eyes." He's
shouting now.*

*I'm under the table. Through the open window I hear
voices.*

*"What, a child's with him? How old? Eight, you say?
Why no nurse?"*

"Nobody goes near. The stink's too bad. All that pain…"

They're talking about me.

The grog was heavy. I dropped the jug.

If I press my hands on my ears, I can't hear his screams.

I was halfway across the lawns when I knew for
certain what I wanted — Isaac's cock. *All* of it. So instead
of making for the fountains to cool off, I headed to the
stables for extra heat.

Isaac tended the horses. At this hour he'd be up in
the hayloft, shoveling forkfuls of fragrant hay so
there'd be great heaps of it for us to roll in when he
pushed up my skirts…*perfect.*

And I was halfway up the ladder to the hayloft when
I heard Madame's shout.

"Lady Saffina? Come back 'ere *now. Espèce d'une jeune putain...*"

Really, such language. She was in hot pursuit — almost as hot as mine. She'd found me feeling myself once too often.

And why not, pray? I was eighteen. I could do what I liked. Yet she still thought a good caning would cool me down.

How little she knew...

Her canings were the best thing about her. She applied them often and well. The very thought of them made me wet and left me dripping. In fact, it was when she first noticed my damp linens that she started getting creative. Then the dampness got worse...and the canings got worse.

It was impossible to resist the urge to feel myself afterward. And when she caught me doing *that...*

But all that did was make me crave... What? I'd no clear idea. But out here in the stables I had a clear picture of what I craved. It was hot and hard and thick and looked very like Isaac's cock, that day I found him fisting himself in the barn and he'd reddened and jerked his hand away.

I liked Isaac. He was tanned and tough with sun-bleached hair and a ready laugh. We'd been friends for a while. He was a few years older than me. He taught me much — how to groom and saddle up horses, how to ride.

He knew his place. He never made advances, but I wished he would. And now I made instinctively for his strong protective arms and his eager, thrusting *maleness*.

That was what I wanted. I was sure of it now.

And this time I'd make sure I got it.

But now Madame was after me full tilt, shrieking like a parrot in her native French. Just as well, if I heard her right. She'd never dare call me a whore in English.

But what I wanted was Isaac. And now here he was, skimming down the ladder to meet me. His breeches already bulged with everything I needed…

And I was on the point of launching into his arms when the far door flew open. Madame dashed in, the thin cane quivering in her hand.

"*Isaac.* Save me." I clutched at his sleeve.

In a flash he took in every detail of my torn gown, my bulging, heaving breasts, one loose and exposed from running. He caught me up, his bold blue eyes dancing, his blond hair all tousled from the hay. His cock already part way out of his breeches flap…

He knew instantly what I craved.

But now here was Madame, about to spoil everything.

And I was just going to snap at her that I was too old for a governess when I saw a look pass between them. In a flash I saw myself at their mercy — Isaac's cock *and* Madame's cane. *Yes…*

I stood, breathless and panting in his arms. My trussed-up skirts showed my stinging backside. The long red welt she'd planted there before I'd bolted still burned my ass.

As she came closer, her tongue darted along her thin lips, scarlet and snake-like. Her black eyes burned into mine. "You disgrace yourself, Lady Saffina. You will go to bed early and receive a severe whipping to correct your behavior. We start now. Hold 'er, Isaac. Push 'er down, *so.*"

"You can't do this," I snapped, still shaky from running. My protest melted already at the thought of how good this would feel. *Especially with Isaac pounding into me afterward…*

"You are a monster, Madame. Wait till my guardian hears of this. I'll tell him the minute he gets here."

Her black eyes narrowed to slits. Her venomous look made her sallow face look even more like a snake's.

Her voice lowered to a snarl. "Oh, your guardian will know. Rest assured. And you will not disgrace me by behaving like a *putain* every time my back is turned. He expects to find you a lady. In the six months since I come 'ere, you grow wild. If you cannot control your indecent lusts, they must be controlled for you. I daresay 'is lordship will agree."

I snorted and glanced downward, thrilling to a glimpse of Isaac's swelling cock. It glowed in a shaft of warm sunshine as he held me fast. I could almost feel it throb.

But Madame had jerked up her head, listening for something. A second later I heard it too. *The jingle of harness.* Some commotion out in the yard. Shouts and the clatter of hooves.

Yet more deliveries? Food, furniture, servants — there'd been no end to it. The preparations for my guardian's arrival had been going on for weeks.

I snorted again, wishing the woman would leave. I wanted to get Isaac into the hay.

We'd talked about this often. He'd told me how it would feel, even how much it would hurt. All that did was excite me more. I hardly cared. I'd take whatever he gave.

I was sick of being a girl. I wanted to be a real woman. Today was the day, and I was damned if I'd let her spoil it, my first breach at the hands — or should I say the *tool* — of my friend and favorite groom.

I glared at her. "My guardian? Why should I care what some shuffling old man thinks about anything? He'll stink of dust and collect moths. He's probably deaf. But he'll make short work of *you* when he learns how you treat me."

Modesty — even *I* had some — forbade me from listing all the reasons I'd be glad to be rid of her in front of Isaac.

He was earnest and well built. He'd told me all about stallions and mares, watching with a gleam when I repeated it all back to him. I'd make him tell me all over again, feeling myself with abandon in front of him while he did so. But he might be surprised to learn that Madame knew all about my tastes for worldly pleasures. She also had strict ideas on discipline as a cure. How little she knew…

Now I sensed another signal pass between them. A shiver ran through me. What were they going to do? In fact, why had she not simply ordered him back to his work and dragged me indoors like she usually did?

"Now?" Isaac's cock jerked again.

I licked my lips, as my wish seemed about to come true. *Really? Both together?* I saw him grin as he glanced my way, taking in my flushed, open-mouthed stare. But he was talking to Madame, not to me.

"How about it?"

She was eyeing him with a thin smile as she fingered the vicious, quivering little cane. "Very well. Hold 'er for me."

I tried to pull away in token protest. Too late. Isaac held me fast, his fingers digging into my upper arms. Madame leaned forward and pulled out my other breast. Now both swung free, bulging right under Isaac's nose.

I saw his cock twitch again, red and glossy now. *Just what I wanted...*

"We're going to give you a thrashing." Her low murmur quivered with suppressed fury. "I've gone easy on you these last six months. Now you're a woman you can take punishment like a woman. And when we've finished, you will pleasure your groom – *on your knees.*"

I writhed in Isaac's grip, my face dangerously close to his hot, throbbing cock.

"Easy there, m'lady." He grinned and jabbed it in my face with an insolent thrust of his hips. "You'll get plenty of it later. Let Madame do her work."

He eyed me with an insolent, open leer. His soft mouth moistened with dribble. His short, fair beard gleamed in a shaft of dust-flecked sunlight.

My governess glared at me and flexed her cane. It was a deliberate attempt to scare me. To make me wait, ashamed to be a wanton, but all it did was inflame me further.

Now her stern look worked its usual magic. I felt a twitch of arousal. At the same time, moisture pooled between my legs.

She bared her teeth as she saw a light, rosy flush dawn over my breasts. "Little 'ussy, even out 'ere. You deserve this."

The first slash of her cane made me shriek. The second made me howl. She'd just lifted her hand for a third when a man's voice, deep and rich, echoed through the barn.

Instantly my captors froze.

"Crude, very crude. What *are* you about?"

We all turned to stare – Madame, her cane aloft, Isaac, fleshy mouth agape and me, ass high in the air, my spilling breasts flushed with shame. Tears of pain already smarted in the corners of my eyes.

I gazed, open-mouthed. This was a gentleman—a real one. I'd seen gentlemen sporting the latest fashions in the pages of *The Lady's Magazine*, but this was no preening dandy.

His clothes were plain and his necktie simple. His manner was haughty to the point of arrogance. His imperious air alone proclaimed him a lord. As he walked slowly across the dusty barn floor, his riding boots kicked up motes of dust.

They sparkled in the sunbeams like floating diamonds.

My universe shifted.

He had what I craved and plenty of it. I could see its hard lines clearly as the shaft of sunlight slanted across his buckskins.

At that moment his eyes locked on mine with a gleam. *He knew.* He knew what I craved, as sure as if I'd said it out loud.

Madame lowered the cane and dropped a deep curtsey. Isaac dropped my arms, hastily buttoned himself and touched his forelock. I struggled to balance, my breasts finally sealing my shame by jerking free of my gown and glowing a rich, rosy pink. Ignoring them, I straightened up, pushed back my hair and lifted my chin.

A vain attempt to look dignified, but I was a lady, after all—by rank, if not deed.

Madame took charge. "*Bonjour, monseigneur. Soyez le bienvenu.* Welcome home, my lord. We did not expect you so soon. This is—"

"Thank you, Madame Junot. I know who it is. And...Isaac, is it? I hear good reports of your work.

Now leave us. I'd like a few moments alone with my ward."

I gaped like a landed fish. "*You* are my guardian?"

His eyes narrowed. As the others scuttled past him, he murmured something to Isaac.

With a scared, shifty look, the groom hoisted a length of coarse rope from a newel post. He dropped it at the newcomer's feet and made for the door.

It swung to with a deafening crash.

The noise echoed off the wooden beams then silence fell. Hay-scented warmth settled around us like a blanket.

My guardian stooped in a graceful curve, scooped up the rope with one hand and walked toward me.

His deep, rich voice flowed around me like melting chocolate. "It's customary to address me as *sir*. When you get to know me better, you'll use it without being reminded. And for your information, much of my collection is still on the road, but thankfully free of moth."

He stepped up close, tipped up my chin with his free hand and smiled deeply into my eyes. His touch felt warm and firm. His fingers smelled clean. For a fleeting second I caught a whiff of chypre from his firm, clean-shaven jaw, and mingled with it, the faintest hint of an aroma from his skin—something *male*.

At the same moment I felt the rasp of hemp as he wound a rough length of rope around one of my wrists. He reached behind me to secure it to the other and swiftly fastened both my wrists at my back.

"And now for a short, sharp lesson in manners."

Home of Erotic Romance

Sign up for our newsletter and find out about all our romance book releases, eBook sales and promotions, sneak peeks and FREE romance books!

About the Author

Nolan Vancey loves stories in all forms, be it words, pictures, songs, or scrimshaw. Whether it's Jane Austen or Tales from the Crypt, when he isn't writing his own stories, he can be found reading or watching something new to him. At other times, he is a musician and family man in his home state of Kansas in the United States.

Nolan loves to hear from readers. You can find his contact information, website details and author profile page at https://www.totallybound.com